THE TIME MACHINE GENE
A PETER AUGUST MYSTERY

MAYA KAATHRYN BOHNHOFF

ANTHONY FRANGIONE

BVC

THE TIME MACHINE GENE

A Peter August Mystery

Maya Kaathryn Bohnhoff
and
Anthony Frangione

CHARIOT BOOKS

September 9, 2025
ISBN: 978-1-63632-346-6
copyright © 2024 by Maya Kaathryn Bohnhoff &
Anthony Frangione

www.bookviewcafe.com

DEDICATION

To my writing partner, Anthony,
for giving me a legit reason to do historical research.
And to the late Elizabeth "Lace" Gilligan,
who taught me that you can have a healthy relationship
with historical research …
without letting it take over your life.
-Maya Kaathryn Bohnhoff

For Justin and Mia.
The energy for the rest of the way.
-Anthony Frangione

1

EPISODES

The first time I had one of my "episodes," I was eight years old and on a playground seesaw at Bellaire Elementary. A hundred other kids ran and shouted, clambered on the monkey bars, plied the rings, or rode the merry-go-round. One moment I was bobbing up and down at the end of a plank with Bobby Swenson as a counterweight, the next I was riding a galloping horse across a grassy plain. And I wasn't an eight-year-old boy anymore; I was a young man wearing chaps, tall boots, and a buckskin jacket.

Wind whipped my face, and the horse's hooves thundered beneath me. I was exhilarated and terrified all at once. The only *real* horse I'd ever ridden was at the Sarpy County Fair. Well, it was sort of a real horse; it was a Shetland pony that I'd fancifully named Black Beauty, even though it was really dark brown. It had been doomed to walk in endless circles at the end of a tether while I pretended to be a cowboy, yippee-kie-ay.

I had dreamed of riding a horse like this, of course, but there was no chance of it happening—or so my parents dictated—until after my twelfth birthday. Why my twelfth birthday, Mom and Dad were unable to explain clearly, but it was apparently a magical age to them, and so it became to me.

Hands on the reins as if I knew what I was doing, I wanted to laugh and cry and scream bloody murder all at once. But the terror ebbed quickly when I realized I actually *did* know how to ride a horse. At least, my grownup body did. I let myself enjoy the experience, not even bothering to ask myself what had happened to the seesaw or Bobby Swenson or the school playground.

This is so cool!

I looked ahead now, tears streaming from my adult eyes, and saw a ramshackle outpost ahead, set close to the dirt road I galloped madly along. A guy stood in front of the outpost with a horse, watching my approach. I felt my body preparing for something and realized, with a jolt of surprise, that I knew what it was.

I got this.

I reined my sweating mount to a gliding stop, flung myself to the ground, then grabbed my saddlebags. As I spun to throw them up behind the saddle of the fresh horse, I was struck by how short I was. That horse seemed awfully tall. Didn't seem to faze me; I fastened the saddlebags down with a leather strap as if I'd done this a million times, and vaulted lightly into the saddle.

This was like a dream, only better. In my dreams I hardly ever did things so expertly. The other guy let go of my new horse's reins and grasped the reins of the horse I'd just dismounted. Then he tipped his hat as I urged my new horse into a full gallop, continuing on the road across the plain.

I, Peter August, was a Pony Express rider! How cool was that? And I realized I knew I was bound for Sacramento, California, where I would receive the huge sum of $100 and three days' rest before having to carry another batch of mail and newspapers back east to St. Joseph, Missouri.

Before I reached Sacramento—someplace I'd never been for real at that point in my life—I knew that I had a rifle in a scabbard under my right knee and wore a gun belt with a single revolver in it on my left hip, mounted backward so I could reach around and grab it with my right hand. I told myself it was a Colt .45 at first, 'cause that was the most famous gun in the world and the one that every movie cowboy carried. But I somehow knew that wasn't right. My gun was called a Pietta .44.

I'd never heard of a Pietta .44 then. Now, I own two.

I rode for uncounted hours on the last leg of the journey, heading toward a strange city that I somehow knew like the back of my hand. There would be beer and food and a big, fat cigar tonight. And maybe a card game and ... I flushed with embarrassment. A girl. Well, a woman, I guess. I distracted myself by trying to remember if I'd ever smelled cigar smoke. I hadn't, but somehow I remembered it anyway and knew I liked it.

My horse galloped into the cool shadow of a twilit forest; elms and oaks rustled in the breeze, and the birds of evening called to each other through the branches. I could barely hear them over the sound of hooves on the soft ground. I could smell wet earth and knew a stream flowed nearby. That made me thirsty, so I took a drink from the canteen dallied to my saddle horn. I gulped some water, surprised at how good it tasted, then stoppered and dropped the canteen. It hit the pommel with a soft clang that spooked me more than it did the horse.

I glanced up and realized we were coming up fast on the stream and that the horse would jump it to get across.

Awesome!

I braced myself for the leap ... and landed at the bottom of the seesaw's arc with a jolt that made my tailbone cry for mercy. Bobby Swenson had jumped off the other end of the seesaw and stared at me with his face all screwed up. The playground was almost empty; the other kids had fled back to the school, answering the bell.

"Jeez-Louise, Petey!" Bobby whined. "What's the matter with you? You were like a zombie or something. The bell's been ringing for*ever*. You want to make us both tardy?" Bobby turned and pelted for the nearest door.

Adrenaline pumping through my veins, I jumped up, wincing, and scrambled after him.

I had similar episodes over the years, each one unique in its own way. I figured they were waking dreams or visions, maybe. I started writing them down when they were interesting, and I even told some of my friends about them ... before I realized they thought I was a raging loon and made fun of me over it behind my back. So, I started telling people I was writing stories; my episodes were scenes I'd come up with. By the time I was in high school, I'd taken my flights of fancy to the Old West, to ancient Egypt, and to some old school where the students wore robes and the study hall looked like Hogwarts.

I kept my journals private; I showed them to no one ... until my last year in the Omaha PD Police Academy. I was dating a fellow cadet—Lauren Canfield. We were what they call *simpatico*. I'd often heard people say of their life partner, "They complete me" or refer to them as a soul mate, but with Lauren, I felt that was true. So, I struggled with whether I should share with her the real-life source of the stories I wrote.

That was decided for me on the evening I proposed. I had a ring—one Lauren had already admired. We'd been drifting toward this moment for months, and both of us knew it. So, I went cheerfully into the Big Evening, anticipating the beginning of our life together. We crossed the Missouri into Council Bluffs to dine at a riverfront restaurant we both liked, and I gave her the ring at a table overlooking the water. There was no question of her turning me down; we both knew we belonged together.

I was still holding Lauren's hand, tilting it so that her

diamond sparkled in the candlelight, when the waiter arrived at our table with a covered platter. He smiled at us as he set it on a folding stand and whisked off the gleaming cover. I blinked and found myself in the cool recesses of an immense, fire-lit hall in which vividly painted columns rose at least two dozen feet to a vaulted ceiling.

"Did you hear me, Amenaru?" said the guy standing next to me.

I blinked and turned to look—or, at least, my body did. The young man peering at me in the shifting half-light of the hall wore a short dress—well, okay, I guess you'd call it a tunic—and a cream-colored head covering. He had on more jewelry than Lauren ever wore, and all of it was gaudy and as brightly hued as the columns rising all around us. Light from braces of oil lamps—the kind that look like little squashed tea pots—glinted off all the bling. I could almost imagine the flutter of lamp flames as distant applause from invisible admirers.

The guy had a name I already knew. This was Har-khebu, acolyte to one Nebemakhet, high priest of the Divine Physician, Imhotep. I'd "met" him before in at least one of my waking dreams. He'd called me Amenaru then, too. Weird. What were the odds of dreaming about the same fictitious person more than once, while not actually repeating the same dream? The last time I'd "been" Amenaru, Har-khebu and I had been attending Nebemakhet during a ceremony that was completely alien to me, yet which I somehow knew every nuance of.

Yeah, I know. Contradictory as hell.

"Sorry, Har-ib," Amenaru said, using a sort of nickname, I guess. "I failed to hear you clearly."

"I asked," said Har-ib, "if you knew whether our lord is out of his bath yet. The hour grows late, and he has an audience with the Pharaoh's minister."

"Do you wish me to attend him?" Amenaru asked, and I felt a lilt of humor in the question. "Perhaps hasten his dressing?"

Har-khebu gave me a grateful smile. "You are so much better at it than I am. When I try to hurry him, he gets angry and adds to my temple duties. He favors you, I think."

"Nonsense. He is only more used to me," Amenaru answered. "I have been here longer than you have."

No, I was pretty sure that I—the real me, Peter August—had just gotten here and really wanted to go back to where Lauren was no doubt waiting for me to say something romantic. I already knew that I could spend long minutes in one of my fugue states while only seconds passed in the real world, but I also knew that the longer I spent *here,* the longer the amount of time passed there, as well.

I—or Amenaru, who was driving this bus—took off for the high priest's bath chamber. I couldn't remember having been there before myself, but my dream-self knew the way. He wasn't surprised that even though the interior of the Temple of Imhotep was lit by brazier and lamp, it was a sunny morning in the open-air atrium that served as Nebemakhet's boudoir.

The man himself had just risen, dripping wet, from a sunken tub set into the floor of the large, airy room. Body servants leapt to offer him soft linen towels, while his dressers stood to one side with his tunic, sandals, headgear, and jewelry.

I approached, bowing and smiling with a wry humor curling in my breast—or Amenaru's breast, or whatever. "Excellent, High One," we said, "you will arrive at your meeting with the emissary of the Pharaoh Sanakht [Son of Amen] as gleaming and effulgent as the sun."

Holy Mother of Pearl—who talks like that?

Nebemakhet returned the smile (I guess he really did favor me ... us ... Amenaru ... whatever) and said, "Ah, you have gently reminded me of the hour, Amenaru. Have I spent too long in the bath? Do you think me vain?"

"Not in the least, Excellence," we replied with another bow.

"You merely wish to show your respect for the Father of Egypt by greeting his emissary in spotless purity."

His dressers had dressed him, at this pass, and he looked mighty fine in his silken yellow tunic and regal jewelry. The last thing they installed on his person was a bright, gold medallion the size of a tangerine that hung on a torque around his neck.

My guy, Amenaru, seemed quite taken with the piece. It had a cabochon of lapis lazuli set in it that would probably have made even my pragmatic Lauren drool, fashioned to look like a scarab with veins of gold running through its half-folded wings. Very swank.

The top dog caught us looking at it and caressed it with the tips of his fingers. "Patience, Amenaru," he told us, apropos of nothing, as far as I knew, but it seemed to mean something to Amenaru. I felt a tickle of anticipation.

Yeah, anticipation—exactly what I'd been feeling while I was holding my fiancée's hand onto which I had just placed a small but still impressive token of my love and admiration. I wanted to go back. Now.

But Amenaru had places to go. "Do you require me to attend you?" we asked Nebemakhet.

He nodded. "Yes, I do require it."

It took him another twenty minutes or so to get his act together, during which I begged to wake up but didn't. At last we headed across an open courtyard to his limo. Or at least, it was the ancient Egyptian equivalent of a limo—an ornate, semi-open box with cushy insides carried by six big dudes with tattoos. We got in, and the big dudes took off at a brisk walk along the Nile, terrifying a flock of birds that burst from the rushes.

I glanced out the open window at them and found myself staring out at the moon rising over the Missouri and hearing Lauren demand, "For God's sake, Peter, *say* something!"

I blinked at her. "Sorry, what?"

She let out a long breath. "Well, that's something. At least you're back to English."

"Back to English," I repeated. "What do you mean, back to English?"

She leaned toward me over the table, lowering her voice. "You've been like—I don't know—speaking in tongues or something. Just babbling gibberish."

"I have?"

"Yeah. I think you scared the bejesus out of the poor waiter."

I glanced across the restaurant to the wait staff's station. Sure enough, our waiter was in a tense tête-à-tête with a couple of his peers, gesturing and casting nervous glances in our direction.

"I'll leave him a big tip," I said.

"Peter, what was that? What happened?" Lauren's eyes were huge and her gaze wary.

"Tell you what, let's eat our dinner and we can take a walk in the moonlight and … and I'll explain everything."

I did explain everything. I told her about my episodes. I showed her my journals. I explained that the stories I made up were really things that happened in my head. About a week after that, she gave me the ring back, crying and protesting that she still loved me but just couldn't marry me because I obviously had mental "issues."

She said, "It's not you—it's me," but I was pretty sure it was me speaking in tongues and disappearing into my head for minutes at a time.

She said something else that no human being ever wants to hear from someone they love: "You need help."

I tried to get help. I had MRIs, CATs, PETs, and other acronyms. I saw a neurologist, a psychiatrist, and a psychologist. No dice. I was like a car that absolutely refused to malfunction in the presence of a mechanic. The fugue states were entirely random; there was simply no way to anticipate them, and when

I had one, I couldn't communicate with the real world to let someone know it was happening. I'd've had to live with one of my therapists 24/7 in order to have someone with half a clue around when I "phased out."

I developed a theory of my own: since I'd always been an avid history fan—even as a child—I'd simply developed such a fascination with some periods of history that I just geeked out, imagination in overdrive, doing really intense what-ifs. Deep down inside, I knew that was utter bull fazoo. While I'd dreamed of being a cowboy as a child, I hadn't studied Egypt before I had the first dream about Amenaru. All my study came after the fact. And though I found no historical references to Amenaru, or Nebemakhet for that matter, I'd discovered that Imhotep was a real person—a significant figure in Egyptian medicine. He was a doctor in the Third Dynasty, under a pharaoh named Netjerikhet or Djoser.

Imhotep was apparently a genius—physician, polymath, philosopher, poet, engineer. He performed a variety of advanced surgeries for that day and age. The Egyptians thought so highly of him that they made him a god after he died. I suppose it was his dabbling in life-extending surgeries that got him written into all those ever-popular mummy movies. From Boris Karloff to Arnold Vasloo, the mummy was almost always Imhotep, cursed for doing blasphemous experiments on folks alive and dead.

Still, I conveniently bent the timeline to keep my sanity. I told myself that my study had been what fleshed out my later episodes. I glossed over what had caused the early ones. I did the same thing when I tried to reconcile with Lauren. She said she wanted to believe me, and I could see that she did. But then she told me why she was really so adamant that we couldn't have the life we both wanted.

"My mother was bipolar," she said. "Struggled with it all her life. Her grandfather, too. If it was just you, I maybe could risk it, Peter. Or if it was just potentially me. But if both of us have some sort of … broken gene…" She shook her head. "Can you tell me you'd want us to raise a family with something like that we might pass along?"

"You're blowing it out of proportion," I told her. "It's just little episodes. Short, benign—"

"Episodes?" she repeated. "You mean seizures. What if you have one while you're driving, Peter? Or crossing a street? Or carrying our child?"

She was right. I knew she was right, but I told her that I'd been free of episodes for months since the one that broke us up. I had, except for the briefest of flashes. She didn't believe me. At that point, I didn't believe myself.

FAST-FORWARD FIVE YEARS. I'd moved back east to take a position as an investigator with the NYPD Detective Bureau (and, yeah, to get way from memories of Lauren). I got promoted quickly and ended up in the Major Crimes Division. We handled kidnappings, homicides, burglaries, extortion, that sort of thing. It was rewarding work, and I was good at it. I was also relatively fugue free, though I'd developed a fascination with all things neurological and psychological and added that to my history addiction. My colleagues called me "the Professor." Except for my partner, Melchior Duarte, who called me "Augie" —something I found as annoying as he found me calling him "Mel".

New Year's Eve of my third year in Major Crimes, something changed. I started having episodes again. Some of them were invisible to anyone but me. They happened while I was on the subway (I'd stopped driving), while I was in bed early in the morning, while I was riding my horse through Central Park.

My horse was a retired police mount named Peccadillo (I have no idea), and I loved him. When I'd fugue out, he'd just keep moving along, and if I failed to recover in short order, he'd take me back to the stable.

Eventually, though, I had episodes in company with other people, and they lasted long enough to get noticed. Sometimes they were funny. Like the time I checked out in the middle of taking a bite of a sloppy Reuben in the diner Mel and I often ate lunch in. I made up a story about getting sucked into thinking about a piece of evidence from one of our cases. It wasn't a lie, exactly, because I *was* bothered by that piece of evidence, but I wasn't going to make the same mistake with Melchior that I'd made with Lauren and admit that I'd been whisked away in my head to ancient Egypt, which seemed to be my go-to time zone.

That's not to say I didn't end up in other places—Vienna, Venice, Rome—and other times, late Roman Empire, Renaissance, early twentieth century. I could see no rhyme or reason to it, no pattern. I just head-hopped all over the place. And I never knew when it was going to happen.

The uncertainty wore on me after a while. As did the way that Mel started watching me after I came inches from walking into an open manhole one afternoon as we bypassed some street work on Lexington.

I lost sleep; I lost weight; I lost confidence in myself. And then, I almost lost Mel.

We were investigating a drug ring that catered to the rich and beautiful. Got called in as backup for a sting operation going down in the back of a seriously upscale nightclub on Bowery—a place ironically called Free Spirits. Right around closing time, Mel and I were to take up positions in a garden courtyard behind the club. We slipped in along an alley access from the cross street and disappeared ourselves among the shrubbery. Little twinkly lights were strung through the trees that dotted the patio. Nice place to wait for the signal from the mole inside the club, telling us the suspects were leaving.

We expected them to go out the front entrance, where the other members of our team were in position to arrest them, but had to be ready for the chance that they'd make the cops out front and try to escape past us.

We'd been hiding in the shadows for half an hour when the twinkly lights blinked out, then back on. That was our signal. We arose from the shrubbery at the rear of the garden patio and made our way toward the rear entrance of the club, guns drawn. I moved down the right side of the courtyard and Mel down the left, so we'd end up flanking the rear exit. Our own backup was behind us at the gate that opened onto the alley.

I was maybe fifteen feet from the rear doors when they flew open and four guys came stumbling out onto the patio. Mel materialized out of the shadows between a couple of tables, leveled his weapon, and shouted, "Police! Freeze!"

They didn't freeze; they tried to reverse course, or maybe they tried to scatter. I don't know. All I know is that one of them lost his balance and collided with a fancy wrought-iron brazier, and another used the distraction to go for his gun.

I stepped out onto the patio, training my weapon on that guy, and found myself somewhere else. The place was dark and still as a tomb. I was standing in a broad gallery in which the only light came from an open door in a short hallway several yards distant. The quiet here was that quivery, intense silence during which you realize you have tinnitus. I smelled the musk of age and felt cold emanating from the plaster walls, marble columns, and tile floors. Then I heard voices—low murmurs that rolled out into the gallery from that dimly lit room up ahead. I moved carefully toward it, ruing the fact that my shiny dress shoes were not the best footwear for spying.

Spying? Is that what I was doing? Why was I spying? I wanted to know what the voices were saying, I got that much. I was focused on that in a way that exiled every other thought. I could hear my own breathing above the ringing in my ears, above the voices from the room. A few more steps and I'd be able to make out words.

My right hip bumped something—a glass display case. I steadied myself and glanced down. In the semi-gloom, I could make out a grouping of Egyptian jewelry and artifacts. Light from the hallway at the end of the gallery gleamed on the centerpiece of the collection—a large medallion with a winged scarab on it.

Okay, I was in a museum.

Down the hall ahead of me, another door opened, more light spilled out onto the tiles of the floor, and a man stepped into the hallway. I froze, knowing that in a heartbeat he'd turn and see me and I'd have to invent an excuse for being here after closing time. But I got a break; he leaned back into the room to shut off the light.

I turned and ran, flinging myself around a corner into a smaller gallery, and thence to an exit that put me outside the building on a stone landing. Chill air plastered itself to my face. Moonlight illumined a short flight of steps and a path that led away into a forested park.

Hearing a commotion from inside the building, I slipped over the stone railing and dropped six feet or so into the shrubs beside the staircase. The branches closed over my head, obscuring my view of the stairs. I huddled in tense silence as a group of men burst out onto the landing.

"Who was it?" one of them demanded. "Did you see who it was, lieutenant?"

"No sir, I did not. I only heard them running down the hall. I'm not even certain they came this way, to tell the truth. I only thought perhaps, because this was the closest exit..."

"Yes, yes. Of course," said the first man—a superior officer, apparently. "Major, you will search the museum. Thoroughly."

"Sir," said a third man, and I heard the door open and close as he moved to obey.

"It will be sunrise soon," the first man continued after a moment. "Lieutenant, are you at the end of your shift?"

"Yes, sir."

"Well, then, go get some sleep. If the intruder is in the museum, Major Myers will find him."

They went back inside, and I all but collapsed beneath my concealing bushes. I had to move now, before the place was overrun with security forces. Who the hell were these people, I wondered. They didn't wear uniforms but had military rank. What were they doing here, in my museum?

I slipped along the wall beneath the shrubs until I reached a point at which a grand old cedar extended its boughs across the sidewalk, dropping a shadow as dark as the night sky into the bushes in which I hid. I used that shadow to flee into the parkland skirting the museum, a building I knew as well as I knew the back of my hand.

I glanced down at my hands, brushing away leaves and dust. I wore a wedding ring—a plain gold band. My fingers were long and awkwardly thin. I realized that I could see them quite well; Dawn was already poking her nose over the horizon. I paused beneath the cedar to get my bearings, listening as the parkland began to wake and creatures stirred in the trees overhead. I heard the musical gurgling of the little creek that ran from here to a culvert some blocks away. I would use it to get home. I hoped my wife, Teresa, would still be asleep.

I turned to go, and noticed that a pigeon had lit on the grass not far off. I would wait until it had flown off of its own accord. The last thing I wanted was to send frightened birds into the air to announce my presence. I peered down through the trees toward the creek … and saw Melchior lying in the middle of the wooded patio with a paramedic kneeling next to him.

2

THE STATE OF FUGUE

I sat on a wrought iron chair at one of the round tables that dotted the courtyard behind Free Spirits. My Glock lay atop the table, inches from my hand, accusing me. I must have made a sound, because another detective—Harley Lewis—appeared out of nowhere to peer into my face.

"You back with us, Peter?" he asked me.

My throat felt tight, like someone was squeezing it. *Mel. What the hell happened to Mel? What have I done?*

"What happened?" I asked, hating the way my voice quivered.

"Jesus, Peter. Don't you know?"

I didn't know. I didn't know what had happened that night in the garden behind Free Spirits. I had to be told that I had suddenly and inexplicably frozen. That one of the drug runners had shot my partner. That I had then run into the darkness of the garden patio and that our backup team had found me leaning against one of the ornamental trees, brushing at my clothing as if it were covered with dust.

Mel took months to recover, and when he came back to work, he requested a new partner. I didn't blame him. I still don't. Nor do I blame any of the other men and women who declined that honor. I was a pariah—the cop no one could depend on to have their back.

Our chief told me the same thing Lauren had years before: "You need help."

He wasn't wrong. I *did* need help, so I did as he advised. I took a mental health leave-of-absence and went to see the division shrink, Dr. Mohan. She realized pretty quickly that my little problem was out of her league. (How comforting is that?)

"I don't usually recommend this," she told me, her Indian accent lilting and precise, "but I think maybe you need to see a hypnotist."

"A hypnotist? You mean like a magician? Like David Copperfield?"

"No, I mean a clinical hypnotist like Dr. Greg Orlov." She handed me a card.

Dr. Gregor Orlov, PhD, Hypnotherapist. Member American Society of Clinical Hypnosis.

"This is real?"

Dr. Mohan nodded. "Hypnotherapy has long been recognized by the psychotherapeutic community as being very helpful in cases in which the patient loses time."

"Loses time?"

I'd never thought of it that way before, but the doctor was right. I did lose time while I was visiting the state of fugue. The question was, where was it going? Or where was *I* going to find it?

"It's not as if I think I'm being abducted by aliens," I said.

"No," agreed Dr. Mohan, "it's as if you are being abducted by history."

DR. ORLOV—WHO insisted I call him Doctor Greg or just Greg —was a large, soft-spoken bear of a man whose resting expression was one of amused curiosity, as if everything I said was intensely interesting and he'd never heard anything like it before in his entire practice. His brown tweed suit looked as if he lived in it the way most people lived in jeans or sweats. I don't mean he was sloppy or unkempt, just that he seemed comfortable in his own skin in ways I couldn't even imagine. I realized that inspired confidence in me, as if his comfort were contagious. Good quality in a therapist.

Naturally, the first half hour of the appointment was taken up by me describing the problem in some detail: the dives into imaginary worlds, the loss of time, my inability to control it (whatever "it" was), my complete ignorance of what triggered it.

"We'll consider triggers later," Dr. Greg told me. "Right now, I'd like to know how all this makes you feel."

"How's it supposed to make me feel?" I asked, maybe a little defensively. "I feel like I'm losing my mind ... along with all the other things I've lost—a fiancée, a career, my peace of mind, my self-confidence ... my partner. When my fiancée broke up with me, she asked me a question that I think will haunt me until the day I die. 'Peter, what if you're carrying our child when it happens?' How's *that* for a confidence killer?"

"Are you angry with her for that?" he wanted to know.

"Angry? Hell no. At least not with Lauren. I'm angry with *me*. With my screwy synapses. I just want it to stop, Doc. Can I call you 'Doc'? I'm not ready for first names, here, and 'Doctor Greg' makes me feel like a kindergartener."

Dr. Greg smiled his big, easy smile. "Whatever makes you most comfortable, Peter. So, let me see if I've got all this: You've been suffering these fugue states since you were a child. And you've 'traveled' to different places—and times—sometimes visiting the same time and place more than once."

"Yes. That about covers it."

"Does it?"

I waited for more, but he just looked at me with that curiously amused expression, which I suddenly found annoying as hell.

"What do you mean?" I asked.

"I mean, what else do you notice about these places, times, people you visit? Is there a common thread or theme? Does it mirror something that's going on in your real life in some way, perhaps?"

I'd already thought about that, as it happened. "No, not really. I don't think the circumstances are what triggers it. At least I haven't observed a pattern."

"Let's talk about triggers, then. Choose three episodes and tell me what you were doing in the real world when you left, and in your imaginary world when you returned."

Having him talk about it as if I actually *went* someplace was eerie, but I went with it. "Okay, first time I was on the playground at school. On the seesaw. Just before I came back, I was riding my horse through a woods toward a stream. I was bummed because I didn't get to jump him across the stream."

He was making notes now. Great. I hoped he wasn't going to try to get me to discuss dream symbolism. I'd already been through that with Dr. Mohan. Sometimes a horse is just a horse.

"And another? Maybe one you've made repeat visits to?"

"The night I proposed to my fiancée. We were having dinner on the deck of the Riverside Inn. The waiter had just arrived and I was suddenly Amenaru in ancient Egypt. Just before I came back, Amenaru was riding in a palanquin along the Nile."

"Really. That's interesting."

"*Why* is that interesting?"

He shrugged, his smile deepening. "Water. There's water in three connections. Can you give me a third?"

I squirmed a little and said, "The night Mel was shot, I found myself in a museum somewhere—I don't know where.

Mel and I were on the back patio of a nightclub that had a secret life as the den of a drug cartel, then I was inside this museum—kind of spying on some military types. Before I came back, I was sneaking through the woods trying to get home."

"Woods. Was there water?"

"Yeah, actually. There was a culvert that opened into a stream near my house."

"Do you remember where your house was? What street; what city; what country?"

I shook my head slowly. "Not a clue. All I knew was that this was *my* museum. I worked there. It was a combination art and history museum. And I knew I had a wife waiting for me at home. Teresa."

The memory filled me with a sudden sense of loss. If things had turned out the way I'd meant them to, I *would* have had a wife. Someone to come home to besides a ginger cat named Matilda.

Dr. Greg nodded as if my thoughts were just flying around out there for him to read. Maybe they were.

"That," he said, putting down his note pad, "is what we're going to try to get at next time through hypnosis."

"Next time? Not this time?"

He shook his head and fished something out of his pocket. It was a big, snowflake-shaped crystal on the end of a sparkly chain.

"This time, we're just going to see how easy you are to hypnotize."

I opened my mouth to make the standard disclaimer that guys like me always make: "Sorry, Doc, I can't be hypnotized." But if life had taught me anything, it was that self-assessments are almost always BS.

I said nothing.

As it happened, he put me under pretty easily. When I came

up for air, I wasn't clucking like a chicken or anything, and I seemed to remember ...

I blinked at him. "Think about rivers. You asked me to think about rivers and what they meant to me."

The doctor's eyebrows rose. "Most people don't remember the key words I use. Tell me, do you manipulate your dreams? Your normal dreams, I mean."

"Yeah. Yeah, I do. Is that good or bad?"

"I don't know. It could be a help or a hindrance. I suppose it depends a lot on what's going on underneath all this."

I nodded. "You mean, I might be hiding from something—or hiding something from myself?"

His smile was back—now almost a grin. "I think you're going to be fascinating to work with ... or maybe challenging is the right word."

Well, on that bag of warm fuzzies, I went home to my cat.

I DID THINK about rivers in the hours I spent waiting for my next session with Orlov. I dreamed about them, but I didn't see how that meant anything. Water couldn't be the trigger that sent me into my fugues. There had been no water on the playground, only a wild menagerie of kids burning off energy. Nor had there been water in the courtyard of Free Spirits or in any number of places I'd "launched" from. I told the doctor as much when I saw him next.

"I think you're barking up the wrong tree, Doc," I said, and he gave me a quizzical look.

"Were there any trees around the playground?" he asked.

I laughed. "None. All tarmac and sand."

I was nervous and expectant. Hoping that I'd reveal some

insight to the doctor that would make him shout, "Eureka! I have found it!" Then he'd cure me and I'd go back to work (maybe even go back to Bellevue and find Lauren) and he'd go write a Nobel Prize—winning paper on hypnotherapy.

And they all lived happily ever after.

Yeah. None of that happened.

Did I remember more under hypnosis? Yes, I did. A lot of it was sensory detail, and a lot of it was about who I imagined myself to be. My Pony Express rider's name was Francis X. Aubry. He went by FX, thought of himself as Fox, and hated that other people called him Little Aubry because of his small stature. I (or he) was a young daredevil out to make a fortune carrying mail across the plains.

The museum guy was a professor of archaeology, and I recalled seeing a sign referring to Salzburg Museum. I could only assume it was the Salzburg in Austria. The odd ducks who'd been crashing my museum made me scared and angry in turns.

I also visited an Egyptian guy named Omari, whom I thought of as the Happy Scribe. We were about to be married to the love of our life.

Then there was the other Egyptian guy, Amenaru, whom I'd already described to the doctor as a priest in the Temple of Imhotep.

"I probably got that one from one of those old mummy movies," I said.

"You think so?" Dr. Greg inquired.

"Well, sure. I've only watched every mummy movie ever made. The mummy is *always* Imhotep, right?" I shrugged. "Well, unless it's a woman."

Orlov tilted his head to look at me quizzically, as if I'd become even more of a curiosity than before. "But your episodes don't exactly follow the movie scripts, do they?"

Was that a rhetorical question? "I guess I embellished."

He glanced down at his notes. "You said the Temple of Imhotep was along the Nile. Just now, under hypnosis, you specified Memphis. There actually was a Temple of Imhotep at Memphis."

I swallowed. "Yeah. I know. I must've gotten that on Wikipedia."

"How long have you been under the impression that the temple was at Memphis?"

"A while."

"A while."

"Okay, since high school."

He quirked an eyebrow. "Wikipedia?"

I sat up straighter in my chair. "Well, I—I must've seen it on a map in geography or history class or something."

"Memphis hasn't been Memphis since around the fourth century AD," said Orlov. "Unless you studied ancient Egypt in high school..."

"Where are you going with this, Doc?"

"I'm not sure yet," he said. "Let's see where it leads. Come on."

He got up from his comfy leather chair and moved to his desk, where he flipped open his laptop and began typing. I followed him and went around to peer over his shoulder. He was googling "Francis Aubry pony express."

There couldn't possibly be—

I was amazed at the number of hits he got. All about the same person. The most detailed account was in *True West Magazine*, an online compendium of all things cowboy that had an article on "the true exploits of horseman Francis Aubry." His name was originally Francois Xavier Aubry and he was French-Canadian. He had been famous for his prowess as a horseman and the speed of his deliveries. Since he was only five-foot-two and weighed in at a whopping 100 pounds, that made perfect sense. If he'd been born in another time, he might have been a jockey.

I just stood and stared at the page of information on Aubry until I became aware that the doctor was no longer reading the text; he was reading me. I reluctantly met his gaze.

"What do you think this means?" I asked quietly. "What's going on?"

"I don't know what's going on, Peter. But I think it means you need to meet my friend Victoria."

I bit back my frustration. Doc Orlov was the second medical professional who wanted to pass my sorry ass off to someone else. "Let me guess, she's a registered psychic, right? Palmistry, tarot, past life regression, that sort of thing?"

Orlov chuckled. "Sorry to disappoint. Vic is a research scientist at the Manhattan Institute of Neuroscience. I think she'll be pretty keen on meeting you."

THE MANHATTAN INSTITUTE OF NEUROSCIENCE (MIN) took up the entirety of an impressive new building with a carefully crafted lived-in look, as if it had been there since the turn of the twentieth century. It was the anchor building in a research park that took up an entire city block. Gardens, walkways, and water features connected the structures around the perimeter of the plaza.

That Dr. Greg was a fairly frequent visitor was apparent the moment we stepped through the revolving doors into the two-story lobby. He waved to the woman behind the receptionist's desk and called her by name. She returned the favor. Apparently, for her, calling a grown man Doctor Greg out loud posed no problem. He clearly knew where he was going, too, and had no trouble getting the third-floor security guard—also on a first-name basis with him—to swipe us through to the labs.

I was impressed. The installation was pristine without being sterile and maintained its artful sense of age. The colors were muted without being pastel (I *hate* pastels); the floors in the corridors we traveled were wood-grained tile that gave way to gleaming quartz in the labs.

Doc Orlov escorted me to the main laboratory used by his friend's team. It was a large, well-lit, open space with a scattering of tables and desks and anonymous machineries. I saw large, flat-screen computer displays everywhere—some showing brain scans and what I assume were brain waves. Flanking the main area were several offices with glass windows that looked out on the lab. Oddly, it smelled of lemons. I suspected one of those environmentally friendly cleansers.

Vic turned out to be Dr. Victoria Shehata, PhD. She had one degree in neurology from Johns Hopkins and a second in computer science from MIT. I don't know if she was pretty keen on meeting me, but she was both pretty and keen (in the smitten fanboy sense). She had thick hair the deep color of honey, which she wore in a ponytail; large, chocolate-brown eyes that her wire rimmed glasses failed to hide; and a shy smile that could have lit Gondor's beacon fires all the way from the mines of Moria.

I can't recall when I've had such a strong reaction to a woman, other than Lauren. And it was a different reaction—not *hubba-hubba* so much as She's All That with some I'm-out-of-my-freaking-league thrown in for good measure. In a word, she was impressive.

I met the other members of her team as well, and once I'd shaken hands with Victoria Shehata and pulled myself out of her dark gaze, the others actually registered. For the record, they were Drs. Drew Hastings, Otis Chen, and Sophie Marais. Drew was a distinguished-looking man in his forties, going gray at the temples; Sophie and Otis were the youngest members of the team—twenty-somethings doing their post-grad work. He was a graduate of Cal Tech, she of Université Paris Descartes. He had a lock of enviably straight, jet black hair that was constantly falling down between his eyes, and was full of edgy enthusiasm. She had a lovely accent, intricately braided hair, and skin the color of polished mahogany. Both proved to be wicked smart.

Dr. Shehata—Victoria—ushered Drs. Hastings and Orlov and me into her office. Here, the impression of being in a vintage building intensified. She clearly liked art deco. We seated ourselves at a small round table to the right of her desk, and I found myself wondering what the heck I was doing here. I'd allowed Dr. Greg to share my "circumstances" with his colleagues, and suddenly feared that they'd think I was a raving lunatic.

As if she'd heard the thoughts aloud, Dr. Shehata said, "Peter, my first priority is to assure you that you're not losing your mind. I think you're experiencing something profound and important. Something that science needs to pay attention to, learn from, and learn to explain."

"And control?" I asked hopefully.

She tilted her head in much the same way Dr. Greg always did and said, "I suppose that might be part of the equation. But let me ask you this: What do you think is causing your … fugues?"

I took a deep breath. "I've thought about that a lot, and I can only imagine that somehow I've picked stuff up by osmosis that I didn't realize I was absorbing. I have an eidetic memory— known that since I was a kid. So, I think that somewhere along the line, I saw an article, a story, a photograph, maybe even an ad for a TV show or movie, and spun it into a series of … daydreams."

I glanced up and caught Shehata and Orlov exchanging *looks*. Drew Hastings scribbled notes.

"Okay," I said, "cut it out. What do *you* think is happening?"

"Based on the experiments my team has been doing," said Dr. Shehata, "I think you're experiencing something we call genetic cognitive transference, or GCT. In other words, you're experiencing the memories of someone in your genealogical tree —essentially, traveling back along your ancestral timeline."

I was gobsmacked, as they say (damned useful expression), and in my moment of complete gobsmackedness, all I could think of was—"Past life regression? You mean reincarnation? Like Shirley MacLaine? I thought that went out with leg warmers and poodle-mullets. Is this some sort of new-age, sprouty—"

"It's not that," Shehata was quick to assure me. She glanced at Hastings. "Or at least, we have reason to doubt that it's that. What we do know is that some rare individuals seem to have the ability to flash back to events in the lives of their ancestors."

"Some rare individuals," I repeated. "How many? How many have you found?"

"So far, less than a dozen," said Dr. Shehata. "And the first one found us. He's why our team is here at MIN in the first place. You'll meet him if you agree to work with us. His name is Theron Cornell, and he's had experiences similar to yours all his life. For a while, he was our only data point, and then we found a few more—none with experiences quite as vivid as yours or Theron's and none as frequent, but all seeming to be able to recall the memories of people they were related to."

"How do you know that's what's happening? How do you know they're not just psychotic or something?" I asked.

"Really, Peter," said Doc Orlov. "You're not psychotic. If you were just psychotic, Dr. Mohan could have diagnosed you, and you never would have met me, or Vic and Drew. Psychoses are a dime a dozen; you're a special case."

This did not fill me with joy.

"We know," said Drew, as if Orlov hadn't spoken, "for the

same reason we know that you're not *just* psychotic; we've verified that the 'visions' our subjects have had correspond with
events in the lives of known historical figures—but from decidedly different viewpoints. We've verified the *process*, but we lack
a way to trigger and control it. We know that it happens; but we
don't know how or why. That's our first order of business in
Project Backstory—trigger and control."

"Okay, so we're not talking about my past lives, then."

"No," said Drew. "Decidedly not. You're experiencing
someone else's memory—a neuronal memory."

I shook my head, and Victoria picked up the explanation.

"Our working theory is that each individual's neurons carry a
genetic memory from their ancestors that allows them to experience key events in that ancestor's life as if they were their own.
We've been trying to trigger this mechanism in a variety of
ways, but have had mixed success. You—" And here she gave
me a heart-stopping smile. "You, Peter, present us with a rare
opportunity to work with someone who has frequent sponta-
neous episodes of GCT."

"This is going to sound incredibly stupid, but how do you
know this isn't past lives?"

"Because," said Drew dryly, "there can't be more than one
Anne Boleyn."

"Beg pardon?"

"What Drew means," explained Victoria, "is that we've
encountered several individuals who have memories of the same
ancestor. Two of them were in the same extended family, but
others seem to have little in common until we perform a
genealogical search. Then we find common ancestry. That,
alone, is enough to give us more faith in our theory."

"So, how would—I mean, what would you do with me?"

"If you're willing," said Victoria, "we'd like you to come in
on a regular schedule so that we can catalogue the experiences
you've already had and see if we can't figure out what triggers

them. I can tell you, for example, that Theron's are triggered by scents. We're just not completely certain which precise components trigger his episodes. We were just starting to nail that down when ... when he developed health problems that precluded him keeping up rigorous work with us."

"Scents," I murmured, and felt my mind already beginning to sift back through my oddball memories. "Would you need me to come in every day?"

"Of course we'd *love* that. It would be ideal. You'll be afforded a stipend. We wouldn't expect you to aid our research without compensation."

Compensation? Hell, I'd pay *them* if they could help me turn these episodes off. "I'm sure Doc Orlov has told you that I'm no longer employed. I'm on leave, so I've got all the time in the world. I don't mind telling you, Doctor Shehata, if you can help me figure this out and get my life back, that would be compensation enough."

Her eyes lit up with what I can only imagine was scientific zeal, and she leaned across the table toward me, holding out her hand for me to shake. "You can call me Victoria," she said. "How soon can you start?"

"Tomorrow's not soon enough," I said, and meant it most sincerely.

3
PROJECT BACKSTORY

When I checked in at the institute on the Monday after my first visit, they gave me my own keycard that doubled as an ID badge. Then they sat me down in a comfy chair, attached electrodes to my head, and had me talk them through every one of my episodes. They monitored my brain activity, recorded every word on video, and took notes as I spoke.

That took most of the day; it was late afternoon by the time I'd finished. My voice was raw, despite the fact that they'd kept me well-hydrated and given me several breaks for meals and exercise. Dr. Shehata—Victoria—referred to me as a "treasure trove." Drew Hastings even lost a little of his reserve when he told me that they'd never had a subject with as rich and diverse a set of episodes as mine or as well self-documented. Yes, I also gave them copies of my stories.

They sent me home, then, Victoria asking me to think about whatever scents or other catalysts might have been present in the environment when I dove into one of my fugue states. Their plan was to pore over the beginnings and ends of the episodes themselves, looking for some sort of common denominator. By the time I saw them again the next morning, I'd thought about scents quite a bit and had developed a theory of my own. Well, maybe it was more of a hypothesis.

"Maybe," I told Team Backstory, "Doctor Orlov is right and water is a common element. I know I told him there was no water on the playground at my elementary school. But, of course, there was."

Otis flicked aside his errant forelock and made a wry face. "Drinking fountains?"

"Rain birds. It's what they called those sprinkler heads that spin around shooting water," I clarified, when I realized the whole team looked puzzled. "If the trigger is scent, then my brain might interpret any scent of wet earth or wet foliage in the same way."

They exchanged meaningful glances, and I swear I thought Otis was going to bounce right out of his chair. They were off and running. While Victoria and Otis prepared some experimental scents for me to inhale, Sophie and Drew showed me brain scans they'd done of their benefactor, Theron Cornell, as he received his trigger scent. What they called the olfactory bulb was lit up like Christmas.

"This is what we would expect to see if you are reacting abnormally to olfactory input," said Sophie.

"Abnormally?"

"What you're looking at," said Drew, "is essentially an olfactory seizure. The scent of a particular mixture of spices sends Professor Cornell into a fugue state." He tapped the screen, and a series of scans opened up to the right of the first image, showing a completely different set of brain parts firing. "Here, you can see what's happening in his brain as he is experiencing the shift in consciousness to its new perspective. After he's been in the fugue state for several minutes, his brain shows relatively normal reactions to whatever stimuli he's receiving in that state."

"And he's come back from this fugue state and been able to describe what happened? Like I did?"

Sophie nodded. *"Précisément.* Yes."

I'd remembered all of my episodes. Right down to the news headlines of the day whenever I'd been able to see them. My squad of professors had noted all of that, too.

Victoria and Otis reappeared, carrying several potted plants and a tray full of other items. They didn't have to tell me why. I submitted willingly to having more electrodes attached to my head and a gadget that looked a lot like an old-fashioned beauty salon hair dryer bonnet placed atop those. I figured that was to take pictures of the inside of my brain while they shoved wet things under my nose, which was exactly what they did.

Nothing happened. At the end of several hours of trying different combinations of wetness and earth and clay and plants, Sophie suggested we might have to go on location with the experiment to determine what scents might work.

"Commercially sold soil one uses to pot the plants," she said, "may not produce the sort of scents experienced outdoors—and all but one of Peter's episodes began outdoors. *Peut-être*—I mean to say, perhaps—this is where we need to seek our catalyst."

This was what led to me taking a late afternoon walk with Victoria Shehata along the banks of the Hudson in the quaint tourist hot spot, Sleepy Hollow. The river chuckled happily along; the sun lowered in the sky and the day shift animals gave way to the night shift. Crickets came out; day birds tucked themselves away in their nests. We got as close to the water as we could, wandering along a cobbled path that had water seeping up between the stones in the lowest spots. I inhaled deeply of the moist air, taking in the smells of wet earth and stone, river reeds, soggy grass, and tree bark.

Nothing happened. I glanced sideways at Victoria. She watched me, no doubt hoping that I'd do a backflip into the state of fugue.

"Maybe I'm trying too hard," I said. "Maybe I need a distraction." *You're plenty distracting,* I didn't say. "So, ah, 'Shehata'—that's an unusual name. Sounds Japanese. No offense, but you don't look at all Japanese."

She laughed. "I'm not. Not even a little. My father is Egyptian and my mom is Scottish. I take after Mom, which Dad says is a good thing. He thinks he's funny-looking. Mom and I think he's pretty handsome. He's also quite tall."

"You're pretty tall yourself," I said, noting that though she was wearing flats, I could look almost directly into her eyes. I'm six-two; I figured she was pretty close to six feet.

"I do take after Dad in that one particular. We share a nickname, too: Stilts."

The light was failing here, among the trees. I was about to suggest we turn and go back when a strange, haunting bird call echoed across the waters of the Hudson. It sent chills all the way from the top of my head to the soles of my feet. I shivered, wriggling my shoulders to dispel the sensation.

"What?" Victoria asked. "What are you reacting to?"

"Loons. I swear to God that is the creepiest birdcall I've ever heard. Gives me the yips."

Victoria walked around in front of me and looked directly into my eyes. I had the impression she was checking my pupils for dilation. "Peter, that was more than just the yips. You checked out for a moment—just stood there shivering and blinking, like…"

"Like someone walked over my grave?"

"Yeah. Did you … go somewhere?"

I frowned and shook my head. "No. It was just like deer in the headlights stuff. Brain freeze. But that might mean something, right? That might mean my fugue trigger is something similar to a loon's call."

She smiled—no, she grinned. "It means we've got someplace to start."

We went back to the institute, during which trip the irony of a noisy loon throwing me for a loop struck me. Beside me, at the wheel of her car, Victoria chuckled. It was a warm, cozy sound, like Matilda the Cat's purr.

"Funny, isn't it," she said. "I mean, that the sound you responded to was the call of a loon, of all things."

I turned to look at her. "What—d'you think I'm ... loony?"

The chuckle became a full-throated laugh. "No. Far from it. I think you're remarkably sane under the circumstances."

When we got back to MIN, Victoria had Otis go online to collect birdcalls. Then she and Drew set up an experiment in which I listened to a barrage of sounds: crows cawing, owls hooting, doves cooing, and loons making a case for being equated with insanity. Meanwhile, they watched my brain dance. I was full of vim and vigor and hope that some birdcall to the left or right of looniness would trigger an event.

It didn't.

A certain type of birdcall—loon, mourning dove, owl—gave me that walked-over grave feeling, but none of them threw me into a fugue beyond a frozen moment in which I heard the shower music from *Psycho* playing somewhere in the distance.

What did it all mean? I had no idea; Victoria had no idea; none of the other members of Project Backstory had any idea. And yet ... and yet there was this *sense* hanging at the edge of my perception that we'd learned something about something. I just couldn't get that last tumbler to fall into place.

"You respond the most strongly to the loons and the doves," Victoria told me as she pointed out the part of my brain that was all fired up with no place to go. "That's the auditory cortex which, for lack of a better term, looks like it's getting ready for an auditory sneeze."

"A sneeze is a type of seizure, isn't it?" I asked.

She nodded, looking tired. It was past normal people's quitting time, but we were still here—Victoria and I at her lab station, Otis and Sophie poring over brain scans at the conference table by the floor-to-ceiling windows in the main lab. Drew had stepped out to take a phone call from his wife and little girl, so he could tell his daughter good night.

"But it's not the kind of seizure we've seen in Theron's results," Victoria said. "It's all buildup and no release."

She sat back and stretched while I tried not to notice how catlike and sensuous she was, even in the dark blue lab coat she usually wore over her street clothes. I distracted myself by noticing that it was late enough that the janitor had come in to clean up and empty the waste bins. He paused in the doorway, consulted his watch, and gave a resigned shrug. Then he headed for the nearest trash receptacle.

Victoria followed my gaze. "I think Charlie is trying to tell us he'd like us out of his domain," she said. "I'm starving, Maybe we should pack it in for the day and go get some dinner."

"Pizza?" I asked, hopefully. "I know a great little place over on Lex."

She opened her mouth to answer, but a startled exclamation from Charlie made us both jerk our heads around to look. He grappled with a trash bin, trying to pry the lid off. Even as we watched, he lost his balance and toppled against the coat rack by the door. The rack scooted sideways, the trash bin flipped over, and I found myself standing on a balcony overlooking a Venetian canal with a cup of something hot in my hands.

I'd seen enough travel guides to know where I was. There wasn't another city in the world exactly like Venice. Yes, Hamburg has more canals and—to hear the Hamburgers tell it—*superior* canals, but *this* was unmistakably Venice. The question was *when* was it Venice, and how long would I be here before I got back?

I took a sip of the hot beverage, which curled steam into the cool, crisp air from a small cup that had no handle. I held it Japanese style—thumb on the top rim, pinky beneath the bottom rim. The strong, almost smoky scent of coffee reached my nose a moment before the flavor hit my tongue. It was potent and reminded me of the Turkish brew I'd had at one of my favorite restaurants. I had no doubt you could stand a spoon in it.

As I registered this, and wondered if I remembered when coffee had come to Italy, a rattling sound came from the room behind me. I turned to see that someone was tapping on the half-open door of a luxurious parlor.

"Come in," I said, and a young woman entered and curtseyed politely.

"Master Augustino," she said primly, with lowered gaze, "Master DaVinci is here to see the duke."

Well, that more or less settled the time period.

"The duke is out, Cinzia. He is dining with the bishop this morning."

"Yes, sir. I mentioned this to Master DaVinci, and he says he is inclined to wait. Shall I put him in the winter parlor or on the patio?"

"The patio, I think," I (or my Augustino forebear) said. "The weather is yet mild. I shall entertain him until the duke returns."

I finished my burly Italian Joe and set the empty cup aside before straightening my (posh) robes, closing the balcony doors, and heading downstairs (through an absolutely amazing household) to the patio. There, I found Master Leonardo DaVinci seated at a table beneath a pergola with a fresh pot of hot chocolate, a plate of baked delicacies before him, and a large leather folio propped in the chair next to him.

I, Peter August, was starstruck with awe and wonder. I was meeting *the* Leonardo DaVinci. Himself. The ultimate Renaissance Man. My host, however, was merely pleased to see an old buddy.

"Leonardo! A pleasure," my host said suavely. "I see that Cinzia has taken good care of you."

The great man rose, smile lines radiating out from his eyes, and embraced me heartily, touching his cheeks to mine in quick, practiced succession. I was … er, surprised, but my host found it completely natural.

"Good day, Cristofano," our pal Leonardo greeted us. "Yes, Cinzia has been most attentive. She knows how well I have come to love a cup of hot chocolate these cool autumn mornings."

I seated myself across from him and poured a cup of the steamy stuff for myself, taking a biscuit from the tiered plate the girl had left. "I daresay, the chocolate and pastries are really why you are here, old friend. The duke is merely an excuse … am I right?"

AMIRITE? Really? Renaissance guys talk like high schoolers from Queens? Of course, I suspected we were actually speaking Italian, but it sounded like English to me … or at least, I understood it as if it were English. Fascinating. Something for Vic and company to puzzle over … if and when I got home.

Of course, you'll get home, I told myself. *You always get home.*

Somehow that comforting logic seemed to have little effect on my anxiety. I suspected that something about Charlie's trash bin juggling had triggered this episode and I was eager to get back to my modern self to figure out what it was.

Leonardo was saying something, but I was distracted by the splash of water fifteen feet to my right across the ornately tiled courtyard. My host turned his head to look. A pair of small, brightly colored ducks played in the water, reminding me of something.

Waterfowl. Specifically, loons.

My mind raced. Fox Aubry had been riding through the woods in the gloaming and had surprised some birds. Amenaru had been traveling along the Nile in the early morning—surely there were waterfowl of all kinds in the reeds. Other examples flooded my mind. Did different trigger sounds produce different effects?

My thoughts milling, I turned back to my old buddy, Leonardo, and inquired how his latest painting was coming along.

"Well," he said, stroking crumbs from his beard, "the subject is lovely enough, though she has trouble sitting still for long. I barely have time to catch the curve of her cheek or the tilt of her head before she's glancing here and there, peering at this and that, asking questions. This last session, I placed her so that she could watch the flower vendors in the square below my studio. I believe she is quite taken with a red-haired young man and he with her, if his frequent glances through the window serve as evidence. If I don't finish the painting before spring and am forced to complete it at the Castle Sforza, I suppose I shall have to hire the young buck to travel to Milan with your master's household. Or have him arrested." His eyes twinkled.

"If he is as smitten by your subject as you suppose," I said, "I doubt he'd find being arrested and made prisoner in the duke's castle much of a hardship."

His subject, I knew (because my host did), was my master's daughter, Bianca. She was fourteen this year and, though she was illegitimate, was much sought after by pining minor nobles and their scheming parents. She was also Ludovico Sforza's only daughter, and he was as much in her thrall as Leonardo's red-haired flower vendor.

"In fact," Leonardo told us now, "it is Mistress Bianca's portrait I have come to speak to the duke about. In spite of my beautiful subject's inconstancy, I have completed two preliminary sketches of her and wish him to select the pose he feels does her the most justice." He patted the folio propped in the neighboring chair.

I opened my mouth to ask if I might see the drawings, when the duke himself appeared in the doorway of his patio as if he had been summoned. He was a tall, lean man with an angular, handsome face and a thick head of dark, curly, shoulder-length hair. He looked as if he ought to be playing bass for a power rock band. He had a way of looking down his rather elegant nose that lent him a great deal of gravitas. Or would, but for the way his mouth curled up at the corners as if he were seconds away from laughing.

I liked him on sight. My ancestor liked him from long association. Leonardo seemed to like him too, though possibly that was because he enjoyed his patronage. I mean, how do you not like someone who pays you to do what you love? AMIRITE?

Leonardo and Cristofano rose smoothly to bow to the duke. Leonardo exchanged pleasantries with his patron, then Sforza turned to me and instructed me to make certain the preparations for the banquet he was giving this evening were well in hand.

Thankfully, I made my good-byes and went off to do just that. In the back of my host's mind I pondered the urgent question as to when we might encounter a loon, a mourning dove, or an owl. Was there an open body of water besides the canals and the ocean? Would another sound throw me out of this fugue?

I had no answers. All I could do was sit tight as Cristofano Augustino went about his duties. They took him to the kitchens, to the servants' hall, even to the stables. All the while I prayed he'd have to go near a canal. While on our way back from the duke's luxury horse hotel (Peccadillo would have been green with envy), I caught a break. Cristofano's route from the stables to the main palazzo took him to a tall set of thick wooden doors. He reached out a hand for the latch, then changed his mind, turning left, instead, to skirt the building. The next thing I knew we were on a walkway above the canal that flowed past the palace.

The scent of salt water wafted up from below, and the sounds of the city—the splash of oars, the shouts of boatmen as they navigated the canal, the lapping of wavelets against stone—stopped me in my tracks. I scanned the waters hopefully for loons. My ride-along with Amenaru led me to hope they favored the Mediterranean at this time of year.

From the corner of Cristofano's eye, I saw flashes of stark black and white, pointed beaks, neck rings. Ooh, baby.

Sing, you little creeps! Sing!

But they didn't sing, and I was getting ready to gnash my mental teeth when Cristofano brought himself up short with a murmured, "Dear God!"

Why, I have no idea. He was clearly in distress, and leaned heavily against the parapet that overlooked the canal. We heard a wild flutter of wings, and about half a dozen doves burst from beneath the parapet. We tilted our head back to watch them fly away, and I blinked as they banked into the morning sun.

Victoria stared into my eyes, her hands clutching mine.

"Whoa," I said artfully, and winced. What was that *noise*?

"Stop!" Victoria cried, and the cacophony ended.

I turned my head, discovering that I had electrodes pasted to my scalp and chest and the lab's hairdryer-hood scanner popped down over my skull. Otis Chen stood by the door to the lab with a trash bin in his hands, peering at me through a cascade of hair. From the dents along the bottom, I suspected he'd been banging that bin on the floor for some time.

"Episode duration, ten minutes, twenty-eight seconds," said Drew from behind me.

I tried to turn to look at him, but couldn't. Victoria let go of my hands, took a last glance at her monitor, and started to pull the electrodes off my chest. Sophie appeared out of nowhere to lift the MRI hood and free my head of electrodes as well. When I was finally able to look at Drew, he turned his monitor around so I could see it.

"This is what your brain did when Charlie dropped the trash bin, Peter," he told me. His expression was one of banked excitement.

Drew, I had come to know, was a lot like Egon of the original *Ghostbusters*. I could imagine him saying, with deadpan sincerity, "Peter, I'm terrified beyond the capacity for rational thought." Or, in this case, "Peter, I'm excited beyond the capacity to Snoopy dance."

What his monitor showed was a brilliant explosion in my auditory cortex.

"That's a seizure, right?" I asked. "That's what my fugue state looks like."

"To be more accurate," said Egon Hastings, "that's what the *catalyst* for your fugue state looks like. Your fugue state looks a bit more normal."

He showed me that, too. My fugue state was more muted and diffuse, but I knew from having pondered many scans of my brain that even this was not quite normal.

"So that was it?" I asked. "The sound the trash bin made when it hit the floor?" I shot a glance at Otis, who looked pretty beat after ten minutes of trashing bins.

Victoria nodded. "Metal on stone. It sounded like a gong. What I don't get is why it took so long to bring you back. Maybe Otis's banging was overload."

I shook my head, raking my fingers through my hair—or at least trying too. I'd gotten lazy about getting it cut and it had gotten a bit out of control. "That's not what brought me back. The birds. The birds are what brought me back. There were mourning doves nesting around the duke's palace."

"*Le duc?*" echoed Sophie in Français, dark eyes wide.

"Two distinct triggers," murmured Victoria, ignoring her. "You're sure?"

"Very." I glanced to where Otis was trying to set the trash bin upright again. "Careful with that, pal. I don't really want a return trip to the Renaissance, Leonardo DaVinci notwithstanding."

"*Vraiment*? You met Leonardo DaVinci?" asked Sophie, in what I can only call a church voice.

"Hey," I said, holding up crossed fingers. "We were like *that*."

4

CORNELL

My debriefing took a little over an hour, during which I related everything I could recall of my visit to Renaissance Italy. I was exhausted by now, almost punchy, but I managed to be coherent. Only Victoria and Otis stayed for my report; Sophie had a meeting with her doctoral adviser the next morning, for which she insisted on being well-rested, and Drew had gone home to his family. His daughter, Eva, Victoria told me, had been ill and he worried about her constantly. With Drew, it was hard to tell. I've known few people more focused.

Vic and Otis recorded everything I said so we could go over it again in the morning. I knew I wasn't likely to forget anything, but they didn't know me as well as I did. I took a cab home because I didn't own a car (for obvious reasons beyond being a single guy living in NYC); Otis and Victoria took a cab and left their cars in the parking structure because neither felt safe to drive.

Knowing what my fugue trigger was changed the way I moved through the world. I mean, I'm a detective—or I was—so I tend to notice things other people might miss, or react to stimuli they might screen out. But now, I found I was listening for certain types of sounds and watching for their potential sources.

On my way home that night, I found myself noticing every freaking metal container on every corner the cab passed. I noticed every construction site at which, during the work day, metal might be expected to come in violent contact with some other hard substance. When I got out of the cab, I noticed the metal trash bins sitting along the curb in front of the row of brownstones on my quiet street. The sound of a garbage truck engine—which at that moment I realized was quite distinctive—sent me bounding up the front steps of my building, into the lobby, and up the stairs to my second-floor apartment, loudly whistling "Eine kleine Nachtmusik" for good measure.

I didn't go to bed. Well, that is, I *tried* to go to bed, but my mind refused to shut off. I found myself going over previous episodes of *Peter August—Time Diver*, cataloguing and reaffirming what this evening's unexpected experiment had shown. Beside me, Matilda snored peacefully. There were times like this, I thought I might prefer being a cat. Finally, I got up, went into my kitchen, and made a cup of hot, black tea loaded with cream and sugar. Then I sat at the kitchen table with a notepad and pencil. Matilda followed me to hop up and make like a cat loaf on the chair to my right. She was immediately asleep, deep in dreams of chasing geckos she'd never catch. She muttered a couple of "eks", but didn't wake.

My episodes were not so frequent that I had them every Wednesday during trash pickup. I could only think of one Wednesday since I'd been on leave that I'd had a fugue, and that had been before the weather started to turn; I'd been out on the balcony overlooking the street. It struck me, though, that I was often in bed when the sanitation guys came for the trash. That would possibly explain some of my more vivid dreams.

I wrote *trash cans* on my notepad.

I'd had another episode while crossing the park catty-corner to my apartment. There were trash bins there, but they were those big stone jobs. The lids were metal and had holes in the centers. I supposed that if someone threw something particularly hard into the bin, it *might* make that gong sound. I frowned, trying to remember the exact place I'd had the fugue. I even considered getting dressed and going over to look, but I wasn't that desperate. It could wait until morning.

Dumpsters went on the list, along with *manhole covers, water pipes, sidewalk elevators,* and *playground equipment*. I pondered the list. After a moment of thought and recall, I added *fire escapes*, which tended to clang when trodden upon or—in the case of the retractable ones—when the pulleys were activated.

This was good, I told myself. If I could keep my head in the game, I might be able to manage this thing. And if I could manage this thing, I could go back to work. Heck, maybe now that I knew what the trigger was, Doc Orlov could give me some sort of post-hypnotic suggestion that would make me less susceptible to particular sounds. I didn't care about the bird-calls. If I never fugued again, the worst I'd ever get out of a loony tune, a hoot, or a coo was a brief moment of hyperventilation. So what if they gave me the yips, at least they didn't shoot my neurons down a time vortex.

At the end of my list making, I was relaxed enough to try sleep again. This time, I succeeded, and woke up with early morning sun streaming in my bedroom window. I showered, dressed, fed Matilda, and headed off to pick up breakfast at the café across the park.

The air was crisp and fall-like, and a fitful breeze gallivanted through the trees like a playful puppy. The joggers all looked perky and fully awake. Annoying, really.

On a whim, I took a loop through the section of the park where I'd had an episode a couple of weeks before. It was near the center of the green space at the confluence of several paved walks, where a fountain was set in the middle of a circular plaza. I also saw two trash bins—both solid cement and pebble with metal lids.

I stopped near the fountain, trying to remember if I'd seen anyone tossing stuff into one of the bins the day of my episode. I hadn't, though I supposed that must have been the trigger.

I heard a soft pinging sound and turned. That was when I saw the flagpole. It stood on the edge of the circular plaza between two of the radiating paths, a Parks and Services pennant and a state flag flying from the top. The halyard that held them aloft swayed in the breeze. The pinging sound was the halyard rubbing against the flagpole.

The *metal* flagpole.

No way that cable was heavy enough to make my trigger sound. My eyes followed the cable's ascent. High up on the pole, a big old carabiner snap hook held the two ends of the halyard together. I felt all my senses go on point, and my fight-or-flight instincts kick in. I skipped backward three steps, nearly colliding with a jogger, but taking my eyes off the carabiner seemed about as logical to me in that moment as turning my back on an armed murder suspect.

Even as I started to turn and bolt for the café, the breeze buffeted the flagpole, and the carabiner struck the hollow metal with a blow I never heard, because I was on my knees in the Temple of Imhotep, offering dates and incense at the altar.

I knew, of course, that Nebemakhet was the one who ate those dates. I aimed a glance at him as I rose from my worship and saw that he was already eyeing them. Sun glinted off the medallion at his throat. I, Amenaru, was more than a little jealous of that singular honor. If I were older, I might have been the one to ascend to the high priesthood and receive the amulet and its secret. Nebemakhet was only a handful of seasons my senior, though he was of a more illustrious family ... or at least a more opportunistic one.

How many times, Amenaru wondered, as we completed our last bow toward the altar, would he have to listen to the high priest going on and on about how the great doctor had entrusted him with the amulet? How many divergent details would he catalogue regarding the circumstances under which the bestowal had been made? The story was slightly different every time Nebemakhet told it, which had led Amenaru and Har-khebu to suspect that their superior had not so much been given the piece as he had simply taken it from the Great Scribe's personal effects.

The only thing consistent in Nebemakhet's story was his claim that the amulet would lead him to some great Knowledge about life and death that Imhotep had been given by the gods— possibly through his mother, who was a demigod herself—and that, at the right moment, Nebemakhet would reveal that Knowledge to the world ... and so on and so forth and blah, blah, yada, yada.

Amenaru shook his head. *What words are these?*

Whoa. That was interesting. Had he heard my thoughts? Was there some sort of reverse leakage across the neuronal memory? How was that even possible?

I didn't have much time to contemplate that, because Nebemakhet was even now leading the way to the library where Har-ib and I put in most of our hours transcribing moldering old texts into shiny new ones. This was a large, impressive room with tall ceilings, ample light from windows on all but one side, and braces of oil lamps, so we minions could work into the night. The one complete wall was covered with shelves and cubbies containing bound tomes and folioed sheaves of loose pages and scrolls of every size and fabric. There were even a few stacks of clay tablets near the bottom.

I studied the far-off eaves, listening for the sound of wings in the rafters, or something that might get me the heck out of here. As far as I knew, I was rooted to the ground in a park in

New York City where any pickpocket might steal me blind or any beat cop mistake me for a homeless drug addict who'd fixated on a flagpole. Chafing accomplished nothing, and Amenaru and I took our place at our writing desk and fished a text out of the basket on the floor next to it.

We set up our tools—a pot of water, a palette with reed pens, and a block of pigment—and examined the first candidate. It was quite faded, and Amenaru knew from the get-go that this one was going to be a bear. While he scratched his head over the washed-out glyphs, I reveled in the sudden realization that I was reading Egyptian hieroglyphs and understanding what they said. This tablet was about the internal organs. My host was delighted.

Great. I was squeamish about giving my horse shots, and Amenaru was into viscera. I know, you're wondering how a major crimes detective can be squeamish about needles. Corpses are part of my work; cutting into live people or sticking needles into my old buddy Pecs is just different.

I wondered how long Amenaru and I would work before we had to take a leak. Maybe we'd see some birds on the way to the little scribe's room.

We dipped a sharpened reed in water and let a drop of the liquid out atop the block of pigment. The tip made *slick-snick* sounds as we rubbed it in the black slurry. We blotted it slightly and set it to the blank papyrus on the table. The reed whispered as we translated the old glyphs into the more nimble hieratic.

Huh. I could now read hieratic.

We wrote a lovely series of characters describing the removal of a human kidney, pausing to re-wet our reed at intervals. Before we moved on to the next body part, we looked up at Nebemakhet, whose writing desk was set up facing his apprentices. It did not escape our notice that he was writing with one hand and caressing his medallion with the other. He'd been doing that a lot lately, and Amenaru and I couldn't help but wonder if it meant he was planning on making his big revelation soon.

"Attend to your work, Amenaru, not to mine," he told us, without even looking up from his own scribbling.

"Yes, sir," Amenaru said, and I shivered as a crisp wind frisked around the legs of my jeans.

I came back to myself quickly, not knowing how soon the sound of that damned carabiner striking the flagpole—which I could hear clearly now—might send me somewhere else. It seemed I had some sort of grace period, but I had no idea how long it was. I turned and loped toward the café, chilled and desperately wanting that cup of coffee.

How had I done it? How had I come out of my dive?

As I was about to leave the park, I glanced back over my shoulder at the fountain plaza. A woman was just rising from one of the stone benches, flinging crumbs from a small, white bag onto the ground while a horde of greedy (and very fat) birds of sundry types scurried around her feet.

I contemplated this during the time I spent standing in an unusually long line at the Morning Grind and throughout the cab ride to the institute. Was it possible that if I heard the bird-call in *my* present, it would pull me back from my ancestor's? Or had there been a bird in the eves of Nebemakhet's library? Or had I responded to a different but similar sound in Amenaru's environment? I supposed there was only one way to find out, so I steamed into the lab, coffee in hand, ready to propose an experiment (for *science!*).

The proposal died on my lips; someone new was in the lab this morning—a forty-ish man, taller than I by a few inches and with much longer hair. I'd let mine grow out from its on-duty-detective sleekness into curly anarchy, but this guy had a *mane*. It was a well-styled mane that fell gracefully to his collar, and was tastefully silver at the temples. In a police procedural, he'd be the homicide chief of detectives or, better yet, the lead prosecutor—the DA who always gets his man ... or maybe Sherlock Holmes.

On the other hand, he'd be the guy in a horror film that you trusted until you found his fangs a bit too close to your favorite neck. Either way, in my beat-up brown bomber jacket, with my hair falling in my eyes, I felt downright scruffy. The components were James Dean; the effect was Dean Winchester.

Now, this first impression was possibly due to the fact that the new guy was engaged in an intense and seemingly intimate conversation with Victoria Shehata at her lab station, and I was already fighting a strong attraction to her. One I probably shouldn't indulge. She wore no rings, but other than that clue I had no idea of the existence of a possible Significant Other, nor did I think it appropriate to ask. I mean, we'd known each other for less than a week.

And, of course, there was the Peter August curse ...

At the sound of the door swinging closed behind me, Victoria swiveled her chair so she could peer past the new guy. I took the expression on her face when she saw me as pleasure and relief, which she confirmed when she jumped up from her chair and took a couple of strides in my direction before stopping and shoving her hands into the pockets of her lab coat.

"Peter! Thank God you're all right. I was getting worried. You weren't answering your phone."

I pulled my phone out of my pocket. Sure enough, I'd gotten three messages from Victoria at about the time I was editing the Ancient Surgeons' Manual. I realized only then how late it was. I must have been frozen in that plaza for a while. That explained the long line at the café. So far this week I'd slipped in just ahead of the morning office crowd. Today, I'd hit it in mid-rush, which had held me up even more. Add to that the rush-hour traffic ...

"Sorry," I said. "I—uh—I had a ... a thing."

"A thing?" asked the new guy, who'd turned to appraise me.

I do mean "appraise," by the way. I felt as if he were assessing everything from my anarchic hair to my aging leather sneakers and beat-up jacket. After that thorough once-over, his smile surprised me with its genuineness.

"You must be Peter," he said, and came over to offer his hand. His voice was a warm baritone and sounded as if he'd just popped across the Pond via Heathrow. "I'm Theron. Theron Cornell."

I felt as if I should babble some exposition. *Ah, Theron Cornell, PhD, MD. Neuroscientist, philanthropist, and award-winning inventor of medical equipment? Pleased to meet you.*

I didn't do that. I simply shook hands with the man and noticed that he looked a little pale.

Vampire?

"By 'thing,' do I understand that you mean you had an episode?" Cornell asked. His pale eyes locked with mine—hopefully, I thought.

I nodded. "Yeah. A flagpole in the park across the street from my apartment has a metal fitting that smacks the pole when the wind hits it just right. This morning, it hit just right. My trigger is—"

"Yes," said Cornell, "I know. Victoria has been keeping me abreast of your progress. Gongs and birds. My triggers are olfactory—spices. Pumpkin pie spices to be exact, but we never did determine what components were key before I had to withdraw from the program for health reasons."

I did not imagine the regret in his eyes or the tightness around his mouth. His incapacity bothered him a lot, I was willing to bet. I remembered, suddenly, why I'd been so eager to get here this morning.

"Listen, Victoria—something happened this morning. The flagpole triggered a dive into Amenaru, but I think the return trigger was something in my environment *here*."

"Here? You mean … ?"

"I mean in *my* environment, not Amenaru's. When I left, he was transcribing a surgical procedure from an old parchment onto papyrus. He was indoors—not a bird in sight."

Theron Cornell and Victoria exchanged glances, then Cornell said, "But there were birds in *your* environment?"

I nodded. "A woman was feeding a flock of pigeons and other lowlifes. I assume that was it, anyway. There might've been birds all around in a park. But it suggests a line of experimentation, doesn't it? Send me somewhere, then see if loons in the lab bring me back."

Victoria looked excited for precisely one second, then she frowned. "What if they don't, Peter? What if it was something in Amenaru's environment you weren't aware of?"

"Look," I said, "I've never been stranded anywhere for more than about twenty minutes in real time. I'm willing to take the chance if it gets me a step closer to figuring out how all this works."

THE FIRST ORDER of business was to isolate the birdcalls that gave me the worst heebie-jeebies. Otis had found recordings of three that seemed to produce tremors of equal magnitude. Then they plugged me in and hooked me up to the hairdryer and had Otis fetch a trash can and a metal baseball bat.

Theron Cornell watched the whole exercise with intense interest. I was at least as curious about him as he was about me. From what I knew of him—which, granted, wasn't a whole lot—he was as much a loner as I was. No wife, no kids, no significant other of any kind. Was he that way for the same reason—the constant fear of fugues?

Doesn't matter, I told myself, trying not to think of Lauren.

You're not going to be "that way" for much longer. As soon as we'd figured out how these triggers worked, I was off to Doc Orlov for The Cure.

"Ready?" Otis asked me.

"As I'll ever be," I told him.

I saw him wind up; I didn't hear the sound that sent me diving into an Egyptian ancestor.

It wasn't Amenaru this time. It was Omarius Statius Prisca. I'd been here before and knew by now that my ancestor was a young minister—a *vicarius*—at the Memphis court of a newly appointed Roman consul named Flavius Anthemius. I was a man of letters, a scholar, a deputy consul.

I was also in a dither about my clothes. Tonight was the night that I would ask the magistrate Honorius Donatus for the hand of his daughter, Sennia, in marriage. I, Peter, already knew that his answer would be yes. (Spoilers: I'd watched these episodes out of order.) Should I make an effort to hide that from my host? Did I need to? How permeable was the membrane between the two of us, after all?

Omarius (Omari to his closest friends and family) was at last satisfied that he was as dashing as all get out, and left off staring into the highly polished piece of metal he used for a mirror. I was overwhelmed, suddenly and unexpectedly, by a wave of love and affection so intense it was almost as if I were experiencing it myself. Hell, it was *exactly* as if I were experiencing it myself. Focused on the object of his adoration as he was, I couldn't help but imagine her through his eyes and heart—the beautiful, angelic Sennia Donata. She of the golden-brown hair and olivine eyes, whose complexion was autumn wheat, whose voice was dove song (wouldn't that be handy?), and whose love was the sweetest honey.

Did I mention that Omari was a poet? I swear he was composing verses all the way to his beloved's family home, where there was a small gathering this evening. Sennia's father,

Honorius, knew what the visit was all about and approved. Omarius was from a good family and, even at his young age, was moving on an upward path in local government. Perhaps he would one day be prefect or an adviser to caesars.

It was not a comfortable place for me to be, inside this kid's head. I wondered, again, about the permeability of the neuronal barrier between us, and wished I had a better grasp of neuroscience. While he watched the road between his horse's ears, I scanned peripherally for water fowl, looking to the Nile for salvation. But we arrived at Sennia's family villa in short order and dismounted, handing our horse off to a stable hand before running lightly up the steps.

We were announced and admitted to the main hall by a steward. Before we had taken two steps into the residence, there she was, standing at the top of a grand staircase dressed in a gown of indigo with gems sparkling in her hair. Omari and I were overcome. I tried to step out of the stream of emotion, but found I couldn't. Omari's love for Sennia washed over me in a deep wave that stirred up ghosts from my own past—a night on the banks of the Missouri that should have been a beginning, but was an ending instead. A new ghost, born moments ago, had Victoria's face.

Victoria … When would she bring me back?

Omarius ripped our attention from the object of his adoration and turned to answer the hearty greeting from her father, who had appeared in the doorway of his salon.

"Peter, are you back with us?" Victoria asked me.

I blinked and, for an instant, still saw Sennia Donata. It took a moment for me to pull the two women apart, but then I was firmly back in the lab, getting grinned at by everyone on the team but Drew and Cornell (neither of whom I could even imagine grinning). I was slow in coming to why they were grinning at me in the first place, but when I got it, I felt as if I'd just done   something   extraordinary—climbed   Godwin-Austen, maybe, or cracked a murder case single-handedly (which, I can tell you, *never* happens).

"What was it?" I asked. "What brought me back?"

"We tried owls this time," said Otis cheerfully. "Had to crank the volume a bit, but it worked like a charm."

My excitement faded quickly when I realized that, of course, these guys couldn't follow me around with a recording device playing me birdcalls to release me from a fugue. Nor could they keep me from diving into one if I happened to get blindsided by a rogue gong player or some city worker mishandling a manhole cover.

"Okay, so now you can bring me back, and that's great—really, it is—but you can't babysit me twenty-four-seven. And frankly, I don't see me making my prospective partners download hoot owls and dove coos and loon cackles to their phones so they can drag me back from other-when. There has to be some way that *I* can trigger my trigger."

Cornell perched on the corner of the workbench at which I sat, and considered what I'd said with a furrowed brow. "You seem to be at least partially present here, physically, even in the midst of your episodes. Just now, your eyes were moving and you reached up a couple of times to smooth your clothing."

"Yeah, I was standing in front of a mirror, checking myself out before I went to visit my sweetheart." I glanced at Victoria and felt a strange tickle of Sennia worship—odd, because the two women were not much alike to look at. "My host was Omarius," I explained.

"Omarius," Cornell repeated. "That was the deputy consul, yes?"

I nodded.

"So then," Cornell mused, "you sometimes echo *here*, what's happening there?"

"Yeah, I guess so. Lauren once told me I was speaking in tongues, and the night my partner was shot, I, uh, I apparently dove into some bushes, mimicking what was happening in my head."

"If that's the case," said Cornell, "maybe there's some way you could signal someone at this end when you want to be retrieved."

"Yeah, maybe. Except that I'm not exactly in control of my destiny at that end. I mean, these are memories, right? So they've happened a certain way." For some reason I was reluctant to mention the possible leakage I'd experienced with Amenaru and possibly Cristofano. I wasn't sure how that fit into Victoria's theories.

What Cornell had said had made her eyes light up. "It's possible, though," she said, "that you'd be able to trigger a retrieval just by producing a particular brain wave. For example, if you mentally recited mathematical equations, it would cause your brain to exhibit abnormal activity."

She was more right about that than she knew. My relationship with math was strained, at best. Abnormal activity was a given.

"So, when you see abnormal activity you bring me home? Sounds dicey. What if my abnormal brain activity is due to something other than the times tables?"

She looked resolute. "We can figure that out, Peter. We can figure all of this out."

There was a moment of awkward silence, then Cornell asked, "What do we know about this particular ancestor—do you have any idea about what time period he lived in?"

"We've got some history students researching the names," said Victoria. "Nothing on Omarius or Sennia so far, but we have located Omarius's boss, Flavius Anthemius. He was a Roman Consul in early fifth-century Egypt."

Cornell mulled that over, then shook his head. "I have often wondered what it is that determines who and when one goes to when they fugue."

"One of many questions," said Drew, "that we hope to answer."

"The only question I hope to answer," I said, "is how do I control this or stop it?"

They all looked at me as if I'd started speaking Latin (which, possibly, I had).

"Stop it?" Victoria echoed. "Peter, do you have any idea how rare a gift this is?"

"Gift? It's a lifelong curse, Vic. It's cost me more than I can calculate. Yes, I want it to stop. Trust me, I've thought about stop-gaps—noise-cancelling headphones, listening to rock and roll whenever I'm in an unpredictable environment. But news flash, everybody: I'm a detective. That's all I've ever wanted to be. And a detective moves and lives in unpredictable environments. It's unavoidable. I had a life of sorts, and I'd really like to get back to it."

They all looked at each other as if trying to decide by telepathy who was going to speak for them. It turned out to be Theron Cornell.

"If you're worried about making a living, Peter, I'm willing and able to pay you handsomely for the work you do here. But the fact is, Project Backstory needs you. In the two years they've been doing this research, there have been only two subjects whose connection to ancestors has been strong enough to provide the sort of firsthand view of the past that historians and educators crave. Only two. Yes, other individuals have these experiences, but so far, the few we've encountered have episodes that are so limited—lasting only moments even in the subjective time of the episode—that they were virtually impossible to reproduce."

"It's true," Victoria said, possibly because my face was wearing my skepticism. "We mostly collected anecdotes—stories like the ones you told us, but none anywhere near as detailed, as rich, as reliable as yours."

"Mine and the other guy," I corrected. "You said there was another one like me."

She tilted her head toward Cornell. "Theron is the 'other one' like you."

I saw where this was going. "So, you're telling me, I'm it." I looked at Cornell. "You really can't do this anymore—you're sure?"

"Show him, Victoria," he said.

She sat down at her computer while Otis lifted the hairdryer off my head and pulled all my leads. The large monitor on the workbench next to me blanked then displayed a new set of images. They were still brain scans and vital signs, but Theron Cornell's, not mine.

"This was Theron's last episode," Victoria said, "from just before fugue to return. Watch the heart monitor."

I did. It wasn't pretty. Theron Cornell's heart rate spiked and went ragged when he fugued, labored while he was in the episode, and flatlined for two terrifying seconds when he returned. His brain scan wasn't much better. The bright flower of consciousness seemed to contract before it stabilized, and even I could tell that stability wasn't at a normal level.

"I recovered, obviously," Cornell said quietly, "but there is a real possibility that if I were to dive into my ancestral past again, it might kill me. A heart transplant might at least give me stability, but I have a rare blood type—the rarest, in fact. Heart donors are practically nonexistent. At least with my trigger being what it is, it's more easily avoidable than yours."

I took a deep breath and let it out. "Obi-wan, you're my only hope—is that about it?"

Victoria nodded. "Yeah, that's about it."

"Explain to me why this is important—this research you're doing. Historians, linguists and archaeologists will be tickled pink, I get that, but what else?"

"How can you ask that?" asked Drew quizzically. "What we

might learn about human neural development alone is priceless. Understanding how this can possibly happen, what causes it, why it's so strong in some individuals and virtually absent in others ... Can you understand how valuable this information could be?"

"At this moment, what I understand best is how valuable a *normal* life could be."

Victoria swiveled in her chair, leaning forward so she almost touched me. "We're not asking you for the rest of your life, Peter. Not even for years. A few more weeks, maybe a couple of months. The more we learn about the mechanism of your— your—"

"Time diving?"

"That's as good a description as any, I guess. The more we learn about it, the more we're likely to be able to control it. There must be other ... time divers out there. We're looking for them all the time, through advertising, through referrals from therapists like Greg Orlov. So many are hoaxers, so unstable or so convinced these are their own past lives, they skew their own narratives. I have to hold out hope that we'll find more like you so we can learn more. And now that we've established the triggering mechanism for you and Theron and seen how we can fully manipulate it, it'll be easier to replicate our results with new subjects. But would you consider staying with this for a while, at least?"

They all stared at me the way I imagine kids look at their dad while standing at the front door with a stray kitten, but Victoria's dark gaze gave me the most unease, because it turned my steely resolve to something with the consistency of soggy pie crust.

"All right. I'll consider it," I said. "But I need to know there's some way to get my life back."

We seemed to have a truce. I recorded my observations from the most recent trip—brief though it was—describing my home and Sennia's, our dress and jewelry and the parts of Memphis I'd seen, in painstaking detail. They had me go back over my recent trip to Amenaru as well, lingering on the sophisticated nature of the medical texts he was transcribing. They wanted me to take another dive, but I protested that I was a little strung out after my dual fugue day and that I wanted to think about their proposition that I stay with the project longer.

What I really wanted to do was see Dr. Greg about the power of hypnosis.

5
LEAKAGE

"I was a bit surprised to hear from you," Greg Orlov told me as I seated myself at the little conference table in his office. "How are things going at the institute?"

"They're going," I said evasively.

He quirked an eyebrow. "Meaning?"

"Meaning we've made a lot of progress in a fairly short period of time."

"But?"

I hated that he could read me so well. "Okay, here's the situation: We know what triggers my episodes and we know how to get me back if I fugue."

"But?" he said again, his expression unchanging.

"But that doesn't help me get my life back, because getting me back to reality requires outside help from someone who knows what the hell to do when I go full zombie."

He shrugged. "Is that insurmountable? Like you just said, you've made an amazing amount of progress in a short period of time. Vic's team is pretty sharp, technologically. I'm certain they'll eventually find a way to let you break out of your fugues at will."

"D'you understand how any of this works?" I asked.

"Victoria has shared some of her theories with me, sure. You have a neuronal link to individuals in your genetic tree. You can share their memories as if they were your own."

I opened my mouth to say something about leakage going both ways, but edited myself right out of the gate. "Yeah, there's a definite sense of being in two places at once. But the operative term here is 'eventually'. I want out *now*. Now that I know what this is—how it's triggered, how I get back—I want to figure out how to make it go away. That's why I've come to you."

"What do you think I can do?"

"Give me a post-hypnotic suggestion."

He smiled. "Cluck like a chicken instead of fugue?"

I wasn't in a joking mood. "I was thinking more of not leaping back into my family tree when I hear someone bang on a piece of metal."

He studied me solemnly for a moment, then said, "It might be possible. It depends a lot on timing. That is, on how quickly the part of your brain that's experiencing these seizures reacts to the sound. Tell me, when someone bangs on a piece of metal, how much of the sound are you conscious of hearing?"

That was easy. "None of it. If I'd heard it, I would have realized what was causing this a long time ago."

"It's possible, then, that a posthypnotic suggestion to do something else when you hear that sound would fail to short-circuit the neural mechanism. For one thing, Peter, I'd have to *make* the sound in order to direct you to ignore it. Now, I might be able to hypnotize you and instruct you not to react to any sound you hear until I wake you. Then again, I might just send you off to the Spanish Inquisition. If we're going to try this, we should probably do it at MIN so that, if you fugue, Vic can bring you back."

I looked down at the knees of my jeans. "Yeah, about that. I was kind of hoping not to bring the Backstory gang into this.

They're not exactly on board with me shutting this down. They think it's this great, valuable, earth-shaking gift I've been given and they want me to keep at it—at least until they can find someone else with my ... profile."

"Ah. Meaning someone with a strong genetic connection, a proven ability for cognitive transference, an eidetic memory, and the instincts and training of a police detective?"

Well, when you put it that way ...

"You think I should stick with it, don't you? For science, and all that."

He rocked forward in his chair, elbows on the table, hands clasped before him, looking very doctor-like. "I think you should do whatever you need to do to maintain your mental and emotional health. But it *is* a pretty cool gift, isn't it? Isn't there a part of you that revels in it?"

I started to deny that, then hesitated. Yeah, there was a certain heady sense of adventure about all this, but ... "I don't revel in losing people, Doc. Lauren and Melchior were the people I've been closest to in the world except for my parents. And they're gone. Not gone, gone—not dead—but I'm pretty much dead to them. Because of this so-called gift. A gift that's made it damn hard to let myself get close to people. I'm not a natural loner, Doc. I've had to learn how to be one. How to conceal a big part of myself from just about everyone."

Except for Victoria and Team Backstory. I couldn't ignore the sense of relief I'd felt when I realized Peter August's weird, scary, Mitty-esque secret life wasn't weird or scary or even off-putting to any of them.

"I get it, Peter. I do," he told me. "Like I said, I don't know if I can do what you ask, but I'm willing to try, if that's what you want. I'll need to be able to replicate your trigger sound and whatever it is that brings you back."

"Loons," I said absently, already contemplating the nature of blessings and curses. "Loons, doves, or hoot owls."

"Should be easy enough."

He got up and moved to his desk, where he opened his laptop and started searching for bird sounds. I noticed he had one of those old, metal trash cans beside his desk. I figured him giving the can a good kick should trigger an episode.

"If this works," I said, "it will shut it off permanently, right?"

"Well, that's another thing I don't know," Greg admitted. "Usually, you give someone an affirming action to perform. In other words, you suggest to someone that they *do* something when they hear a particular sound or word or see a person or object. In this case, we're telling you *not* to do something. Although, I'm thinking it would be best to give an affirming action as well. It might serve as a distraction. But whether it would be permanent or not, I don't know. It might wear off and the old behavior reassert itself."

"Actually, what I was wondering was, if for some reason I wanted to time dive again, you could turn the suggestion off."

He shrugged. "I don't know. Do you think it likely that you'd want to do that?"

I thought of Team Backstory, especially Cornell and Victoria. "It's ... possible, I suppose."

He gave me the eyebrow again. "I have hoots, coos, and whatever that is that loons do. You want to do this?"

I stood. "Not today. I've been having these episodes for years. I guess a little longer won't hurt. And I guess they need me. I'm a rare specimen," I added wryly.

Greg smiled at me. "You are that," he said.

TEAM BACKSTORY WAS UNDERSTANDABLY PUMPED when I told them I was willing to stay with the project a bit longer—at least until they had all the mechanisms catalogued. I felt a little sheepish when they revealed that they'd spent the remainder of their time at the lab the day before brainstorming ways they could detect when I wanted to be reeled in. Otis had even begun to noodle with ideas for a software/hardware solution so I could self-retrieve.

"There are already smart phone apps that sense footsteps, heart rate, blood pressure—that sort of thing," he explained. "I figured Vic and I might be able to design an app that would detect a particular neural condition that you generate when you're in fugue and cause your phone or smart watch to erupt into birdsong."

I thanked them all kindly but didn't hold out much hope that it would be something that would impress a police review board. That sort of thing might be the ticket for someone with a less dangerous job, but even going into a fugue for a second in the wrong circumstance (such as when smoking out a drug ring) could be disastrous. Besides, I couldn't imagine a worse time for my cell phone to burst into song.

Sophie was back today, smiling and perky after what she said was a *merveilleux* conference with her doctoral adviser, but Drew was out. His daughter had a doctor's appointment and he wouldn't be in until late in the day, if then. He'd provided us with another pair of hands in the form of Harald Hilmirsson, his grad student assistant, whose job it was to monitor and annotate vital signs. Harald was a big, handsome blond kid. I thought he and Sophie had sort of "clicked" from the jump. Yin and yang. Kind of cute. Made me feel lonely just looking at them.

Theron Cornell was off doing whatever it was that terrifyingly brilliant and rich scholar-philanthropists did. That kind of surprised me. I figured he'd want to monitor the process ... or maybe monitor Victoria. I wondered if there was something going on there. I mean, Theron Cornell was definitely more her intellectual match than I was.

When I went under that day, I was thinking about something Cornell had asked: Why did my dives take me where and when they did? Why did I visit Amenaru and not his daddy or his great-grandpa? Why Omarius and not one of his and Sennia's kids? I decided to try a little science experiment of my own. As we prepped for my dive, I tried to concentrate on Amenaru. Specifically, I wondered if there was a way I could test leakage.

I began the thought as Peter, sitting under the hairdryer in MIN's lab, and finished it as Amenaru walking the hallway with an armful of papyri. He was toting them to the high priest's private apartments to leave them for his perusal. Nebemakhet was not in when he arrived, so he set the pages on the high priest's private writing table.

Doing my peripheral scanning, I noticed that Nebemakhet's dressers had yet to gather his vestments and carry them to the bath. His jewelry lay in an open box—bracelets, a circlet for his mighty brow, and the Amulet of Imhotep. Seeing it from this angle awoke a memory from the night Melchior was shot. My Austrian ancestor had seen a medallion much like it in a museum display case.

Coincidence? Or something else? A chill scurried down my backbone on icy little feet. I'd never thought much about esoteric concepts like destiny or fate or divine intervention. I hovered between belief and agnosticism when it came to the idea of a deity. I wasn't sure what to make of a scarab medallion turning up in two different time periods I had visited.

Amenaru, having completed his duty, afforded the amulet a long, covetous look, then turned on his sandaled heel and headed for the door. I, on the other hand, wanted a closer look at the bloody thing. Really, *really* wanted a closer look. I wanted to pick it up and examine it.

Quite suddenly, my host reversed course, made a beeline for the amulet, and lifted it out of the box. Reverently, he brushed the tips of his fingers over the lapis carapace of the scarab.

Hot damn—had I done that?

Turn it over. Look at the back, I suggested.

He did. I saw hieroglyphs carved neatly into the underside of the pendant. Several rows of them. They looked like this:

I knew what some of them said. I just had no idea what they *meant.* I mean, neither of us—Peter nor Amenaru—knew the significance of the symbols or how they could possibly hold the secret of Imhotep's earthshaking Knowledge (with a capital K).

The topmost word was a name: *Imhotep.* Made sense. It was his medallion, after all. The next symbol was Anubis, god of the Underworld, Egyptian Grim Reaper. Inside the rectangle were the glyphs for Hapi, Duamutef, Imsety, and Qebesenuef—the four sons of the god Horus.

Ever seen *Close Encounters of the Third Kind?* Great film. There's a great scene in that great film in which the Richard Dreyfus character—Roy—is seated at the dinner table with his family (who already think he's two tacos short of a combination plate) making a science fair sculpture out of his mashed potatoes, while insisting, "This means something. This is important."

That's what I felt like as I stared at the little mini-cartouche on the back of Imhotep's amulet.

Before I could connect any dots—or even snatch a context in which those dots might appear—I heard the sounds of approach from the direction of our master's bath. Amenaru and I were in complete agreement about beating a hasty retreat. Which we did, after quickly but carefully returning the amulet to its box.

That was close, I thought, and was surprised when the words came out of Amenaru's mouth. Seconds later, I was back in the lab, standing about two feet from the hairdryer with my electrode leads in disarray. I knew Backstory must have pulled me back—an idea reinforced by the way they all stared at me.

"What?" I asked. "What happened?"

"We were going to ask you the same thing," said Otis. "You stood up suddenly and said something weird. We thought we'd better bring you back."

"I was probably speaking Egyptian," I said absently, still thinking about leakage.

The Imhotep doodad showing up in two time zones was odd enough, but I'd *interfered* with Amenaru. Or at least, I thought I had. I mean, he was certainly *interested* in the amulet, but he wouldn't have dared handle it. At least that's what he told himself repeatedly. Had my words come out of his mouth, or had we simply thought the same thing? If I *had* influenced him, what did it mean? How much control did I have over a host? Could I make him do something completely against his will? If I did, might it change his future—and the present?

That was a scary thought. It was one thing to ride along with a host and something else again entirely to have one hand on the steering wheel. I was, I realized, dancing around the real issue: If this was a neuronal memory, how the hell could I have any effect on my ancestor at all?

I felt a strong urge to tell Victoria, but then cautioned myself to silence. I wasn't sure I'd done anything to Amenaru, really.

He might've picked up the amulet on a sudden whim. I needed to be sure.

"Peter? Did you hear me?" Victoria looked worried.

"Sorry. Thinking. You heard me say something. Out loud."

"That's what I was saying," she said. "Or at least that something your ancestor said in the memory, you said out loud here. Honestly, your brain waves didn't show distress, but your voice sounded urgent. We thought we'd better pull you out."

"I want to do another dive," I said. "I'll try to give you some distressed brain waves and I want to test a theory I have about how I can choose an ancestor to visit. That time, I was thinking about Amenaru and that's who I went to. Might have been coincidence, though, so I'd like to try again."

"Can we debrief first?" Victoria asked. "You weren't gone very long. What happened with Amenaru?"

"Not much. He's really fixated on his boss's jewelry, though."

She nodded. "The scarab necklace you mentioned."

"Yeah. He—um—he picked it up. There's writing on the back."

That generated some excitement, so I sketched the hieroglyphs for them and translated the symbols. Then I gave my usual detailed report. After that, I dove again, this time choosing my Austrian relation. In the back of my mind was a half-baked idea that I'd try to get a look at the scarab in his museum—to make sure, I told myself, that it wasn't the same one Nebemakhet wore.

And yes, that was where I landed, in the museum in Salzburg, Austria. I was in an office, doing some sort of paperwork. I've always hated paperwork. Crime reports—yeah, those I liked; trying to lucidly describe a crime scene or an interrogation or an interaction with a witness or perp. What I hated was the kind of make-work Eckart was doing. This was his name, I now knew, because I joined him as he appended his signature to an acceptance form for some new acquisitions. Eckart Metz. *Professor Eckart Metz.*

Presently, Eckart was focused on his acquisitions approvals. He was not thinking at all about the contents of a particular display case in his Egyptian gallery. This was as good a time as any to test my leakability. I willed us to get up and go into the Egyptian gallery to the case with the scarab necklace in it. I thought it strongly and positively, as if I were just going to get up and do it.

Eckart hesitated a moment, then frowned and stood up. He went to the door, then glanced back at his desk. I gave another mental shove and he shook his head and went out into the museum. He went straight to the Egyptian gallery; he knew where it was, after all, though I didn't. He made a beeline for the display case, crossing beneath a looming statue of Anubis that had once supported the roof of a temple at Karnak, bypassing a scale model of an Egyptian funerary barge and a stone sarcophagus.

There it was, in a beam of sunlight, being admired by a gaggle of school children—the lapis scarab. But was it the *same* lapis scarab? How could I find out?

The teacher accompanying the kids—who were about nine or ten—caught sight of us and smiled broadly. "Professor Metz! How nice to see you! Children, Professor Metz is the curator of the museum. Does anyone know what a curator is and what he does?"

She fielded a series of answers, and my host gave his own description of a curator's role. At that point, I made a little suggestion: *Let's talk to them. Let's tell them about the bug bauble. Heck, let's take it out and let them look at it.*

He did, letting each child touch the big, blue scarab, which I noticed was loose. He told them it was thought to have belonged to a great Third Dynasty Egyptian doctor named

Imhotep, whose name was inscribed on the back of the piece with some other symbols whose meaning was in question.

"You aren't sure what it says?" a little girl wanted to know.

"Well, you see," Eckart explained, turning the amulet over so they could see the back of it, "the hieroglyphs here are very worn and scratched. We can barely make them out. There are other names on the piece as well. At least one of them is the name of a minor deity who was a son of the god Horus. That's the god with the head of a hawk or falcon."

The kids all thought that was pretty cool.

I thought that if the amulet held any secrets beyond the images on the back, they'd probably been just as thoroughly lost. I imagined the sketch I'd made of those symbols. What did they mean? Were they important to anyone besides Nebe-makhet? How could the names of Horus's kids lead to some great, earthshaking Knowledge?

His explanation of the artifact exhausted, poor Eckart dithered for a moment before returning to his office, still shaking his head. Here, we both got an unpleasant surprise. A gray-eyed man in a gray suit sat behind our desk, kicked back in our chair with his fingers steepled before his face.

The professor went from bemused to apoplectic in two seconds flat. Who did Gray Suit think he was, taking over our office? His agitation added heat to my own realization that this was the guy who'd scared us out of the Egyptian gallery that night—the guy who'd had us scrambling under bushes and hiding in the woods ... while my partner was getting shot in my present.

Eckart's distrust of this guy exploded into anger that threat-ened to overwhelm his good sense. As words of outrage formed in his mind and made their way to his tongue, I snapped back into the lab at MIN like an overstretched rubber band.

"I wasn't ready to go!" I said the moment I had gathered my wits somewhat back into my general vicinity.

Sophie, who was now seated at the laptop they used as my control center, blinked at me, clearly taken aback. "But your brain waves, Peter ... You were clearly very setup."

"You mean upset, and yeah, I was. So was Eckart. But I didn't want to *leave*! I wanted to find out who the asshole was that we were spying on the last time I was him. He was sitting in my office like he belonged there." I swiveled my head around, looking around for— "Victoria!"

"Right here," she said, popping into my peripheral vision. "How did it go?"

Drew appeared behind her, holding my sketch of the glyphs from Imhotep's amulet. He must have come in while I was diving.

I put my hands up to grasp the hairdryer. "Look, can we do away with this thing now? The electrodes give you a good enough look into my noggin, right? And this is so ... undignified."

She smiled and lifted the encumbrance off my head. Then she sat down facing me. "Talk to me," she said. "Were you able to pick your destination?"

I nodded. "I was. I went right where I wanted to go—to see Professor Eckart Metz in Salzburg, Austria. So, I'm two for two. But Soph, here, pulled me back before I was ready to come."

Sophie scowled at me and murmured something in French that I was glad I didn't understand.

"Anyway," I said, "here's what I'm thinking: I can't exactly say 'Beam me up Sophie' while I'm sharing someone else's consciousness, but if I hummed something—say, 'Eine kleine Nachtmusik' or 'Louie, Louie'—something you could hear—"

Victoria laughed and shook her head. "You forget, Peter, you're not in charge when you time dive. You're a silent passenger."

Well, there it was.

I felt a wave of—was that *guilt?*—and knew my face was

turning pinkish. "Yeah, but I'm not always completely silent *here*. Besides ... um, there's something else I've been experimenting with and ... I've been meaning to talk to you about it. I'm not sure what it means, but I'm pretty sure it's a Thing."

She frowned, expression wary. "What?"

"When I visited Amenaru before and again just now with Eckart, I was able to ... well, to guide them. To influence their behavior."

She stared at me. Drew stared at me. Sophie stared at me. I could just about feel Otis staring at me from his workstation behind me. Harald wasn't around or he would have been staring at me too. Then they did the shared glance thing that tends to make the subject feel like the adults in the room are talking over his head and getting ready to break out the straightjacket.

Finally Drew-Egon said, deadpan, "That's impossible."

"No, it's a fact. I did it. Twice. I made Amenaru pick up the Imhotep amulet so I could get a better look at it, and I made Eckart leave his paperwork and go out into his museum for the same reason."

Again, with the significant glances. I got it. I did. I had to consider their position: They couldn't see what I saw, or hear what I heard. All they saw were my brain waves and body language, and all they heard was the occasional mumble of dialogue in a foreign language. My accounts of my episodes were all they had to go by.

"Peter," said Victoria, "it's entirely possible that both men would have done exactly what you wanted them to do on their own. You were sharing their consciousness, after all. You might have simply felt their intentions as if they were your own."

I shook my head. "No. That's not the way it was. Amenaru was on his way out the door of Nebemakhet's chambers when I *made* him turn around and go back. Trust me—he did not want to pick up that medallion. He was terrified of Nebemakhet knowing how much it fascinated him. Yeah, he wanted to know why it was so special to his boss, but he was not going to tempt fate. I made him do that. Same deal with Professor Metz. He was in his office doing paperwork when I put the idea in his head that he needed to go check out the medallion in one of his Egyptian displays. So, he did, though I know he couldn't figure out why he was doing it. He almost turned back. I, uh, I even had him give a little talk on the thing to a bunch of school kids."

"You did all this," asked Drew, "to test your theory? That's impressive."

"Well, that and I had to be sure it was the same medallion."

Victoria leaned forward in her chair. "The same—you mean the same medallion as in Amenaru's timeline? The Imhotep amulet?"

"Yeah, weird coincidence, isn't it? The back of it is so trashed that they can only read the name Imhotep with any certainty. They're not one hundred percent certain of the other names. But I am, for what it's worth." I nodded at the sketch in Drew's hand. "The lapis scarab is loose, too," I added.

"I wonder if it *is* a coincidence," said Victoria.

"What else could it be?"

She gave me a look. "Peter, think about what you've just told us. You're not just *experiencing* your ancestor's memories; you're somehow—as improbable as it seems—in actual contact with them. I'm not a physicist, so I can't even begin to conjecture about the real nature of time. That's more up Theron's alley. I know we humans experience time as a linear series of events. Maybe it's more than that. I don't know … which is exciting and intimidating in equal measure." She fixed me with her most direct gaze and pushed her glasses up the bridge of her nose. I found the gesture endearing. "Are you sure, Peter? Are you absolutely sure that you somehow co-opted your ancestors' thoughts and actions?"

"I'm sure."

I explained, then, how I had accidentally discovered my leakage. About how what I knew of my host had been dictated by their own inner dialogue up to that point, while after, I'd been able to provoke disclosures. The entire team looked ... well, blown out, is how they looked.

"This changes everything," said Victoria in an airless voice.

In the silence after, I knew what they were thinking, because I'd been thinking the same thing. What we were doing had the potential to change history.

6

TWO'S COMPANY

We took the weekend off. Well, in a manner of speaking. It was something in the nature of a time out. I wasn't to do any more time diving—at least not intentionally—until Team Backstory had a chance to consult with Cornell about our discoveries and discuss the scientific and moral implications of the program.

Could we go on, knowing that what we did might change the course of history?

You may notice that I'm using the collective pronoun "we" a lot, here. If you thought that meant I was starting to feel as if I were a member of Team Backstory and not a sacrificial guinea pig, you'd be right. I had begun to own this, which probably means I'm certifiable, but I'd thought I was nuts before. Victoria and crew had rescued me from that unhappy possibility. I now stared down the barrel of the threat that Theron Cornell would pull the plug on this whole venture just as I was beginning to get into it.

He came in the following Monday morning and sat down with us in Victoria's office, where we laid out our findings.

Assembled into a bullet list, they were curious, exciting, impossible, and disturbing.

Here's what we knew:

1. There was a Common Element in two time periods the Subject (me) had visited—the so-called Amulet of Imhotep. (Curious.)
2. The Subject can choose a host to visit. (Exciting.)
3. The Subject can signal the team that he wants to be removed from the fugue state. (Also exciting.)
4. The Subject can influence the thought and behavior of the host. (Impossible and disturbing.)

What we *didn't* know was even more disturbing. We didn't know if such meddling would change history through thought, word, or deed.

"What if," I asked, "I think about cell phones or guns or impressionist paintings or helicopters too vividly in the wrong company? What if I cause my host to say or do something that alters his relationship with someone? What would have happened if I'd stayed in Eckart Metz's head a moment longer and kept him from saying whatever he was going to say to Gray Suit?"

On that appalling thought, I realized that I'd already changed that interaction by pulling Eckart away from his desk and into the Egyptian gallery in his museum. If I hadn't done that, Gray Suit would have come to the door of his office as an unwelcome visitor, not an intruder who'd misappropriated his desk and made him angry enough to say something we all might later regret.

That made me sweat. What if I'd already done something literally world-changing?

After we'd put all our cards on the table, Victoria said, "So there it is, Theron. And of course, the question is: Can we consciably continue this line of research, knowing that we might alter the timeline?"

"Can we consciably *not* continue, knowing what we might learn?" Cornell countered. He turned to me. "Peter, you're a police detective by trade and training. I suspect that means you're trained for silent observation of a situation, yes?"

"Yes, of course. Ideally, a detective is nonreactive."

"Do you think you have the capacity to be nonreactive while you're in an episode?"

"Under normal circumstances, I'd say yes, absolutely." I heard what I was saying and laughed out loud. "Normal. There's nothing normal about any of this. But ... yes, I can sit in silence and just watch. My question is: What might I have done already, without realizing I was doing it? Is what we can learn from this worth the possibility of changing the world?"

Theron Cornell opened his briefcase and took out a sketch pad. He looked at it for a moment as if considering its contents. Then he asked me: "Do you believe in kismet, Peter? Destiny, fate, divine intervention?" He smiled enigmatically and added, "Or quantum physics?"

"Jury's out," I said. "Why do you ask?"

He flipped the sketch pad open and handed it to me. In the center of the page was a good, detailed pencil sketch of Imhotep's amulet.

"I made that sketch after my last time dive," Cornell told me.

Stunned does not even begin to cover it. "Y-you've seen this amulet before?" By which I meant *before I did?*

He nodded. "In the Temple of Imhotep ... I think. At least, it matches the description you've given of the place and of the man you call Nebemakhet. And, of course, this amulet."

"Why?" I wondered aloud. "Why this amulet?"

"I don't know. I'd like to, wouldn't you? Nebemakhet insists it holds the key to some great Knowledge about life and death. Given what Imhotep did for a living, that's a pretty interesting claim. Here's what I *do* know: We talk about a space-time continuum for a reason. We perceive time as a river, a line or an arrow that moves in one direction. There is evidence to support the idea that this is not so. Time and space are both in constant and nonlinear movement. What we might discover from this research is a better understanding of the reality of time. We might discover, for example, that there are loci in what we call history that are especially meaningful. Points that are crucial, but that somehow never yield their potential."

"I'm not sure I follow," I said, and checked the faces of the others to see if they were getting something I wasn't. Didn't think they were.

"Whatever knowledge was supposed to be accessible by virtue of this medallion seems to never have emerged," Cornell continued. "Where did it go? You said Nebemakhet talked about revealing his secret knowledge soon. We haven't been able to find his name in any of the histories. You and I are the only two people I know of who can vouch that he even existed. That suggests to me that he never found out what Imhotep knew or at least that he never revealed it."

"Or," I said, "that it turned out not to be so earthshaking after all."

"Entirely possible," Cornell conceded. "But then, why is this artifact a locus for two of your ancestors and one of mine?"

"Because our ancestors only thought it was all that?" I guessed.

"Peter, if Nebemakhet revealed the amulet's secret and it wasn't 'all that,' as you put it, why would we—you and I—be drawn to it as if it were? In fact, I'd ask by what fluke of the universe did you and I come to be working on the same project?"

"Maybe that's not so cosmic as it seems," said Otis. "I mean, at some level we're all related. Fiftieth cousins or something. So if you go back far enough, you're bound to find some crossover.

Everyone's family tree is pretty overgrown after enough genera-
tions, right? And we've been scouring all of our networks
looking for candidates. *And,*" he added, as if the idea had just
popped into his fertile brain, "it's also highly likely that certain
gene groups are stronger in the Force than others, and so more
likely to manifest this ability and to be discovered to do so."

Everyone turned to look at him. Then, Cornell shook his
head and chuckled.

"The Force? Meaning some of us have more *midichlorians*
than others?"

Poor Otis blushed, turning his complexion to rose gold.

Theron, still smiling, extended a hand, as if in apology. "No,
seriously, Otis, there might be a sort of truth to that, at least in
concept. Vic, I do believe we may be served by doing a bit of
genetic testing."

The upshot of our big conclave was that we determined to
soldier on with Project Backstory, with me being extra careful in
my ride-alongs while trying to get as much information about
the amulet as I could. With that in mind, when we resumed our
work, I went back to visit Amenaru.

Right out of the gate, the situation was somehow different.
Nebemakhet had two sub-priests the last time I visited; now he
had three. Okay, I thought, our boss has brought in a new
recruit. His name was Abet, but Amenaru knew little about him.
I saw no reason to pry.

Because of this development, I assumed I must have arrived
a fair amount of time after my last dive, but a visit my host
made to our master's chambers caused me to seriously reassess.
A missive from the court of Pharaoh was delivered by a royal
courier, and Amenaru was deputized to run it to the high priest.
He was surprised to see the new guy, Abet, attending our master
in his private rooms. Nebemakhet was holding forth on some
aspect of the greatness of the Divine Doctor, and Abet was absolutely riveted.

I noticed, as Amenaru entered the room, that the page on the master's writing table was one we had brought to him during my last time here. I reluctantly fed my host a gentle question: How fast had our dear master gotten through checking the materials we'd brought him?

"Sir," said Amenaru, as we handed over the Pharaoh's letter, "when do you expect to have completed your assessment of the tablets I brought you?"

Nebemakhet raised his sleek brows. "It has been only two days since you delivered them to me, Amenaru. I expect I shall be finished by Imhotep's Feast Day."

That was several days off. Amenaru sighed inwardly. That his master was taking his sweet time with the editing only meant more work for himself and Har-khebu.

The high priest looked down at the missive in his hands. "Ah, I see that this is an invitation for me to attend our lord at a reception in two days' time. Wait a moment and I shall send back a reply."

He moved to his writing table, pulled a bleached, blank papyrus from a basket that hung from its edge, and took up his stylus. His water and ink block were still on the writing surface, so he bent over the table for a moment, deftly penning a reply, while Abet and I watched. The amulet dangled from its torque, swinging slightly with every scratch of the high priest's reed pen.

I caught movement out of the corner of Amenaru's eye and directed our attention to the new priest. He had raised a hand to his throat and caressed the empty air above the collar of his tunic as if he were the one wearing Imhotep's precious medallion. Every investigative instinct in my head went on instant alert; even Amenaru's hackles were raised. Who was this guy and why had he appeared on the scene with an amulet fixation already in place?

When Nebemakhet dismissed us, I mentally crossed my

fingers and prodded my host just a bit, trying to assess what he knew about the new guy. The answer was next to nothing. Abet had just appeared at the temple gates several days earlier with a story about relocating from Fayum, which was about a day to our south. This puzzled Amenaru, because Fayum was the religious capital of the crocodile god, Sobek. What would prompt an acolyte of an old-guard powerhouse like Sobek to switch allegiance to a newly minted deity?

"Pardon, Abet," said Amenaru—I swear, without prompting from me—as we made our way down the broad corridor that led from Nebemakhet's chambers to the forecourt where the guards and couriers hung out. "Do I understand rightly that you come to us from Fayum?"

Abet seemed to consider that simple question for several steps before he said, "Yes. I come from Fayum."

"You must surely have trained as a priest of Sobek," we observed. "How came you to serve the Temple of Imhotep?"

Abet turned his head and gave us a look I can only describe as calculating. "As I explained to High Priest Nebemakhet," he said, "I have always revered the great Physician and been most impressed with his unearthly grasp of the human body and soul."

"You seemed most impressed," I ventured (and yes, I was in the driver's seat for this one), "with the memento of Imhotep that His Excellence Nebemakhet wears. I, too, admire it. Did he tell you that it holds the key to a great secret?"

"No," Abet said neutrally. "Every high priest I have known claims to have some secret knowledge. I think it is their way of being superior. It is a very pretty necklace, all the same."

Even Amenaru thought that was a suspiciously lukewarm response, given Abet's evident fascination with the "pretty necklace." He opened his mouth to say something more, but I was already humming "Louie, Louie," and a second later, I was back in modern Manhattan.

The first words out of my mouth were, "There's something going on in the Temple of Imhotep."

HAVE you ever woken up from a dream absolutely certain that it made sense, only to have that illusion fall completely apart when you tried to tell someone about it? That's about what happened when I tried to explain to my teammates what I'd meant when I said, "There's something going on in the Temple of Imhotep."

This new priest appeared out of nowhere, sounded unduly alarmist when I admitted that he came from Fayum, and more so when I gave his rationale for why he'd dumped Sobek for a younger god.

"That doesn't seem all that outlandish," Victoria said. "I imagine there was all manner of trading up when it came to deities. In fact, some accounts indicate there really wasn't that much conflict between god cults. They're all children of Amenre, after all."

Well, when you put it that way …

"Yeah, but this would be trading *down*, Vic. And this new guy was riveted on Nebemakhet's scarab bauble from the get-go. Then he denied it. Something's not right."

"Scarabauble?" she repeated, saying it as if it were all one word.

I barely heard her because I'd just realized something. "The timeline," I said.

"What about the timeline?"

"The last time I visited Amenaru, I took the high priest a batch of pages to read and correct. Pages Har-ib and I transcribed. In temple time, that was two days earlier. In Amenaru's memory just now, Abet had been there longer than that, but he wasn't there when I took Nebemakhet those pages. Do you see the problem?"

She'd been sitting forward in her chair with her elbows propped on her knees. Now she sat up straight, a frown creasing her forehead. "You're telling me he wasn't there in the original timeline."

"Yeah. And you're going to tell me that's impossible, right?"

She paled. "The last time I told you something was impossible..." She didn't need to finish the sentence.

"Exactly."

They sent me back right away. It was night and Amenaru was getting ready to turn in.

Damn. I hesitated to make him do something radically different than he was inclined to, but it turned out I didn't have to. He was feeling troubled about some things (some of which were my fault) and decided to wander down to the shrine of Imhotep to pray for guidance and inner peace. I let him do that. It was actually rather inspiring. The flicker and flap of flame from the braziers and lamps, the shifting light, the warm scent of incense, all filtered through Amenaru's feelings of devotion to Imhotep and the God Father Amen-re ... that was a heady combo.

I didn't put out my own feelers until he made his way back to the priest's quarters. I admit, I prompted him to think about Abet, and discovered that the new priest made him uneasy. It didn't take much to get him to swing by the new guy's quarters to see how he was doing.

He was gone. His couch hadn't been slept on.

Amenaru was inclined to celebrate this; me, not so much. I put the idea in Amenaru's head that Abet's absence was something the high priest needed to be told about immediately. He was gleeful. He had come to dislike Abet in the brief time the older man had been here. It was his opinion that Abet was ingratiating himself with Nebemakhet by listening to his tall tales and flattering him. He clearly had designs on replacing Amenaru in the high priest's regard.

Padding on bare feet, we made our way to Nebemakhet's quarters in high dudgeon. We slipped past the privacy screen in the doorway and felt the hairs rise up on the back of our neck. We felt the movement in the room like prickles on our face.

We froze. Someone stood at the doorway of Nebemakhet's sleeping alcove, peering in. Even as we watched, the Other moved from Nebemakhet's bedroom to a dressing cabinet along the near wall, atop which was the box containing his jewelry. The patch of moonlight the cabinet sat in revealed that the skulker was Abet. His back was to us.

Amenaru took over at this point, stepping fully into the room and moving to lay a heavy hand on Abet's shoulder. Abet jumped and turned, letting go of the box.

"So, Abet," Amenaru hissed, "you are a common thief!"

I was surprised when Abet grabbed hold of Amenaru's shoulders and shoved us out of his way so he could escape into the corridor. We gave chase and caught him before he'd gone fifteen feet, pinning him against the wall. He fought back, striking us repeatedly and trying to break away. His flailing arms struck a lamp stand, toppling it against the stone wall. One of the little clay lamps fell and shattered on the floor. In the fitful light, I could see the determination in Abet's eyes morph into utter confusion.

"Why would you steal the master's amulet?" Amenaru demanded. "Why?"

Abet frowned as if he were having trouble understanding the question. "Must have it," he mumbled.

"Why?" Amenaru asked, and I added, "What did his excellence tell you about it?"

The frown deepened and Abet shook his head. "Resurrection?" he asked, as if the word had just now entered his vocabulary.

While Amenaru considered what he should do, I pondered the imponderables. I was pretty sure I'd just seen another time diver abandon his host. That was a chilling thought. I felt kind of sorry for Abet. He probably had no idea in the world what he was doing in Memphis. He'd stopped fighting back and huddled against the wall as if he needed it to hold him up.

"You have no idea why you're here, do you?" we asked him.

He looked at us, fear warring with confusion in his eyes. He shook his head. "It seemed to me a good idea, I simply cannot remember why."

In the end, we escorted him back to his rooms and advised him to pack up his few belongings and return to Fayum. Amenaru simply wanted him gone; I reasoned that if he was a time diver's host, I wanted to make his getting back to the amulet as logistically difficult as possible. As for Abet, he just wanted to return to his own temple. He did not wait until morning, but took off into the night.

I hummed my way home, knowing that Amenaru intended to sit up all night to make sure Abet did not come back.

7
THE AMULET OF IMHOTEP

"You're telling me," said Victoria carefully, "that there's another time diver in the Temple of Imhotep."

The whole team was in her office with the door shut against the possibility of someone from outside the team entering the lab. The faces of the people around me were grim. For good reason. But, suspicious me, I was instinctively watching them for ... something.

"I'm saying I think that's a possibility, even if it's improbable. As near as I can tell, this guy changed the timeline by appearing in a time and place he wasn't before. Amenaru might've accepted his presence as merely being awkward and inconvenient, but I was in the unique position of being a sort of objective third party. My last visit to Amenaru, Abet hadn't arrived yet, but this time, Amenaru's memory said he had. And just now, I think I may have seen the moment his ... rider dismounted. It was like watching water drain out of a cracked glass. It was eerie." I shivered at the memory. "He was after that amulet. No question."

"But Imhotep's amulet is famous among the priesthood at

that time, yes?" asked Sophie. She seemed hopeful that there was some simple, benign explanation for Abet. "Your ancestor is fixed upon it, as is his *associer*, Har-khebu. Perhaps its fame has spread."

"But why?" asked Otis. "Why does everyone want the amulet? I mean, yeah, the high priest says it holds a 'secret'"— he made air quotes around the word—"but it sounds as if it's more of a status symbol. What time diver would care about an ancient Egyptian status symbol that eventually ends up gathering dust in a museum in Salzburg, Austria?"

"Resurrection," I said.

Victoria made a wry face. "What?"

"When I pressed him, Abet mumbled something about resurrection."

"*Résurrection?*" Sophie echoed. "You think someone believes this amulet can raise the dead?"

"It was a more superstitious time," I said. "People believed stuff like that back then. But that's not the point. The point is that someone who can do what I do seems to believe it—or at least they believe the amulet is valuable in some way. Presumably, some non-superstitious way. In fact, we're talking about someone who's willing to do *more* than I can do ... that is, *if* they wrenched their ancestor away from his life in Fayum and forced him to travel all the way to Memphis to enlist in service to the new god on the block."

The thought was clearly as stunning to the rest of the team as it was to me.

"Who could do *such* a thing?" asked Sophie. "And why? Is someone else trying to replicate our research—our processes?"

"I'd say they did a damn sight more than try," said Otis. "I'd say they succeeded with flying colors."

"The question is," said Drew, "*when* are they from? Now, or a future in which the GCT process might be more stable?"

Well, there was an unnerving thought.

My brainy associates spent the remainder of the day reviewing everything they'd published on genetic cognitive transference in research journals, every email to colleagues, every lab note—hard copy and digital—that might've leaked. When they were done, they realized that other neuroscientists might, if they extrapolated from their published work, be able to replicate some of their results. Well, someone with Mensa-level smarts who read publications targeted at other people with Mensa-level smarts and a deep interest in neuroscience. Oh, and who either happened to suffer episodes of neuronal memory or had a close personal friend who did.

I didn't want to say it aloud, but the only person I could think of who fit that description was Theron Cornell. While I supposed it might be possible for him to fake illness to turn aside suspicion (something most people learn to do in grade school), I had to ask why. I mean, let's suppose for a moment that he could fake a heart condition. His illness gave him a motive for wanting the secret of resurrection, I guess, but that same illness—if real—made it impossible for him to attain it … maybe.

Victoria was clearly not thinking along the same lines I was. She called Theron Cornell as soon as we were as sure as we could be that there was another time diver poking their nose into the same historical period. Theron had us suspend operations until he could come down to the institute; the wait made me feel as if someone had staked me to an ant hill. I didn't realize it showed until Sophie begged me to stop pacing and insisted that I also take my house keys and spare change out of my pocket. She also cut me off from caffeine.

Sophie, I learn, can be very intimidating when she's annoyed with you. When I tried to sneak a cup of coffee, she barred the way, with a look that said: *Judge me by my size, do you?* A slightly taller, much prettier Yoda with a French accent.

When we'd briefed Cornell fully on what we suspected, he

was grimmer than anybody else in the room. Real or pretend? Was he that good an actor, or ... ?

I caught my thoughts and gave myself a mental rap upside the head. It was a stupid idea. He was the guy underwriting the whole operation. He had the entire Backstory project team at his beck and call. Why the heck would he need to insert himself into the proceedings when I was already busily researching the strangely attractive and mysterious amulet? Even if he believed the thing could cure his heart condition, why would he risk moonlighting in order to get close to it?

In the end, we decided that the lab should be swept for listening devices, just in case, and that I needed to get more intel on the object of all this attention. That meant another dive back into Amenaru's life stream. I was able to fine-tune my dive by concentrating on the aftermath of Abet's disappearance—which turned out to be pretty eventful.

Amenaru was doing his morning devotions in the shrine when I dropped in for a visit. Not long after, Nebemakhet summoned us to his rooms. His Excellence was in a dither because his newest acolyte had vanished. That he'd also taken his few belongings hinted that he meant to stay vanished. Nebemakhet wanted to know if Amenaru knew anything about it.

Now, my natural inclination was to plead the Fifth and pretend ignorance. Amenaru had other ideas. He was fiercely protective of his boss (notwithstanding he was also envious of him) and damned proud to have intercepted the thief. So he straightened his spine and told Nebemakhet all about finding the strange priest poking around in his esteemed quarters in the middle of the night, and about having caught him with his thieving fingers on the precious box.

Nebemakhet was gobsmacked. For a moment, all he could do was stare at us bug-eyed while I mentally crossed my fingers and hoped Amenaru hadn't just made an error in judgement.

Then His Excellence said: "Where is he, then? What did you do when you found him?"

"I fought him, High One," Amenaru said, flexing his biceps (which were actually rather impressive). "You can see the proof of this in the hall beyond your chambers. During our battle, we toppled a lamp stand. You can yet see where it struck the wall and will note that one of the lamps is missing. It shattered during our fight. I cleaned it up and will have it replaced today."

"But, Abet? Where is he now?"

"I have no idea, Excellence. He toppled me, as well, and escaped into the night." Amenaru did not care to tell his boss that he had rather intentionally let the guy go. In part, this was because he was confused as to why he'd let him go in the first place. That had been my idea, not his.

The high priest's face went pale, then red, then he opened his arms and swept us into a swift, emphatic embrace. That lasted only a moment before he stepped back, wrapped his hand around the amulet, and stared at us with glistening eyes.

"Amenaru, you were truly sent by the gods as my protector! Abet might well have slain me, had you not intervened. I owe you my life. What gift might I bestow upon you to repay such loyalty and courage?"

Amenaru was on the verge of asking for his own private study and library, but I couldn't let the opportunity pass. "The gift of wisdom, High One," I said. "I know that great Knowledge was given into your wise keeping by Lord Imhotep. I doubt I have the capacity to comprehend more than a drop of the ocean of such wisdom, but it is my humble wish that you share a few drops so that I might aid you in safeguarding it."

Amenaru was quaking with (he must assume) his own audacity, but relaxed when he saw the expression of deep satisfaction on the elder priest's face. I seem to have struck the right chord; Nebemakhet waved us to an ornate chair and seated himself upon his divan.

"You have proven your loyalty to me, Amenaru, and since—as you say—you have not the capacity to comprehend this Knowledge, I will shed upon you but a dew drop. The Divine Physician has put in my hands the Knowledge of Resurrection."

"Resurrection?" we gasped.

He nodded sagely. "The god himself committed to writing a process by which the soul of one person can be transferred to the body of another whose spirit has fled, thus reanimating it." *There!* his expression seemed to say. *I have blessed you.*

"So let me get this straight," I said, forgetting that I was supposed to be an Egyptian priest and not a Manhattan cop. "You put the soul of one person into the body of someone who's … who's *dead?*"

He inclined his head in the affirmative. "Indeed."

"And you'd want to do this if…"

Now he smiled as if I'd just stumbled upon a great truth—which, as it turned out, I had. "You'd want to do this if someone, for example, had a sickness that caused them to exist in great pain or was crippled … as the Pharaoh's young son may be crippled." He frowned and shook his head. "I have been treating him from infancy. He has always been sickly, and his limbs seem to weaken daily."

"And this Knowledge of Imhotep can save him? But how is it done?"

Nebemakhet was almost as pleased with my astonishment as he was distressed by the prince's illness. "That is Imhotep's secret, of course. But he taught, did he not, that the throne of the soul was the intellect? He told me, before he passed into the next life, that he believed he could move this throne into a new abode."

"But the Knowledge isn't *in* the amulet…" I thought out loud now, my eyes on the scarab in question.

Nebemakhet laughed. "Of course not! The amulet is but a key.

The papyrus that contains Imhotep's wisdom is where no living man would think to find it, under the eternally watchful gaze of the gods. When the time is right, Amenaru, I will draw forth the Papyrus of Imhotep and use it. And you shall be at my right hand."

Our collective consciousness was electrified at this point. Amenaru was psyched about the idea of being Nebemakhet's right-hand man; I grappled with the idea of moving "the throne of the intellect" from one body to another. We were in seriously Frankensteinian territory here.

As soon as Nebemakhet dismissed us, Amenaru hummed "Louie, Louie."

THE SECOND THE electrodes were off, I stood up and started pacing. "I don't even know where to start," I said. "My head is still buzzing."

"You were gone for only ten minutes," Sophie informed me, tapping a key to begin recording my commentary.

"Yeah, well, it was an action-packed ten minutes."

"Did you find out anything new about the amulet?" That was Victoria, who leaned against the corner of my workstation, an iPad in one hand and a stylus in the other.

"Nebemakhet called it a key. A key to the location of a papyrus on which Imhotep recorded..." I hesitated. How to put this. I decided to put it as close to Nebemakhet's description as possible. "It's a papyrus on which he recorded a procedure for moving—and I'm quoting here—'the throne of the soul' from one person to another. He planned on revealing this procedure at a point the Pharaoh's sick son was beyond his capacity to help."

"The throne of the soul?" repeated Drew. "What does that mean?"

"Nebemakhet said it was the intellect. I know this is going to sound creepy and weird and impossible, but I think maybe he thinks Imhotep was considering transplanting a human brain."

"A brain?" repeated Victoria. She took her glasses off and began polishing the lenses with the hem of her lab coat. "That's … I was going to say 'impossible,' but I'm beginning to think I'll have to eradicate that word from my vocabulary. But it is literally unheard of except in science fiction stories."

"Imhotep is said to have performed surgeries that were advanced for the time," Sophie observed, "and archaeologists have found mummies of people who clearly survived brain surgery by many years."

Victoria shook her head. "Yes, but this…"

"You'd think," I said, taking another lap around the workstations, "that if the procedure was known that far back in history, it would show in our modern medicine. But it hasn't. So, presumably that means that Nebemakhet never recovered the Papyrus of Imhotep and it stayed buried wherever Imhotep hid it."

"Or," said Otis, "it didn't work and it was buried with Nebemakhet—figuratively speaking. That sort of transplant is still only dreamed of."

Yeah, I thought, *by people like Theron Cornell, whose heart is failing*. I didn't say it, of course, but I now was considering a motive for someone from *this* time period to want to unearth something from that one. Someone with a failing body might very much want to have brain transplantation be a Thing in the twenty-first century. And it was the sort of Thing that a great many people might consider off-limits.

I tried to deep-six my questions about who the other time diver was as I resumed my detective work in Memphis. I was determined to figure out what became of the Amulet of Imhotep and why Nebemakhet had never revealed the secrets of this papyrus. Or, if he had revealed them, why they did not resonate through the ages.

Victoria and Cornell had an intense dialogue about that as I prepared to dive back into Amenaru. I listened while pretending not to, looking for any hint that Cornell was trying to manipulate our expectations or shift our attention elsewhere.

"I would think," Victoria said, "that this sort of knowledge would have been swept up by the Muslim scholars and made its way into the European universities."

"In which case," Cornell countered, "it would have been in texts like Ibn Sina's *Canon of Medicine* or Ibn Rushd's encyclopedias. It wasn't. That much we know."

"Here's the question, though, Theron," she said as Otis started the preflight test of my electrodes, "if Imhotep did pioneer some sort of brain transplantation, and unearthing it in the past would cause it to be viable now..."

Her hesitation made me glance over at her; she looked queasy.

"... should we keep the knowledge alive, or make sure it stays dead?" she finished.

"That," said Cornell, "is a troubling question."

That was the end of the conversation for the time being; Sophie hit a key on her keyboard and launched me into the past. I wanted to be a bit later in Amenaru's life stream, but I didn't know how to go about that. After all, all my early dives had been random, or nearly so. I knew, now, how to select *who* to visit, but I was still a bit foggy on how to select *when*.

In the end, I thought *later* as I dove, and found myself staring out at the Nile as Nebemakhet and I were being carried along in his limo by the big tattooed guys. This made me a little nervous. I had no idea what season it was or if loons nested in the marshes. For all I knew, one would burst into crazed song at any moment and send me packing back to twenty-first century Manhattan.

Nebemakhet was talking, and I caught up with him in mid-sentence. "… may be upon us," he was saying. "Today will tell."

I wasn't sure what today would tell, so I gently prodded Amenaru to see how much he knew. What he knew definitely piqued my interest. We were on our way to the court of Sanakht in answer to an urgent summons; the Pharaoh's son was in great distress and he wanted us (or rather, Nebemakhet) to rush to his aid. What we found when we got there was hard for me to take.

Yeah, I know—violent crimes detective, yada, yada. But this was a kid. A little boy whom Amenaru knew to be about twelve, but who looked more like seven or eight. His arms and legs were so thin and wasted, the joints looked enormous, and he moaned in obvious pain. I stood by while Nebemakhet examined him carefully, gave him a potion of some sort, and applied pungent herbal compresses to his joints.

When he finished with all of this (which did seem to help), he stood back from the boy's bed, turned to the Pharaoh and his Queen, who hovered nearby like any concerned parents, and said, "My lord, I have done all within my earthly power to help your son. I must now invoke the god himself and beg of him superhuman knowledge and wisdom. Pray that he will bestow them."

He bowed, as did I, and led the way out of the room. We had no more than emerged into the corridor outside, than he grasped the amulet tightly and said, "It is time, Amenaru. It is time for me to bring forth the god's own Knowledge."

"What would you have me do?" we asked him as we stepped into his limo.(Okay, it's more properly called a *palanquin* or a *litter*, but *palanquin* is just too damned fussy and a *litter* is a box on poles, right? So, it's a litter box. I will not admit to being carried around in a litter box.)

The High One frowned thoughtfully, then said, "I must receive the Knowledge of Imhotep alone. You will go at once to the shrine of our god and pray for the success of my work this night."

I sighed. If I were going to lay eyes on this marvelous papyrus, I was going to have to figure out a way to get to it once it was in Nebemakhet's possession. Who knew—maybe that was how the Knowledge failed to surface later in the timeline. Maybe I or we or Amenaru absconded with it.

I realized this was the longest I'd ever been in an episode, but I was determined—if I was not unmanned by a loon—to stick it out until I at least knew where Nebemakhet was headed. Maybe I could follow him. For now, I might as well sit back and enjoy the cooling, wet-scented breeze off the Nile.

"Where will you go to receive this knowledge," asked Amenaru, surprising me. "if not the shrine of Imhotep?"

"I will go to the gate of his abode."

Amenaru and I puzzled over that, but before we could come to any conclusion, we heard a cry from outside the limo. Our transportation lurched, then shuddered, then pitched toward the river, tumbling over several times before plunging upside down into the murky water among the reeds. In a heartbeat, we were submerged in silent gloom. Amenaru thrashed, seeking the open windows of the box, but Nebemakhet did the same thing, and the two men ended up punching and kicking each other. I tried to exert some sort of control, to force my host to yield to my emergency training—calm down, figure out which way is up, methodically locate a window, squeeze out. But he couldn't be calm; he was drowning. I could feel his panic pounding through my head, feel the burning of his lungs as he fought the urge to breathe.

I came close to panic myself when a sudden thought struck me: If I was in a host when he died, would I die too? I knew that old saw about dying in dreams was total fiction, but this was *terra incognita.* I had no idea if I, Peter, could survive Amenaru's death. And here, beneath the waters of the Nile, I couldn't even hum a few bars of "Louie, Louie." I was stranded.

I felt Amenaru's consciousness slipping; in a second he'd have to draw a breath that would kill him. His mind fogged over and I found, to my horror, that it had an effect on *my* thought processes as well. I felt suddenly light, disembodied, the world around me gray—but not the gray of the river. It was as if I were floating through a thick cloud or a fog bank. Then I saw a flash of radiance like sunlight on water.

Okay, I thought, *this is bad.*

Amenaru breathed in. I had never felt anything like it. It was beyond pain. I tried to focus on the watery sunlight; it reminded me of the fountain in the courtyard of the Sforzas' summer palace.

"Don't you agree, Cristo?"

I blinked and pulled my gaze away from the courtyard fountain where sun and water did a flirtatious dance. Ludo Sforza sat at the marble-topped table in the light of a brisk fall day. His gaze was on a pair of sketches of his daughter, Bianca.

Huddled in Cristofano Augustino's head, I resisted the urge to gasp for air. "Cristo," as the duke had called him, was not drowning. He stood placidly in the sun-dappled courtyard, admiring his friend Leonardo's work. I hunkered down, letting my host do all the talking and thinking, while I ordered my chaotic thoughts.

"Personally," he said, "I find the one of her glancing back over her shoulder captures a certain quality of her nature."

"That sly stubbornness, you mean," said Sforza amiably. "I like it too, but I am not sure it would commend her to the parents of her suitors. This other portrait"—here he waved at the more formal profile—"makes her look more a princess, don't you agree?"

Cristo admitted that he did, while I tried to herd my little gray cells into orderly obedience. What the hell had happened? Had I just survived the death of a host? How had I ended up here instead of back at the institute?

Sunlight on water. I'd thought of sunlight on water and this fountain, and I'd leapt straight from one ancestor to another. I wondered what Team Backstory made of *those* brain waves? Could it have been that simple—that in the absence of loons or hoot owls, I could direct myself away from a dying host? But why here? Why now?

"I do agree," said Cristo. "But I still favor the other. You could have him do both, of course, or you might have him use the truer image in the religious work you desired to have him paint for the palace chapel."

Sforza smiled at us. "Ah, she would make a brilliant Madonna, or perhaps an angel or a saint. Bianca, patron saint of mules."

We all laughed, and I decided I had my head together enough to go home and report. I was about to excuse us so I could go whistle a merry tune, when Sforza smiled broadly and rose from his chair, his eyes on the patio doors.

"Bernardo, have you finished it?"

We turned to the doors. A tall, middle-aged man with graying hair stood in the doorway, an ornate wooden writing box tucked under one arm. Cristofano nodded to him deferentially. I felt his admiration as diffuse warmth. His interest was piqued, and he hoped the duke would not dispatch him on some errand or household task so that he might get to hear the poem the duke had commissioned for his beloved daughter's social debut.

My interest was piqued for an entirely different reason—a reason I could not have described if my life depended on it. I'll try, anyway. Something in the other man's bearing and expression seemed too wary and too tentative. This was Bernardo Bellincioni, the Sforzas' court poet. He was as much a fixture here as I—or rather, Cristofano—was. Yet, I'd swear when he stepped across the threshold, his attitude was that of a first-time visitor, his eyes scanning the layout of the patio, his posture eloquent with uncertainty.

I was convinced—possibly without any real evidence—that I was in the presence of another time diver. Was it the same one I'd met before?

8

SABOTAGE

Bernardo read his poem. I remember that his voice was fluid and resonant and that the words rolled off his tongue, warm and lovely and quite appropriate for the coming out of a young Sforza—legitimate or no. I don't remember the words themselves, though. I was occupied with wondering if there was a way I could identify the other time diver.

Did he recognize me or at least register my presence? Since I'd been lying low in the back of Cristo's head, I hoped not, and he didn't seem to be throwing me any suspicious glances. So far so good. I'd scrapped the idea of calling for an extraction, because I was now focused on my new goal.

Why was this guy here? (I'm assuming it was a guy—I hadn't changed genders in any of my dives, but I had no way of knowing if that was a constant or just me.) Did his presence mean the Amulet of Imhotep was here as well? I mean, clearly it hadn't been completely destroyed by what I assume was Nebe-makhet's untimely demise; it was going to end up in a museum in Austria. But maybe it had been lost for centuries. Maybe it reappeared here.

Where, here? I'd seen no evidence that Ludo Sforza was a collector of Egyptian antiquities. Testing that theory, I presented my host with a mental image of the scarab medallion. Beyond a moment of surprise and bemusement, I got nothing.

Okay, so Cristo had never seen the thing. That didn't mean it wasn't here. I determined that I needed to keep a close eye on our old buddy Bernardo. Our boss made that more difficult by dismissing us to take care of the preparations for Master DaVinci's arrival; he was to be the duke's guest here and at the Castle Sforza in Milan where he would finish Bianca's portrait.

I found the house in a state of controlled chaos; everywhere servants were packing up for the removal to Milan. I let Cristofano take the lead, which meant giving orders to the staff, poking our nose into the duchess's rooms to make certain her transitional gowns were carefully handled, ordering luncheon to be served, then returning to the guest wing to make sure that Master DaVinci's chambers had been freshened and a fire set in the grate.

By the time all the chores were done and Cristo had eaten an early supper, the servants were lighting the lamps in the hallways. I was getting a bit nervous about how long this was all taking, and put the idea into my host's head that he really ought to find Bernie and tell him what a great poem he'd written. Bianca's coming out was going to be one of the best and biggest ballyhoos of the winter season. He went along eagerly—it helped that Cristo and Bernardo were members of a mutual admiration society.

We reached the second floor to find that Master DaVinci had arrived in time for the evening meal. The duchess had apparently withdrawn to her own rooms, leaving the three men to hang out in the dining room, sipping wine and chatting amiably. Some perverse demon made me blend Cristo into a dim corner of the outer corridor where we could eavesdrop.

The conversation wasn't anything particularly interesting at first; it was Bianca this, Bianca that, Bianca would have the best gowns for her debut, et cetera. Leonardo's sketches were prominently displayed on a table beside the fireplace, and Bernardo weighed in on which one he felt was the most like the girl. Then he did something I did find interesting. He turned the conversation—awkwardly, I thought—to the master painter's engineering pursuits.

"Have you, by any chance, brought with you any of those marvelous sketches you do of mysterious machineries?" Bernardo asked, after praising the exacting detail of DaVinci's technical works. "I find them utterly fascinating, lyrical, almost poetic in their form."

This raised Leonardo's eyebrows. He was clearly not used to Bernardo waxing poetic about his technical sketches. "Well, yes," he said, "but they are in my portfolio in my rooms."

"I could have a servant retrieve them, if you wish," suggested Ludo, reaching for a bell that sat on the table next to his wine glass.

Bernardo raised his hands. "No, no! Do not bother, Your Grace. There will be plenty of time for me to enjoy them during our journey to Milan."

The conversation went on for several minutes after that, then Bernardo claimed he was about to nod off and excused himself to go to bed. Cristo was all for intercepting the poet in order to praise his work, but I gave him a sharp nudge and, instead, he stepped further into shadow. Bernardo went on by and, as I thought he might, took a right turn into the guest wing. That engaged even my ancestor's curiosity, so it was easier than I expected to get him to follow.

We moved at a leisurely pace, because I wanted us to catch Bernardo in the act of whatever he was in the act of. When we reached Leonardo's rooms I was not surprised to find Bernardo bent over the writing table in the suite's fancy parlor, shuffling through DaVinci's sketches.

What the hell was he up to?

As we peered through the door he'd left slightly ajar, Bernardo pulled a blank sheet of paper from a sheaf on the table top, produced a pen from his own writing box, dipped it into Leonardo's inkwell, and proceeded to scratch something onto the piece of paper. We could tell that he was both sketching and writing, and both of us wondered why.

Cristofano leapt to the conclusion that, for some reason, the poet was copying his friend's work. As you might imagine, this upset him a bit. In fact, he was furious. It was all I could do to keep him from throwing open the door in a dramatic gesture of "aha!" and storming into the room.

I counseled him—in the persona of the Voice of Reason—to let Bernardo finish what he was doing so as to have the maximum evidence of his crime. So, we spent several long minutes out in the hallway, watching Bernardo work. I chafed at not being able to pace and wondered if Leonardo DaVinci had somehow come in contact with the amulet or the papyrus, while poor Cristo wondered why he looked at his own left wrist twice, expecting to find out what time it was. Finally, the poet/time diver finished what he was doing and stowed his pen.

And that's where it got weirder. He didn't take the paper; he blotted it, blew it dry, and shuffled it in among the other sketches. Then he shoveled the whole kit and caboodle back into DaVinci's folio. Cristo and I were both surprised as all get out and decided that absence was the better part of valor. We dashed around a corner and waited for Bernardo to sneak out and hurry down the main corridor to the rooms reserved for non-family household members. As soon as he was out of sight, we hustled back to the room and in.

We were sweating by the time we found the sheaf of sketches Bernardo had disturbed, but it wasn't hard to find the new drawing; it looked nothing like Leonardo's work, for a number of reasons. The one that struck me most was the subject matter. These were not the drawings of a brilliant Renaissance Man; these were modern ideas—twenty-first century state-of-the-art tech broken down into simple terms and diagrams that someone of DaVinci's caliber could understand with some serious wood-shedding. They were essentially schematics for a robotic or bionic assembly—one that mimicked a human being part for part.

What the hell.

I staggered for a moment as I grappled with the realization that this seemed to have nothing to do with the Papyrus of Imhotep. What was it? Was it a fresh attempt to accomplish the same end in a different way? The one thing I was sure of was that the other time diver was trying to plant modern technology in the past.

I was deep in my own thoughts and not paying much attention to what Cristo made of this. I snapped back to awareness when I realized that we were in motion, striding angrily out of the room with the offending drawing in hand. Cristo didn't know what Bernardo's game was, but he was determined to find out. I tried to stop him, but the strength of his outrage made that difficult.

Just when I thought I'd gotten him under control, we came face-to-face with Leonardo DaVinci in the second-floor gallery. He was on his way to bed, looking a little worse for wine. We tucked the schematic behind us and smiled, wishing him a hearty good night. He slapped us on the shoulder, said good night, and wandered unsteadily toward his rooms. We let out a sigh of relief, turned, and saw Bernardo (or not) peering at us from the staff wing. He'd apparently doubled back to follow up with Leonardo.

I met his gaze and shivered at the keenness of it. This was not the Sforzas' court poet. This was someone else.

"Bernardo," I said carefully, "you are not yourself this evening. Return to your proper place."

I saw the awareness dart through the dark eyes, saw the jaw set and the mouth harden. Then the other time diver was gone, leaving behind a confused poet. We escorted him to his suite of rooms, chuckling with him about the strength of the duke's wine, then went to our own chambers. There was a roaring fire in the grate. We tossed the anachronistic drawing into it, and I sang my way home.

When I opened my eyes in the lab, I found myself staring into the face of an exhausted Victoria. Strands of hair had escaped her pony tail and floated around her face. She had taken off her glasses and was watching me, concern in her eyes. Outside, darkness had wrapped itself around the building; inside, the lights were all on, but Victoria was alone.

"Peter," she said, her voice sounding dry and husky. "You're back. I was getting worried. You had a metabolic spike hours ago and I almost brought you back then, but you sort of settled down and I wasn't sure … What happened?"

Wow. Where to start.

"Amenaru died," I said simply.

She paled visibly. "He … *died*? Are—are you all right?"

To which "I'm working on it," was the only response I had to give. She distracted me from what I suspected was going to keep me up all night by recording and dissecting my experiences until neither of us was able to concentrate. Both of us needed cabs to get home.

OKAY, so this is what we knew that we knew when we discussed my double-dip the next morning with the whole Back-story team—minus Cornell, who was giving a speech at Boston College.

1. A time diver could experience the death of a host without apparent harm to himself.
2. A time diver could make lateral leaps from one host to another without benefit of triggers upon the death of a host. Question: Could they also do it if the host was unconscious, asleep, or in distress?
3. There had been another diver in two different time zones. Both times this person was trying to change history—once by recovering alleged technology related to life extension or reanimation, once by introducing modern bionics technology into a timeline. Questions: Was this the same person? Were they from now or from a future in which GCT was a more developed process?

Victoria and I had stayed late enough the night before to assemble this somewhat coherent series of points, but going over them in full daylight with a tankful of caffeine and a group of inquiring minds was a different proposition. Otis saw, at once, what our tired brains had been too foggy to grok the night before.

"I don't think this person is trying to resurrect a particular ancient knowledge (you'll pardon the term) and put it in play. He's trying to bring about a specific result in his home era by whatever means necessary. At least, that's the way it looks to me. And that suggests that this isn't about monetary gain; this is personal." He looked around at the rest of the team, his errant lock of hair bobbing over the bridge of his nose. "That make sense to anybody else?"

It made sense to me. I came *that close* to mentioning Cornell's name, but I bit my tongue and said something else instead. "What if this bionics tech were to connect with Imhotep's resurrection process? I mean, a straight transfer of one person's brain into another person's body is ... well, it's messed up, is what it is. But if the body is bionic..."

"Cyborgs?" said Otis, wrinkling his nose. "Maybe that's better ethically. Robotic, biomimetic transplantation instead of ... well, Frankenstein. No host has to die to keep the other person alive."

"I think the central question," said Victoria, "is what will we do about it? We're the ones who opened this can of worms. Whether the other time diver is from now or the future—and I can't believe I just said that—*we're* responsible for furthering the technology. The genie's out of the bottle now; we can't put it back."

"Then surely we must try to stop it," said Sophie.

"How?" asked Drew.

"Well, look," I said, pacing around Victoria's office, uncaring if I drove everyone nuts, "if this guy is dedicated to seeding some sort of life-extending tech into the past, he's going to try again, right? So, where's the most logical time and place for him to go?"

Victoria made that thoughtful scientist-staring-into-the-middle-distance face (which, I admit, I found really attractive) then said, "The most surefire way of getting these ideas into the mainstream of Renaissance thought is to plant them in the medieval education system."

"The what?" I asked. "I didn't think there *was* much of a medieval education system. Isn't that why they call it the Dark Ages?"

"Ibn Sina," said Sophie eagerly, ignoring me. "I would channel this into the works of Ibn Sina."

I'd heard that name before. Cornell had mentioned it. "Name rings a bell," I said. "Why would anyone want to get this stuff to this Ibn Sina?"

"Ibn Sina," Victoria explained, "was an eleventh-century Persian polymath and philosopher. Incredibly prolific. You may have heard him referred to by his westernized name: Avicenna. We still have about forty of his medical texts and more than twice as many of his philosophical works. They were taught in all of the great European Universities of the Middle Ages. His volumes on human physiology form the basis of modern medicine. If this knowledge makes it into one of those texts, it will spread like a virus."

"The question is," said Drew, "which text?"

I was clueless on this point and stood well back out of the way to let the professionals handle it. They decided that the most likely target would be Ibn Sina's influential medical encyclopedia, *Al-Qānūn fī al-tibb* (aka *The Canon of Medicine*). My part in all this was to grope in the murk of my genealogical line for an ancestor living in the time period this guy was working on these volumes—so, in the years before 1025 AD, when the last one was published.

I was confident I could find such an ancestor, but before I embarked on my mission to the past, there was something I had to do. Watching the team work, I had come to the inevitable conclusion that I had to level with Vic about my Theron Cornell concerns. So, before I launched, I took her aside into her office and struggled to give her potentially devastating news about her dear and trusted benefactor.

"Listen, Victoria," I said as I closed the office door behind me, "there's, ah, there's something I need to get off my chest before we get further into this."

She shrugged and gave me an uncertain smile. "O—okay."

Before I could open my mouth again, her expression changed with lightning speed, a dawning light of comprehension flooding her eyes.

"Oh, Peter, I'm so sorry. We've completely hijacked your life, haven't we? You only wanted to stay with this until we figured out triggers and controls and now you're up to your neck in historical intrigue. I promise you, if you can just help us stop this—this sabotage—"

Caught by surprise, I raised my hands to stop her. "No, no, it's not that. Really, Vic. I'm a detective doing detective work. Granted, it's weird detective work, but you're not hijacking me. I have as much skin in this game as anyone else. That wasn't what I was going to say."

She shook her head. "Then ... ?"

"Why don't you sit down?" I said, as if it were my office, not hers. I waved her toward the little conference table.

She went to the table but perched against the top. She wore her hair in a braid today and I was finding everything about her distracting, from the sparkle of her earrings to the little wisps of hair that had escaped the braid, to the color of her eyes behind her glasses—a sort of deep, chocolaty garnet.

"Peter, what is it?"

I hesitated, scrambling momentarily to recall what "it" was. "I want you to think about something. I want you to consider who might fit the description of the other time diver. Someone who knows what they're doing, who's had the benefit of your research, and who has an urgent personal reason to want this particular technology to be well-developed in the twenty-first century."

"Or later," she said. "In fact it's more likely that our other time diver is from our future. That would explain how he seems to have the benefit of our research."

"Or he's from right now, monitoring everything we do."

She tilted her head in that characteristically Victoria way, frowning slightly. Her braid draped itself across her shoulder. "What are you saying? We've had the place swept for bugs; we're clean."

I took a deep breath. "Maybe it's not a bug; maybe it's a mole. Ask yourself how well Theron Cornell fits the profile of our mysterious ride-along."

Her jaw literally dropped and she stared at me. "Theron ... that's ridiculous, Peter! Why—?"

"Hear me out. He knows almost everything you know about GCT; he's a natural time diver; and he has a deep personal reason for wanting this type of biotech to be developed by now. *And* he's got the educational background to seed the past with modern ideas."

Now her eyes shot sparks at me and her lips clamped shut as if she held back a lot of choice words.

"You're mad," I said. "I get that. And you're going to argue that Cornell wouldn't have any reason to seed bionic tech into the past since it's his team tracking down the papyrus. And I'd argue that he could be just hedging his bets—making sure that he's covered. Or maybe he tried to introduce the bionics because the guy's got a moral compass. In any event, he's got motive, means, and opportunity." I ticked them off on my fingers. "In case you haven't noticed, he's never here when I have one of my run-ins with our time diver friend."

"Of course, he's not here. He's got a foundation to run. He doesn't..." She crossed her arms across her chest and shook her head. "What do you expect me to do with this, Peter? Do you expect me to confront Theron with your ... suspicions?"

"No. All I want is for you not to tell him about our new attempt to stop him—or whomever—from hot-wiring modern medicine. Just tell him about Amenaru dying and the sideways leap."

"And the bionic tech?"

I thought about that. "Not yet. I'd kind of like to see his face when he hears that."

She continued to fix me with that smoldering (and not in a good way) gaze, then shook her head again and said, "All right. Fine. I won't tell him about the bionic tech or monitoring Ibn Sina. But, Peter, if you're wrong..."

"I may be wrong. I hope I *am* wrong. I don't want it to be

Cornell. I like the guy. I just have to look at probabilities. You understand that, right?" I gave her the best, most earnest look I could manage. Lauren had called it my "killer-wolf-puppy" look.

She sighed, uncrossed her arms, and straightened from the table. "Let's do this. As soon as you eat something. You may have to be there awhile, and your blood sugar was pretty rocky along toward the end last night."

I honestly hadn't thought of that before, but she was right. When an ancestor I was visiting ate, my own body back here in the lab got zilch. The fact that she cared about my blood sugar made me feel ridiculously happy.

9
WRONG PLACE, RIGHT TIME

My internal agenda, as I dove headfirst into my genealogical past, was to find the ancestor closest to Ibn Sina in time and location. So, it came as no surprise to me to end up in Egypt again, but this time in eleventh-century Alexandria, sharing consciousness with a host I'd never met before—Thabit Hadad, scribe.

I knew from my preflight briefing on Ibn Sina that he was living in Persia in the city of Hamadan. That, according to my host's memory, was about ten days from Alexandria by camel train, which I was pretty sure wasn't nearly as cozy as Amtrak. I contemplated having Victoria reel me in and trying to find someone closer, but I had a strong feeling this was the best I was going to do. Besides which, I quickly discovered that my host, Thabit, wasn't just a scribe by trade; he loved his job. He considered himself a student of the scholars whose works he copied and illuminated. Ibn Sina was a rock star as far as he was concerned. I hoped I could use that to my advantage.

I joined Thabit in the middle of his workday at an impressive library on the seaward side of the city. He had a writing desk beneath a skylight in a sunny room where he copied and annotated scholarly works and translated texts into Arabic from a variety of other languages. Apparently Thabit was fluent in four or five.

I stayed with him for an entire one of his days, getting the lay of the land, as it were, figuring out how I could appeal to him in a way that would convince him to venture a journey to Persia. When he knocked off for the day and went home, I discovered that he lived with his parents and several siblings in a pleasant villa with a view of the sea.

His family was great—his father taught the Qur'an and calligraphy at a neighborhood school, his mother did amazing embroidery that she sold in her eldest son's shop, and loved to cook great, elaborate meals. His two younger sisters were in their teens—sweet, sunny girls who were both learning their mother's craft. The elder one was preparing for her upcoming wedding.

I stayed with him even as he settled onto his couch for the night because I wanted to see what happened when he went to sleep. I didn't leap sideways or back or anything. It was kind of like being left alone in a dark house. Naturally, I wondered if I could have any effect on his dreams. Before I either hummed my way home or discovered I was stuck here for the night, I decided to give it a try. I started thinking about Ibn Sina (okay, so sometimes I lack finesse). How cool would it be, I thought, if I, Thabit Hadad, could transcribe the works of such a great man?

I spent several minutes contemplating the glory of illuminating one of his philosophical or medical works and, just for an extra kick, I planted the idea that, as much as I loved my work here in Alexandria, it could sometimes be a bit boring...

To my relief, I was able to swing an extraction and popped back into the lab with an elapsed time of two hours. I puzzled about that, because there didn't seem to be a consistent ratio of real time to past time. I debriefed with Victoria and Sophie, half-listened to Otis telling me about the automatic retrieval system he'd set up (I caught something about a microphone triggering the loony-tunes), then took care of my mundane concerns before getting prepped to dive back in.

"What's the matter, Peter?" Victoria's question alerted me to the fact that I was scowling. She leaned over my shoulder, placing my electrodes. She'd just attached one to my left temple.

"It's Thabit," I admitted. "He's got such a great gig. Loves his work—and he's good at it—his family is amazing…"

"And?"

"And I feel really skeevy about taking him away from all that. I mean, what if he's supposed to meet his future wife during the time I've hijacked him to Hamadan? Or what if he's supposed to die in a freak library accident? Steering a host is one thing, but dragging him two weeks from home in the wild hope that he can get a job with his hero—that's something else again. What if Ibn Sina doesn't bite?"

"You said Thabit is a good scribe and calligrapher. Do *you* think he's good enough to work for Ibn Sina?"

"I *think* so. I mean, I don't really know, do I? *My* handwriting sucks."

She laughed and I had the absurd expectation that she was going to kiss me. Or maybe I just had the absurd impulse to kiss her. Not sure about that. All I know is that we just sort of stared at each other until Otis cleared his throat. Then I cleared my throat, Victoria said, "Right," and Sophie giggled.

Okay, so I'm not smooth. But to cut myself some slack, I hadn't even thought about having a relationship with a woman since Lauren. What would have been the point? I was still not actually *thinking* about it—just sort of pre-thinking about thinking about it. About having the *right* to think about it.

I went back to Alexandria with the impression that roughly a week had passed since my first visit. I was jazzed to discover that, in idle moments, Thabit was daydreaming about working for Ibn Sina. That was a plus. There was also a minus: the group of scholars that my host worked for was considering promoting him to lead calligrapher, managing a team of other scribes. He was barely thirty years old and about to become head of a whole calligraphy team. He'd be able to choose the projects he worked on.

Ultimately, it was that aspect of the possible promotion that gave me the opportunity I was hoping for. Could any of the projects that came through his library here be as exciting as working directly with the great polymath? What came bubbling up out of Thabit's soul when I gently posed this question was something he'd never admitted to anyone; being part of Ibn Sina's coterie was a dream he'd held for years, but lacked the courage or ambition to consider seriously.

This, I thought, *is what it looks like when Fortune smiles.* Question was, could I fan that spark enough to get Thabit to hop the camel train to Hamadan?

It took two visits to do it, but in the end, Thabit Hadad gathered up the best samples of his work he could find, bought himself passage in a caravan to Baghdad, and from there to Hamadan.

I made two more short dives to make sure my guy stayed on track. I suppose I could've tried to reunite with him in Persia, but I was nervous about it. I mean, what if he changed his mind in Baghdad, turned around, and went home?

The camel train was two days out from Hamadan when an outbound courier met us with dire news. Persia's great poet, Baba Tahir, had died, and the entire city was in deep mourning. I didn't know what to make of that, because I had only a vague idea of who Baba Tahir was, but Thabit knew. He was grief-stricken at the news, and I was caught in the explosion.

That night, when we made camp, Thabit got out his portable writing box and sat down to compose a poetic tribute to Baba Tahir in his finest hand. It took about half the night, and when it was done, I have to admit, it was a work of art. I'm no poetry aficionado, but the words were lovely, graceful, and not at all smarmy. The calligraphy and illumination were gorgeous—I didn't need to be an expert to see that. That he did it by the light of a full moon, the flicker of lamplight and a cleverly placed mirror, was the stuff of legend.

Finished with his tribute, Thabit fell into his bedroll and slept, while I went home for dinner.

My two skips and a jump had taken about half the day, and my debriefing took a good bite out of what was left. Vic and I were still hung over from last night's sleep dep, and I suggested we knock off early and go get something to eat. I smoothly framed the invitation so it didn't sound as if I were inviting a specific someone to dinner, but Victoria was the only one who bit, so we ended up at a noodle house appropriately called The Noodle House.

Over huge bowls of curried shrimp soup that smelled like heaven in a bowl, we talked about why we ended up doing what we were doing. Turns out she came from a science-y family. Her dad was a professor at MIT, her mom was the head of the Anthropology Department at Amherst, which I suspect explained how well-versed in history and archaeology she was. She admitted a fondness for digging things up.

"Me, too," I said, über-aware of how lame that sounded. "I mean, I love figuring stuff out. Problem solving."

She grinned. "Uncovering mysteries—addictive, right?"

"Not that I'm saying any of what I've done as a cop is, you know, in the same league as what you do."

She speared me with a look. "Why not? You solve crimes. You save lives. I don't think I've ever saved any lives. If I'm lucky maybe something I do in my career will save lives down the line. Or at least change them. I suppose all scientists hope for that—to change lives."

"Well," I said sincerely, "you've changed mine."

She blushed. I loved that, until I realized it could mean that

I'd embarrassed her. That the thought of me coming on to her made her uncomfortable.

"I mean," I added quickly, "that I never would have found out what was going on in my head without you. I would've just thought I was crazy. I would've thought I was the only one with this ... gift. I would have been alone with it. That's not a good feeling."

Like I'd told Dr. Greg. I lived alone but I was not a natural loner. I'd always had a partner until the night I almost got Mel killed. I was used to being paired with someone. Two heads are better than one and all that. I was starting to think of Victoria as my partner—a fellow detective working a case with me. That was good, I told myself. If I could think of her in that light and not as a woman I was attracted to, it would make all this much easier.

I returned to Hamadan first thing the next morning. Thabit Hadad's thoughts were like a yarn ball that'd been thoroughly terrorized by a rambunctious kitten. Why had he come here? What had made him think this was a good idea? What should he do now?

Since parts A and B were all my doing, I went to work on part C: what to do next. The answer, insofar as I was concerned, was *find Ibn Sina*. He was famous hereabouts, so it merely required asking the owner of the caravansary where the camel train ended up where the great master might be found. Ibn Sina's school was located at the fringes of town in a wooded parkland which, I have to admit, I did not expect to find. I'd always thought of Iran as being desert (and we'd certainly crossed a lot of desert to get here), but Hamadan was in the foothills of the Alvand mountains and was surrounded by acres of grasslands and crop-producing fields and forests.

I got directions to Ibn Sina's school, but the moment I started across the courtyard of the inn to follow them, the helpful inn-keeper said, "Oh, but he will not be there today.

Today, he is at the salon of al-Hamadani, celebrating the life of our dear Baba Tahir."

We got directions there, instead, and on the way, Thabit began to doubt himself again. The thought of walking up to his hero and begging for an audition (or whatever the scribe's equivalent is), especially in the midst of this time of mourning, was terrifying. It seemed just plain wrong to my host.

Okay, it seemed wrong to me, too, but I knew how important it was for us to weasel our way into the great man's inner circle.

Thabit tamped down my anxiety pretty firmly and resolved that he was not going to beg Ibn Sina to give him a job interview. He would not—could not—be so disrespectful of as great a man as Baba Tahir. I didn't have the heart to push my own agenda. I could only hope that, in the time we'd have to spend here before he could arrange passage in a caravan home, I could find a way to put Thabit in Ibn Sina's path.

Al-Hamadani's salon was the prototype for those art salons that came out of nineteenth- and twentieth-century Europe. What does a New York detective know about those? I admit that most of what I knew came from old movies … that I watched because one of my episodes in high school had taken me to just such a salon where I was the proprietor and an amateur sculptor with delusions of godhood. I hadn't liked my ancestor all that much, but I really got off on the atmosphere of his salon. It had been filled with elaborate ornamentation and Persian carpets, too, although the clientele was different.

This salon was in a whitewashed building with blue shutters. A short, broad flight of steps ran up to a series of graceful arches edged with painted tiles. Inside the blue doors, we passed into a crowded courtyard. Men clustered at tables, lounged on divans, or stood along the walls all around the room. The air was filled with the scents of mint, pipe smoke, and cooking. In the far corner, I saw the Man himself—Ibn Sina —sitting on a divan, his attention on an old man who was reciting a poem that Thabit recognized as one of Baba Tahir's early works.

"And do you truly say, 'Why are you troubled, pray?'" the old fellow crooned. "You have me, soul and body…"

I focused our attention on Ibn Sina. He was a slender man with a close-cropped beard, an aquiline nose, and hazel eyes. He wore his hair cropped to collar length and topped with a small, plain white turban, wrapped around a brown fez. (I now knew firsthand how skillful a wrapping job was required to keep that head gear in place. And I'd thought *ties* were too much trouble.)

We worked our way toward the front of the group—me thinking about how we might wangle a private meeting with Ibn Sina, Thabit not thinking about anything except being in such an exalted gathering. By the time we reached the inner circle, another man had arisen to praise Baba Tahir. I felt Thabit's pulse quicken as the idea came to him of presenting his own tribute poem to the gathering. The thought made him feel brave and terrified at the same time. Me too, actually.

And so, once the other gentleman had finished and received hums, ahs, and knowledgeable commentary, Thabit stepped forward to read his magnum opus.

"I heard of Baba Tahir's passing while inbound from Alexandria," he told the gathering. "Our last night on the road, I could not sleep, my heart was so burdened with grief. Wakeful, I composed this tribute to the Great Poet of Hamadan, which I would humbly beg leave to read to you."

There were murmurs of agreement (I mean, seriously, who would say no to a tribute dedicated to a fallen hero?), then Ibn Sina smiled graciously and inclined his head, gesturing for us to begin.

Thabit pulled a thin folio from his belt pouch and opened it to the pages he had written. His reading was kind of weak at first, so I gave him a shot of confidence. His voice got stronger, and he forged on with growing passion for the subject. He was actually pretty good at this. Not only did he put lots of feeling into it, but he had a sort of musical rhythm to his reading. Almost, but not quite, chanting.

When he was done, we were met with complete silence. Dread reared its ugly head. Poor Thabit almost turned and ran. But then came the murmurs of appreciation and approval.

In the midst of this, Ibn Sina spoke. "You composed this yourself, you say?"

"Yes, sir," said Thabit humbly.

"And you did the calligraphy and illumination yourself, as well?"

"Yes, sir."

Ibn Sina held out his hand toward us. "Please, young man, may I see the pages?"

Hands quaking, we handed the poem over. Ibn Sina examined the pages of the poem closely, concentrating on the first page, which was where my host had put most of his creative energy when it came to the drawing style of the illumination.

When he finally handed back the pages, Ibn Sina said, "You have a marvelously fine hand, young man. You say you have come to us from Alexandria—what is your name?"

"I am Thabit Hadad, gracious sir. I was a scribe in the college at Alexandria."

"It does not surprise me that you are a scribe by trade. Your skill with a pen is obvious. Why have you come here all the way from Egypt?"

I felt our face flushing. "I came to see you, Master. In the hope that perhaps I might be so privileged as to be allowed to copy your works."

Ibn Sina smiled again. "We will speak of this later, Thabit of Alexandria."

That, I thought, *was one hell of a job interview.*

I SPENT MORE subjective time in Ibn Sina's household than I had anywhere else in my travels. Thabit had impressed the socks off the old master and was happily transcribing manuscripts by day three. I, meanwhile, kept my eyes open for any activity from my time-diving adversary. There was none. Zip. Zilch.

I popped in and out of Thabit's head over a period of about a week in real time. I suspected everyone I met of being The One, only to be disappointed. I also used my new position to pore over all of Ibn Sina's available works to see if I could see any sign at all of modern technologies or concepts, or of ancient brain transplants. I paid special attention to the newest works of the master. He was editing the last of the fourteen volumes of his encyclopedic *Canon,* and I—or rather Thabit— was one of the scribes charged with copying them for distribution. Even in the newest material, I saw no hint of modern-day "sabotage".

I was stumped. I wondered if Ibn Sina was working on something even newer than *The Canon.* Maybe our saboteur had chosen a vehicle for his work that was less high profile than the doctor's magnum opus. I decided to follow up on that. I took the initiative one afternoon as I delivered fresh pages to my new mentor to proofread, to ask if he was working on anything new, now that *The Canon* was complete.

He laughed and raised his hands as if to fend off the idea. "Let me rest, dear Thabit! Do I not deserve a respite?"

"Of course, Ali-jan," we responded, daring to use the affectionate, yet respectful version of his personal name. (You gotta love the Persian culture for coming up with so many different levels of courtesy.) "It's only that I am eager to know what destination your exceptional mind will arrive at next. Have you any idea?" I added hopefully.

I should tell you that Thabit, during all of this, was quaking a bit at the depths of his own boldness. He'd gotten comfortable in Ibn Sina's presence, but daring to ask him to share his thoughts like this—well, Thabit hadn't thought he had it in him. Possibly, he was correct.

"As it happens," said our mentor, "there is a collection of essays I have been working on for some time—a compendium of the physical and metaphysical, of philosophy and faith. I have titled it, at least for the time being, *The Book of Salvation*."

"Salvation?" I repeated. "Is that its primary subject then?"

He wagged his head, a half-smile on his face. "A rather mystical title, to be sure, though the topics range from the mundane to the philosophical to the spiritual."

"But you have not yet completed it?"

"It is a work in progress and, though I might complete it shortly, were I to try, I find I prefer to dawdle."

Well, damn.

"Sir," said Thabit, before I could open our mouth, "I would be honored beyond measure if I might be the first to copy and illuminate this compendium."

Score. This so obviously pleased Ali-jan that he pressed a hand to his breast, bowed his head, and said, "Perhaps you would peruse my draft of the book? It is quite rough…"

We knew, Thabit and I, that our master's idea of "rough" meant exquisitely penned but with marginal annotations. I prodded a bit, and Thabit said this aloud, which pleased the master even more. We left his parlor with the aforementioned draft in hand and stayed up all night reading it, continuing into the morning of the next day. Nothing in it even hinted at bionics or brain surgery, let alone resurrection. When Ibn Sina wrote about the soul, he wrote from the conviction that it was the essential element of a human being for which the body was a mere vessel or a reflection composed of material elements. Bringing the dead back to life, let alone doing it in the body of another individual (who obviously had to die first) seemed to run counter to his philosophy. I began to suspect that even if he were to stumble across technology that could lead to bionic bodies for dying humans, he might not wish to save it for posterity. If body snatching were involved, I was willing to bet *rials* to *lavash* that he'd never go for it.

Still, this was too important to leave up to a single time diver's speculation. I needed to get a look at the piece of the manuscript that Ali-jan was working on now, or at least get a sense of it. To that end, I made certain that the master was out when I took back the draft of *The Book of Salvation* and the pages of *The Canon* I'd copied that day. Those, at least, would give me an excuse for being in the master's private offices.

I lucked out. The pages he was working on were in a neat stack on one side of a low, beautifully hand-carved desk. I knelt beside it and reached for the manuscript. Thabit balked at the effrontery.

Aw, come on, I thought, *you want to, and you know it. You're just eaten up with curiosity about what he's writing now.*

He was, too; but he was too polite to peek. I gave him an extra shove, and we picked up the pages and skimmed them. This manuscript had nothing about bionics or brain transplants or anything related, either.

My disappointment warred with Thabit's excitement at the ideas his hero promoted. He shook his head and put the pages back where we'd found them. I took pity and let him have his *squee* moment; he smiled as he carefully arranged his copied pages of *The Canon* atop the master's desk. As we straightened to leave, we heard a noise at the door, and Ibn Sina emerged from behind the ornately carved privacy screen.

"Thabit-jan!" he exclaimed. "You've finished reading the volume already?"

"I have," we said. "I must admit, it took me the entire night to do it, but I couldn't stop reading. It is wonderful, Ali-jan. I look forward to the day you complete it, and it is my happy lot to copy it."

Thabit bowed and made his way to the door, but I had to try one more thing. I paused just shy of slipping out of the room. "Ali-jan, may I ask you something?"

"Certainly."

"In my work at the college, we scribes had occasion to see bits and pieces of arcane knowledge from many parts of the world." That much was true. "A colleague once told me about a scrap of manuscript that spoke of the magical reanimation of the dead and of building a—a golem for a dying man to carry his soul—his mind. Have you ever come across such knowledge?"

Ibn Sina looked completely surprised and perplexed. "I have never heard of such things. If I were you, I would not credit it, Thabit. Such things carry the scent of magic, not of natural or divine philosophy. Such things defy both reason and faith." He paused and peered at us appraisingly. "This subject disturbs you."

"Greatly," we said, in all honesty.

"Do not let it," Ali-jan said. "These are vain imaginings; they have no place in the real world."

He was right, of course. And knowing what I knew, I couldn't help but be disturbed.

10

TRUST NO ONE

"Nothing," I said, when I'd been freed of my head harness and vital signs monitors. "There was nothing there. I pulled poor Thabit away from his family and friends for nothing."

"You're pacing again," Otis informed me.

"It's good for my nerves," I said, shoving my hands into the pockets of my jeans.

Otis snorted. "It's not good for ours."

"What do you think it means?" Victoria asked.

I swung around to look at her. I didn't like what I was thinking. "It means that someone on the team…" I cut off, then tried again. "Are we sure that nobody told Cornell about where and when I was going?"

Victoria blushed to the roots of her hair. "I know I didn't. I haven't spoken to Theron since we concocted this plan. Frankly, I was afraid I'd seem guilty if I tried to talk around it."

"Yeah," agreed Otis. "You're a terrible liar, Vic."

Well, that was a small comfort. I looked from one member of the team to another. "Anybody? No one talked to Cornell?"

Otis, Sophie, and Drew shook their heads. Drew's assistant, Harald, who was helping compile our written notes said, "I've never actually met the man."

"Anybody else who's not on the team have access to the offices?" I asked. "What about security staff? I know you've got security cams all over the place."

"Yeah," said Otis, "but they don't capture audio for obvious reasons. Just video. So if someone was watching us, they'd have to be lip readers to get what we were talking about."

Lip-reading spies and saboteurs were a bit of a stretch, even for me, and I now sort of believed in time travel. I turned to Victoria. "Can you get Cornell to come in? I'd like to get his reaction to all this."

"Are you going to tell him you suspected him of sabotage?"

"No, I just want to tell him that somebody's trying to introduce modern tech to the ancient timeline."

Theron Cornell was in an investor meeting when Vic tried to call him. He came as soon as the meeting was over ... or at least that's what he said. I have to admit that the situation made me more suspicious (paranoid?) than even my years as a detective had. But, when Cornell arrived and I described catching Bernardo Bellincioni in the act of trying to slip modern bionic tech into Renaissance Italy, he went cloud-belly white and gripped the arms of his chair as if he expected it to try to buck him off.

"Say again," he told me.

I did, and added, "Bernardo did a series of sketches for Leonardo DaVinci to play with. Basic bionics, I take it, but enough to give the master inventor raw material he certainly never would have thought up himself."

"And you did what with it?" he asked through stiff lips.

"I destroyed it. Tossed it into the fire."

Cornell relaxed as visibly as he'd clenched a moment ago. He nodded. "Good. You have an eidetic memory, correct?"

I tapped my forehead. "Like one of those old Polaroids."

"Could you reproduce the drawings?"

"I could ballpark it. My artistic skills are mediocre at best, and what I know about robotics, or bionics or whatever, you could print on a postage stamp. But yeah, I can try."

It took me three tries, but I finally produced a decent semblance of the sketches Bernie had made. Enough for Cornell to get a sense of what our saboteur had been trying to accomplish. By the time he confirmed my sense that this was either two separate saboteurs or one with a strong imperative to plant one or both of these technologies in the historical timeline, I was half-convinced he was sincerely disturbed and puzzled by this newest development. Either that or he was a damn good actor.

Believing the latter theory would have been the easy out, of course, because if he were sincerely *not* the saboteur, then we still had a problem. If the fact that no saboteur had turned up in the most likely place to spread contraband tech meant anything, it meant there might be another mole in the organization.

I pondered the idea that Cornell was the other time diver— or that he was hiding another time diver somewhere who had links to the same distant past that he and I did. Maybe, among other things, he wasn't as sick as he made out to be. Or maybe he wasn't the only one engaged in these shenanigans.

I cast an assessing glance at Harald. Was he a man with a hidden agenda or secret connections? It was hard to believe that about the kid. He seemed like such an open-faced sandwich—all ingredients on display. Ham and Swiss. Well, Norwegian, anyway. Which meant that unlike some other members of the team—Cornell, Victoria, Sophie, and me—he was unlikely to have ancestors in the Middle East or North Africa in the last several thousand years.

The upshot of all this pondering was a headache and the fear that I could trust no one. Clearly, the best way to stop the two streams of information from coming together was to subvert or destroy one of them. I had no idea when or where the bionic tech would enter the time stream, but I did know when and where Imhotep's amulet was, and that it was somehow the key to the Great Doctor's "resurrection" process. If there were any chance my worthy adversary was going to keep going after the damned thing, then I had to get there first.

Okay, I acknowledge that "first" is a weird concept in context with time travel, but I had to get the amulet, use it to find the papyrus, and then...

And then, what?

That was probably going to have to wait until I got where I knew I was going to have to go. And this was where I ran into trouble. As much as I wanted to trust Vic and the guys, I realized that was not a good idea. I also realized I was about to do something stupid.

IT TOOK ABOUT two hours for me to debrief from this morning's time dive. Theron Cornell stayed for the entire process. When we were done, he went back over my two run-ins with the time saboteur, grilling me about the other time diver's speech patterns, body language—anything that might contribute to us recognizing him.

Misdirection? Entirely possible. It could be Cornell's way of killing two birds with one stone: reaffirm his solidarity with the team, while making sure he avoided any telltale body language or vocal tics in future visits to the past.

Like I said, headache.

I gave exhaustive answers to everyone's questions, then went home. I ate dinner, waited until about nine thirty p.m., then took a cab back to the institute. The night watchman, Dennis, greeted me with a wave and a smile.

"Hey, Mr. August. You forget something up in the lab?"

"No. I thought I'd just come in and go over some stuff. Is anybody else on the team here?"

"No, sir. At least, not as far as I know. I just came on at nine."

"Oh. Oh, well, that's okay. I was kind of hoping to go over some things with Dr. Shehata, but I guess that can wait until tomorrow." I gave him a jaunty salute and headed for the elevator core.

The lab was, as Dennis surmised, empty and dimly lit. Fine by me. I made my way to the station I usually used for my time dives and considered how to go about this solo. I knew the technical drill; I'd watched Otis and Sophie go through it often enough by now. I didn't need the electrodes to monitor my vitals, but I needed to make use of Otis's auto-retrieval system, which meant I'd need the audio turned on.

I powered up the console, put on my headset, and made sure the microphone was working so I wouldn't get stranded in the olden days waiting for a passing loon. Then I pulled a copy of the amulet sketch out of my jacket pocket and studied it, wishing I could take it with me. Eidetic memory notwithstanding, I wasn't willing to trust that I'd gotten every detail completely right. I needed to get my hands on the original.

I wanted to return to the day our boss had made Amenaru his right-hand man, but late enough in the day that I'd get a shot at the amulet without an awkward off-with-his-head moment. Question was, how close could I cut a dive? I was about to get an answer. I focused as intently as I could on the day Nebemakhet made us Teacher's Pet, thought about bedding down for the night, and hit the trigger key.

I came to Amenaru as he was saying his evening prayers—

right in the middle of a prayer in praise of the gods for moving Nebemakhet to elevate him. He was still glowing from that signal Moment. Seemed like a good time to hit him with a shot of amulet envy.

If, I reasoned, playing Little Voice in the Head, *I can get another look at the amulet, surely I will be able to divine the location of Imhotep's papyrus.*

Amenaru hesitated, then took the bait. Up we got and headed for our master's chambers, hopeful that he had already retired for the night. We hurried from the sanctuary of Imhotep's shrine, down the steps, and into the corridor that led to the priest's quarters. Turning the final corner, we came face—to-face with a large human obstacle. We leapt back several feet and landed ready to fight; I instinctively brought Amenaru's hands up into a *tae kwon do* block.

The large obstacle stepped into the lamplight and turned out to be Har-khebu.

"Har-ib, you startled me!" said Amenaru, relaxing.

But I saw the look in Har-khebu's eyes. This was not the look of our friend and fellow priest; this was something else. A tingle of dread coursed up our spine. I was convinced beyond reason that we were face-to-face with another time diver and that, if we didn't act fast, my mission was about to come to an abrupt end.

I spurred Amenaru to attack Har-khebu, but he was now confused. Har-ib was his friend. Why did he suddenly want to fight him?

He hesitated just long enough for the other priest to grab our shoulder in a vise grip and drag us toward him. I readied myself for a punch that never came. His eyes boring into ours, Har-khebu rasped out two words: *"Destroy it."*

His grip slackened and he fell unconscious to the limestone floor.

What the hell?

Amenaru was stunned. Me too, but I had the benefit of knowing what Har-ib (or his future relation) meant. He was right. Yes, I'd seen the amulet lost with Nebemakhet in the Nile, but I also knew it didn't stay lost, and I suspected that we'd changed the timeline enough that even its eventual defacement couldn't be taken for granted. I had to keep anyone from being able to find Imhotep's papyrus ... or at least anyone but me.

Galvanized, we bolted to our master's quarters, pausing outside his door to listen. He was sawing logs quite lustily in his little alcove. His chambers were dark; the only light came from a lamp stand outside the door. We let our eyes adjust to the darkness, then pulled off our sandals and slipped silently into the room, crossing to the chest where the amulet sat in its ornate box.

Now, I've seen lots of movies where the good guy stops to admire his work and gets taken out by a lurking baddie or the palace guard. I was determined that was not going to be That Guy. We grabbed the amulet without hesitation and padded back out of the room. We were yards away before we stopped to get a good look at the back of the thing so I could fix it in my memory. In the moments it took me to do that, Amenaru was already thinking of putting it back; I couldn't let him do that. I had to destroy it, and I had to be the only one at the lab who knew that I had destroyed it and how. I forced a trembling Amenaru to carry the medallion back to his quarters. I found myself focused on the scarab. Was it possible that part of the "secret" of Imhotep was beneath it or within it? Did I want to know?

Amenaru was intrigued by this, despite the fact that he had no firm idea of why he was doing what he was doing. He scrabbled among his belongings for a ceremonial knife and used it to pry the scarab from its base. There was nothing on the flip side but a rough etching of a square with a tiny depression along one leg and an ankh at the center.

Okay. Imhotep and the gods on one side and the symbol for the human soul on the other. I suppose that made sense in light of what the papyrus was supposed to contain.

Time to finish the job. We dropped the thing on the stone floor, smashed it to smithereens with a bronze vase, and tossed the pieces into three different braziers. Then, while poor Amenaru dithered in confusion over what he had done, I sang like a bird.

Otis's auto-retrieval system worked, thank God. I blinked, closing my eyes in Memphis and opening them in Manhattan. At the workstation across from mine, Theron Cornell was slumped in a chair wearing a headset and an oxygen mask that I realized must feed him trigger scents. His face was a deathly shade of gray. I pulled off my headphones and hurried to check for breathing and a pulse, praying he was merely unconscious.

He was. But he was also not responding to several attempts to rouse him. I called 911. Then I went back to trying to wake Cornell. My mind raced through the implications of him diving into Har-khebu. I tossed the cosmic ones to the side. It would take a geneticist to explain some of that; I was more concerned with the other ramifications. He'd urged me to destroy the amulet. Why do that, if it contained a link to something he needed to keep him alive? More to the point, if he were the saboteur and had an ancestor in the Temple of Imhotep, why snag some poor schmuck from Fayum to play cat burglar?

I came to the reluctant conclusion that I'd been wrong about the saboteur. Whoever had been driving Abet was hell bent on getting the secret of resurrection. Har-khebu/Theron had been insistent on its destruction. There was still another time diver.

"Peter..."

I glanced up into Cornell's face. His color was a bit better, but he still looked like he'd been through a wringer. Sweat stood out along his upper lip, and he breathed with effort.

"That was a pretty big chance you took just now," I told him. "You could've killed yourself."

"Chance I had to take," he said, his voice barely audible. "Don't know who to trust except you. Did you...?"

I hesitated, knowing what he was asking me. I had to make a decision here. Either I trusted him or I didn't. "Yeah, I destroyed it."

"Don't let anyone else know what you did. Not even Victoria. Don't let them know about what happened here tonight."

"I have no intention of letting them know. Trust me."

"I do ... Listen. You need to find that papyrus."

"And do what with it?" I asked.

"If you can find a safe place to hide it—someplace we might be able to retrieve it from in the present—it would be of great interest to scientists now. But if you can't..."

"Message received. But, you realize you've got skin in this game, right? I mean, if this tech was discovered in the distant past..."

He shook his head. "Doesn't matter. Moral implications..."

I nodded. "I gotta ask you, Theron. Have you always known Har-khebu was your ancestor?"

"No. In my ... episodes, I never caught a name. Had no idea how to pry. I was just a silent passenger. Wasn't until you started describing things in detail that I realized I'd seen all of it

—the temple, the amulet, the other priests. I wasn't sure Har-khebu was my host, but I had to take the chance."

"You'd've made a good detective," I told him. I heard voices out in the corridor beyond the lab and realized the EMTs had arrived. "Sounds like our ride is here."

Cornell grasped my arm. "They'll get me to the hospital. *You* need to go back. You need to get to the papyrus before someone else does."

He was right, of course. Dennis, the night watchman, and I saw him off to the hospital, then I slipped back up to the lab, mumbling something about important records being left out. I sat down at my workstation, mulling the best approach. I went back to the sketch I'd made of the back side of the amulet. Stared at it. A line here and there wasn't identical to the original, but it was pretty damned close.

Imhotep was on top of Anubis. Or maybe *over* Anubis was a better way of putting it. Did that mean Imhotep thought he was a bigger god? Well, no, he hadn't been a god before he died, and he'd presumably had the scarabauble made to protect his big secret. Maybe it meant he thought he would conquer death? And what about the rest of it? Four minor gods in a box? Not just any gods—Horus's boys. What did that mean?

What I needed, I decided, was to think like an Egyptian. I plugged myself into the rig and dove back to Memphis. I made sure I returned *after* my destruction of the amulet. Best not to muck up the timeline even further. It was early morning in subjective time, and the Temple of Imhotep was in a frenzy. All anyone knew was that the Amulet of Imhotep had been stolen, and it seemed that Har-khebu (who was alive, but wobbly) had tried to stop the thief and gotten cold-cocked for his trouble.

While Har-khebu couldn't remember beyond running to the sanctuary on some dire mission that had to do with the amulet, Amenaru was beside himself. I was happy to fill in the blanks in his chaotic memory. I overrode my ancestor's perfectly understandable terror and confusion to add further nuance to the story: Har-ib had come to us in a dither with a tale of someone trying to steal the Amulet of Imhotep. He'd already been bludgeoned by the thief and fell senseless at our feet. Small wonder he couldn't remember what had happened. I, Amenaru, had run to the master's room, but it was too late. The amulet was gone and we'd seen no sign of the thief, though I suspected it was that fake convert from Fayum (if he really was from Fayum, which I sincerely doubted). I then (as Amenaru's memory told me) had gone back to help Har-khebu and dispatched servants to wake Nebemakhet.

I have to say, I felt really sorry for what I'd put my poor ancestor through. I'd been so focused on destroying the amulet and getting back to the lab that I hadn't even considered what he must have made of his own inexplicable behavior. He had a hazy memory of going to Nebemakhet's rooms, but everything after that was almost entirely blank except for going to find Har-ib in the hallway and calling for servants to attend him. What he —or rather, what I—had done to the amulet was so murky as to be incoherent, I suspected because it made no sense to him.

I did the best I could to replace the murk with my own preferred narrative: He had been at prayer, was warned by a wounded Har-ib, ran to save the amulet and failed, then raised the alarm and tended to his fallen friend. Third run-through was a charm; he calmed down and reassured himself that, yes, it had happened just that way.

His thoughts went to the amulet without my prompting. Why had the thief taken it? Yeah, I knew that there really was no thief, but Amenaru believed in him and was worried. Had the motive been simple greed? The medallion was a beautiful piece of work made from precious metal and semi-precious stone, after all. Had it been professional or religious rivalry? Or had it been more than that? How much did the thief know about the Amulet and what it portended? Nebemakhet and I were allegedly the only people who knew its secret. Had the thief somehow known it as well?

When at last we were alone with the high priest, we asked him if he feared the thief's motives, but the older man scoffed, saying that the thief could have no idea that the amulet was a key to anything, much less be aware of what the glyphs meant. Only a priest of Imhotep would understand such things.

What if Nebemakhet is wrong? What if the thief divines the meaning of the glyphs before Nebemakhet shares them with me? Amenaru wondered.

Or, I countered, *before you figure them out for yourself.*

Our pulse quickened. Amenaru was immediately on board with the idea of deciphering the glyphs. He thought he remembered them; I knew I did. We got out writing utensils and a sheet of papyrus and sat down at our little writing board to sketch. Amenaru was surprised and pleased that he'd remembered the text so well. I let him have his moment of self-congrats, then focused him on the meaning of the symbols.

We scanned the glyphs: *Imhotep.* Got that. This is the key to his Knowledge. But why was he figured as being *over* the God of Death? Was that a sly reference to cheating the god, somehow? Of resurrecting?

Amenaru didn't give that idea a second thought: Anubis was the god of mummification and the protector of the tomb in which Imhotep now resided. It was a simple reference to the location of the Divine Doctor's earthly remains.

Good grief.

No wonder I hadn't seen the connection. I'd screwed up Anubis's job title. He wasn't the god of Death; he was Protector of Tombs. Amenaru got it after only a moment's thought: *The papyrus is in Imhotep's tomb.*

Well of course it was. After all, what had Nebemakhet said on the day of our promotion? "The papyrus is where no *living* man would think to find it, under the eternally watchful gaze of the gods." This was something that, I realized from his stray thought, had caused Amenaru to poke around in the Divine Doctor's shrine, turning over icons, feeling around under benches, tapping on slabs.

Pleased with our epiphany, we turned our attention to the rest of the symbols—the ones inside the rectangle. They were, without doubt, the names of Horus's sons: Hapi, Duamutef, Imsety, and Qebesenuef. Those were obviously the gods whose watchful eyes Nebemakhet referred to.

Duh.

The question was, where was Imhotep's tomb? I prodded Amenaru's memory only to find that he had no idea. The location of the god's tomb was known only to his successor, Nebemakhet, and Amenaru and I both knew that by no means would he or anyone else get the priest to divulge its location.

I knew something that Amenaru didn't; in a matter of days— if my reading of the temple calendar was accurate—Nebemakhet would go on an errand that would convince him it was time to

unearth Imhotep's secret Knowledge, but he and Amenaru
would both die before he could take that fateful step.

I retreated into my host's subconscious to ponder the
imponderable. What should I do? Should I dive to the day of the
priests' deaths and try to prevent them? Should I simply make
myself unavailable for the trip to the Pharaoh's court so that
only the high priest died? If he died, then the information about
the location of the god's tomb would fall to Amenaru—and me
—but that was too close to murder for my comfort. Besides,
who's to say that it wasn't the weight of the litter with two full
grown men in it that had caused the porter to trip and drop his
shaft?

I could think of only one other possibility I was willing to
consider, and that was to go back home and do some research
on Imhotep's tomb. Maybe it had been unearthed in the inter-
vening centuries and I could simply dive back to the time of its
discovery. That was especially attractive because I already knew
how uneven the passage of time was between the two zones; for
all I knew, the other members of Team Backstory were moments
away from walking in on me.

In the end, that prospect drove me to return to the lab. It
was about two a.m. and the place was quiet as a (pardon the
expression) tomb. I went home, planning on getting some sleep.
Yeah, right. When I got back to my apartment, the first thing I
did was call the hospital to check on Theron. After establishing
that he was stable and resting, I curled up in my comfy chair
with my cat and my laptop and surfed the Internet.

By four-thirty a.m., this was the sum total of my knowledge:
Imhotep's tomb was at Saqqara near the pyramid of his
Pharaoh, Netjerikhet (aka, Djoser)—a pyramid allegedly
designed by Imhotep himself in his role as the Pharaoh's architect. Alas, Imhotep's burial had never been found. The closest
thing to intel on its location was a legend that it had been
discovered and looted at the end of the Roman occupation of

Egypt, a few years before the fall of Rome. The evidences of this were items in a stash of artifacts that eventually made their way up into Europe—artifacts that became part of Hitler's collection before and during WWII.

At four forty-five a.m., I nodded off in my chair, wondering if I'd lose money on a bet that more than one of those artifacts had ended up in a university museum in Salzburg, Austria.

11

BUSTED

I was a bit late getting to the lab that morning. I woke up with a start at 8:33 a.m. when Matilda the Cat leapt onto my chest and stuck her nose in my face. The message was clear: Where the hell is my breakfast, Monkey Boy?

I roused myself, fed Matilda, took a quick shower, and jogged across the park to the Morning Grind for a large triple-shot latte and a scone. I took a cab to the institute with no idea in the world what I would find when I got there. What I found was a team of scientists who looked as if their funding had been pulled ... or something horrific had happened to its source.

I took a tighter grip on my coffee cup and stepped through the door of the lab. "Hi, sorry I'm late ... uh, what's wrong?"

Victoria looked up at me, stricken. She sat at the monitoring station, hands between her knees as if she were trying to keep them from shaking. She wore jeans and a Failure is Not an Option sweatshirt, her hair in a messy bun that was already starting to unravel. I suspected that meant her morning had been far from normal.

"It's Theron," she said. "He had a heart attack last night."

I crossed the room slowly, carefully, trying to read her face. "He did?"

"Apparently, he came in to do some work and his heart..." She stopped and pressed her lips together as if trying to stop the words that came next: "Peter, what if he was trying to time dive? What if he was the saboteur after all?"

I set the coffee cup down on the workstation, guilt rising out of my heart like a swarm of angry bees from a poked hive. It was a feeling I was used to at this point in my life. "'Was' you said—he's not ... I mean, is he...?"

"He's in surgery," said Drew. His face was haggard and pale. "The operation is somewhat experimental. Apparently he has an abnormal valve in one chamber of his heart."

I should have called the hospital again this morning, I thought. *I should have...*

In my head, my mother's voice said, "Peter, don't 'should' on yourself." It was a lesson I'd taken much to heart until Mel. Right now, it left me clueless about what I should do next: let Victoria think that maybe Cornell was our adversary, or tell her the very truth that he had made me promise to keep between us?

"Are you sure he was time diving when he had the attack?" I asked. The fact they weren't asking *me* told me they had no idea I was involved.

Victoria took off her glasses and wiped them on the hem of her sweatshirt. "Dennis says Theron came in to do some work after hours. He found him while he was making his rounds, slumped in a chair in the lab. Dennis called 911."

Okay. That meant someone had instructed Dennis not to tell anyone what had actually happened. That someone could only have been Cornell. I felt even more compelled to keep our secret.

"Does this mean we're taking the day off?" I asked. "Victoria, I completely understand if you want to go to the hospital..."

She shook her head. "If I were sure Theron was the other time diver, maybe we could afford to back off, but if he's not, I'm pretty sure he'd want us to stay on task. We either need to figure out where our saboteur is going to strike next, or..."

"Or," I said, "we need to find the Papyrus of Imhotep and deep-six it."

"Neither of those options sounds terribly likely," said Drew, "considering that we have no idea where the papyrus is or how the amulet can lead us to it."

"Then I guess we should keep after it."

"What are you thinking, Peter?" Victoria asked.

I settled on a half-truth. "All throughout this ... experience, I've felt like I'm being led around by the nose. Particular ancestors have—I don't know—pulled me to them, I guess. The thing that connects two of them is Imhotep's Amulet. What if it connects them all? I'd like to try visiting a different time zone. See if I can find the amulet—or a connection to it—there. Maybe one of those connections will lead me to the papyrus."

"The glyphs on the amulet still don't make any sense to you?"

Unlike Victoria, I was trained in the art of lying. I made a face and shrugged. "No, but maybe they'll make sense to one of my ancestors."

"Which one?"

"Well, I was thinking maybe Omari Prisca. He's well-educated and Egyptian. Maybe he'll catch something in the glyphs that I haven't."

Victoria frowned. "What about Amenaru? Wouldn't he be the most likely to understand the glyphs?"

Well, damn.

"He hasn't shown any sign of it," I lied. "I suspect that code is meaningful only to Nebemakhet, and he's not talking. The only way Amenaru could get that information, I figure, is for Nebemakhet to die. I thought of making Amenaru call in sick the morning of his drowning so he gets whatever bequest Nebemakhet leaves for his successor. That's assuming they recovered Nebemakhet's body or Amenaru remembers what the back of the bauble looks like."

Victoria looked horrified. "That would be ... No, I wouldn't want you to do that. But what if you could find the high priest's last instructions? Surely they must explain *how* the amulet is the key, or at least give some clue about how you should read the glyphs."

"If all else fails," I said. "I mean, who knows how long that could take? And what if I made Nebemakhet suspicious of Amenaru in the process? God knows what might happen to a priest suspected of—of espionage."

Victoria let it drop there and we started prepping for my visit to Omari's time zone. I'd done some homework on this in the wee hours of the morning. The problem with my plan was that I had only a ballpark idea of when the tomb might have been found. I'd narrowed the Roman presence in Memphis down to a three-month period in 408 AD. I'd accounted for such variables as the type of weather necessary to travel, histories of a Roman march into Egypt, any tidbits about their triumphant return to Rome with swag. It wasn't as narrow a window as I'd've liked, but it was something.

Of course, I kept that to myself.

I arrived in Memphis on a fine spring day and caught up with the Vicarius Omarius Statius Prisca as he was answering his boss's correspondence. Flavius Anthemius was off in Constantinople receiving his promotion to consul, and Omari was feeling pretty good about life. His boss trusted and liked him, and had spoken to him openly of his own career potential. Plus, he was soon to be married to his beloved Sennia Donata. It was a heady sensation. He was looking forward to what amounted to an engagement party tonight at her family villa.

This, naturally, came into conflict with my own plans,

which were to have him spend his evenings staking out the necropolis at Saqqara. He was, I discovered, aware of a legion of Roman troops in the area that had been dispatched to put down any thought of rebellion on the part of the Egyptian citizenry. The empire was a little frayed around the edges, notwithstanding Emperor Arcadius's efforts to hold it together. The troops were camped on the outskirts of the city, toward Saqqara, as it happened, and had with them a large contingent of camp followers that included folk known to indulge in theft and grand larceny at the expense of the local populace.

Omari's concerns about this were peripheral, really, but I impressed him with the idea that his handling of potential looters in Anthemius's absence could make or break his career. I mean, really, if the more unscrupulous soldiers and camp followers took it into their heads to raid the necropolis, and we were able to thwart them, wouldn't that look great on our permanent record? We should really go out and take a look around for any signs of trespass—and soon. The longer those folks were in Memphis, the more likely they were to start thinking of ways to pad their assets when they got back to Rome.

Omari pushed back hard against what he supposed were his own rogue thoughts. Yes, he recognized the real threat, but pilfering and tomb robbing had been going on for centuries. That, all by itself, inclined my host to have a rather "meh" attitude toward the idea of skulking around the City of the Dead on the night he was supposed to be celebrating his formal engagement. Omari and his ersatz Conscience—that is, me—had a running battle over this idea. I kept raising the issue of his performance as vicarius during his boss's absence; he kept batting it away as being needlessly fretful … until I produced a forceful image of Djoser's step pyramid from a photo I'd found on Wikipedia: debris everywhere, the steps looking like they were covered in dirty shag carpet, the lowest tier half-eaten by sand.

It worked. He was horrified. Djoser's tomb complex was still a famous landmark hereabouts and a source of regional pride. It was part of a tribal identity that distinguished Egyptians from other citizens of the Roman Empire. But horrified or no, he was still not willing to give up an evening with his beloved to surveil some dead guy's final abode.

Fine. I compromised. Party first, then stakeout.

During the celebration, I sat back and let Omari take the lead. No little voice sounded in his head, nagging him about being vigilant on behalf of Flavius Anthemius; no weird urges struck him, making him choose water over wine or figs over artichokes. For him, the evening was a delight: food, drink, family, friends, and the magical, beauteous Sennia.

They sat together in her father's great hall during the meal and entertainment, sharing a divan and a lot of coy and smoldering looks. They fed each other bits of food and touched each other tentatively.

This was not as detached an experience as it sounds. I wasn't watching the happy couple from the outside, thinking, *Aren't they cute?* I was on the *inside*, looking into Sennia's eyes and sensing every bit of her beloved's emotional and physical attraction. Omarius Statius Prisca was so in love with Sennia Donata Honoria that I felt as if I were in love with her too. This was not good; when I got back to the lab, I already knew, those feelings didn't automatically turn off. They were, for some reason, likely to slop over onto Victoria.

When the festivities were over, Sennia walked us out to her villa's courtyard, stealing a moment alone with her hubby-to-be. I hung back in a corner of Omari's mind as they discussed the time and place of their wedding—little more than a fortnight from now in her family villa—and the various visits to oracles, shrines, and church that must be made in advance. I tried not to get too caught up in the kissing and caressing that happened after that. I tried to concentrate on The mission.

Sennia stirred in our arms and pulled out of a kiss. "Is your mind elsewhere, my love?" she asked, gazing up into our eyes.

We were in awe of her beauty. She wore little makeup, but her eyes, outlined with kohl, seemed huge. They were filled with the light of the waning moon that hung over the rooftops of Memphis. I could smell her perfume mingled with the cool, moist breath of the Nile.

Whoa.

"No," we said. "Our mind is right here with you."

She laughed musically. "*Our* mind? Are you more than one?"

Oops.

"Indeed there are two of me, Sennia," we ad-libbed. "One attends to the business of state so that the other may be dedicated to you alone, with nothing in his heart but Sennia." That last was all Omari and, by God, he meant every word of it.

The ride back to the consulate was physically uncomfortable. At least until I was able to distract my host from the heady charms of his fiancée. Damn, but he was a stubborn cuss ... and horny as hell. I informed him that the best antidote to his present overheated state was a brisk ride out to Saqqara and some time spent tramping among the tombs in the cool spring air.

Back at the villa, we changed into dark clothing, wrapped our head and shoulders in a burnoose, and chose a dark horse from the stables. Our body servant inquired where we were going and asked if we didn't require an escort. Omari considered it. I pushed back. More men meant more danger of being spied by the very people we wanted to spy on.

The necropolis was six miles from the consul's villa. At an easy lope, it took us twenty-five minutes or so to reach the verge of the tomb complex. We tied our horse in the shadow of a low mastaba and looked for a place from which to scan the area. The perimeter wall that enclosed the pharaoh's tomb provided the best combination of height and orientation. If we climbed up to the top of the wall, we would get a great view of the surrounding tombs and shallow wadis. If anyone were out there poking around in the dark, we'd see them the moment they lit a lamp.

We made our way to the gates of Djoser's plaza, keeping to the shadows as much as possible. Once inside, we trotted up a flight of stone steps to the top of the wall and began our watch. I decided the best approach would be to scan a segment of the necropolis visible from our vantage point, then move quickly to a new position atop the wall and repeat, taking in a slightly different area each time. The parapet was just high enough that we could stoop below its lip if we bent over at the waist.

The sun was sneaking up on the horizon when we finally decided there would be no activity out among the graves this time. We woke our horse and rode back into Memphis, wondering how many nights we could keep this up before sleep dep became a problem. Well, it wouldn't be a problem for me, but poor Omari …

Huh. Would I gain more control over him if he were sleep-deprived? Interesting idea. I seriously pondered it when we entered the green zone and the chill dry of the desert was replaced with the cool damp of the Nile. I wondered if there were a more efficient way to carry out this stakeout. I mean, one man for all that territory—it'd be awfully easy to miss something.

"Peter! What happened?"

I blinked and realized I'd been unceremoniously ejected from Omari's head. Victoria looked at me with concern in her big brown eyes and a frown creasing her forehead. I fought the urge to reach up and try to smooth it away … or kiss her.

Focus. "I guess I got too close to the Nile too near dawn."

She checked her watch. My grace period after a trigger sound had settled in at around ten minutes, so I had to wait at least that long to return. "Do you want to go back right away, or take time to debrief?"

I glanced down at my watch, not exactly seeing the dial. "How long was I gone?"

"Four hours, three minutes," said Otis from behind me.

Go back or debrief. If I debriefed, I'd have to come up with what I was going to tell the others in short order. They didn't know I'd destroyed the amulet and thought I was looking for it in this time zone. Still, I opted to debrief, telling Victoria that my host was pretty much ready to hit the sack, anyway.

I walked through the visit, editing as I went. It didn't require all that much editing. I recorded Omari's worries about tomb robbers, and theorized that this might be the connection—after all, Nebemakhet's Amulet was looted from Memphis and ended up in Austria.

"I still think maybe you should give Amenaru a try," said Victoria. "What if you go back and let him get a really good look at Imhotep's Amulet? I think there's a strong possibility he might recognize what those names mean. And that might tell you exactly where the papyrus is."

"Yeah, but what if he figures it out, then takes it into his head to go look for the papyrus on his own—as in, while I'm not on board?"

She gave me a strange look. "Well, obviously, you'd have to push him to go get it while you *are* 'on board,' as you put it. Don't tell me you're suddenly shy about guiding your host."

I was out of dodges. I couldn't simply tell her—right in front of everyone—that I'd already gone back days before Amenaru and Nebemakhet drowned in the Nile and destroyed the amulet. Or that we'd figured out where the papyrus was ... without knowing its exact location. I couldn't just blurt out that this was why I was lurking around a necropolis in 408 AD Memphis because, if I did, the saboteur would know he needed to give up on the amulet altogether. I wanted him (or her) to believe it was still in play.

Victoria looked at me strangely. She opened her mouth to say something … and her cell phone rang. She pulled it out of her sweatshirt pocket, looked at the screen, and answered, heading for her office as she did.

I let out a breath of relief. Saved by the bell. Or rather by Blue Oyster Cult's *Godzilla*. But not for long. She'd been in her office barely a minute before she poked her head out and beckoned to me to come in.

"It's Theron," she said.

Dread coursed through me. "You mean it's the hospital? Or it's Theron calling from the hospital?"

"It's Theron," she repeated. "He wants to talk to you."

"Hey," I said when Victoria handed me her phone, "how are you doing, man?"

"I'm in recovery. Not a cure, but a help." His voice sounded husky, but not all that weak. "Listen, Vic is having misgivings about both of us right now. I know I asked you to keep our secret. Maybe keeping it from her wasn't a good idea. If you can bring her in without anyone else—meaning a possible mole—finding out, you probably should."

I glanced at Victoria. Her expression was a nonverbal threat.

"Maybe better coming from you," I said.

"I seriously doubt it." The coward hung up on me.

I turned off the phone and handed it back to Victoria.

"What's up, Peter?" she asked. "Why are you so reluctant to prod Amenaru to—"

I pointed at the phone. "He didn't tell you…?"

"He didn't tell me a damn thing except that he wasn't our saboteur and you'd explain. So explain. You've been acting weird since you came in this morning. Why don't you want to try getting the amulet into Amenaru's hands?"

"Because I destroyed the amulet. Last night."

"You ... what? Wait—you were here last night? With Theron?"

I nodded. "I'm the one who called 911."

"Then what are you looking for in 408 AD?"

"The Papyrus of Imhotep. Amenaru figured out that it's in Imhotep's tomb."

Victoria's eyes lit up. Apparently archaeological discovery trumped personal umbrage. I'd have to remember that.

"You know where it is? That's fantastic! Then you can—"

I raised my hands. "There's a little problem, Vic. I know the papyrus is in the tomb. I just don't know where the *tomb* is."

She stared at me mutely for a full five seconds, then said, "Start at the beginning."

IT WAS NOT A COMFORTABLE CONVERSATION, and the worst of it was watching her take in that Cornell hadn't trusted her. That he'd thought maybe she was the mole.

"How could he think that?" she asked me—rhetorically, I'm sure. "How could *you* think it? I've been here every time you time dived."

"It's not about *you*, specifically. It's more that, if we don't know who our saboteur is ... the best policy is to trust no one. Frankly, Otis is right—you're a pretty bad liar, Vic. You might give something away by showing your own discomfort. But, I think you raise an important point—the person doing the diving isn't necessarily the person doing the spying. And if you know where and when you're going, does it matter when you do it in real time? I mean, couldn't our saboteur end up in the same past moments even if he or she is leaping from a different point in time?"

The anger melted from her eyes as she pondered the scientific principle in that. Maybe she was even a little impressed that I'd thought of it.

"Time travel paradoxes," she murmured.

"Why not? I mean I'm not physically going back in time; my thoughts are, or my mental energy is. I don't pretend to understand how this works."

"That makes two of us," she admitted, then hit me with a laser beam look. "Okay, Detective. What do we do now?"

"I'd prefer we don't announce to all and sundry that I know the papyrus is in the tomb. Since we don't know when our saboteur may try to introduce modern tech, it makes the most sense for us to concentrate on taking the papyrus out of the timeline altogether. Our saboteur doesn't know where the papyrus is and doesn't know that the amulet is out of play. His only way of finding any of that out involves using a guy he has to drag all the way from Fayum. He —or she—may figure out right away that it makes the most sense for him to find a place to insert the tech into the timeline, but if we're lucky, he'll waste some more time in the Third Dynasty."

Victoria nodded. "Frankly, his tech is dangerous, but it's only lethal if combined with Imhotep's alleged resurrection process. Do you still think Omarius Prisca is the best link to the papyrus?"

I nodded. "I know some Roman tomb raiders will find Imhotep's tomb—or at least artifacts from it—sometime in the next several months, Omari's time. And the only way I can think of to connect with them is to have Omari stake out the necropolis."

"Sounds deadly boring," she said, deadpan.

I took it from the subtle snark that she was recovering from the shock of having secrets kept from her.

"I think I should go back in, but I also think we need to keep the rest of the team in the dark."

"Agreed."

She straightened, put a smile on her face, and went back out into the lab where the rest of the team were trying, pointedly, to look as if they had not been watching us through the glass half-panels of Vic's office.

"Theron is out of surgery," she announced brightly. "He's awake and doing well. So far so good."

"Good to hear," said Otis, "but what was the big discussion about—or are we allowed to know?"

"Theron was concerned about the approach we're taking. He thinks we should be figuring out where the other time diver would insert his tech instead of trying to decipher what the amulet says."

Drew quirked an eyebrow. "Does that mean we're going back to plan A?"

Victoria shook her head. "No, I agree with Peter that instead of chasing around trying to pinpoint something that could literally happen in a thousand places in the timeline, we should concentrate on later time zones that are potentially connected to the amulet."

Sophie, Otis, and Drew exchanged glances, then Sophie asked, "Could we not do both? What if I were to look for other scholars whose work in medicine or mechanics might serve our saboteur? Ibn Rushd's or Henry Gray's work in medicine has greatly influenced twentieth and twenty-first-century experimentation."

Now it was Vic and I doing the eye dance. I tilted my head a hair, hoping she'd read it as a yes—if one of these three folks was our saboteur or his mole, then having them off doing other stuff was a plus.

"That sounds like a great idea, Sophie," Vic said. "I think Ibn Rushd might be the best place to start. Develop a timeline for his publications and work back from there. It would make sense for our time diver to insert the tech at the earliest possible point."

Sophie went off to her corner to dive happily into the data streams while I prepped to go back to Omari's neck of the desert.

I aimed rather purposefully for the day after his engagement party and got there to discover that my ancestor was adorning himself for yet another visit to his sweetheart. Damn, but this guy could be focused—just not on what I needed him to be focused on right now. I tried to inject doubt into his plans for the evening; maybe he should go back to Saqqara and watch for skullduggery.

He shook off the idea with a shrug of bemusement. That would be redundant. After all, what could he accomplish that the men he'd dispatched to keep watch over the necropolis could not do far more efficiently and effectively?

The clever boy had done me one better—well, six better, to be more accurate. He'd assigned half a dozen of Flavius Anthemius's crack troops to hide among the graves and keep watch on his behalf. They would go out at sunset and return at dawn with explicit instructions to send their fastest rider to him if they saw anything suspicious.

What this meant, of course, was that I had to reverse my polarities, as it were. I had to go to my ancestor in his evening and stay with him until dawn. Seeing how fond he was of parties and hanging out until the wee hours with his lady, this could be either incredibly boring or exciting in ways that were way too distracting.

On the off chance that he might have some knowledge of dynastic lore, I presented my host with a memory of the Amulet of Imhotep, trying to judge if he'd ever seen such a thing, or heard of it, even in legend. He had not, but he *had* heard tales of the papyrus—or at least rumors that the Divine Doctor had left behind a secret cache of his most revolutionary procedures and wisdom.

I conjured a flash image of the glyphs from the back of the amulet. Omari recognized them immediately as the names of the deities who guarded Egyptian tombs. In this case, apparently the tomb was Imhotep's. So what? Any Egyptian who could read hieroglyphs would get that from the images. Omari had no idea *why* the tomb of Imhotep should be of interest to him, and I had no way to tell him. Unless, of course, I was going to cast myself in the role of divine revelation—an angel or a ghost from the gods sent to present him with the secret of eternal life. Except I realized by his ornamentation that my guy was a Coptic Christian and probably wasn't likely to give two figs for the old gods.

I'd only managed to get him wondering where the heck he'd seen those glyphs before. I generated the idea that he must have come across them in his reading of old papyri. Or maybe had seen them on a frieze in one of the temples hereabouts. Yes, that was it; there must've been some reference to the tomb of Imhotep at his old shrine on the banks of the Nile.

My dusk-to-dawn stakeouts of the Vicarius Prisca took place over a series of evenings during which my host sometimes worked late into the evening on his master's business, partied into the wee hours at the home of his in-laws-to-be, or slept like a rock, worn out by the other two pastimes. Every night his men went out to the necropolis, and every morning they returned with nothing to report. Here in the lab, this was also taking time —too bloody much time. If I could've jumped ahead to just the right spot, I'd've done it in a Manhattan minute.

In Omari's waking hours, my only intel about anything important came from the captain of the consular guard, Citro Superstes. As Omari slept, I could only mess around with his dreams, planting the idea that the Romans knocking about Memphis annoying the crap out of the populace were Up to No Good, and that he would prove his mettle as vicar if he could keep them from desecrating the tombs of the pharaohs. I poked about in his memories, hoping to find that he harbored a special admiration for Imhotep, but he didn't. He was somewhat of a scholar, but had no interest in Imhotep as either a god or an author, preferring Christian philosophers like Origen.

At the Manhattan Institute of Neuroscience, days passed and I began to wonder if I was barking up the wrong tree. Then, on the fourth day of my poking about in Omari's brain—which was equivalent to about two weeks in his timeline—he was woken from a sound sleep by a member of his surveillance team.

"Vicarius Prisca," the soldier greeted us when Omari had wrapped himself in a robe and come out into his sitting room, "our vigilance has borne fruit; two of the watchers confirm a party of men making their way into the necropolis. Given that they are dressed in dark clothing, our captain believes they may be tomb raiders."

We could not have been more awake if someone had poured icy water over our head.

"I will ride out at once," we said, and ran to dress the part of spy, forgetting for the moment that we were to be married in the morning.

12

TOMB RAIDER

Remember where this all started—with little Petey August racing across the Midwestern plains in his grade school idea of a dream job? Well, let me tell you that riding hell bent for leather through the star-spangled night beyond Memphis was like being that kid again. I half expected to wake up on the seesaw at Bellaire Elementary. It was surreal. The moment in which we shot from the river vale into the desert air was like surfacing after a dive into cold water, or as I imagined the moment an Air Force test pilot "slipped the surly bonds of Earth" and all that.

The excitement was both daunting and appealing to Omari; I found I had to focus to keep our wits about us. He was drifting toward treating this as a Grand Adventure, while I was flashing back to a certain drug bust gone pear-shaped.

We reached the outskirts of the necropolis and slowed our mounts. Our guide—the guard who'd been dispatched to get us —indicated we should dismount. Together we made our stealthy way to where a second soldier sheltered behind a crumbled bit of wall. He, in turn, led us to where his captain, Citro Superstes, watched. Citro picked up the role of guide dog and tippy-toed us into the lee of a more recent tomb whose limestone-clad sides gleamed weakly in the light of a sliver of moon, causing me to assume that this grave-dweller still had family in the area.

Citro peered around the corner of the tomb, beckoned to us, and pointed, but we'd already seen what there was to see: A shadowy group of figures was milling around the base of Djoser's stepped mastaba. We expected them to dig. They didn't dig; they began to pull rock fall and debris away from a cleft between the larger pyramid and a smaller mastaba in front of it. After fifteen or twenty minutes of concerted effort, they hauled out a large piece of heavy fabric—a sail, I thought, that had apparently been used to cover their work.

A cold chill swept through us. This could only mean that they'd been working the site for some time without my watchers detecting them. We glanced up at the moon and it struck me: They'd probably been working the site for months, coming out only when the moon was new or, like tonight, a barely visible sliver. It also meant we had no idea if they'd entered the tomb or, if they hadn't, how close they were to getting in.

I was torn. I mean, this might not even be the Tomb of Imhotep, even though the location was a good candidate. And it might yet take the tomb robbers days, weeks even, to break through into the burial chamber.

What I needed, I decided, was to see what sort of stuff the diggers were bringing up in those big old baskets they carried in and out of the hole. There were approximately fifteen men involved, moving about in the deep shadows between the structures, dumping their baskets somewhere I couldn't make out, then returning for another load. They were all dressed approximately the way Omari was—dark pantaloons, tunics, and anonymous burnooses. We'd fit right in.

I gave a thought to checking in with Victoria, but realized I didn't know if I could cut a dive quite as close as necessary to keep my hands on Omari's reins, as it were. I didn't want to bail on him in a crucial moment. So, I prodded him into considering a little reconnaissance. Omari was all over it. I knew the kid was a romantic, but now he'd also gotten his Egyptian pride in high gear and was determined to thwart the grave robbers' nefarious plans.

We sent Captain Citro back to gather his men after settling on a signal we'd give to call them to attack if necessary. Then we slipped through the incredibly Stygian gloom to the flank of the baby pyramid behind which the diggers milled. Extra baskets sat in a jumbled row next to a refuse pile in which the men dumped debris. As we watched, one of the men popped out of the mouth of the tomb with his basket held aloft.

"Decurion!" he called.

This got the attention of a burly fellow we hadn't noticed before because he wasn't moving, and had no basket in his hands. If we'd tried to slither closer, we'd've tripped over him. He had been sitting against the lowest tier of the mastaba, to our left, and now stood and strode to the mouth of the hole in the ground.

"Look, sir!" the digger said, holding up his basket.

His excitement crawled like ants across my face; I scratched my nose. Or, well, Omari's nose. You get the picture.

We took the opportunity to slip into the cleft, snag one of the baskets, and hurry across the uneven ground to where a gaggle of men now stood, peering at the digger's find in the light of a hooded hand lamp. We saw two items: ornamental lamps fashioned of metal and richly decorated. Even in the dim light, the colors in their ornate patterns were vivid. The decurion rubbed at one of the lamps with his cloak and the metal gleamed. So did his teeth when he smiled. I half-expected a genie to appear.

"You've found the door to the burial chamber then," the

decurion said. "This was surely from a lamp stand in the outer chamber."

"Yes, sir!" said the digger eagerly. "And in the corridor below, we can see part of a painting."

The men all made appreciative noises, and we joined in, nodding and echoing the fist-pumping gesture that is still in use even in the twenty-first century.

Grinning now, the ringleader of the group tossed the lamps back into the basket, instructing the digger to place them in "the farthest hamper." We followed his gesture and saw a row of camels lying in the sand on the far side of the little mastaba. Well, that is, we saw camel-ish shapes in the darkness. Their low snorts and grumbles were the only thing that distinguished them from the rocks. The digger ran off to comply while the decurion lowered himself into the hole ... which I realized was some yards to the left of center in the facade of Djoser's pyramid —like the etched rectangle on the back of Imhotep's amulet.

I almost did a face-palm. Of course. The square with the ankh in it was the pyramid viewed from the top, and the little rectangle was the entrance to a second tomb—Imhotep's tomb.

The other men ran to dump their baskets on the slag heap and brought them back empty. Mine was already empty, so I let myself down into the hole and followed the head guy's lamp-light through a long descent followed by an equally long, level corridor. Our fearless leader turned three times in a tightening spiral, ignoring any other corridors along the way.

The experience was not a comfortable one. I am not claustro-phobic, but trekking through that dark, dusty, crunchy-under-foot place with what I knew to be tons of rock and quarried limestone and sand overhead gave me a great appreciation for the condition. By the time we got to the spot where the lamps had been found, other members of the crew had already dug a great deal of debris away from the suspected doorway. By the

light of lamp and torch, the frieze they'd revealed was spec-
tacular.

"Dig! Dig!" commanded the decurion.

I realized he was wearing a Roman legionnaires' uniform
beneath his dusky cloak, with rank insignia on one shoulder
that meant his day job was commanding a squad of horsemen.
Another man in uniform stood farther down the corridor,
watching the proceedings with obvious interest. We couldn't
make out his rank.

"Clear the door!" the decurion ordered, so we did.

I pitched in alongside everyone else, fairly certain that no
one was likely to be counting heads at this juncture; one extra
man would not be noticed. In the flickering light, all guys in
burnooses looked about the same.

It took roughly forty minutes to clear the door and another
slightly lesser amount of time to stick a pair of pry bars into a
seam in the frieze and pry the slabs apart. If the crew had been
composed of archaeologists led by Henry Jones Junior and not
tomb raiders, it would have taken a lot longer, but the two
legion officers ran out of patience pretty fast and abandoned any
attempt to preserve the artwork on the doors and surrounding
frame. When we finished with the pry bars, the thick slab doors
lay in pieces around the entry. Omari and I felt vague guilt at
having been party to this desecration, but we couldn't exactly
hail our men from underground. It wasn't like we were wearing
a wire. If we were to serve the greater goal, we'd have to wait
until they were above ground to catch them red-handed with the
goods.

We all stepped through the ruined archway and into the
burial chamber in complete silence. Even I could tell this was
the real deal and not one of those decoys that are sometimes
used to discourage the looting of royalty. At the time of his
death, Imhotep had been a celebrity and a national treasure, but

he was not a pharaoh, and his godhood had been conferred upon him after his burial. His vault was hidden, but not obscured.

We experienced a suspended moment of disbelief as we stared at the painted walls; the collections of funerary goods; lavishly decorated containers; folded stacks of cloth that were probably garments for the afterlife; figurines of ships, horses, chariots and carriages, courtiers and servants, even a house—all the goodies the deceased was supposed to need in the afterlife.

In the center of it all was the sarcophagus. No mere giant sandstone shoebox, it was a giant sandstone shoebox supported by four sturdy pillars two feet in height that were painted to look like the pillars in the arcade that ran from Djoser's pyramid to the gates of his tomb complex. The walls looking down on the sarcophagus were covered with friezes and glyphs, with an altar of sorts at the head of the big stone shoebox.

It seemed we all took a deep breath of the dusty, still air, and exhaled before the decurion ordered: "Grab what you can and get it above! Get anything metal or jeweled first. Load the hampers. Best we clear this out tonight."

My first thought was for Victoria. Was there any point to letting her know what was happening?

Omari's first thought was for his men: Did he dare signal them to attack once he was above ground? Should he? They might overcome the two officers, but if these men were also legionnaires and not simply hired diggers, then they would not be easily overwhelmed. These guys all moved as if they were used to taking orders spit-spot, and they'd called the head guy by his rank, not with a generic honorific. That sort of hinted that they were legion regulars, not local guys hired to do a night's work. Plus, they didn't speak Latin with a local accent, which hinted they weren't from around here.

My money was on them all being soldier boys. Not good.

I brought my mind into tight focus. The first thing I needed to do was confirm that this was Imhotep's tomb. I moved to the altar on the wall opposite the head of the sarcophagus and picked up stuff to put in my basket. I gave Omari his head and he started looking for glyphs that would tell us something about the inhabitant of the stone box behind us. On the altar was a sort of diorama with little figures in it representing the household of the deceased—*ushebtis*. We picked up one that was seated on a little throne and turned it over. There it was—the name Imhotep. It was also on the top of the frieze decorating the wall behind the little shrine.

Great. We kept picking up *ushebtis* and other swag and putting them into the basket. This was where I needed to be in the driver's seat, because Omari's thoughts were beginning to tell me he believed he had fulfilled his duty here; he'd discovered a plot to rob the tomb of a local deity and now needed to get the hell out of Dodge. He'd already decided he was going to take his first basket of stolen goods up top and sneak it back to the spot where he'd parted company with his guard. I couldn't let that happen because I needed to figure out where the papyrus was.

While Omari methodically loaded our basket, I brought to mind the amulet glyphs: Imhotep, Anubis, four minor gods in a box. Where in this tomb would I find four minor gods in a box?

As I contemplated this, I realized a couple of disturbing facts: One was that behind me, the two officers were using their pry bars on the sarcophagus. The second was that other diggers swiftly moved items that might very well be necessary for the symbols on Imhotep's amulet to make any sense.

A shot of adrenaline hit our nervous system like a triple latte with an espresso chaser. I turned Omari around, pretending to look for other goodies to loot, and tried to see anything that might go with the glyphs. The papyrus was no doubt well-hidden, but where? I looked for caskets, boxes, folios, anything that might conceal a scroll or set of bound pages, but the torches and lamps filled the space with a jittery dance of light and darkness that threw the shadows of the diggers far up the walls and across areas of the chamber that might contain exactly what I was looking for.

Omari, meanwhile, recognized the symbols flashing before his mind's eye as something he'd had out-of-the-clear-blue thoughts about weeks ago. What could that mean? Could a Christian possibly be receiving communications from the god Imhotep, he wondered?

Sure, why not?

Save my wisdom! I lobbed the idea into Omari's head like a revelatory grenade. *These men desecrate my tomb! For the love of God, save my greatest wisdom!*

I presented Omari with the amulet glyphs again.

Heart pounding, we looked this way and that, turning finally toward where the two legion officers worked at disinterring the Divine Doctor. Two things struck me at that moment. Thing one: As a pyramid in two dimensions and viewed from the top is a square, a sarcophagus is a rectangle. Thing two: at this end of the rectangle, tucked beneath the overhang between the chubby little columns, was a tray—another rectangle—and nestled into a series of holes in the top of that rectangle were what Omari immediately recognized as Imhotep's four canopic jars.

Each jar was topped with the head of a god. Guess which ones.

Yep, Horus's boys: Hapi, Duamutef, Imsety, and Qebesenuef. Each one guarded a different set of Imhotep's internal organs. The jars and the tray they sat in were stunningly decorated with cloisonné and gold.

The papyrus must be hidden in the tray.

The decurion and his buddy snarled and grunted and called for help down at the foot of the sarcophagus. While others answered the call, we stooped down, grasped the tray firmly, and pulled it into our basket. It was made of metal and was fairly heavy, but I didn't let that deter us. Omari assumed he was the recipient of divine intervention, and if he had been chosen to rescue the wisdom of an old god—or possibly a prophet that had been mistaken for a god—he was up to the task.

We hefted the basket and carried it out into the dimly lit corridor. A few of the other men had already taken baskets to the surface and were returning with empties for another load. We kept our head down as if struggling with our basket, and wended our way into the open air. A quick look around showed that we were alone for the moment, though we could hear voices coming from the line of camels.

We set the basket down and hoisted the tray, turned left instead of right, and started toward where Omari's men would be waiting. We'd just reached the open end of the gap between the tombs, and raised an arm as a signal, when we heard a noise behind us.

I felt a blast of pain that left me blind as a bat and alone in Omari's head.

I ONLY KNEW Omari wasn't dead because I was still with him, locked inside his head. I could see nothing, and what I heard and felt was muted, as if wads of cotton batting walled me from the outside world. I couldn't sing "Louie, Louie." And thinking the music was not enough to get my body, sitting in its chair in Manhattan, to so much as twitch, apparently, because no one yanked me out of my flesh and blood prison.

After the initial shock of being cut off, I figured out what must have happened. Someone must have realized we weren't with the team (or at least that we were trying to make off with some of the swag) and thumped us on the head. Omari was down for the count, so all I could do was wait for him to wake up. It was weird, being able to sense motion and hear mumbly conversations without having the slightest clue what was happening or what was being discussed. I was aware that someone had pulled off Omari's burnoose, and that it had caused a lot of fevered discussion. I suspected it was because the tomb raiders—being Roman citizens—recognized the medallion that he wore beneath his ninja clothes as an official badge of rank. Possibly, that's what saved his life.

I hunkered down in a corner of my ancestor's catatonic brain and recited poetry, puzzled over song lyrics, critiqued series TV plots, and pondered the nature of life and time. I had no real sense of time passing, and figured that not enough time had gone by in the lab to alarm Vic and make her bring me home. So it was that, hours later, it seemed to me that the movement I dully sensed had become somewhat regular and more pronounced. We rocked back and forth, forth and back. A creaking sound seemed to echo the motion in some way I couldn't put my finger on, and it all grew steadily more noticeable.

Then, I saw light—weak and muddy at first, then brighter and more coherent. Suddenly, I could see again, if blearily. Omari had opened his eyes a crack, and I took in an expanse of wooden planking beneath our cheek, thick wooden dowels only inches away from our face and, beyond that, desert flushed with ruddy light.

Whisky Tango Foxtrot. Where were we … a moving jail cell?

We tried to move, and our head protested loudly and painfully. Omari uttered a groan that was completely involuntary, and someone grasped our shoulder and shook it.

A voice said urgently, "My lord! My lord, do you wake?"

It was Citro. When Omari mumbled something in the affirmative, Citro helped us sit up. This caused more pain and some nausea, which I tamped down with a firm thought. I *hated* throwing up with a passion. As long as I was on board, Omari was *not* going to hurl.

Sitting up, with Citro checking out the lump on the back of our head, we realized the true and dismal reality: We were in a cage—a foul, nasty, wooden cage with big noisy wheels and no protection from the elements. It was being pulled by a couple of thick-legged horses and surrounded by mounted Roman soldiers.

The fact that Citro was here was disturbing. The fact that he was the only one of the half-dozen men we'd dispatched was even more so.

"The other men," we croaked. "What happened to them?"

Citro didn't answer, so we turned to look at him. His face was bruised and abraded and wore as dark a look as I've ever seen.

"Three are dead, Vicarius. Two are in a cage somewhere behind us. One—Lycus Nazarius—escaped. I believe he was wounded, but as far as I know, they sent no one after him. God willing, he will be able to give report of our kidnap and of the thievery we witnessed."

Omari tried to nod, winced, and gave it up as a bad move. "The tomb goods they stole—are they with this train?"

"Yes, Vicarius. Somewhere behind us in the column, I believe."

"How long have we been traveling?"

He correctly surmised that I was trying to figure out how long Omari had been unconscious. "You slept as one dead for the better part of this day. The sun is setting," he added.

It took me a moment to realize that he was right. I'd taken the ruddy light and long shadows of horses and men to mean it was early morning and that we were traveling south. Instead, we were traveling northeast with the sun riding low to our southwest, angling across the desert—to where?

That's when it hit us—this was the day of Omari's wedding to Sennia Donata. It had passed without him. For Omari, this realization caused one kind of unbearable agony; for me, it caused another. Lucky me, I got to experience both. His heart was breaking and he was filled with self-loathing. If he had not been so caught up in his desire to impress his consul, if he had focused on his wedding and marriage, he would not now be in a cage on his way to an uncertain fate, leaving his beloved to feel abandoned.

His anguish only made mine worse: This wasn't the first time I'd yanked an ancestor out of his natural habitat, but when I'd done it to Thabit, he'd been thrilled to pieces and had flourished in his new environment. I'd given Thabit everything he wanted; I'd taken it all away from Omari. And to make matters worse, I may have sabotaged my own reality—my own *existence* —by taking Omarius Prisca away from the woman he was supposed to marry.

But away to where? Were we going to Carthage? I might be able to escape if we ended up in Carthage, or convince someone I was a deputy to Consul Flavius Anthemius and arrange a rescue. Whatever our ultimate destination, I had to report in to Victoria. Omari wasn't going anywhere, and I could at least let Vic know what was happening and take care of some of my more mundane housekeeping duties.

As I began to hum "Louie, Louie," I realized I could smell the sea.

13
THE NEW WORLD

"Who am I?"

Those were the first words out of my mouth when I resurfaced in Manhattan. I had eyes only for Victoria, and fought to keep from grabbing her to make sure she was real. I slowly realized that the rest of the team was there (Drew, Otis, Sophie. Huzzah!), all staring at me as if I'd taken leave of my senses. Maybe I had, but I was terrified. I must have changed *something*, after all. I'd taken Omari away from his family, his friends, his bride. Unless—and it seemed a dismally thin hope—he was able to prove who he was to someone at the thieves' destination and hitch a ride back to Memphis. Or maybe they'd ransom him.

Maybe, I thought, *I'm not even Peter August anymore.*

Victoria was visibly worried. "Who *are* you?" she echoed. "You're you. What—?"

"Not helping," I said. "Am I Peter August?"

She glanced up and around at the other members of the team. "Um," she said, "yes, you're Peter August. Who else would you be?"

I pursued the point. "Detective? NYPD Major Crimes Division? On leave for ... psychological health reasons?"

She nodded, and something in her eyes told me she got it. She understood what I was freaked out about. "What happened, Peter? Did something go pear-shaped?"

I spent all of a nanosecond flattering myself that she'd started to talk like me (next, she'd be picking food off my plate) before I responded to her question. "Yeah, you could say so," I said. "I managed to get my ancestor thumped on the head and hauled off to God-knows-where by tomb raiders."

"Oh, my God," Vic murmured. She straightened, lifting a netlike cap from my head.

"Did you find the amulet?" Drew asked, frowning.

"Not exactly. The long and short of it is that I convinced Omari to impress his boss by trying to keep grave robbers out of the necropolis. Instead, we got caught trying to remove evidence. When I left Omari, he was in a wooden cage on his way to the seashore ... *on his wedding day.*"

"*Mon Dieu,*" said Sophie. "*Ce n'est pas bon.* That can't be good."

"But it can't be all bad, either, right?" asked Otis. "After all, you're still here. You're still you."

He was right. There was a good deal of not bad in that. It must mean that Omari would be able to free himself and get back to Memphis and that Sennia wouldn't hold it against him that he'd decided to go play master spy on the eve of their wedding. I relaxed a bit, but just to be sure ...

"You've got my CV on file here. Can you tell me if my parents are still Marija Lepak and Frank August?"

Otis turned to his computer and said, "Bio for Peter August, MIN associate."

"Retrieved," the computer said in a pleasant female voice.

Well, that was new. So, I realized, was the net-cap that Vic was placing carefully on a stand.

"Parents of Peter August," said Otis.

"Marija Susannah Lepak and Franklin Peter August," the computer voice said.

Otis swung back to look at me. His hair was different, I realized. It was cut into a center-parted curtain style that I was pretty sure went out of vogue in the early 2000s. The little errant lock was gone. My face must've been doing something weird, because he frowned and said, "What? Those are the right names ... aren't they?"

"How long has your computer had a voice interface?" I asked.

Otis frowned and shrugged. "As long as I can remember."

Damn. I swiveled my chair around, looking for my smart phone and house keys. I saw no house keys. The phone was postcard thin and curved and set into an armband.

"Where are my house keys?"

I could feel gazes collide over my head.

"You don't have house keys, Peter," said Victoria reasonably. "No one has house keys in this day and age. Your house..." She trailed off, her gaze on my face. "When you dived, you had house keys."

I nodded.

"We all had house keys," she guessed.

I nodded again. "Most of us, anyway. Otis had his in an app on his iPhone, but he still had a physical key as backup. Let me ask you this—how's Theron doing?"

Now she looked wary. "He's doing great. His new heart is functioning way better than the original. He'll probably be in tomorrow, if he passes the stress test. How was he when you left?"

"Still in the ICU. He'd had surgery, but only to repair a heart valve. You're saying he got a whole new heart. He has a rare blood type; how'd they find a donor?"

"There was no donor. His new heart is a bionic, grown from his own..."

I shook my head.

"What? What are you saying, Peter?"

"That the timeline has changed. History has changed. When I dived today, your computers did not have voice interfaces and I had house keys and a handheld smart phone and there were no bionic hearts *anywhere*. And Otis's hair was ... different. Just so I'm clear—we're still trying to keep brain transplantation from becoming a Thing, right? We're not trying to put a genie back in the bottle."

Vic nodded. "Yes. There's no sign of brain transplantation being even a *theoretical* Thing at this point—though the Chinese did make some noise about doing a head transplant. Or, well, a full body transplant I guess."

I didn't want to get into that sticky wicket. "So, our saboteur seems to have gotten the bionic tech into the timeline somewhere. I'm assuming not to the point of us giving people android bodies."

Victoria's mouth twitched and Drew said, deadpan, "No. No android bodies."

Well, that was something, anyway. Since we didn't have a clue where our time diving tinkerer had put the biotech, I saw no feasible way to undo it. And, honestly, I wasn't sure it should be undone. If there were something horrific about it, I wasn't likely to find out by playing twenty questions with Team Backstory. Besides which, the tangle of time-related ramifications was giving me a headache.

Plus, I was starving and had to pee.

"Okay, look. I need to take care of some mundane matters like eating and such, and then I need to get back to Omari."

"Peter," said Victoria, "it's really late. You were immersed in Omarius Prisca for most of the day. I really think you need to sleep. You look exhausted."

I glanced at the windows. The light filtering through them was clearly coming from the epically tall light standards in the central plaza. Above, the sky was as dark as it could be in Manhattan on any given evening, given the light pollution. I felt exhausted, too—mentally and emotionally. I just wasn't sure I could sleep knowing that Omari was sitting in a cage on his way to Big Question Mark. (Yeah, I know—at least in some respects, that ship had sailed.)

Vic knew exactly what I was thinking. "You have time, Peter. Which means Omari has time." She reached across me and snagged my phone, then handed it to me. "Here. Call yourself a car, go eat. Go home. Get sleep. Feed your cat. Hm. Maybe not in that order."

I was hit with a wave of … gravity, I guess, because I suddenly felt more grounded. There was still Matilda. I nodded, attaching the phone to my arm without even thinking about it— as if it were habit. Muscle memory, I guess.

"What about you?" I asked. "You need to eat, too, right? Maybe you can debrief me over dinner."

"Good idea." She addressed the rest of the team. "Let's all knock off. We can pick this up in the morning."

The team dispersed.

Not until I stood on the sidewalk outside the institute did something Victoria had said strike me. "Call myself a car? You mean an Über?"

"A what? What's an Über?" She pointed at my phone. "You call a city car."

I held my arm out toward her. Muscle memory did not apparently run to electronic apps. She tilted my arm in a way that caused the screen to light up, then showed me which icon to tap to hail a car—a car icon, appropriately. I tapped it. A window opened on the little screen telling me my request had been accepted; a cheerful voice said, "I'm on my way. ETA two minutes."

"Is there still a Thai place on Thirty-fourth?" I asked Vic.

She nodded, then asked, "Is it really weird? Coming home …
but not?"

I reluctantly gave that some serious thought. "You're still
here," I said. "That's home enough."

She smiled brilliantly as the car pulled up in front of us. It
looked like a Prius mostly, and it was made by Toyota. The car
had no driver. I reached for the rear door. The car beat me to it,
popping the lock and swinging the door open.

"Good evening," the car said in a warm, natural male voice.
"Where would you like to go?"

Damn. This was like being with one of my hosts. It was more
disconcerting than I cared to admit.

"Lemon Grass," Victoria said. "The one on Thirty-fourth."
She turned to look at me as the car pulled silently out from the
curb. "This is hard for you, isn't it?"

"Yeah. Right now, I'm not feeling at home anywhere. It's like
things are the same, but not. And I don't know what I don't
know."

She responded to that by taking my hand and lacing her
fingers through mine. "I've got your back, Detective," she said.

I wondered if that was the secret to attracting a woman: act
vulnerable and look like a deer in the headlights. I wasn't acting,
though. I was navigating strange waters here, in more ways than
one. Still, it was cheering to know that the way to a woman's
heart was through her heart.

We debriefed over dinner and, yeah, we picked stuff off each
others' plates, which I think meant we'd moved to a new stage
in our relationship. Next would be finishing each other's
sentences.

"How much are you going to tell the others?" I asked when
she'd turned off the recording feature on her phone at the end of
the debriefing.

"Only what we need to. The biotech might have already been

planted, but we have no way of knowing whether or not that's enough for our guy. For all we know, he might've done all this so he could buy stock in a biotech startup."

"I doubt that. I still think this is personal," I said, then yawned.

"To some people, money is intensely personal," she observed, then added, "Time to go."

I gave the car my address and found myself studying the streets for differences as we made our way to my building. My place still looked like the same old row house, but the streetlights were different—their light seemed more natural, warmer. And in that light, the building looked different, too. Cleaner, as if the old gold of the bricks had been power washed. I wondered what else would be different.

I reached for the car's door handle, only to realize there wasn't one.

"Open right rear door," said Victoria, and the right rear door opened.

I gazed up at the building through the open door. "Uh, I don't have—"

"House keys," we said in perfect unison.

Vic laughed. "I'm sorry. I'd forgotten. You just go up to the front door and put your hand on the metal handle in the center so your thumb is in the little depression on the..." She could see I wasn't following. "Here, I'll show you. Go ahead and get out."

I did. I stood on the sidewalk feeling like a complete idiot. No, like an alien that had woken up on a strange world that only looked familiar at first glance. Or like a guy who'd been in suspended animation long enough to miss out on a whole lot of technological innovation ... or a doofus who'd somehow been complicit in screwing up the timeline.

Behind me, Vic told the car to wait, then got out onto the sidewalk and took my arm. "Come on, Detective, let's get you into bed."

I made a funny noise; I swear it just came out.

"I didn't mean it that way," she said, and gave me a half-joking glare. In the natural light of the new-fangled streetlights I could see she was blushing. Cute.

The front door of my building had no key-able lock. It had a depression in the center of the door panel with a sort of handle set into it. The handle was six inches tall and three inches wide and rounded toward the outer edge—like the spine of a thick book.

"Just grasp the handle. It will read your fingerprints and let you in."

I grasped the handle. It was warm to the touch. The door responded with a click, a beep, and a vibration. I pulled. The door pulled back the other way, yanking itself out of my hand. Then it swung open.

"Hands free," Victoria informed me.

"You come here often?" I asked before I could stop myself.

"My house has the same kind of lock."

The door swung open and I squared my shoulders. "Think I have any other surprises waiting for me up there?" I nodded toward the stairs. "I mean, how advanced is domestic tech? Do I get into my apartment the same way?"

"More or less. You probably have a latch with a thumb pad. That's pretty standard." She gave me a long, assessing look. "Do you want me to come up and help you navigate the new world?"

"I do. And that's not a pickup line, I promise. I just want to make sure I can get in the door. After that, I'll be fine, I'm sure. I mean, unless I have a voice-activated shower or something."

"There are voice-activated showers," Victoria told me, "but I doubt an apartment building this old has one. Unless, of course, you had one installed."

"I doubt I'd do that."

"Luddite."

She walked upstairs with me, while I scanned the place for more changes. I saw a tiny elevator in the back of the entry.

"Voice activated," she said when she caught me looking at it. "They're all like that now. The mechanical buttons are just backup."

My front door had what looked like a standard door handle with a thumb pad on the top. I assumed it would read my thumbprint. It did, and the door clicked open. Entry lights came on automatically. Down the entry way, at eye level, a round panel set into the wall lit up, showing the number 68. The heater went on, then the living room lights. My furniture looked pretty much the same, except for my wall-mounted television, which was bigger and flatter than I remembered it being. I glanced down at the coffee table where I kept the remote. I saw no remote.

I pointed at the TV. "Voice-activated?"

Victoria nodded.

I wondered what else I was missing. And that was when I thought of Matilda the Cat. Vic had said I should feed my cat, but that didn't mean it was Matilda, who'd been my companion since kittenhood. My heart started to race. I pivoted and headed for the kitchen, calling the cat's name.

Vic followed me.

The kitchen lights came on, illuminating the water fountain and food dish in the corner by the breakfast nook. They looked different—I could see that both were automatically refilled—the food from a hopper on the top, the water from a tube that ran under the cabinets. My other appliances looked a bit alien, too. Okay, I'd confirmed that I still had a cat, but ... At this time of night I knew where Matilda would be. I turned again, hurrying past Victoria, and made a beeline for the bedroom.

She followed me as far as the doorway. The lights in the room came on as I crossed the threshold, though dimmed. The clock radio I kept on the bedside table was gone, replaced by a svelte metal stand. I guessed it was for my wrist phone. But there, in the middle of my bed, was Matilda, her gingersnap-striped body curled into a sleek, plump circle snuggled into the down comforter.

I exhaled. All was right with the world.

Grinning, I turned back toward Victoria, making a sweeping gesture at the bed. "This makes it all okay," I said.

She glanced from me to the bed and back. "Excuse me … ?"

"Mattie the Cat! I still have Matilda. I need sleep, but I'm okay. I think I needed…" I turned to look over my shoulder at the sleeping cat. "I know it's dumb, but having you and Mattie both still … you know…" I trailed off and shrugged. "So, I'm good, Vic. I'm fine. And if the Morning Grind is still across the park, then I'm better than fine. I'll see you at the institute in the morning."

She hovered in the doorway, looking uncertain. "Are you sure?"

"Yeah, I'm sure. Hey, I know how to call a car and feed my cat. I'm good."

"Okay," she said, but seemed reluctant to move.

I crossed the room, took her hand, and walked her to the front door. "Go home and get some sleep, Vic. I'll see you first thing in the morning."

She nodded. I nodded. We stood there for a moment in silence (awkward), then she leaned in and kissed me.

Cool. I was a little too punchy from my strangely alien experience in my own time zone to fully appreciate it, you know, *viscerally*, but I put my heart into it.

"Sleep well, okay?" she said, when we came up for air.

"I believe I shall," I said with some conviction.

Victoria laughed, gave me a second swift, soft kiss, then let herself out. The door clicked shut behind her. I stood and stared at it for a moment or two, then rambled back to the bedroom, where Matilda the Cat had awakened and stretched her sleek self with a silent yawn.

"Hey," I said.

She looked up at me and mewed. You know, one of those inquiring mews that has a definite question mark at the end.

"Well, the thing is," I told her, "I'm not sure, but I think I may have a girlfriend."

Matilda blinked and yawned again, then jumped off the bed and headed for the kitchen—which is feline for, "So what? Big deal." By the time I'd showered and pulled on the scrubs I used for PJs, she was back in her spot on the comforter. I arranged myself around her and started to drift off, realizing just before I did that I was nervous about what the morning would bring. And not just for Omari, but for me. I was legitimately disturbed by how many more improbable things I might have to believe before breakfast.

14

OMARI

Before I left for the institute, I called Greg Orlov to make an appointment to talk to him. I was relieved to find he still knew me and remembered our previous conversations.

"What's up?" he asked. "Are you going to want me to hypnotize you so you don't experience fugue episodes?"

"No, nothing like that. I just have some things I may need help working through."

Without spoilers, I talked about this changed world I now lived in, but I wondered if I'd also end up talking to him about my (potential) relationship with Victoria. That was an undiscovered country. I'd avoided relationships for years because—well, because. Vic was different. She knew everything about me and my fugue states, including how to snap me out of them. That wasn't likely to freak her out, so if this little social experiment failed, I had nothing to blame but my charming personality.

Yeah, I probably would end up talking to Orlov about that.

The Morning Grind was right where I'd left it, but the espresso machine had an artificial intelligence unit that competently and efficiently made my drink while the human behind the counter got the requisite baked goods. I had a moment of angst when it came time to pay, and was confronted by another thumb pad. Apparently, ApplePay—which had been all razzle-dazzle when I'd dived yesterday—was now hopelessly passé. It seemed I had a bank account somewhere that required only a registered fingerprint to access. Any pay point with one of these AI units could use the universal system. I assumed the tech was pretty widespread if a mom and pop shop like Morning Grind had it.

I was on my way into the institute, crossing the foyer when I saw another evidence of robotic prevalence. A kid of about ten or so was leaving the building with a couple I assumed were his parents. I noticed him because he walked a little oddly. It took me a moment to realize that was because his legs were encased in a sort of wireframe or exoskeleton made of fine silver filaments that attached to a wide belt at the waist and what looked like soccer pads at the knees. A thin cable ran from the belt up to the kid's head where a barely-there mesh cap covered his hair. It was not unlike the cap I now wore to time dive.

The father caught me looking. "Something wrong?"

"No, I just … that's amazing. What tech can do for people nowadays."

The man exchanged glances with his wife, who shrugged eloquently as if to say, *Where's he from, Outer Mongolia?*

Felt like it. I smiled and continued on my way to the lab. I tried to pretend that everything was hunky dory, as my mom used to say, but deep down inside, it wasn't okay. *I* wasn't okay. Where I'd begun to almost enjoy my trips down memory lane, I was now reluctant to go. I was leery of the changes I might wreak on my ancestor's world and of returning to find further changes in my own.

Still, I put on my detective face and debriefed the team—selectively. As far as they were concerned, I was still looking for the amulet and remained at least one step away from knowing where the papyrus was. In reality, I knew exactly where the papyrus was. I just couldn't get to it.

When Theron came in, Victoria invited the two of us into her office—allegedly so I could bring him up to speed, but really so I could give him a more honest reporting of my activities.

He looked good. Hale and healthy. The signs of strain and illness that were in evidence the last time I'd seen him were gone. That was a huge relief. I couldn't help but feel as if I'd had a hand in making his original heart go south.

"Hey," I greeted him, shaking his hand. "You look great. For which I am really, really happy, seeing as how I contributed to the demise of your former heart."

He chuckled. "No, Peter, that was all on me. If I'd been swifter on the uptake, I might've been able to tell you to destroy the amulet *before* you dove, instead of making that eleventh-hour save. And if I'd trusted Victoria, and she'd trusted me, you wouldn't have felt the need to go rogue. So, what's the situation?"

I ran through my adventures with Omarius Prisca, omitting the fact that my own existence had become weird because of it. Victoria, however, was not about to let that slide.

"Something changed in the timeline while Peter was 'away,'" she told Theron. "Whether it was something he did, or something our saboteur did, robotics, bionics, and AI have apparently gone ahead in leaps and bounds. That biomimetic heart you were given was barely a gleam in some researcher's eye when he dove last."

Cornell couldn't cover his unease. "So, our saboteur was able to insert modern tech into an earlier time zone."

"Or zones," said Vic. "We really have no way of knowing. All we know right now is where the papyrus is."

"And that," I said, "is my cue to get back to Omari. I bet I can break him out of jail. I mean, I must've been able to, right, or I wouldn't be here. As me, I mean. And with the same set of parents."

I dove immediately, and came to my ancestor's senses with stomach cramps and the sensation of riding a carousel—horizontally. I smelled fish and brine and other things I didn't want to think about, and I—or rather Omari—was wet and miserable.

Open your eyes, already, I thought.

He did and wished he hadn't. We were in a small, dark enclosure inside a large, dark enclosure. We were still in a damned cage, wrists shackled and connected with a foot-long length of chain. We saw other cages, with multiple occupants. We were alone in ours. We also saw boxes and barrels and bags of whatever, and a ladder going up to the only source of illumination—a thick grate that allowed a dim gray light to filter into the gloom. With every rolling movement, the place sloshed, creaked, and groaned like a whale in its death-throes.

The reality hit me like a pile driver: we were on a ship bound for God knows where. First thought: *I have to go back.* Second thought: *No, wait—where's the canopic tray?* I had to make sure it was here before I tried to extricate us from this situation.

I scooted around to face the other cages. "Citro!" I called. "Citro Superstes!"

I heard a prodigious shuffling and grunting and then he called back to me, "Vicarius! Are you all right? Are you well?"

"I've been better," we said.

Surprisingly, Citro chuckled. "I suppose that is true of all of us, sir."

"Citro, do you know if the goods these robbers stole are with us on this vessel?"

"I believe so, sir, but I am not certain."

"The men who captured us—are they here?"

"I have seen the decurion with my own eyes, and his—"

Whatever he'd been going to say was interrupted by the grinding of the grate above. In a moment, a pair of sandaled feet appeared on the topmost step, followed by legs, a torso, and a head. In a moment, I saw the decurion with my own eyes—well, Omari's eyes, anyway. Another man climbed down into the hold as well—the other officer. Omari's knowledge base supplied the word *optio*. Seeing the two of them made me hopeful that the artifacts were here as well, but I wanted to be sure.

"You there, Decurion!" I made Omari demand (and he really, really didn't want to demand anything). "Where are the tomb goods you stole from the sepulcher of the Divine Doctor?"

The two officers exchanged glances that were either surprised or impressed with our audacity (or maybe just mocking), then the decurion said, "You're a bold one, aren't you? It hardly matters where your precious tomb goods are, boy. They are ours now, and you are in no position to take them back again."

"Don't be so sure of that," I growled, while poor Omari thought, *What am I saying?*

The decurion lunged toward us, unsheathing his sword on the fly. I'm not sure if he intended to run us through, but the ship pitched just then and he stumbled and nearly fell into a briny puddle about three feet from our cage. He recovered, snarling, while his optio harrumphed and said, "Decurion! Remember our commission. One less slave is much less coin."

The red-faced decurion, still snarling, pulled himself upright and made do with sweeping his sword across the bars of our cage, making a horrific racket. We shrunk back against the rear wall.

"That's it, you filthy Egyptian! Cower before a true Roman patriot!" He jerked his head at his optio. "Get them up on deck. You'll get a crust of bread and a dipper of water and a measure of time topside. Then you're back down for the duration."

He stood aside and watched as the optio unlocked the cages and let us out. We gave a moment's thought to escape, but had no idea how far we were from land. Besides, with my hands shackled, swimming was impossible. Of course, the decurion had to trip us as we tried to navigate the ladder, but we made it up on deck and were pleased to see that all the members of Omari's guard who'd made the trek from Memphis were here and seemed to be in good health.

"Vicarius," said Citro, drawing near as we shuffled toward the water barrel up on deck, "you fill my heart with courage with your bravery. I regret that we were unable to save you from this fate. I pray we might have another chance."

"You just might," we told him.

We got our dipper of water and a chunk of bread as big as Omari's fist, and turned to take in our surroundings. We were under full sail in a stiff, soggy breeze, scudding across the choppy, gray Mediterranean. The sky was deep pewter with silver at the seams where clouds bumped up against each other, shaking loose fits of cool rain.

I wondered how I might make certain of the artifacts when I saw a bevy of sleek black and white heads bobbing off the port rail. Uh-oh. I glanced at the grate over the hold. It was still open. I might be able to sidle over to it and—

"*Damn* it!"

Victoria glanced up at me from her station. "Back already? You were only gone five minutes."

"Add cormorants to my hit list," I growled and lowered my hands, realizing that I was holding them up to my face as if getting ready to take a bite of crunchy, dry bread. I flushed, realizing how silly that pantomime must've looked from this end. What other embarrassing things was I doing in other-when that I was echoing here?

"I need to go back earlier," I said. "He was on a ship. Probably headed for Rome. I think I just got Omari sold into slavery."

"Not ransom?"

"Not by the sound of it."

She came to stand in front of me. "Do you need to do anything before you go back?"

"No. Let me focus on earlier. I'll let you know when to pull the trigger." I closed my eyes and felt her hesitate for a moment before she went back to her station. Seconds later, with the pack train's arrival at the seashore targeted as a point of entry, I gave her the thumbs-up.

This was more like it. Omari was still in the creaky little cage with Citro, rocking and rolling toward a shoreside habitation of some sort. It was bigger than an encampment but smaller than a village. I saw a few permanent structures inside a stockade and a bunch of tents—some immense—outside the wood and stone walls. Okay, probably a fort of some kind or a military outpost. Along the shore was a wharf area at which a number of ships and boats of different sizes were tied up. Further out were two large vessels—Roman galleys like the ones you see in history books, with thick masts and two banks of oars.

I set Omari's mind to looking for any opportunity to escape. They'd have to get us out of these cages. Perhaps we could escape then, or catch the attention of someone who might care that these guys had kidnapped the favorite sidekick of the new Consul of Memphis. Omari was right there with me on that. He was, in fact, pretty darn certain that if he just slipped the right word into the right ear, he'd be out of this cage in minutes.

Our parade made its way through the field of tents, through the gates of the stockade and down to a cluster of wharf-side buildings with their own gated enclosure. At first, our cages were rolled into the lee of the inner wall while our captors led their horses to what I assumed was a stable, wrangled their gear, and talked about what they might have for supper. There were three wagons loaded with boxes, casks, bags, and chests that they parked caddy corner to our cages close to the entrance of a stone and stucco building that looked like a barracks. Those wagons almost certainly contained the loot from Imhotep's tomb.

There was a lot of activity going on in and around the barracks; soldiers and other men passed in and out as they secured their gear. We watched for anyone who looked as if they might have some official capacity in the township. I found myself praying for a prelate or some other member of the Christian clergy. Someone we could appeal to on moral grounds.

The sun was no more than an afterthought by the time we finally saw someone who fit the bill—a slightly built youngish fellow in fancy robes and wearing a large ornate cross. He made his way toward the barracks with a leather folio tucked under one arm.

"Father!" we called, rising to our knees in the cage. "Father please! I need your help!"

The priest (or maybe he was a monk) stopped and turned to look at us. "Who are you? Why do you call to me?"

"I am Omarius Statius Prisca, vicarius to Consul Flavius Anthemius of Memphis. I and my men were captured by thieves and brought here against our will. If you can help free us, it would surely please God and Consul Anthemius as well. I'm certain both would reward you greatly."

He looked uncertain, glancing this way and that. He took a step toward us, hesitated, then took another. "How can I know you speak the truth?"

How *could* he know? Though we were still in the remnants of some fine clothes, Omari had been stripped of his signet ring and medallion of office.

"The thieves have stolen all my possessions, Father. I have nothing but the clothes I wear and the testimony of my men, here."

"Yes, Father," said Citro earnestly, pressing his face against the wooden bars of our cage. "We do give testimony. This young man is who he claims to be; the rest of us are members of his guard, all captured by Roman soldiers in the commission of a tomb robbery."

That brought the priest up short. "Roman soldiers?"

He turned to look over his shoulder at the barracks from which we could all hear the sounds of loud chatter and broken bits of bawdy song. He frowned, fingering his cross.

"Father, please!" we begged. "Please release us. The lock is a simple one, but it is beneath the carriage and we can't reach it."

He took another step toward us, then stopped again and looked right at me with obvious fear in his eyes. "I don't doubt your story, Vicarius, but these men know me." He gestured at the barracks. "If I were to free you, God only knows what they might do to me or to the people of my church." He shuffled forward a few more feet and lowered his voice. "Who might I tell of your troubles? Perhaps I can help in that way."

"This port must be part of some prefecture," Omari said, while I was still considering the question. "Inform the prefect or the pro-consul that Omarius Prisca—an official of the Roman Empire—has been so foully treated. These men must be stopped, Father. If they are willing to desecrate tombs, what else might they dishonor by theft?"

He clutched his pendant fiercely, no doubt thinking of what these guys might steal from his church, then nodded, turned on his heel, and continued toward the barracks.

Okay, that was something, but not good enough. Who knew if there were even a prefect in the immediate vicinity? By the time the good Father delivered his message to someone, we'd most likely be on our way to Europe, probably via Rome. What else could we do?

We conferred with Citro and the other men, but came to the same conclusion as ever: we could hardly plan when we had no idea what they were going to do with us. For all we knew they might leave us in here until the ship sailed.

In the event that our captors did remove us from the cages,

Citro came up with a sort of plan that involved him and his men (Canus and Kaeso, by name) attacking our captors while we did our best to escape. Not much, but it was something, and I appreciated that they were willing to make such a sacrifice on Omari's behalf. My respect for my ancestor increased; if he was this beloved by those in his service, he must be a pretty good guy. Naturally, that made me feel even worse about having landed him in this glorified horse trailer.

In the meantime, Omari and I amused ourselves (in a dark sort of way) by trying to reach the locking mechanism under the floor boards. It was just far enough beneath the wagon that even as slender a man as Omari couldn't reach it. The bars were simply too close together.

Omari fell asleep finally, and I considered returning to Manhattan, but I couldn't leave since I had no idea when I'd see the opportunity that I hoped would allow us to escape and return to Memphis. So, I sat there in the darkness of Omari's head, thinking about timelines and paradoxes and that sort of nonsense. It struck me that I—Peter August—sill existed in a timeline that put Omari on a ship to Rome, and me with him. What did that mean? Did it mean that we had successfully escaped in *this* timeline and that reality was reflected in *that* timeline, or did it mean that Omari managed to escape from Rome and return to Egypt? Or none of the above? Did it mean that every time I dove back into an ancestor's life, I created a shiny new reality that overwrote the old one or existed side by side with it?

I was giving myself a headache, so I moved my thoughts to the escape plan (such as it was). If I got the chance, I would make a beeline for the stables where I could hide and/or swipe a horse.

I'm not sure how much time had passed before Citro's hand clamped on Omari's shoulder and shook it.

"Vicarius!" he whispered harshly. "The decurion!"

I roused Omari with a little jolt of adrenaline (which I was pleased to find I could administer from my back brain driver's position) and helped focus our bleary eyes on the figures approaching from the lighted doorway of the barracks. It was more than the decurion, of course. His optio was there, along with a couple of other guys holding lanterns ... and manacles. I suspected that, if they got those on us, it was game over.

They came right to the cages and unlocked them, obviously intending to remove us. Citro positioned himself in the door of the cage so that he'd be the first one out. He kept an eagle eye on the other two men, who were being released from the cage next to us. When the door in front of Citro opened, he didn't move. He waited until he saw the other cage door swing free, then let out a mighty roar and kicked out powerfully with both feet. Kaeso, who'd squeezed into the doorway of the other cage, did the same. He and Citro both followed this up with a direct attack on the men carrying the lamps.

Canus leapt from his cage as well, connecting a powerful punch to the head of the nearest soldier. Omari didn't need much urging from me; he slipped from the cage and ran, full-tilt-boogie (as Mel might have said) toward the stables. It meant crossing an open courtyard for fifty feet, but Omari was young, fast, and scared spitless.

He *flew*.

15

SAVING OMARI

The stable was empty of anything but the officers' horses and tack. I gave a moment's thought to how long it would take me to get a bridle on one of these guys and gallop out of here. But I could hear the sounds of pursuit out in the courtyard and knew our only chance now was to hide.

I'd grown up around horses and stables from the age of twelve. Some people find horse habitats smelly. I find them fragrant with hay and horse and oiled leather and various grains. Having played ninja games with a bunch of other horse-loving kids, I knew every good hiding place most barns or stables had to offer. I manhandled Omari and slipped into the stall with a horse I suspected belonged to the decurion himself, merely because of the size of the stall and its position in the barn. It was a roomy box stall made of wood and stuccoed brick or stone, and it had a wooden hay rack from which the horse had been munching meditatively when we barged in on him.

"S'cuse me," we murmured and went feet first into the rack, pulling the hay over us. The horse, being a horse, snorted, then went back to eating. Omari, like me, loved the scent of hay, but had to fight the urge to sneeze.

Seconds later, we heard the pounding of feet and the heavy breathing of at least two men. The horse whickered and moved toward the doorway of his stall, which was blocked by a rope lattice to keep him in. The men slowed to a walk and one of them said, "I've no treats for you now, Eonus. I must first catch a stupid slave."

Omari recoiled from the last word. So, they weren't planning on ransoming us. I wondered if there were any way to convince them they should. I just as quickly realized that if we were to escape, Imhotep's canopic tray, with its hidden papyrus, would sail for Rome without us.

Okay, so we could hide until the decurion gave up or went to look somewhere else, then sneak over to the loot wagons and find the tray. We might even be able to free the other men; we'd given them stern instructions to surrender the moment we were out of sight, so we had reason to hope they were still alive.

With my mind made up, I perked up Omari's ears and listened to the sounds of the decurion searching the nooks and crannies of the stable. Judging by what we could hear, his companion picked up a wooden pitchfork and attacked a hay stack across the way. We heard him throw the pitchfork down with a snort of disgust, sneeze, and proclaim, "Well, he's not in there."

"Careful, Lar," warned the decurion. "This one is likely worth twice again what we will get for the others. He's a vicarius, after all, which means he is likely scholarly and educated. The praetor will pay handsomely for this fellow."

The praetor. So, they already knew whom we were going to. Omari was deeply affected by that. How could they be so brazen? Wouldn't a praetor care that they'd kidnapped another Roman official?

Sometime later, the decurion opined that the "damned Gyp"

must've gone out the back of the stable. "Let's go check the paddock," he said, and the two men trotted out the rear of the building. We had spotted a large fenced pen back there, in which the mounts of the rank and file legionnaires were kept.

Omari was of a mind to spring up right away and try to get a bridle on one of these horses. He thought taking good old Eonus here would be a great bit of get-even, but I tried to convince him that if the decurion was half as fond of the horse as he seemed to be, it would only make him more inclined to hunt us to the ends of the earth. So, I kept Omari from moving until the sounds from the paddock had ceased. And it was a good thing I did, too, because Lar and his buddy came rolling right back through the stable when they were done searching the horse pen.

Let that be a lesson, Omari, I told my young forbear. *Those guys would have had us dead to rights.*

And they still might, I realized, for the first thing our dear decurion did when he stepped out the front door of the stable was holler for his men to "Mount a search! Search the whole village! He won't have gotten beyond the gates," he added in an aside to his optio. "They'll be closed for the night."

Well, there was an important piece of news.

We'd started to wriggle out from under the hay when we heard the unmistakable sound of footfalls and realized that the two soldiers had swung about and were coming back into the stable. One of them—the decurion, I thought—came to Eonus's stall and opened the rope net to let the animal out. He saddled and bridled it, then led it out of the stable into the barracks forecourt. He gave an order to his optio to secure the barracks and rode off to look for the escapee.

We waited until we could hear no sound coming from the courtyard, then climbed out of the hay bin. The stable entry was lit by a single lantern hung from a post above the lintel. The courtyard, on the other hand, had four big braziers—two by the door of the barracks and two arranged to either side of the village gate. The corner of the yard where the tomb raiders had parked their booty carts was mostly in darkness. Problem was, in order to get to it, we'd either have to cross a lot of open space or sneak around the edges where we'd have to negotiate several pools of light.

We opted for plan B, and set out along the front wall of the stable. We were pretty much in deep shadow from the moment we left the building, but as we approached the barracks, the shadows faded and squirmed in the light of the braziers. Praying no one would come galloping in through the gates on the other side of the forecourt, we crept up to the brazier that sat to this side of the barracks entry.

I didn't have to prompt Omari through any of this—we were of the same mind: get to the canopic tray, remove the papyrus, and slink off somewhere to hide. Sandwiched between the brazier and one of the thick stone columns that bracketed the barracks entry, we peered toward the wagons. We could see that the cages were still there, though no one was in them.

What did that mean? Did it mean Omari's men had sacrificed their lives for us to escape, or had the legionnaires simply recaptured them and moved them somewhere else? We both sincerely hoped for the latter and suppressed the thought that Citro and those other brave souls might have gotten themselves killed on our behalf. We recalled the decurion's words about the value of slaves and decided to take comfort in it.

Hearing nothing from inside the barracks, we slipped swiftly across the doorway and behind the second brazier. We waited there again, eyeing the wagons and listening to the snap and flap of the flames just overhead. We took a deep breath and crept along the front wall of the barracks toward the corner of the yard. If we could just get under the closest wagon ...

We were within spitting distance when we heard voices coming from the doorway behind us. We made a wild leap for the wagons, hitting the sandy, hard-packed dirt and skidding under the nearest one, rolling until we were in almost complete darkness. The roll was stopped by the wheel of a second wagon. Omari did a great job of stifling his grunt of pain, then we hunkered in the shadows, trying to be silent as the sand.

"What was that?" asked a male voice. "Did you hear something over there?"

"No," said a second man, "but I think I saw something move under that wagon."

Oh, hell, I thought, and Omari growled. I mean, he literally growled like an animal. My ancestor was apparently a man of many talents.

One of the soldiers snorted. "Ah, it's just one of those damned dogs, cadging for food. Guard the wagons well, you stupid cur, and I'll bring you some table scraps."

Omari growled again, and the soldier laughed and headed off across the forecourt toward the front gates. We caught our breath and waited a few minutes before rising and moving toward the rear of the wagons. They were parked in a rough row along the wall. I moved into the deepest shadows behind the one closest to the barracks and began poking around, looking for a way to see beneath the sailcloth the raiders had used to cover their loot. Not until we were able to pull up one corner of the cover did we realize the immensity of the task. Here, away from the direct light of the braziers, there wasn't enough illumination to tell an ushebti from a turkey leg. Of course, there were no turkey legs among the booty, but you get the point.

Omari fought despair; his shoulders slumped.

Nope. None of that, young man, I thought. There had to be a way to go about this systematically and increase our chances of finding the tray before the sun came up. We reached into the wagon and felt the nearest object. It was large and wooden, with some sort of cold, metal ornamentation. Peaked top. Omari recognized it as the altar box that was supposed to represent the abode of the deceased in the next life.

We felt farther afield. Something even larger, also wooden. We tapped it. Thick, too, by the sound of it. We loosened the tarp more and made our way up the side of the wagon, feeling along the object.

Holy mother of pearl. They'd snatched the whole inner coffin. I wondered if Imhotep was still in it. The thought chilled my host to the core. Stealing the god's stuff was one thing, but stealing the god himself—that took a level of *chutzpah* he was pretty sure there was a special level of hell for.

Moving on, we quickly determined that this wagon held the largest pieces of the funerary gear. There was nothing smaller than a dog house in here. That made sense, and it hinted that the thieves were at least good at their jobs; they'd get precious little out of an artifact that was wrecked because they'd done a poor job of packing. I had to force Omari to move on to the next wagon, impressing him with my logic until he accepted it as *his* logic.

It took us long, precious minutes to loosen the sail on the second wagon enough to reach in and pat down the contents. We started on the darkest side, deciding it made more sense to search the more exposed side only if we absolutely had to. This wagon was piled with handmade wooden crates that apparently contained small items from the tomb—lots of *ushebtis*. There were ceremonial implements, too, and cups, cutlery, small weapons—things with a metallic feel. Another crate held the same sorts of things, but no canopic tray. We hadn't found the model ship yet, either.

Gritting our teeth, we moved around to the more exposed side of the cart and worked the tarp loose. This was more of a challenge, because we had to keep our head down so we wouldn't be spotted from the yard or the barracks. On this side, the crates seemed to contain tiles, or at least pieces of something hard but not metal. Most were about the length of Omari's forearm, several inches thick and smooth on one side. They felt like stone, but not. Too light, maybe, or too ... something.

It hit us both at the same moment, I think. These guys had actually chiseled some of the friezes off the walls of Imhotep's tomb.

Bastards.

I felt a sudden kinship with Indiana Jones. Omari, of course, had no idea in the world who Indiana Jones was, but he was even more outraged than I was. Cursing silently and inventively, we made our way to the third wagon and went to the rear on the side nearest the wall. The rear wheel of the wagon was pressed up against the wall and the sailcloth tarpaulin was trapped beneath it.

Of course it was.

We crouched down and crawled beneath wagon number three to reach wagon number two, which contained sharp metal things. For a refreshing change, we found what we were looking for in the first crate we tried: a heavy knife with a wide, flat blade. We slipped back under the wagon and emerged on the other side to crouch by the wheel and hack at the tarp. It was a good knife and pretty sharp, all things considered, but it still seemed to take forever to free the sailcloth.

When it tore free, we thrust our hands into the darkness and found that—bingo!—this wagon seemed to contain the delicate, midsized items. The first thing our questing fingers found was the little wooden ship. Heart rate climbing, we made our way across the back of the wagon, feeling carefully for the animal-head lids of the canopic jars in their boxy tray.

It was not at the rear of the wagon. I found myself praying it was not in the middle of the load as we made our way around the edges, loosening, tugging, and feeling our way forward.

Of course, it *was* in the middle of the load. Which meant that we were going to have to climb in after it. We found the little ship again. And by little, I mean not as big as a real ship. It was a good-sized model—three feet long with a two-foot mast—and lying on its side. We carefully drew it out and lowered it toward the sand. A spar parted from the mast and disappeared into the gloom between our feet. Sand crunched; Omari bit his tongue and tried not to yelp as the thing connected with his ankle.

We set the ship down and reached back under the sail—here was a cask of some liquid, there was a jewelry box with metal bands and (ouch) a sharp locking mechanism. We pushed further into the wagon, reaching. There, at last, our fingertips met an etched metallic surface. We hoisted ourselves into the wagon bed, breath coming in short gusts, heart tripping over itself. I began to wish I'd studied yoga, though I'm not sure it would have helped Omari.

We felt upward to a fluted rim, and above that ... a curved something with a long, pointed snout and upright, equally pointy ears.

Duamutef! Hurrah!

Grasping the rim of the tray, we pulled.

Whatever made me think it would be that easy? It was caught on something. It took me a moment to realize that the offending snag was Duamutef's jaunty ears. We poked upward at the sailcloth and freed it on the second try.

We'd wriggled backward about six inches when it got stuck again. Again, we poked at the canvas cover, lifting it until we could get a good grip on the canopic jar to wiggle it out of the tray.

That was when someone grabbed our ankles.

Omari's hands tightened on the canopic jar and the tray as we were yanked backward across the wagon bed. I forced him to let go. The last thing I wanted was for these guys to figure out what we were searching for and examine it more closely. Not that they'd realize what they had, but they could sure put it back into public knowledge where it could be tripped over by the Wrong Person.

Whoever had our ankles ripped us free of the wagon and dumped us onto the hard, sandy ground. A large foot pressed against our belly. It was the optio, Lar.

I thought about administering a karate chop to his knee and trying to run, but a glance to my right showed many pairs of feet beyond the wagons, and a second soldier working his way toward us with a lantern. There was nowhere for us to run.

"Well, well," said Lar, peering down at us in the flickering light of the approaching lamp. "Not such a bright boy after all, are you, to try to stow away in one of these wagons? We'd have found you when we unloaded them in the morning ... or didn't you think of that?"

"No," we mumbled, "I didn't."

"Your men will be pleased to see you, anyway." He paused, then gave us a mocking grin. "But no, I wager they won't, seeing as how they took their lumps for trying to help you escape. Now, get up, boy. We sail at dawn. You're going to Rome."

He removed his foot and we got up. Omari, at this point, was happy to dust himself off and call it quits. I wasn't. I had one more last-ditch effort to make.

"Hear me out, optio," I said. "I am vicarius to the newly made Consul of Memphis. Whatever you think I might be worth as a slave to your praetor, I assure you I am worth many times more if you ransom me back to Flavius Anthemius."

The optio looked at me quizzically, then glanced at his decurion, who had appeared from the gloom to stand next to him. "Did you hear that, Paulus Serranus? He thinks we might ransom him back to his consul." He looked as if he found the thought mighty amusing.

Decurion Serranus certainly did. He burst out laughing. "Now that's an interesting idea. Which do you think might accord us the most certain benefits: to deal with a Roman who has always paid us well for both goods and slaves and never questioned our methods, or to take our chances with an Egyptian overlord who could just as easily have our heads for kidnapping his favorite deputy as paying us to get him back?"

Well, when you put it like that…

"You forgot about the part where the deputy tells his consul how we desecrated the tomb of a local god," added Lar.

Paulus Serranus nodded in mocking consideration of the point. "Ah, I had forgotten about that."

"I wouldn't tell him," we said. "You could arrange an exchange using a courier. You could—"

"We could cut out his tongue, I suppose," said Lar helpfully.

"I'd be no good to my consul without a tongue!" Omari objected, and felt enough sheer terror for both of us.

The decurion spread his big hands in an age-old gesture of "what ya gonna do?" and said, "You see my problem. If I were to ransom you to your consul, you'd be no good to him *without* a tongue and no good to me *with* one. But Praetor Festus will pay quite well for a man of your quality, tongue or no … assuming you're better at your job than you are at escaping."

They both had a good guffaw over that one. I have to admit, I was tempted to laugh right along with them, mostly from relief that it hadn't occurred to them that we weren't trying to hide ourselves in their booty wagon, but remove something from it.

Our captors hauled us into the barracks and installed us in a slightly more comfortable cage than the transport, with fresh straw on the floor. Citro and the other guards were each in separate cages; apparently Paulus Serranus had learned his lesson about making us roomies. The men were disappointed to see their master returned to them in chains, but when the legionnaires had left us alone in the dim light of a dying fire, Citro expressed relief that we were alive.

"I only wish you were not to share our fate, Vicarius," he told us, "for I've no idea what that shall be."

Oh, right. He hadn't already experienced the romance of our shipboard adventure. (Neither had Omari, but he seemed to take my veiled memories of it as his own imaginative dread.)

"They say they will sell us to a praetor, likely in Rome," we said. "He is apparently someone they do a lot of business with. I couldn't get them to even consider ransoming us back to Consul Anthemius." We took a deep breath and tried to settle comfortably into our bed of straw. "I hope none of you get sea sick."

"I don't know, sir," said Canus, the youngest of the three guards. "I've never left Egypt until now."

Great. Another notch in my bad karma belt.

"But," he added with a grin, "I've always wanted to see Rome."

I appreciated the attempt at optimism. So did Omari, but he was still inclined to depression. He'd never been out of Egypt either.

He went to sleep. I went back to Manhattan.

16

MARCELLUS

All I could see was a pair of large brown eyes; Victoria was watching me that closely when I surfaced from my dive fugue.

Startled, I yelped. "What?"

She straightened and let out a pent-up breath. "Thank God, I was just about to bring you out by force. You've been gone for hours."

"I had a lot to do." I glanced around, noticing that the lab was empty except for the two of us. "Where is everybody?"

"Otis and Sophie went home, Harald and Drew are down the hall, working out a new process, and Theron's out getting us dinner. I assume because you came back on your own that everything's all right?"

Hell. How did I know? "We couldn't escape. We ship out for Rome in the morning. Omari's morning, anyway. So, situation normal: all—"

"But you're still … here."

She'd been going to say "alive," I was pretty sure. I was kind of glad she hadn't. It's a special kind of weird knowing that one wrong move on your part could erase you from existence.

"Here's what I'm wondering," I said. "I'm wondering if there are just some pieces of History or Time (capital H, capital T) that refuse to be rewritten. That just have to happen. What do they call them in science fiction—time-locked?"

"Like Omari ending up in Rome?" she suggested.

"Yeah. I mean, I've been assuming he was supposed to marry Sennia Donata, but maybe that's not the case. Maybe he marries —or at least, impregnates—someone else." I shook my head wryly. "It's weird. As much as I influence the way Omari thinks, I'm pretty sure he does the same to me. He's so certain, in his heart of hearts and soul of souls, that Sennia is his other half, that I think I accepted that as reality."

"You didn't believe that before?" Vic asked. "That we each have a sort of soul mate?"

"Well, I did once upon a time," I admitted. "Back when I fell in love with Lauren. After that, not so much." I cleared my throat and dodged her gaze. "But lately ... lately, I've been giving it some thought."

"Because of Sennia?"

I tilted my head and made myself meet her eyes. "Maybe. Then again, maybe not."

She smiled and leaned in for a kiss. Just as our lips touched, Theron Cornell's voice said, "Good God, I can't leave you two alone for a minute. Such unprofessional behavior."

A glance past Victoria's blushing face showed that he was smiling and that the smile went all the way up into his eyes. He held up a couple of white takeout bags that smelled strongly of curry. "I brought debriefing materials," he said cheerfully.

"Great," I said. "I'm starving. Cognitive transference is hard work."

We dined in Theron's onsite office, which was right next to Victoria's, and I told them what had transpired in Wherever-the-hell-it-was North Africa. I raised the issue with him, too, about moments in history that couldn't be undone.

He was skeptical. "This is not an episode of Doctor Who," he told me.

"Then again," I said, "maybe I didn't try hard enough to escape. Or maybe it was stupid of me to try to get at the tray as soon as I did. I could've waited until they'd all given up looking for Omari and gone into the barracks. Like old Paulus said, he wasn't likely to get out of town with the gates all locked up and guarded."

"You weren't able to escape, after all?" asked Drew from the office doorway. "What was it you were trying to get—a tray?"

I glanced up to see Harald peering over his shoulder. "Uh," I said. Brilliant.

Theron stepped in smoothly and with no outward indication that he was lying through his teeth. "Peter thought he'd found a likely location for the small ornamental items from Imhotep's tomb and got himself caught trying to get to it. Fortunately, the artifacts will likely be on their way to Rome with his imprisoned ancestor."

Drew looked at me. "Then you'll be able to keep after the amulet there?"

"That's what I'm hoping. From what I've been able to glean from the moonlighting soldiers, they sell the slaves and the artifacts to the same Roman official."

Drew shook his head. "Things never seem to change, do they? Someone is always on the take. Well, I just thought I'd check our progress before I went home. It's Eva's birthday. Liz and I are taking her to a hockey game." He shrugged as if he didn't see the appeal of this, then turned and disappeared back into the lab.

Harald stood in the doorway a moment longer, then looked at me wistfully and said, "I sure wish I could do what you do, Detective. Time travel, I mean. It must be quite a rush."

"Oh, yeah," I said. "It is. Quite a rush."

He smiled, waved vaguely, and left, humming tunelessly.

"What're Drew and Harald working on?" I asked. "A new process, you said?"

"They're working on an interference system," Vic told me.

"Beg pardon?"

Theron chuckled. "They're attempting to build a system that will allow you to navigate the world without fear of trash cans being knocked about. Drew is working on a subcutaneous chip that would detect sounds with the wave profile and decibel range that would trigger one of your episodes, and automatically cancel them out—hence, interference system."

"They'd also be able to produce a retrieval tone only you could hear," added Victoria. "In case the interference mechanism failed for some reason."

Subcutaneous. I knew what that meant—under the skin. "Uh-huh. And where would they put this little bit of tech?"

She tapped the side of her head. "Probably behind your ears. One on each side right up against the mastoid bone. They've been experimenting with a little device that would go in your ears and screen out any sounds that fit the offending profile. They're pretty close on that one," she added. "It would be a nuisance to have to wear ear plugs all the time, but it could at least serve as a stop gap."

I was surprised at the strength of my reaction—gratitude, and a profound sense of hope. If I could control this thing, I might be able to go back to my work with the NYPD. I might even be able to explain to Melchior what had happened to me so that he'd understand that I wasn't a dangerous nut case. I realized, at that moment, that I wanted to keep my cake and eat it, too. As much as I wanted to go back to detective work (ideally, partnered with Mel), I wanted to keep working with Project Backstory ... and Victoria.

"That's great news," I said, and meant it. "But for the time being, I'll have to rely on you to get me out of trouble." I glanced from Theron to Victoria. "I suppose you'll tell me it's too late in the day to go back to Omari."

"I think tomorrow is soon enough," Theron said.

He called his private car to drop us each at our respective homes. I hadn't seen where Victoria lived before. I'd assumed she was an apartment-dweller like me, but no—she had an entire brownstone of her own over in Queens. I found myself wishing she'd invite me in. She didn't, and I wasn't going to presume—at least, not in front of Theron.

"See you tomorrow," she said, leaning over and giving me a quick kiss on the lips. "'Night, Theron," she added, then slid out of the backseat. The door closed itself behind her.

Theron, who sat in front, gave me a significant glance over his shoulder. "I have to say, it's nice to see Victoria letting something—or someone—distract her from her work. She's been married to it for quite some time."

"Why aren't *you* distracting her from her work?" I asked bluntly. "I mean, you're both good-looking, accomplished people. A matched set."

He faced front as the car began to move again. "Victoria and I have a profound friendship, and have from the start of the project, but ... to be frank, up until recently, I thought of myself as damaged goods. I will admit to having moments when I considered what a brilliant match Vic and I would make, but my heart has never been robust, and I felt it was wrong to inflict that on someone I was fond of. Losing a friend is one thing; losing a partner—as you well know—is something else again."

Yeah. I knew that, all right. "You could've just said 'it's complicated.'"

He glanced back at me again, then chuckled when he realized I was kidding.

"Seriously," I said, "I'm glad you told me that. It's nice to have friends who understand ... stuff."

"Yes," he agreed. "It is."

He dropped me off at my apartment; I got in without mishap, and Mattie the Cat was thrilled to see me. We spent the evening confirming that our music collection—in the cloud and on CD—still existed pretty much without change, and that I could now say, "Computer, play Incubus, 'Morning View,'" and have it just happen. I listened to Incubus and Vivaldi, reading from my souped-up iPad while Matilda slept peacefully in my lap.

I fell asleep on the sofa and dreamed about Omarius Prisca. It was the first time I'd dreamed of one of my hosts. It was a vivid dream. So real, I found myself trying to manipulate it the way I did my host ... and actually succeeding. I'd always been a little manipulative with my dreams, so that was nothing new. It took awhile before I fully realized I was dreaming, not time diving.

We were sailing. I was locked up with Citro as we'd been on the cart from Memphis. I couldn't see Canus or Kaeso. Nothing much happened in the dream except that I kept peering through the bars of my cage trying to see the rest of the cargo hold— trying to guess where the artifacts were. Shapes came and went in the darkness, but nothing screamed, *Tomb goods here!*

For some reason it was important to me to understand why I'd dreamed Citro into the cage with me when I already knew he'd been in his own pen. I realized, as the dream slipped away without me knowing diddly about where the papyrus was, that Citro and I had become partners in this adventure and that I— Peter, if not Omari—wanted and maybe even *needed* a partner. Always had. If I had no human partner—having lost first Lauren, then Mel—I'd ally myself with animal partners like Peccadillo and Matilda.

Did that bear on my ability to connect with long-dead ancestors? Did I have some sort of connection imperative? Before I went too far down that rabbit hole, I woke myself up and crawled off to bed, leaving a disgruntled ginger cat behind.

BY MORNING, I'd decided I didn't need to rejoin Team Omari at sea. My ancestor was a smart kid who could pretty much take care of himself. Plus he had Citro whom, I realized, reminded me a bit of Melchior. So, I aimed for a later time when Omari's feet were planted firmly on the soil of Italia.

Now, I want it to be clear that I like being on the water. I am not the least bit prone to sea-sickness. But taking a sea voyage in the aromatic darkness of a galley hold isn't quite the same thing as scudding down the Hudson in a sloop or even gliding down the South Platte in a tractor tire inner tube. So, I wasn't being a weenie about an unpleasant three-day cruise across the Mediterranean. It's just that there was no way for Omari to escape and nowhere for him to go. I also trusted he was curious enough about where the artifacts were on his own account.

Omari wasn't bothered much by the time he spent moldering in the hold of Paulus's nasty galley, but he missed Sennia the way I missed Lauren right after our breakup. No, worse. He viewed their separation as his own damned fault (even though it was my damned fault) and was tormented by the knowledge that, for Sennia, a day that had begun in joy had ended in fear and disappointment and anguish. By the end of her wedding day, his beloved would have felt the full weight of his disappearance with no idea in the world where he'd gone or why. She might think he'd abandoned her ... and his patron and his career in government. Or she might believe him dead. Either way, she would know nothing for certain. The fact that his entire guard had disappeared with him merely deepened the mystery, because Omari was the only who knew where they'd gone and why.

For Omari, that was sheer torture. Me too.

I rejoined him as he stood blinking in the bright sun in the inner courtyard of a villa. It reminded me a bit of Ludovico Sforza's summer home in Venice, but the courtyard was bigger and the ornamentation less fussy. The air was pleasantly balmy. I was disoriented for a moment. I'd obviously overshot my target by some months. It felt like spring, Omari's clothes were clean and new and quite grand, and his body felt healthy and strong. He carried an armload of cloth on long, thick wooden cards. A glance down at his hands revealed that they were clean except for some ink stains on his right thumb.

"Marcellus!" a woman's voice called. "Whatever are you doing dawdling there? Bring the fabrics to us ... Marcellus!"

My inclination was to look around to see who the heck she was talking to, but Omari responded with a jolt.

"I'm sorry, madam," he said, and moved forward, carrying the bolts of cloth to a shaded pergola draped with grapevines and wisteria.

A man and a woman sat at a marble table in the shade, goblets of some beverage in front of them. The woman was roughly in her forties, at a guess, and had striking features and glorious black hair. Her husband (as I gleaned from Omari) was a bit older, and was handsome in a craggy sort of way.

The woman reached out and tugged gently at the fold of cloth on the topmost bolt. "This one, I think. Don't you agree Drusus?"

Drusus rubbed his chin speculatively. "I prefer the gold," he said, "but you will no doubt ignore my opinion, as you always do—and always should—and will choose what is best."

Wow. That was one of the most backhanded compliments(?)

I'd ever heard. I couldn't decide if he was buttering her up or dissing her. Maybe both.

She smiled at him so sweetly and sincerely, I knew she'd taken it as a compliment. Then she turned her smile on me. "The blue and turquoise will do nicely, Marcellus. We should like all of the draperies in the banquet salon made up of this. And do tell that ridiculous man that, in the future, he should bring his wares to us himself, rather than impose upon you to do it. Whatever is he thinking to waste your time so?"

I had no idea what "that ridiculous man" was thinking since I had no clue who he was. Omari—or rather, Marcellus, as he was apparently known here—was tickled by her disdain. I gathered from his thoughts that the ridiculous man was the weaver who supplied the praetor's household with fine linens, and who somehow and for some reason had pawned off his duties onto his client's personal servant.

I probed Omari's memory gently. Was I a steward here? His fleeting thoughts about the duties he would rather be tackling than carting fabric around, portrayed him as sort of a Man Friday—a cross between a castellan, a secretary, and a valet. A personal assistant, in other words.

That was great, I thought, as we made our way back to the front of the villa. A PA would be in the perfect position to find the canopic tray somewhere among the household goods. I put the image of the tray in Omari's head, but he batted it away with a flash of annoyance. He was frustrated. He'd looked high and low for Imhotep's tomb goods but had found only a portion of them. Some were still packed up in a storage building somewhere and others were about the household. In fact, we passed the little ship on the way to the portico where the weaver's cart sat. In all the time Omari had been here, he had seen neither hide nor hair of the canopic tray.

In all *what* time, I wondered? Omari's memory supplied the answer: *Two years.* He'd been here for two long years. I was stunned. So stunned I just curled up in his head (figuratively speaking) and STFU.

"You there," he called to the boy standing by the weaver's cart. "Tell your master that Praetor Drusus Memmius Festus and the lady Varia prefer this fabric for their banquet salon. And tell your master that when he comes to take measurements for the job, he will present himself in person or his goods will not be received."

"Yes, sir. Thank you, sir," the boy said, bowing. "The blue and turquoise. Yes, sir." He snatched the bolts from our arms and placed them carefully in the cart, with the chosen pattern uppermost. Then he clambered up into the driver's box and nudged his pony with one dangling foot.

Two years.

I stuck with Omari-Marcellus as he went about his tasks for the rest of the day. He thought about Sennia non-stop, notwithstanding one of Lady Varia's maids, Liuva, had made it clear she desired him and sought to improve her status through marriage to the praetor's man.

When he wasn't thinking of Sennia with a mixture of despair and longing, he was wondering where the hell the canopic tray had gone. He knew the master hadn't sold it; he did the books for house and business and knew which artifacts had left through sale. He did not, however, take inventory of Drusus Festus's storehouses, nor did he have many opportunities to visit them. He'd thought of sneaking away from the house at night and trying to break into them, but he doubted he could do that without being caught.

He thought fondly of Citro and Canus and Kaeso. Citro was in his master's household guard, while the others had been sold to one of Drusus Festus's associates in Mediolanum (that's Milan to you). He toyed with the idea of enlisting Citro's help in trying to get into the storehouses, but he didn't want to cause the poor man any more grief than he already had.

I, on the other hand, seized on that connection, because I was determined to get Omari out of this fix *and* find the canopic tray with its precious and dangerous cargo. If Citro could help, I knew he would. To that end, I began to inflate my host's sense of his capacity for espionage. Once his praetor and lady had retired for the evening to their respective chambers, he was his own man, free to go where he would. I suggested he could go down to the wharf-side warehouse district for an evening stroll.

He countered this with a fond thought of his favorite watering hole—a public house on the banks of the Tiber.

Good enough. *Let's go there tonight.*

He didn't argue the idea—supposing, of course, that it was his own. So that evening, after the praetor and his wife had turned in, we headed off to the Inn of the River Pike where Omari drank, pretended he was a free man, and listened to other bound servants' scathing conversations about their masters or their fellow slaves.

Omari did not participate in those discussions. He had no real complaints about his boss other than that he was not Flavius Anthemius, and headquartered in Memphis. Both Festus and Lady Varia treated him well and with dignity, and had from the moment they realized how well-educated and intelligent he was. He was also fluent in several languages—which I supposed made sense for a consul's sidekick. The empire was nothing if not diverse and cosmopolitan.

It was in this venue—which was pretty close to our master's storehouses—that I worked at directing Omari's thoughts toward exactly how close they were and how easy it would be to pay them a visit one of these nights. The more we drank, the harder I worked on him. What did he have to lose, really? He'd been over the master's books with a fine-toothed stylus, had peered into the various nooks and crannies of homes and businesses owned by his many associates and friends. Many of them had displayed evidence of Drusus

Festus's largesse, but none of it had been recognizably from Imhotep's tomb.

By the time my man dragged himself out of his chair to make his careful way home, I had convinced him that he was ready to become a master spy. At his next opportunity, he would choose a storehouse and pry his way in.

I made a rather interesting discovery in the course of my manipulations; Omari's drunkenness did not make *me* drunk any more than his being asleep caused me to snooze. His reflexes were slower, of course, and though I could conceive of moving more swiftly or walking in a straighter line, my effect on his body was less dramatic than when he was fully present. It was a lot like driving a big car with loose suspension ... or riding a curmudgeonly, lazy horse. You could get results, but you had to work twice as hard to get them.

Now, you're probably wondering if I had any epiphanies about the wisdom of trying to *fix* Omari's life in pretty much the same way I'd screwed it up. The answer is yes. Yes, I did. It absolutely did occur to me that I was repeating a behavior I'd pursued with disastrous results, while hoping for a different outcome. And yes, I realize that is the classic definition of insanity. But really, what did Omari have to lose that he hadn't lost already?

I mean, besides the obvious.

Answer: He had *nothing* to lose. As much as he liked his praetor and the other members of the Festus household, he was not ready to resign himself to living out his life as a slave. He had, all on his own, kept tabs on the comings and goings of African legates in the hope that Flavius Anthemius might visit Rome again and he could just happen to bump into him.

Of course, even that idea had its dark side: What would Consul Anthemius make of the fact that Praetor Festus had kept Omarius Prisca as a slave knowing that he had been a consul's right-hand man?

We managed to get safely home. I had planned to deposit Omari in his room at the villa then scarper back to Manhattan, but as we turned into the corridor that led to the elite servants' quarters we found our way blocked by an attractive young woman carrying a lamp. She was barefoot and wearing a simple linen shift that, in the lamplight, was vaguely see-through. Her hair—which was thick, wavy, and the color of autumn maples—tumbled over her shoulders and fell across one green eye.

"I saw you from my bedroom window," she told us breathlessly, her voice a low purr, "where I sat dreaming that you would come to me, at last. Marcellus, why do you spurn me? Tell me how I may please you!"

Omari had stopped in consternation, disjointed and conflicting thoughts flashing like electric pulses in his tipsy brain. Liuva was winsome, seductive, really, really hot, and he was *so* lonely.

But I don't love her, he argued against his physical reaction.

The thought was clear and bell-like, and the emotion that went with it was equally vivid. He didn't just not *love* this pouting vixen, he didn't even *like* her. He thought she was vain and shallow and, of course, nothing like his beloved Sennia.

On the other hand, she was sexy and she obviously wanted him and she was *here* ... and slinking closer with every breath.

I pulled back into my corner of his consciousness. Should I interfere? Bug out? I didn't know what to do. I suspected that if Omari did take Liuva up on her tempting offer, he'd live to regret it, but what if *this* was my many times great grandmother?

Discretion is the better part of valor. That's my story and I'm sticking to it. I Louie, Louie'd my way out of there as fast as I could, and whatever happened next, I hoped never to know.

Now, remember that my body back in Manhattan often echoed what was happening with my host in whenever. When I came to myself in my usual chair in the lab, I became keenly aware of this. Recalling the last time I'd come back to find Victoria staring into my eyes, I kept them tightly closed, wishing I'd paid more attention to the little meditation exercises I'd learned along with my martial arts training.

"Peter? Are you all right?"

She was right there, gripping my wrists. I could smell the lemon verbena scent of her hair and feel her breath on my cheek.

Focus, Detective August, I told myself. "I need a moment to reorient myself," I said. "Just ... just a moment." I took a deep breath.

She let go of my wrists and straightened, but continued to stand in front of me. I saw her even with my eyes closed—eyes bright, that puzzled, concerned wrinkle between her brows. She moved, and I knew she was flipping her braid over her shoulder, the way she did when she was impatient or worried.

This was not helping.

"Um, Vic," I said, shifting in my chair. "Could you get me some coffee? I really need some caffeine." What I really needed was a cold shower ... or at least ten seconds of not being completely aware of her.

"You need *something,*" she said wryly, "but I don't think caffeine is it."

I could feel my face flushing. "A moment, please?" I begged.

She gave me the moment. I opened my eyes. Otis sat ten feet away, gaze glued to his computer display. It might have been my imagination, but he looked as if he were trying hard not to laugh. His mouth kept twitching.

I took a deep breath and let it out. Better. Humiliation does wonders for the libido ... thought no one, ever. I took off my headgear and put it on its stand, then stood up, realizing that what I wanted right now, besides the obvious, was a stiff drink. Coffee would have to do.

I started for the kitchenette/break room in the front corner of the lab and met Victoria coming out. She held out a cup of coffee.

"Not sure this is really the best thing for you right now," she told me. "You seem pretty amped up. Can you tell me what happened, or would you rather I not know?"

"Thanks," I said, accepting the coffee. "Omari went out to the pub and got a wee bit plastered. We got home to find his lady's maid waiting up for him."

Victoria just gaped at me. "Pub? Lady's maid? When the hell were you?"

I crooked my finger and headed for her office. I gave her the whole rundown from fabric to ale and everything in between. Including what Omari and I were plotting.

"Two years, Vic," I said when I'd dumped the whole Megillah into her personal recording device. "He's been a slave in that house for two years. He's not miserable, except for the being torn up about Sennia part, but he's not free—he just pretends to be free a couple of nights a week."

"Do you want to try again, earlier?"

I shook my head. "No. He's got an idea. Or, I guess *we* have an idea."

"Getting into a warehouse?"

I nodded. "Could be as easy as that. Find the thing, then get rid of it or hide it where it won't surface again until we want it to."

She looked skeptical. "It's never as easy as that."

I finished my coffee and dropped the cup into her recycle processor. "I better get back. If he's going into that storehouse, I need to be there."

I took care of my mundane business, grabbed a snack, then dove back to Omari, aiming for the next day. Got it in one. It was late afternoon and my man was having a chat with the head cook in a pleasant little courtyard off the kitchens. There was to be a banquet later in the week, and Omari was making sure the head chef had all the bases covered.

I did not want to know what had happened with Liuva, so I didn't pry or poke or peek. I did feel him out about his master and mistress's activities for the evening, though. They were booked. A dinner gathering at the home of one of his business associates. I was expected to attend. So was Liuva. He was nervous about that, but avoided thinking about it as circumspectly as I avoided *making* him think about it.

Okay, no warehouse crawl tonight, then. Instead, we found ourselves curried and dressed in our best and on our way to a small banquet at the home of a wealthy Roman merchant—one Herculius Magnus. We rode in the carriage with our respective bosses and kept silence while they chatted about their own upcoming party plans.

So, here's how this works, if you're a slave at one of these shindigs: You go to the big do with your master or mistress. You take their cloak and you collect any prezzies they're offered as they arrive and carry them to the house steward who will see that they are kept safe until they can be loaded into your coach. If your boss needs something during the party (except food— that's for the house staff to take care of) you make sure you're within hailing distance so you can provide it.

Say, for example, our praetor needs to seal a contract over the purchase of some property. You bring him his seal (which you wear around your neck), papyrus, and a stylus, as necessary. If he gets cold, you bring his cloak; if he drops food or drink on his garments, you bring him a change of clothing and help him into it in an adjoining room or curtained-off cubby intended for just that purpose. And yes, these guys really do bring extra duds, and anything else they think they might need, to a house party. Liuva was carrying our mistress's makeup kit—a flat, ornately carved box with a leather strap and a brass mirror built into the lid. We wore our respective burdens in shoulder satchels.

After our bosses disembarked from their coach and exchanged the initial ritual greetings, they were ushered into a large, round vestibule. From there, the Festuses went on into the banquet hall while Liuva and Omari were released to loiter where we could be swiftly summoned.

The banquet hall of Herculius Magnus's palazzo was a long oval in which low tables had been arranged, leaving a space at center for the dinner show. The perimeter of the room was bordered by a series of columns made of reddish-brown stone—probably red marble—that supported a second-floor gallery. Since the evening was cool, the spaces between the columns were hung with rich fabrics of gold and black. Braziers added light and heat to the space. The air smelled of flowers and incense. A group of musicians filled the air with soft music from a variety of instruments. Very luxurious.

Once we were dismissed from the banquet chamber, Liuva and I sought the steward and put the baskets containing the Festuses' goods in his hands. Then, it was time to withdraw to the second-floor gallery where the servants would gather to chat, keeping one eye on the hall below in case our folks needed us.

I was sweating this part of the evening because I suspected that once we were free of the need to be silent and circumspect, we'd have to deal with Liuva. As we crossed the villa's large, open vestibule to the staircase, Omari happened to glance into a large alcove that was lit with two braces of lamps. There, on prominent display, was a large, ornate wooden doll house. A very familiar doll house, peopled by similarly familiar dolls—the *ushebtis* from Imhotep's tomb.

I did not have to prompt Omari to stop and stare at it. He was doing that all on his own. Was it possible that the rest of the funerary artifacts (or at least the ones we cared about) were here? We glanced feverishly around the vestibule, wondering where there might be more of the same. Surely the steward would know.

Omari started to turn back from the staircase, then hesitated. What about Liuva? Would she be watching him? We glanced up the gallery steps. She stood right at the top among a small cluster of slaves from a local proconsul's house. She didn't watch Omari, she *glared* at him—at us—through twin green Death Stars. Even as our eyes locked, she scrunched her mouth so hard her lips disappeared, then whipped back around, laying a hand on the arm of a tall young man with a swimmer's legs, bronze skin, and blue-black hair. He looked down at her with an expression that said he thought this was his lucky day.

The relief that washed through us wasn't mine alone. Omari mentally reviewed the array of stony silences, glares, and childish pouts he'd received since he'd rejected Liuva's advances. He hoped she was serious about pursuing her new target.

Me too.

Their kids will be gorgeous, I thought generously, as we reversed course and returned to the glorified coat-check room overseen by the steward.

"Thanos," said Omari, without my prompting, "the wooden house in the alcove there—it is a marvel. I thought I recognized it from my master's inventory."

Thanos nodded. "Indeed, it has become Herculius Magnus's favorite piece. Your master alleged it came from the tomb of an Egyptian god." He laid not-so-subtle emphasis on the word "alleged," his eyes narrowing slyly. "You are Egyptian, are you not?"

"I am, and I can vouch for the fact that the house is, indeed, from the tomb of the divine physician, Imhotep. I helped bring it out of the ground. [All true.] Has your master any more funerary ornaments you wish me to verify?"

"No. Which is a source of great disappointment to Magnus. I know Praetor Festus heeds your advice. Perhaps you might hint that another of these treasures would greatly please his good friend."

We inclined our head in agreement. Maybe that would offer a chance to find out what other "treasures" the praetor had.

We trotted up to the gallery to keep watch on the banquet hall. Liuva ignored us completely in favor of her hunky lackey. Omari surprised me by taking the initiative to ask a number of the other slaves if their masters or mistresses had received gifts from Festus. The way he did it was sheer manipulation; I could take lessons from this guy.

"Did you see that marvelous little house in the alcove downstairs?" he asked, as if preening. "It was a gift from my master."

Several of the PAs simply looked disgruntled. Others lifted their chins and described what Drusus Festus had bestowed on *their* households. Most tried to make it sound as if this or that box or casket or whatever was far and away better than the child's toy down in Magnus's lobby. To our mingled disappointment, we recognized none of the artifacts they described as being from Imhotep's tomb.

I was able to try the same ploy on a few other slaves in the course of the evening, but got *bupkis*. I spent the bulk of the banquet watching our master partying below, when I wasn't noshing at the servant's table in a room off the gallery. Meanwhile, I tried to inspire my host to further deeds of great adventure, stoically ignoring the disasters I'd already caused.

Between us, we came up with a not-half-bad plan, so I kicked back a bit and took in the unique experience of living a piece of history. I mean, the closest most people came to witnessing a Roman banquet was watching BBC reruns of *I, Claudius,* and here I was, hanging out at one.

It was boring. Even the chatter about the Visigoths skulking about in the countryside failed to raise our blood pressure.

Omari, who'd been to these things before, was even more bored than I was. That is, until he saw his master toasting a neighboring table with a bit of a wink and a nod. Omari stood up a bit straighter by the gallery rail, following the direction of Festus's toast. A woman at the end of the other table winked and nodded back. A moment later, she stood and made her way between two columns into the shadows beneath the gallery. A moment after that, Festus excused himself and did likewise, leaving his wife to chat with the woman next to her.

Was a business deal in the offing? Omari wrapped a hand around his master's seal. Ought we go put ourselves within easy reach?

Hey, why not? It would certainly be more interesting than hanging out up here.

I let Omari drive, since he seemed to know the layout of the palazzo. He made his way to the rear of the curving gallery and down a narrow flight of stairs to the ground floor, then hurried through the broad lamplit corridor that skirted the banquet hall.

Doorways opened at intervals onto a fan-shaped patio. As we swept around the curved flank of the building, we saw Praetor Festus and the unknown woman standing in the shadows near one of the doorways. They stood facing each other, speaking in low voices. Our master handed the woman something that she seemed to find of great interest. She held it up in the light of a lamp stand to examine it. It was a figurine.

No. It was an *ushebti*.

That brought us up short. Our pulse quickened and we hesitated in the lee of a support column. Did we appear as if by magic, hoping it would make us look clairvoyant, or wait until we were called for?

Just as Omari made the decision to forge ahead, the entire scenario changed. Drusus Festus hauled the woman into his arms and gave her a kiss that made me want to shout, "Get a room!" The kiss went on for a good ten count and, when they finally parted, the lady said in a husky voice, "Until the appointed eve." Then she (and the *ushebti*) disappeared through the curtains, returning to the banquet hall.

Our philandering master watched her go. When he leaned slightly in our direction, we realized that he was going to return to the banquet hall the same way he'd left it—through the columns we currently sheltered between.

Yikes.

I did not have to impress my host with the urgency of the situation; he turned and fled.

17

I, SPY

In all my travels down the cognitive transfer highway or slipstream or whatever, I had never quite figured out what made the difference between ending up when I intended to and not ending up there. I think it may have had something to do with concentration. The tiniest bit of indecision or a stray momentary thought about something else and I might find myself days or weeks or even years off.

At least, that was my theory. So, when I dived back to Omari again, later that same afternoon, my time, I fastened my attention on *the very next day* like a disgruntled terrier fastens its jaws on a mail carrier's ankle. I managed it, but it was later than I'd intended. I'd wanted to have the day to work on Omari whom, I realized, didn't fully understand what he was hoping to do with the papyrus he believed (without any proof of his own) was hidden in Imhotep's canopic tray.

I was surprised and pleased to find that he was thoroughly dedicated to the idea of finding the tray, freeing the papyrus, and returning with it to Memphis where he intended to turn it over to one of the local physicians—Flavius Anthemius's personal doctor being the most likely candidate. He seemed to have taken my urgency for finding the papyrus and translated it into terms that made sense to him: The special knowledge of the Great Physician ought to be in the hands of his acolytes and country-men. The human impulse to avoid cognitive dissonance by simply making it go away usually has dire results. In this case, I was hoping it would work for the larger good.

Having partied the night before, my master and his wife had settled in for the evening. Drusus Festus had given Omari the night off, and he had decided to make use of it. As we did the night we invaded the necropolis, we chose dark clothing and covered our head and the lower part of our face with a cowl. We armed ourselves with a short sword and two hand lamps with a length of additional wick and a flask of oil (Omari's idea). These we put in our satchel and left the villa through the kitchens. Omari considered going to the Pike for some liquid fortitude before he went a-spying (or a-thieving, if we actually found what we were looking for), but I talked him out of it. If someone at the tavern became at all curious about the way we were dressed, the heist was off. If he got plastered, likewise.

Omari knew his way around the wharves pretty well. Even in darkness broken only by a half moon and the lights of the occa-sional inn or brothel, he knew his way to his master's ware-houses. Turned out he had made this trip several times during my long absence, trying to get up the courage to stow away on a southbound ship. But he was marked as a slave now with a tattoo on his neck just above the collar bone; if he was caught trying to steal away, his fate would not be pretty. He wanted to leave Rome as what he had been—an Egyptian dignitary.

I was surprised at how much he'd been thinking about this. He'd begun to consider the idea that he could snatch salable goods from one of the storehouses in such a way that the theft would not be discovered for some time. He could then wait for the opportune moment to disappear. His Plan A was to feign sickness when the master and mistress were away in the countryside at their rural villa—a trip they made in the heat of summer. Though this year, with the Visigoths cutting up a ruckus to the north, they might stick pretty close to home.

Whenever he was able to escape, Omari planned to go south by land to Parthenope, where he could sell enough of his loot for a makeover. He hoped to convince Citro to go with him; he was ashamed of having cost his chief guard his freedom. He thought maybe no one would question him about his legal status if he looked the part of a nobleman and had a bodyguard and money to throw around. He wondered why it had taken him so long to get up his courage for this.

I didn't offer an opinion on that.

We reached the wharf at last, and crouched for some time in the lee of a nearby building from which we could see the entire row of warehouses. We waited to see if there was a watch posted on our master's properties (there was) and what course their rounds took.

There were three storehouses—a big one and two smaller ones. The big one (I'll call it Warehouse A) was farthest from my hiding place, which made the smaller ones (Warehouses B and C) more attractive targets. Warehouses A and B fronted on the river, while C was tucked in behind B. The buildings were separated from each other by alleys just wide enough to admit a cart or wagon. None of them seemed to have windows; they were just stone boxes with wooden doors—the largest of the three had a front door big enough to drive a wagon through. Made sense.

There seemed to be four watchmen. One of them was always at the front of the property at a station overlooking the wharf. He had a stool to sit on, a brazier to keep him warm, and an awning over his head in case of inclement weather.

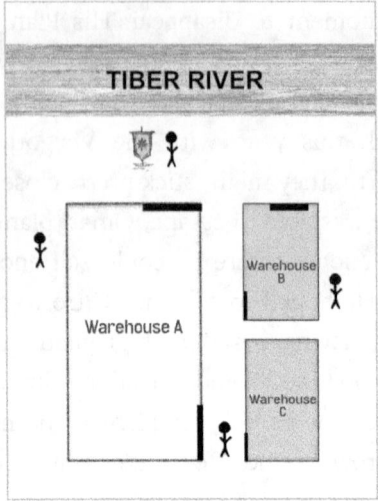

Omari remembered disembarking from the galley here, chained together with Citro and the others. He recalled the bleakness of the day and how the clouds had dumped rain on their heads as if all the angels in heaven (and possibly the ancient gods) wept for them.

Ouch. I did not need that little extra shot of guilt.

I directed my host's attention to the sides and backs of the buildings. If one guy was stationed out here, what were the other guys doing? Was there a pattern, or did they simply wander about at will? Omari had never been any closer than this, so he had no idea if there were other points of access toward the rear of the buildings.

Well, let's find out.

We slipped back along the side of the building we were using for concealment, then moved carefully toward the Festus storehouses, stopping beneath a loading dock that ran the entire width of the place. If I looked toward the river, I could just barely see the guard station on the wharf side. Closer to hand, I had a view of the sides of both smaller warehouses and the transverse alley that ran between them. I could also see the rear of Warehouse C and the opening of the long-axis alley that ran between Warehouse A and its smaller siblings.

Turned out there was a pattern to the guards' movements. The three roamers would circle the trio of buildings twice, keeping a distance between them of about the length of one of the smaller storehouses—which was approximately half the length of Warehouse A. For every two times they circled the outer perimeter, one of them would cut through the long alley between the buildings from back to riverfront, then relieve the guy at the guard station. That guy would get up and take his place in the rotation.

We watched one iteration of this from the shadows of the next-door loading dock, then started thinking about logistics as they repeated the pattern. We noticed two things: (1) no one ever cut down the crosswise alley between buildings B and C, though they swept it visually, and (2) during the time the guard at the front of the complex (Guard 1) was being relieved, nobody had eyes on that alley for several moments. While Guard 2 crossed the open area at the front of the buildings to take up his place at the guard station, Guard 3 had turned the rear corner of Warehouse C, and Guard 4 was just reaching the front of Warehouse A.

Okay, that was it, then—the only real opportunity to get close to the storehouses was during the changing of the guard.

I waited patiently for that to happen—Omari, not so patiently. Our muscles tensed as Guard 3 turned the rear corner of Warehouse C—the warehouse closest to us. We slipped a few paces toward the front of the complex, then dashed across the brick-paved yard and into the access between the two smaller warehouses. We found no real place to hide—just grass and weeds growing up between the cobbles, so we threw ourselves flat to the ground, tight up against the rear wall of Warehouse B.

We craned to see if there were a window or door in sight on either building. We saw neither.

The sounds of tramping feet came in stereo from two directions. We ducked our head, hoping we looked like one more clump of weeds. The feet moved on without hesitation. That gave us some time to get up and move to where the cross alley met the long-axis one. We peered up the length of Warehouse B. Yes, there was a door with a low loading platform and, judging from how much of the guard station we could see from here—which was most of it—I estimated that this door was in plain view of the guard posted at the station. That was a no-op.

We ducked back against the wall as Guard 3 strode across the rear mouth of the central alley. When he'd passed, we glanced back up at the inner wall of Warehouse C. We saw a door and loading dock there, as well.

We took a second to remember where all the guards were, then slipped swiftly and quietly down the side of Warehouse C to the loading dock. We crouched beneath it and waited. A guard crossed the front of the main alley without doing anything more than glancing down the aisle.

So far, so good.

We swung ourselves up onto the loading platform, then rose and moved to the door. It was about the size of the door on a modern day self-storage unit. It was made of solid planks of hardwood and recessed into the thick wall of the storehouse. If we flattened ourself up against the door, we'd be nearly invisible from the mouth of the alley.

We felt for the latch; it was held fast by a metal lock. I was momentarily disconcerted, but Omari knelt against the door and squinted at the thing in the light of the half moon. He knew this kind of lock; they were used everywhere. Question was, how many pins did it have and what would it take to lift them?

Footsteps at one end of the alley forced us to press ourself against the door and freeze. The footsteps moved on without hesitation, and I let Omari examine the lock. It would take a key with at least three pin lifters. The guards *might* have keys, but Festus would unquestionably have a set at the villa. We were disappointed, but it seemed as if the only thing we could do was to go home and try to find those keys ... or, I thought, make a simple set of lock picks.

Omari was taken aback by that idea. Lock picks? How did one make lock picks? I slowly released that simple intel so it would feel as if he were thinking it through. Who knows, maybe he was. Of all the ancestral hosts I'd inhabited, Omari and I were the most similar in our thought processes. He was quick on the uptake, too. Sometimes quicker than I was. Right now, for example, he'd already realized that making lock picks would be the safest thing to do. As castellan (sort of) we had access to *household* keys, but had no idea where the keys to these storehouses were kept. Getting caught being too interested in them or worse, trying to lift them, would be very bad. Lock-pickery was the way to go.

We were both so focused on the lock that we heard the sandy crunch of footsteps at the far end of the alley only seconds before they hesitated.

Oops.

We froze again, plastered right up against the door. Our head was turned toward the rear of the building, so one eye could see half the gray figure of the guard as he paused to peer in this direction. Which, of course, meant that if he had good night vision, he might be able to see a bit of us. Omari considered making an animal noise, but thought better of it. Even a bird call might intrigue a hungry soldier (and send me packing back to my time zone).

After a moment, the guard muttered something under his breath and began a noisy ... well, "dance" sort of describes it. It took us a moment of tense watching to realize he was searching for something—most likely a hand lamp and a flint. Not good.

We considered trying to run. Omari was young and physically strong, but there were four of them and only one of us. We'd lost track of where the other guards were.

The guard at the end of the alley gave up on trying to find his lamp. Instead, he took a step into the aisle. And drew his sword. Moonlight raced down the length of the blade. I introduced Omari to a number of words in a language he'd never heard before. He was getting ready to bolt, but I held him still with all my will.

The guard had come five feet up the aisle when a second guard appeared in the opening behind him.

"Hoy! Tertius!" the newcomer called. "Where are you going? It's not your turn to relieve the wharf watch."

Tertius stopped and gestured toward the loading dock. "Thought I heard something back there. Some scratching."

"What, you mean like one of those big old rats that Lurio caught last week? Did you fancy some hunting, then?"

"Rats?" repeated Tertius. "Ugh. I'd forgotten about those." He hesitated a moment more, seeming to peer right at us, then swung about, sheathed his sword, and returned to his well-worn path.

"Better hurry," said his buddy. "Or Nonus will catch us both up."

Swearing under his breath, Tertius trotted off across the rear of the big warehouse. His comrade chuckled then began walking the perimeter again.

Omari's heart pounded like a bass drum and he strained to run. I made him count to ten before we slipped from the loading dock back to *terra firma*. From there we crept to the narrow cut between Warehouses B and C. We played weed tuft again until we heard the sounds of guards moving up the central aisle behind us and across the alley in front of us. After they'd moved on, we got up and padded to the corner of Warehouse C. A quick peek around the corner showed a guard disappearing from sight at the rear of the warehouse. The aforementioned Nonus, no doubt.

We waited for a six count, then cut diagonally toward the neighboring building. We didn't stop to reconnoiter, but kept running. We thought we heard a shout behind us, which only made us run faster. We were determined to return at the next opportunity to try again, but with a lock pick.

Omari was so jazzed by the evening's adventure, he couldn't sleep. Instead, he resolved to stay up and make himself a skeleton key. I knew a bit about picking locks, so I stayed with him to help him fashion a crude set of picks from metal cotter pins we filched from the stable. In feeling the lock, we thought it had three pins, but we made four lifters just to be sure. Each one was about the length of our hand and shaped like an Allen wrench. We wrapped the handles in fabric borrowed from the housekeep's rag bag. They weren't bad as makeshift lock picks go.

By the time we finished up, Omari was exhausted and fell into his bed. He was out the moment he lay down. I took the opportunity to go home and eat whatever meal was appropriate —dinner, in this case. I dined with Victoria at a little Persian place not far from the institute and debriefed over steaming plates of *fesenjoon*.

She was worried. "Peter, are you sure it's wise to get Omari wrapped up in something like this? I mean, what if he gets caught? They might throw him in prison, or worse. Then you really might disappear." She hesitated, then added, "Maybe you should let Liuva catch you."

"No," I said, reflexively. "That's not the answer. It would feel … icky."

She tilted her head and gave me a look. "You said she was beautiful."

"Yeah, so?"

She shrugged. "So, what's 'icky' about going to bed with a beautiful woman?"

"She's not Sennia."

"You're not Omari."

I stared at her. She was right. I wasn't Omari, and Sennia wasn't my beloved.

"She's not you," I said.

She reached across the table and took my hand. "Peter ... maybe we've gotten too involved, but if anything happened to you..."

"If 'anything happened' to me—meaning I was zapped out of existence—I doubt you'd remember any of this. Theron would've gotten his heart fixed and he'd be your time diver, not me. You'd never even know I'd existed in some other timeline."

She met my eyes. "I'm pretty sure I would know."

We ended up back at my place, and if Mattie the Cat minded that a human female had usurped her spot on the pillow next to mine, she didn't let on. I took this as a good omen.

WAKING up to Victoria was a revelation. Not just that she was beautiful in the morning with her makeup awry and her hair in disarray, but that it felt so natural and right for me to wake up with her next to me. We woke at the sound of my alarm, which was a rotation of songs from my music library, and popped our heads up at almost precisely the same moment. A second later, before I'd even had time to register that I, Peter August—not Omari Prisca or Eckart Metz or Fox Aubry—was in bed with a woman, Matilda poked her head up out of the comforter between our feet.

We all stared at each other for a moment or two, then the cat got up, stretched, and walked up the length of our bodies before deciding she preferred Victoria to me.

Well.

"I guess she approves of me," Vic laughed as the cat head-butted her chin.

I was struck by two things. One was how different (and amazing) she looked with her honey-colored hair loose around her shoulders and falling into her eyes. Two was how much I wanted to make love to her again and ... okay, *three* things. Three being that I was in love with her, and would have been, regardless of what Mattie Cat thought.

"Vic ... ," I said.

She was making kissy faces at the cat, but stopped to look up at me. Matilda turned to look at me too. Apparently, the expression on my face spooked the cat; she scampered off the bed. It seemed to spook Vic, too, but she froze in place.

"Oh," she said. She pulled the covers up to her neck. This, I suspected, was code for "oh, no, what have I done?"

I felt my throat constrict. I'd overshot the runway.

"Oh," she said again, "you're regretting last night already, aren't you?"

"What? No. *No!* I am absolutely, one hundred percent *not* regretting last night ... unless you are."

She seemed surprised. "Me? Oh, Peter, *no.*" She dropped the covers and reached out to touch my cheek.

I fought to keep my eyes on hers. "That's good, because I..." I stalled for a moment, afraid to say what I was thinking. Which was ridiculous. I was one of New York's finest, a detective and a time diver. I had been in life-or-death situations any number of times, had busted drug dealers, captured murderers and rapists. Now, here I was, face-to-face with a woman I loved, and I was in a freaking panic.

"Oh, come on, August," I said aloud. "Don't be a wimp." I took her hand and kissed the palm. "Look, I don't know if you're ready to hear this, or if you'll ever be ready to hear this, but I have to say it. I'm in love with you."

Her eyes widened and she drew in a deep breath. Then she pulled me in for a kiss that lit up every nerve ending in my body and short-circuited half my synapses. We got to work a little late that morning.

18

INSIDE MAN

In Omari's head, it was like Mission Impossible. Even the morning after his near-yikes experience, he was committed to the proposition that he was now a master spy. Impressionable boy, Omari-Marcellus.

He performed his duties for Drusus Festus with his mind half on our planned after-hours activities. That impressed the hell out of me. If he was this organized with half his attention on adventures to come, what must he be like without my interference? He completely ignored Liuva's sniping—which annoyed her no end—and focused instead on the conversations between master and mistress.

We discovered the downside of annoying Liuva late in the afternoon when we took some documents to Drusus Festus to read and seal. We'd left the folio of papers with him in his salon (which is a Roman cross between a man cave and an office) and started to go about our business when the lady Varia called us into her parlor.

"Marcellus," she said in her most commanding voice—and she had a commanding voice even in her mellower moods.

"Marcellus, why are you spurning my maidservant's attentions?"

"Madam?" That was Omari. I was speechless.

"Liuva has been in a sorry state for some time and, when I pressed her, she admitted she had fond dreams of becoming your wife—something that Drusus and I would be pleased to allow. I daresay Drusus would be much inclined to grant you your freedom were you to marry."

Omari's ears pricked up at this. Was he being offered a means of securing his freedom? He kiboshed the idea before he'd fully thought it through. Wedding Liuva then fleeing to Memphis would be the act of a scoundrel, and Omari had no interest in becoming a scoundrel.

"That's very thoughtful of you, Madam. You and the praetor have been most kind to me. I could not have asked for a better position," said Omari diplomatically, omitting the fact that he had been kidnapped from a better position.

She wagged her finger at us. "You have sidestepped my question, Marcellus. Why do you make my poor Liuva so miserable?"

Now it was Omari's turn to be struck dumb. I was no Cyrano de Bergerac, but I managed what I flattered myself was a reply that would win our mistress's approval. "Madam, I don't mean to make Liuva miserable. But when I was … taken from my home, I left behind the woman I love. The woman I was to marry in mere hours. My heart is still hers."

She exceeded my hopes; her eyes filled with tears. "What? Drusus never spoke of this to me. You were to have been married?"

We nodded in honest sorrow. Omari was now thinking of Sennia and wasn't that far from tears himself. "So you see," we said, "I have nothing to offer Liuva. My heart is not mine to give."

Lady Varia put a hand to her throat, clearly moved by our

legitimate tale of woe. "Such a faithful heart! Few men are as true to love as you are, Marcellus. I cannot fault you for that."

Something in her eyes told me she wasn't blind to her husband's wandering attention. I felt sorry for her. "Thank you, Madam, for understanding."

"I do understand, Marcellus. Liuva must simply be patient or turn her gaze elsewhere."

We smiled. "Indeed, Madam, I believe she may have already turned it."

Her eyes widened. "Really? Do you know where her interest might lie?"

"There was a young man at the banquet you attended at the home of Herculius Magnus. I'm not certain what house he served, but Liuva seemed to find him ... pleasing."

"Are you sure she was not simply trying to make you jealous?" Her dark eyes sparkled at us.

We weren't sure of that, just hopeful that she was sincerely attracted to the young stud. We said as much, if not in so many words, and the lady Varia dismissed us. With that bullet dodged, we finished our daily tasks with one eye on what we hoped to do when the sun went down.

CLOAKED and armed with a short sword, a hand lamp, and our handcrafted lock picks, we stepped out into the Roman night with purpose. We went directly to our hiding place behind the storehouse next door to Festus's little complex and started tracking the security forces. We'd move only after we'd seen one changing of the wharf-side guard. After that, it should be child's play.

Uh-oh. I caught the tenor of Omari's thoughts with a prickle of alarm. He was influencing me again, and not in a good way. Last night's near-discovery had clearly had the inverse effect of making him cocky. I tried to inject some perfectly sane terror into him, hoping I could at least scare him into caution. I reminded him of the moments we'd spent pressed up against the door of the storehouse watching good old Tertius come stomping down the alley.

This had the desired effect. Omari cooled his jets and began to take the whole thing more seriously. This was good. Last thing in the world I wanted was to have a duel over who was going to sit in the driver's seat. That would be awkward. I wanted us relying on my detective instincts, not his buckaroo banzai ones.

We timed everything perfectly. The dash to the transverse alley, the scramble to the loading dock—both went off without a hitch. Omari kept one ear on the guards while I drove the work on the lock. He was stoked about his suddenly extended capacity for multitasking. He thought it was magic ... literally. He was convinced that God was guiding him. I was not going to be the one to burst his bubble. Besides, God works in mysterious ways.

Squeezed up against the door, I brought out our lock picks and bent to the task of lifting the pins on the primitive lock. The breeze off the river was damp and smelled of water and tarred wood. It also carried the creak of bobbing boats and the hollow sigh of the river currents eddying beneath the wharf. The combination of scent and sound reminded Omari of his wretched journey in the dark hold of that Roman galley. He was becoming increasingly depressed ... and less watchful.

I'd gotten two picks in and was angling with the third when I felt his pulse quicken. A second later—almost too late—I caught the sound of footsteps. One hand on the lock and picks, I flattened us against the door, counting on the thick frame to hide us.

It did. Once that guard had passed, we had somewhere between a minute-and-a-half and two minutes to work. I hauled Omari's attention back to the need for care and urgency. We got the third pick in and began poking around for the pins. We hit one right away but had a bit of trouble with the second. We'd just popped the third when another guard reached the rear end of the aisle. We tried to keep our hand wrapped around the lock picks as we squeezed ourselves into the door frame.

Guard: March, march, march. Crunch, crunch, crunch.

Us: Breathe in; breathe out. Breathe in; breathe out.

The guard was gone a moment later, and we went back to the lock, holding the picks in place with one hand while sliding back the latch bolt. Of course, it squeaked. We hoped the noise would be attributed to the giant rats.

Seconds later, we stood inside the storehouse in darkness so deep it seemed to press against our face. Omari scratched his nose, took a deep breath, and almost choked on the dust we'd stirred up coming in.

We stood for a time with our ear against the door, making sure we hadn't also stirred up interest from the guards. After several minutes, we decided we'd gotten in clean and exchanged the lock picks for one of the hand lamps. To Omari, this was familiar tech, so I let him handle the flint and steel. With the lamp lit, we turned to survey the storehouse and realized the sheer enormity of our task. The place was packed with stuff in crates and casks, or covered with sail cloth.

Great. This was clearly going to take more than one night, unless we got absurdly lucky. Omari was considering prayer and I have to admit, I was giving that some thought, myself.

Omari was all about being systematic in his approach; I didn't have to elaborate on that point. He murmured a prayer, then mentally divided the place into quadrants and tackled the one to the right of the door first. We set the lamp down where we thought it would do the most good and started unwrapping things. Artifacts from all over the place rested here. A lot of them were war-related. There was leather armor I thought must have been from China and wooden shields with Celtic knot embellishments that I'd seen in the history texts I'd devoured as a kid and knew came from Gaul and Britain.

Finally, we came across some items Omari and I both recognized as being from Egypt. We flipped back sailcloth covers, opened crates, and looked for the treasures of Imhotep's tomb—and yes, I am aware of how ridiculously Hollywood that sounds. We spent roughly four hours pawing through the trove. We'd calculated that we'd brought enough oil and wick to last that long. Yeah, we could have brought more, but doing that would have risked overstaying our welcome and being forced to try to sneak out with dawn threatening. When our last wick began to sputter, we gave up the hunt. It was defeating to realize that we'd only gotten to about a third of the first quarter of the storehouse.

Okay, clearly this was not going to work. We could hardly sneak in here night after night. For one thing, Omari was often called on to attend functions with his master. What we needed was a man on the inside. We returned the sailcloth covers to their places and contemplated ways we could suggest to our master that Citro Superstes would make a great addition to his storehouse guard.

Leaving the storehouse presented challenges getting in had not. Coming in, we'd been able to count the rotations of the guard. Going out, we had no idea where the guards were, either in location or in rotation. I joined Omari in silent prayer as we put our hand on the interior latch and slid it back. We took a deep breath and listened. Heavy footsteps sounded just beyond the door.

Omari's urge to dive for cover was hard to fight, but I managed it. I kept our hand on the latch, ready to ram it shut and hide if necessary. Omari was amazed at his own *cojones*.

The footsteps drew level with the door ... and passed on up the aisle.

All right, then. We now knew where we were in the rotation. We counted slowly to thirty, then opened the door inward a crack. Another guard was crossing the end of the aisle. He passed, and we let ourself out onto the loading dock. A beat later, we slipped over the side of the dock and went to ground between warehouses B and C. We waited to hear another guard coming up the side of B from our left. He didn't come. When he continued not to come, I knew something was off.

Maybe he'd had to go off and pee. Maybe he'd seen something that he had to go check out. Something had thrown the whole rotation off and, for all we knew, we were that something.

After several tense moments lying in the weeds, Omari couldn't take any more. Before I realized what he was thinking, he leapt up and ran for the building next door. This time, I knew we hadn't imagined the outraged shouts from behind us—from too freaking close behind us. We ran as fast as we could, zigging and zagging between buildings, leaping over piles of refuse, hawsers, and low walls. We ran until we no longer heard the sounds of pursuit, then we took a circuitous route back to the Festus villa. We stowed our ninja outfit and Omari went to bed.

I headed back to the lab.

LESS THAN TWO hours had passed during my day in Omari's life; it was still early in the day in modern Manhattan. After last night, I was a bit disappointed with that development, especially when I saw Victoria smiling at me from her station. We debriefed quickly with the whole team and I outlined how I hoped to get another set of eyes on the warehouses.

"From what you describe, though," said Otis, "I can't imagine that just one more set of eyes is going to help that much. I mean, the amulet is sort of small. It could be anywhere in that mess—in a box, a bag, a drawer. You might've even blown right past it yourself and not realized it."

I shrugged. "Yeah, I suppose you're right. But to be honest, I'm not even sure I can manage getting Citro attached to the guard. It might look really suspicious if Omari suddenly starts agitating to get his old buddy into the warehouse circuit."

Otis made a face. "It seems as if you're not getting any closer to finding this thing in this time zone. Maybe you should try Dr. Metz's museum again."

Drew shook his head. "That won't work. The amulet has been damaged by then, so if there'd been any additional information in it or on it, it may be lost."

I nodded, perpetuating the lie. "Drew's right. The amulet is too far gone in Austria to be of use."

I DOVE AGAIN RIGHT AWAY, coming into Omari as he hurried to attend his master. He was carrying Festus's writing box and had a packet of papyrus and a bundle of scrolls under one arm. He was tired—no small wonder. He'd had a big night last night and was thinking less of his master's correspondence and more about how he could convince the praetor that he needed a man of Citro's ability working at his storehouses.

The master was in his man cave poring over the correspondence he'd already received. We added several new pieces—petitions, personal letters, contracts. We sat with Festus at his writing table and went over the contracts and petitions with him. I was surprised at how often he asked Omari's opinion and even took his advice. He respected Omari's intellect and business and diplomatic acumen, slave or no. That was great, but it still didn't give us any solid reason to insert our man into his business.

As Festus wrapped up and Omari assembled a basketful of messages to post, contracts to deliver, and petitions to pass to the appropriate officials, I wracked my brain for a way to introduce the idea of adding our guy to the guard. I recalled the "doll house" he'd given Magnus. Could we connect that with the treasures of Imhotep that were presumably still in the warehouse and express concern because Omari was Egyptian? Something like: *Sir, I saw the marvelous artifact you gave Magnus. I must assume there are more treasures from my homeland still in your storehouses. I fear they might attract thieves and* ...

Effing lame.

"Praetor, a moment?" The gruff voice came from the man cave doorway.

We turned to see a soldier standing beneath the arch that led to the hall. Omari recognized him as the chief of the praetor's personal guard, Appius Trimalchio.

"Certainly, Appius. Come in. What do you wish?"

"Shall I return for these papers later, Master?" we asked Festus.

"No, no," he said, "continue what you were doing, Marcellus. There is nothing Appius could say that you cannot hear."

What Appius had to say sent a shot of electricity through us that rooted Omari to the tile floor.

"It's the warehouses, Praetor," he said. "The guards report that, two nights in a row, someone was skulking around. Last night they surprised him and he ran. They pursued, but could not catch him. They believe the intention is burglary."

Festus paled. "You believe we should increase the guard?"

"That would be my advice, sir. That way, if he returns, we would better spare the men to pursue and catch him. Two of my men set off in pursuit last night but abandoned their posts to do so. If the thief was working with others…"

The praetor caught his meaning and nodded. "Yes, of course. You must choose the best men—"

We straightened. "Excuse me, Praetor Festus, if I might make a suggestion?"

The expression on our master's face seemed to be one of relief. "Of course, Marcellus. Give me your thoughts."

"There is a man in your house guard named Citro Superstes. He was the captain of my own personal guard when I … when I was in Memphis. He is a brave and intensely loyal man who is proud of his Egyptian heritage. Correct me if I am wrong, but I assume that there are artifacts from the necropolis at Memphis in those storehouses."

"You assume correctly."

"Then Citro's desire to protect those artifacts would make him an ideal addition to your guard. He would not want to see the treasures of Egypt fall into the hands of unknown thieves. He's also an able leader of men, strategist, and spy."

Festus looked at us speculatively. "I see that you trust him."

"Praetor Festus, I have trusted him with my life and would do so again without hesitation."

The praetor nodded again. He turned back to Appius Trimalchio. "You know the man of whom he speaks—this Citro Superstes?"

"I do, Praetor. And your man is correct. I, too, would judge Superstes to be a fine leader of men. I have observed myself how he tutors and guides the young pups in your service."

"That's good, then," said Festus. "Put Citro Superstes in charge of the storehouse guard and help him to select additional men for night duty. Perhaps some of these 'pups' would be more likely to catch our would-be thief or thieves with the speed of youth."

Wow. That went better than we had any right to expect.

Now, we just needed to get to Citro and give him his secret orders ... if he was up for it.

"Shall I find Citro and send him to you, Praetor?" we asked, allowing him to know we were pleased with his decision (but not *too* pleased).

"Yes, thank you, Marcellus."

We bowed, gathered up the papyri and writing box, and took off in search of Citro. We found him out in the sandy courtyard of the small guard barracks that sat behind the praetor's stables. He was sparring with one of the aforementioned pups, teaching him the use of his short sword with wooden mockups. When he saw Omari, he reflexively bowed, forgetting that they were both now slaves.

"Vicarius," he greeted us, "how may I serve you?"

The pup standing nearby gaped at us. He could see the mark on Omari's bared neck that matched the one on his own and on Citro's. We were all slaves, his expression said, so why was Citro treating us with such deference?

"You are to come with me, Citro. Praetor Festus wishes to promote you to chief of his storehouse guard. It seems there has been someone sneaking around his storehouses at night and he wishes to increase security there. I sang your praises and..." We shrugged.

The corner of Citro's mouth twitched. "Well, I'd best make myself presentable then."

We followed him to his quarters—which were far more spartan than ours—using the opportunity to fill him in on our recent activities and our agenda.

He looked at us with something approaching amazement. "Then you were the would-be thief that led to this promotion?"

We shrugged. "Unintentionally. I mean, I hoped to find the artifacts Praetor Festus had stolen from Imhotep's tomb. This situation is a lucky consequence. You see, I believe the stolen treasures may be in one of those warehouses. If you are willing, I would like you to find them."

He paused in the act of fastening on his cloak. "And then what, Vicarius?"

"First," we said, "I am no longer a vicarius. I am a slave in the house of Drusus Festus, just as you are, Citro. You may call me..." Omari hesitated, considering. Was he Marcellus? Omarius? He settled on his un-Latinized given name. "You may call me Omari, as that is my name. Second, this is a request made on the basis of our friendship, not an order given by a superior. And third, simply report what you find to me, if you would."

Citro gave a nod that was more salute, and we returned to the house together. We left him with the praetor and Trimalchio and headed off to look after our daily tasks which were, frankly, boring. Omari and I were both relieved not to have to play secret agent again, but we made a point of taking Citro aside after his meeting with our master and his new boss, and gave him a little sketch of the specific item we were looking for.

Citro asked a single question: "Why, sir—Omari—is this particular artifact of such importance?"

"Because," we said, "I feel compelled to return something of the Divine Doctor to Egypt. His mummy and its casket are obviously too cumbersome. But the tray containing his canopic jars might be concealed and taken home to rest. I feel this is my sacred obligation."

"Then it is mine, as well," Citro said. "And do not doubt that I shall find them. I suggested to our master and Captain Trimalchio that the first thing I should do is make certain the thief"— here he gave us a look—"did not manage to gain entry."

"But, I told you—I *did* gain entry."

"Indeed. A fact I shall report to Praetor Festus along with a suggestion that we take inventory of the storehouses to ensure nothing has been taken from them."

"Citro," we told him, laying a hand on his shoulder, "I am in awe of your brilliance. And grateful to have such a friend."

Citro flashed a rare smile and went off to prep for his first night of duty at the wharf. I hummed "Louie, Louie."

NATURALLY, my debriefing with the team was self-censored. I told everyone about the storehouses, implying that it would be a miracle to find the amulet in that haystack and that even with Citro on the job, it could take months to find what we were looking for. I was more forthcoming with Vic and Theron, of course, and Theron reminded me that we had (ironically) a time pressure. Sometime in 410 CE, the Visigoths would lose patience with the Roman government and overthrow it.

I returned to Omari about a week in his time after I'd left him. The news from the storehouses was no news. Citro and his team of soldier-clerks had nearly completed their inventory of the warehouse I'd broken into and had yet to find any but the smallest, least impressive of Imhotep's treasures. I made repeated return trips to Rome over the next several real-world, Manhattan days, though weeks had passed in ancient Rome. Each time, Citro gave a negative report. Even more discouraging, he had completed inventory on both of the smaller warehouses and begun work on the largest one. He'd seen no Egyptian artifacts for some time and had found none so far in Warehouse A.

On my fifth or sixth trip back, I found Omari preparing for an evening out with his boss and fretting over what Citro might or might not find tonight. I stuck with it, even though I was pretty sure what he'd find—a big fat zero. The Egyptian artifacts seemed to have been stored in the two smaller warehouses, and their contents had all been catalogued. I was pretty sure Festus had given Imhotep's earthly remains to some bosom buddy or political functionary, and neither Omari nor I had a clue which one. The canopic jars of even a minor Egyptian god were pretty major swag. Chances were he'd given them to someone important—a senator maybe, or a bishop. Though what a church man would want with a pagan saint's innards, I have no idea. A senator or other political figure—someone Festus wanted to butter up—made more sense. He did pay visits to such people on occasion, but had none lined up that Omari knew of in the near future.

Tonight, he was to be the guest at the home of Eliphas Germanicus, a sometime business associate, or so he told Lady Varia, who was content to spend the evening at home.

We took the praetor's coach to the Germanicus estate, which was some miles down the Tiber from his own home. It was after dark by the time we arrived, and my thoughts were on how we might discover which highly placed statesman had scored the canopic tray. We were welcomed into the forecourt of the Germanicus villa by the steward, who greeted our master warmly and bid us enter. Once inside an ornate anteroom, the steward took our cloaks.

Festus turned to us with a smile. "Marcellus, you may let the steward take charge of your writing box and satchel, as well. You will not need them this evening. You will, yourself, be fed and entertained among the household staff. Consider it a night off."

"Sir?"

"I shall do no business tonight, Marcellus."

He turned toward the entry to the receiving hall, and I realized that someone had come to stand in the doorway. It was the woman from the Magnus banquet. The one he'd been snogging under the gallery. She opened her arms and he went into them eagerly, giving us another "get a room" moment. When they finally parted, the lady took Festus by the hand and led him toward a wide set of marble stairs that curved upward to a second floor.

We could only stare. "Well," I said, "if that was Eliphas Germanicus, he wasn't quite what I expected."

The steward chuckled. "That is his daughter, Lady Felicia Germanica. The master and his lady wife are away in the country-side for a day or so. Now, Marcellus, if you will come with me, we have a fine repast laid out for the senior staff."

We nodded and followed him, while I tried to figure out what to do next. I could go back to Manhattan and dive further forward in Omari's timeline, or I could stick with him for the next six or seven hours and get Citro's early morning report.

I was still debating this as we stepped into the receiving hall. Our attention was caught by what we first took as some sort of household shrine, gleaming with brazier and lamplight. Most Roman households had them, often converted from the veneration of pagan *lares* to Christian icons. This wasn't one of those shrines.

It took us a moment to realize that we'd stopped moving and simply stood there in stunned disbelief. In the center of the blaze of light was Imhotep's ornate inner coffin and, sitting before it on a low table, his canopic tray.

19

WONDERS NEVER CEASE

Naturally, I resolved to remove the Papyrus of Imhotep from the Lady Felicia's reception hall at the earliest opportunity. Omari, on the other hand, was more interested in returning the great man's innards to the necropolis they'd been stolen from ... and in returning himself to the arms of his beloved ... if she hadn't married someone else.

In short order, he'd come up with a plan. He was expected to tote around a bag of his master's clothing and goods. It was certainly large enough to hold Imhotep's canopic jars. Festus and his lover could be expected to spend hours doing their thing, which should theoretically give us lots of time to abscond with the jars and the papyrus. The trick would be getting access to the reception hall unwatched. Neither of us thought it would be a big trick, really. While my master and their mistress were at play, things tended to get a little loose in the Germanicus servant's quarters.

Omari argued with himself about the tray. Which is to say he argued with *me* about it. I wanted to grab the whole thing for expediency. Dinking around with the individual parts was a surefire way to get us caught. He wanted to grab the jars and see if there was anything else worth taking. He was still not one hundred percent sure why he thought there was some piece of Imhotep's wisdom encased in the tray. I kept reassuring him that he'd read it somewhere in his literary wanderings. He seemed satisfied with this, though he spent some time wracking his brains, trying to remember precisely where he'd read it. Fortunately, he spent most of his time that evening getting the lay of the land. Both of us noticed that the servants stayed very much to their quarters and the gargantuan kitchens. Not one ventured back out into the main house.

The unfortunate part of this situation was that Drusus Festus's plans to visit his girlfriend were not something he shared with us until the last minute. That meant I had to check in with Omari in closely timed bursts and stick with him until it became clear that the boss wasn't budging for the evening. It also meant I had to string the team along. I told them that I thought we'd found the amulet and that we were planning to lift it.

When Festus visited Felicia Germanica again, we decided to use the opportunity for a dry run. We still hadn't completed working out all the kinks for our complete escape. The basic outline was that we'd take the goods (I made the case that the tray might be worth something for sale or barter) and return to the Festus villa only long enough to grab our pre-packed belongings, snag Citro—who naturally insisted on coming with us— and flee south to Parthenope. There, we would establish our creds and sail for Egypt.

The whole evening went as slick as water off a loon's back. The placement of the tray and the flickering of the braziers in the hall practically guaranteed that it would be morning before anyone noticed its absence. And if we did have time to remove the canopic jars and papyrus, leaving the tray behind, then the theft would take even longer to notice.

Next time, for sure, we told ourselves. Tonight, we'd go back to the Festus villa, pack, and have a quick word with Citro.

No doubt, you are expecting me to tell you that it didn't exactly go as planned. Best laid plans of mice and men, yada, yada. And, yes, that is exactly what I'm going to tell you. Not only did things not go the way we planned, they went spectacularly wrong pretty much from the moment we got back to our master's villa. We'd no more than entered the house when the cook approached us with a puzzled expression on his face.

"Marcellus," he said, "might I trouble you to come back to the kitchens with me? There's someone here asking questions about … well, I think they're asking about you, sir."

The first thing that crossed our collective mind was that someone had followed us on one of our forays to and from the master's warehouses and was going to either report us to Festus or blackmail us.

Tough, we thought. We were going to be out of here in short order. The master had already begun to consider when he could visit Felicia next. She apparently couldn't get enough of him, and her father was off again for a day or two to look at some vineyard or other to the south—apparently in an area not plagued by roaming Visigoths.

We hesitantly followed the cook to the back of the villa where the kitchens and laundry were located. The kitchen was lit with the ruddy light of the hearth fires, the smell of baking bread filling the warm air. Liuva sat at the kitchen's large plank counter with a mug of something in front of her. She did not look happy. She glared at us, then jerked her head toward the stairs that went up to an external door.

"Here he is," she said, "the master's Egyptian favorite. Is he the one you want?"

We only just realized that someone stood at the bottom of the steps. Someone wearing a hooded robe. We swallowed, and peered at the person warily. They weren't all that tall, so if they offered physical threat, we could probably take them. Omari didn't have martial arts training, but I did.

The person stepped into the red light of the hearth and raised their hands to push back their hood. Shaking hands, we realized.

"Don't you know me, Omarius?" she said.

Yeah. She. Capital S. As in Sennia.

Omari hit me with a great wave of emotional chaos, crossed the room in three strides, and flung himself to his knees in front of his beloved. He threw his arms around her waist and sobbed into the front of her robe.

Short form: My ride was a wreck. So was I. So were our plans. I had to fight to keep him from bolting right this minute before Drusus Festus's next visit to his mistress, which would be the very next night.

Ignoring Liuva's Death Star glare, he led Sennia to his quarters, where he told her of how he and Citro had been scheming to steal Imhotep's relics and return to Egypt. Now that God had reunited them, he proposed that he should feign sickness so the two of them could slip off together while the master was away. I played Devil's Advocate; on the other hand, the plan was close to fruition. What harm in carrying it through and returning to Egypt with the artifacts? I played the Sacred Duty Card, reminding Omari that he had assigned himself a Mission, and that he was only a day away from fulfilling it. He was too overcome with joy and passion to listen.

In the end, it was Sennia who got through to my headstrong host.

"I am near the end of my resources, Beloved," she told us, covering our hands with her own, "for I have been seeking you for long months, alone and against the will of my family. I had only a portion of my dowry and the proceeds from selling my jewelry to bring me here. If it were not for the kindness of a priest in Catabathmus Maior, I would not have known you were sent to Rome, let alone have the resources to reach here. If this treasure from the tomb of Imhotep is as dear as you say, then might we not be able to sell some small pieces to finance our journey home?"

Omari gave that several moments of thought while I held my breath, figuratively speaking. It was true he'd described the canopic tray to Sennia as a marvelous treasure. He agreed that some portion of that treasure could help them return to Egypt. I cannot describe my relief. We spent the next hour or so plotting our escape.

That was not, however, the way Omari and Sennia wanted to spend the entire night. After the plotting was all done and they'd exchanged stories of adventure and anguish, they lapsed into silence. Then, he touched her cheek, she turned into the touch and kissed his palm, and that started a sort of cascade effect that I absolutely did not want cascading its way into my body back in the lab. There was only one way out and I took it.

"Peter?"

I blinked into Victoria's worried face, then had a seriously YOLO impulse. I took her face in my hands and kissed her. I heard someone clear their throat and someone else giggle. Tough.

Victoria drew back and looked at me. "Liuva?"

I shook my head. "You're not going to believe this: Sennia. Sennia found Omari. On the eve of his ... mission."

"She what?" said Otis, and Sophie gasped.

"She tracked him down, all the way to Rome. All the way to the praetor's villa."

We adjourned to Vic's office for the formal debriefing, during which I referred to the object of my quest as "the item" or "the artifact" so I wouldn't accidentally refer to it as the papyrus. Afterward we ate a meal. I didn't pay too much attention to which one. I thought about goals—mine and Omari's—and how mixed up they'd gotten in my own mind. His goal—his real goal

—was to return to Memphis with Sennia, make her his wife (not necessarily in that order), and take up his old life of scholarly and diplomatic pursuits. Returning Imhotep's body parts to the necropolis and his wisdom to scholars.

My goal was not to return the papyrus anywhere. I had to either hide it so well it would still be wherever I put it in the twenty-first century, or burn it to ashes. But—and it was a big but—I also felt compelled to help my ancestor get back to Memphis where he and Sennia could give birth to another generation that led, eventually, to me. I will admit, here and now, that I also just wanted the poor guy to be happy. After everything I'd put him through, it seemed like the least I could do.

Vic and I decided I had time for one more dive today. I had mixed feelings about that. Yes, I wanted to set Omari and Sennia to rights and I wanted to finally get my hands on that damned papyrus, but I also had strong feelings about spending the evening with Victoria and whatever that might lead to. Here was a woman that would be neither offended nor frightened if I suddenly started babbling in Egyptian in the middle of my marriage proposal.

I had the feeling she'd even take it in stride if I cried out "Sennia!" in the throes of passion. Question was, if I went back to working for the NYPD running drug busts and murder investigations, would she also take that in stride? Lauren had gotten the cop part of my life, but not the time diving. Vic accepted the time diver; would she accept the cop?

I must have looked extra pensive as Victoria adjusted my neural cap for the dive, because she leaned in close and murmured, "You okay?"

"Yeah, fine. Why?"

"You look worried, and before you came back earlier, you were crying."

I swallowed. "Omari got a little *ferklempt* when he saw

Sennia. There were times he was pretty sure he'd never see her again."

"Softie," she called me and kissed my forehead.

"She reminds me of you," I said—blurted, actually. Like a verbal sneeze.

"Really?"

"Yeah. I mean, she doesn't look like you, exactly, but she's beautiful, intelligent, brave, resourceful..."

"Apparently. She'd have to be to track her fiancé all the way across the Mediterranean to Rome against her parents' wishes." She sent me into the past with a kiss (making Soph giggle again).

I surfaced in the midst of Omari's eleventh-hour planning. Sennia had purchased a horse when she'd gotten to Rome; Omari gave her some of his own earnings to purchase two more for him and Citro. The plan was for her to take the horses and await the two men in a lane that ran along the eastern wall of Festus's villa. Citro had already taken possession of Omari's belongings and would take them there.

Drusus Festus never spent the entire night with his lover. He liked to leave her right around midnight so there was no chance of him being seen coming home in the wee hours. It pleased him to keep up the pretense that he was engaged in business with the lady's father, Eliphas.

Earlier, I mentioned things going wrong. They weren't quite done doing that. Whereas previously Festus and his mistress would enjoy food and drink in her private chambers, for some reason—twisted sense of divine humor, godly boredom, maybe —they didn't do that tonight. They had their meal in the main banquet room, which was right behind the reception hall. The chamber I'd expected would be deserted most of the evening was alight and populated by scurrying servants and slaves, which included both Omari and Felicia's body servant—a strapping young gladiator type.

At long last, the lovers withdrew to the lady's rooms, the house staff cleared the banquet hall, snuffed most of the lamps, and retired to their part of the villa. Omari and I dined with them, then excused ourself to take our master a change of clothing he hadn't requested. The reception hall was lit only by the braziers nearest Imhotep's casket. We carried the mostly empty pack we'd brought with us into the hall and set it down next to the low table that held the canopic tray.

Here, I realized yet again that my ancestor did pretty well for himself when left to his own devices. In my absence, he'd somehow acquired a brass tray of approximately the same size and depth as the one we were about to steal. He pulled it out of our satchel and set it on the floor, then picked up the canopic tray—jars and all—and put it into the big bag, carefully packing the master's change of clothing around it. The last step was to replace the original tray with the fake.

We returned to the servant's quarters to await the praetor's departure. It was one of the longest nights of our conjoined life. Or well, nearly so. Its competition was our shared first night in a wooden cage and my first night alone after Lauren dumped me, after all. We made merry with our fellow slaves and thought of Sennia.

Sometime in the depth of night, my master emerged from his lady's boudoir and summoned us for the ride home. He was fast asleep by the time we got back to his villa; we had to wake him and half-carry him to his rooms. We stood for a moment in the hallway outside Festus's suite of rooms, shivering a bit in anticipation of the adventure to come. There was no need to return to our own quarters—Citro would have already removed everything. There was only one thing to do.

Carrying the heavy satchel, we went out through the kitchens into the rear court where there was a vendor's entrance in the perimeter wall. Citro and Sennia met us in the narrow lane with horses. Mounted, we headed for a main north-south avenue.

"We should take care," Citro said. "There are Visigoth forces in the countryside. They range mostly to the north and east, but we must look sharp to avoid them."

Visigoths. Check. Reason enough to get out of Rome. Now, my question was what I should do—skip back to Manhattan, or stick around and look for the first opportunity to get my hands (well, Omari's hands, anyway) on the papyrus. I was pondering this in the corner of Omari's mind when Sennia cried out.

We glanced over at her to find her pointing upward toward the treetops to the east. The night sky seemed to literally be on fire. Lurid red light washed across the bellies of the low-hanging clouds. The Visigoths had apparently gotten bored with harassing farmers and spooking the Senate and decided to press on into Rome. Before we'd gone a mile, we saw flames leaping above the rooftops and heard the far-off sounds of conflict.

"We must hurry!" Citro drew his sword and urged us forward. He herded us into a north-south street, angling away from what I had to assume were Visigoth hordes.

We cut a zigzag pattern through the streets of Rome, which became increasingly clogged with other fleeing people. Most of them seemed to be heading toward the sea. Citro opted to keep us weaving our way south. So we were pretty much on our own when we reached a small market square and ran headlong into a group of large armed men blocking our southward progress.

We turned west. More armed men blocked that exit as well. Ditto to the east. Naturally, when we did an about-face, we saw more of these guys behind us. A particularly impressive man stepped out from this last group and pointed his weapon at Citro.

"Drop your sword, soldier," he said in strangely accented … Latin, I guess.

Citro looked to Omari, perfectly willing to give his life if we asked it.

Wearily, we shook our head. "Stand down, Citro," we said, and to the Visigoths: "We surrender. I am Omarius Statius Prisca, vicarius to Prefect Flavius Anthemius of Memphis. This is my betrothed, Sennia Donata Honoria and the captain of my guard, Citro Superstes. We were leaving Rome to return to Memphis. I beg you to allow us to continue our journey."

That didn't work, of course, so we passed into the keeping of Alaric, king of the Visigoths, and the Papyrus of Imhotep slipped out of our hands yet again.

DURING OUR TREK out of Rome, I thought about escaping to Manhattan ... for all of a split second. I couldn't bring myself to bail on Omari now. I'd stick it out, at least until I could deliver everyone to some sort of safety. In the meantime, I'd keep Omari's ears and eyes open for any opportunity to ensure that safety.

The Visigoth soldiers took my introduction at face value, and treated us with something like deference. We were taken to the camp of the Visigoth king, and were deposited in a large, comfortable tent that gave a whole new dimension to the phrase "camping out." It wasn't opulent, by any means, but it was far from the spartan quarters I'd imagined I'd find in a military camp. Not long after, Citro was separated from us. I suspected he'd end up a conscript in the king's army unless a miracle occurred.

Omari and Sennia spent the rest of the night alone, but for a servant who brought us bowls of steaming stew and returned our baggage to us—minus the tomb goods, of course. Omari did not sleep and I did not abandon him. We sat up until dawn, watching over Sennia. In the morning, both of us were taken to Alaric's tent to speak to the man himself.

It was an interesting conversation. The first thing the Visigoth king said was, "You told my men you were vicarius to an Egyptian prefect. Why did you seek to mislead them?"

We were a bit taken aback. "I did not mislead anyone. I am Omarius Statius Prisca—"

"Slave."

Sennia made a mewing sound, and Omari's hand went to his neck.

"Yes," Alaric said, "my manservant saw your mark when he brought you food last night. Did you imagine we would kill you if you admitted your low status?"

"No. I imagined that your men might allow an Egyptian juris to return home. I have been a slave for the past two years, it's true. But I am who and what I claim to be—vicarius to the newly elevated Prefect of Memphis. I was taken against my will by tomb raiders, brought to Rome, and installed in the house of a praetor as his secretary. My man, Citro, was also enslaved to the same house."

Alaric sat back in his camp chair and stared us down. "Truly," he said, at last. "Did your master here in Rome know your tale of woe?"

We smiled wryly. "Oh, yes. They were his tomb raiders ... and Roman legionnaires."

The king, who had up until now also been a Roman official, sneered and shook his head. "You see, Ataulf," he said glancing aside at his lieutenant, who stood by watching with a stony expression, "you see how corruption has eaten into the vitals of this society? Roman officials send Roman soldiers off to deprive other citizens of their freedom and property." He turned back to us. "And the fair lady—is she also a slave?"

Sennia did something that we probably should have

expected. She squared her shoulders and came to stand next to us, wrapping her hands around our arm. Then she fixed the king with a direct gaze and said, "I am no slave, sir. I am what Omarius has claimed me to be: a Roman citizen and daughter of a magistrate. My beloved was taken from me on the day of our wedding and I have sought him for more than a year. I had just found him when..." Her voice faltered.

"We were fleeing back to our homeland," Omari said, "when your men found us."

Alaric actually growled. "This," he said, gesturing at us, "is why we have, at last, crushed the government of Rome. They bleed their own people and grow fat on the gore. Well, Omarius Prisca, I would release you, but with that mark on your neck, you would be safe nowhere. And my army is soon to march to Africa."

"Then we could go with you!" Omari blurted.

Alaric shook his head. "You forget what it is we mean to do in Africa, Omarius Prisca. You were a Roman official. You would find no place there."

Damn. "Then what will you do with us?" we asked, putting a protective arm around Sennia.

"I propose to send you north to my capital in Toulouse. There, that mark upon your neck will mean nothing."

"I would be free?" Omari asked.

"You would be free."

Well, that was something. "And my man Citro? He has been the best of protectors and fell into slavery only because of his loyalty to me."

Alaric glanced at his second again, and something passed between the two men.

"You have impressed me, Omarius Prisca, with your qualities of loyalty and perseverance. Is there something you would ask of me, aside from returning you to Egypt?"

We glanced at Sennia. "If we could be married, my lord..."

The Visigoth king smiled. "An easy request to grant. Ataulf, will you find Father Silvio and send him to me?"

Ataulf inclined his head. "A pleasure, sire," he said and went off on his errand.

Feeling as if things might finally be falling into place for Omari, we bowed to our new liege, Alaric. "We shall prove the most loyal of subjects, my lord," we said.

"I shall prove a generous lord, Omarius Prisca," Alaric replied.

He did, indeed, prove generous. Upon discovering what Omari's duties had been in the houses of Anthemius and Festus, he appointed us steward-secretary to Ataulf who, it turned out, was not only his lieutenant, but his brother-in-law. Omari began his life as a married man with a secure job as right-hand man to Visigoth royalty.

You're no doubt wondering about the canopic tray. We asked about it, actually, claiming it was a sort of family heirloom and wondering if we might have it back. The answer was a resounding *no*. It seems the king's steward had the jars opened and was thoroughly disgusted when he recognized the withered contents. While Sennia and Omari cooled their heels in the king's "guest tent," the steward had burned the viscera and consigned the tray to a northbound caravan hauling looted goods to the king's capital.

In a way it was a relief to have the damned papyrus beyond Omari's reach. If it had remained in camp, or if he'd been riding the northbound train himself, I'd've felt compelled to keep after it. Hell, who was I kidding? Omari was by now as motivated as I was to run the tray to ground even though there was a popsicle's chance in hell of him ever getting the papyrus back to Egypt. Besides, I had no doubt that, if he were found trying to pilfer from his new lord after everything Alaric had done for him, Ataulf would have his head on a pike. So, I saw Omari and Sennia off to Toulouse and went back to Manhattan further from the papyrus than I'd ever been.

20

WHERE IN THE WORLD IS IMHOTEP'S PAPYRUS?

"Y ou're telling us we're dead in the water, aren't you?" Otis had a way of cutting to the chase that I found I couldn't appreciate at the moment.

"No," I said. "I'm telling you we need to find another angle. The item apparently makes its way to Toulouse, so…"

"So that's how it ends up in Salzburg," said Otis, following my train of thought.

The whole team was huddled in the lab after my return from the Sack of Rome. I'd parted company with Omari only after making sure his marriage to Sennia was a done deal and discovering that the canopic tray had been absorbed into the general pile of loot the Visigoths amassed.

Victoria and I exchanged glances. We both knew we were talking about the papyrus and Otis was talking about the amulet, but we both suspected that the two artifacts might very well have ended up in the same place. If the amulet had made its way to my ancestor's museum in Salzburg, Austria, in one timeline, then the tray might well have done the same in this new one.

"What do you propose?" asked Drew. "Do you think Omari might find it when he gets to Toulouse?"

"The treasure belongs to Alaric. Omari belongs to his brother-in-law, Ataulf."

"*Vraiment*," said Sophie. "True, but Alaric is not going to live much past the Sack of Rome, and Ataulf is going to inherit the throne and any treasures that go with it. Perhaps in coming years, Omari could find the amulet."

"And do what with it, Soph?" I asked. "There's no way he's going to be able to get back to Egypt with it."

"He doesn't need to," Drew said. "He only needs to get his hands on the amulet so that you can dismantle it and squeeze the location of the papyrus out of it."

Which, of course, I'd already done in a manner of speaking.

"Assuming that information is contained in the amulet," said Theron. He leaned against the wall next to the door of his office, arms crossed over his chest, looking saturnine in a Doctor Strange sort of way and making me wonder all over again what the hell Vic saw in me.

"Nebemakhet said it was," said Drew patiently. "And the glyphs on the back of the scarab clearly relate to Imhotep. The other gods mentioned must be a sort of code. Peter said the scarab was set into the brass mounting. Maybe the code is hidden in the mounting somewhere. Possibly beneath the scarab itself."

I met Theron's eyes. We needed to get the team busy doing something while we figured out what to do next.

"We need to do some more research in the here and now," Theron said, levering himself away from the wall. "We know the amulet ends up in bad condition in a Salzburg museum. What we don't know is where it was before that. Sophie and Otis, I'd like you to see if you can't get a historical perspective on this. What happened to the treasure that Alaric sent back up into northern Europe? Known artifacts from the Sack of Rome might connect us to the more obscure ones. Get on the Internet, bring in experts if you have to. See if you can identify other artifacts that might have been in the same loot train with our item."

He turned to Drew and Harald next. "I'm not giving up on the biotech angle either. See if you can find anything in historical material that suggests a provenance for the bionic and AI tech we take for granted. If we can pinpoint a juncture at which that tech entered the ancient world, we might be able to at least run our saboteur to ground, figure out who he is, and make sure he and the item don't come into contact.

Drew nodded and corralled Harald, who looked as if he were having trouble following the conversation. Theron then beckoned Vic and me into his office.

"You're the detective, Peter," he told me when we were safely behind the closed door. "If this were a heist you were investigating, what would you do next?"

"Go to where evidence presented itself. The amulet is gone, but the tray was from the same heist and it might well have ended up in the same place—Eckart Metz's collection in Salzburg. There's only one way to find out."

Theron nodded. "All right, but what do we tell the rest of the team? They know the amulet in Metz's time is so damaged so as to be unreadable. You've presented it as a dead end. What rationale do we give for your returning there?"

I shrugged. "I tell them I'm desperate enough to hope I can pry what's left of the scarab off the mounting and see if there's anything underneath it. I tell them maybe I missed something. I tell them I want to get the Egyptian stuff out of the museum before it's stolen by Nazis or destroyed by allied bombers."

"I don't know, Peter," said Victoria. "That sounds lame even to me."

"Then maybe we tell them part of the truth—that I've had an epiphany about the amulet and that I think maybe it refers to another artifact that might be in Eckart's trove."

Theron quirked an eyebrow. "When do you want to have your epiphany?"

I HAD MY "EPIPHANY" during the night and came steaming into the lab early the next morning with Victoria in tow. The other members of the team were still wandering in when I launched into an impassioned description of my alleged breakthrough.

"I had a sort of epiphany last night," I said.

"Is that what it was?" murmured Victoria, who'd been with me all night.

I looked at her. "More of a revelation, maybe."

"Don't keep us in suspense," complained Otis. "If you've got something that will keep me from more hours of scouring museum databases, I'm all ears."

I sat at my station and looked up at their eager faces. I felt a wriggle of discomfort about lying to them, but one of them might be our shadowy adversary.

"I kept thinking about the glyphs on the back of Imhotep's amulet. And I think I may have interpreted them incorrectly. I think the reference to Anubis is in his role as Guardian of the Tomb. I think the other glyphs are a reference to another element *in* the tomb. I think the amulet is pointing to a second artifact. A particular piece of funerary gear."

"You mentioned a ship," Sophie said, "and a house."

I nodded, thanking her silently for feeding me lines. "Yes. The ship is the vehicle that carries the soul to the afterlife; the house is where the soul is supposed to live when it gets there."

Sophie smiled brilliantly. "Then, we need to be looking for other artifacts from the same burial."

"Exactly. So, I want to go back to Salzburg and see if any of those artifacts are in Eckart Metz's collection."

Otis clapped his hands together. "Fantastic. Let's get on it."

We got on it. I routed myself to Salzburg, threading the Great Needle of Time in the hope of getting there before A) the Nazis removed anything of import or B) the Allies bombed the crap out of the place. I either needed to remove the papyrus (if it was even there) or make sure it got bombed to oblivion. What I could not do was allow it to survive—most especially, I could not allow it to fall into the hands of the Nazis.

It was not comforting to realize that it had not fallen into their hands in the original un-monkeyed-with timeline. I was beginning to feel as if everything I was doing in the cause of Good was having an equal and opposite effect.

Damn Newton.

I collided with Eckart while on his way to the museum on a particularly blustery spring day. He was in high dudgeon, because a colleague had just told him something that made him realize the Nazis' pains to seem disinterested in the Egyptian trove actually meant that they were *very* interested in the Egyptian trove.

Before I could fully grasp what he meant to do, we burst into the halls of the museum to confront Gray Suit and his cohort. Gray Suit had a name, which Eckart now knew: Berend Beckmann. Herr Beckmann was in the Egyptian gallery, overseeing an inventory of the collection. His minions had laid the artifacts out on the floor of the gallery and photographed, took measurements, and jotted things in little leather bound notebooks.

"What do you think you're doing?" Eckart demanded, planting us firmly in the main entry to the exhibit.

Herr Beckmann turned to fix us with a cool gaze that eloquently informed us that we were a Minor Annoyance. "What does it look as if we are doing, Professor? We are cataloguing this collection."

"I have already catalogued the collection, Herr Beckmann. Your activity is redundant."

"Yes, but you have catalogued everything, even hand lamps and other minutiae. We are cataloguing only those items of religious significance, which we are also assigning inventory numbers so that they may be integrated into the Führer's collection."

An icy chill shot through us—equal parts Eckart's and mine. Only one of us realized the real stakes here. Eckart feared for his beloved artifacts; I feared for the fate of humanity if someone like, say, Dr. Mengele were to get his hands on Imhotep's bloody papyrus.

Calm down, Peter, I told myself. Maybe Beckmann wouldn't see the canopic tray as a religious artifact.

I exerted as much control of Eckart as I dared, prompting him to take a quick visual inventory of the items the Nazis had hauled out. We saw a sort of refuse pile on a tarp in one corner of the gallery floor that mostly contained now-broken shards of lamps, bowls, cups, and other apparent household items.

Eckart's sense of outrage gave way momentarily to wry contempt. How stupid these men were if they didn't recognize the religious significance of those bowls and goblets. Not to mention the *ushebtis* they'd discarded as if they were a child's dolls.

"Herr Beckmann," Eckart said, "I take it you are not an academic."

Beckmann bristled. "I am *Professor* Beckmann, of the Berlin Historical Institute."

Eckart gave him a scorching sneer. "Really? Yet you toss these ceremonial goblets and bowls into the refuse bin? The Führer will be disappointed."

During this little speech, guaranteed to gain Eckart *Professor* Beckmann's enduring friendship, I took stock of the pile. No tray. Beckmann, face going red, directed one of his lackeys to cull the goblets and bowls out of the rejects. Meanwhile, I turned to the artifacts laid out on the floor.

There was the tray—scraped, dented, but still obviously valuable—in a group of similarly sized artifacts.

I took the reins and prodded my host sharply. We moved to pick up the tray, then turned back to Beckmann. "And this," we said, holding it carelessly. "A simple serving tray, you wish to keep? You think this will impress your leader more than goblets that once held ritual wine and ale?"

Beckmann looked as if he might explode. "It was described as a funerary item in your own inventory. Are you saying it is not?"

"We are staffed by students from the college," we said. "They sometimes make mistakes in evaluating our finds."

"He's lying."

Beckmann and Eckart both spun to face the speaker. It was one of those very students—an undergraduate named Elmar Pagel, who occasionally helped his professor in cataloguing acquisitions and keeping the gallery records up to date. He was now apparently helping the Nazis dismantle the collection we'd taken pains to gather.

The young man stepped forward, his eyes intense. I felt a mental shiver that had nothing to do with Eckart's feelings about his dear artifacts ... or about the lies I'd made him tell just now to protect them. I was facing the other time diver. I was sure of it.

"That is a canopic tray, unless I am very much mistaken," he said. "The jars have been lost, but you can see the insets intended to hold them. Professor Metz has some ulterior reason to protect that artifact. He seeks to mislead you. I can only wonder why. Perhaps it has some significance beyond its apparent purpose."

Beckmann's narrowed gaze moved to the tray. "Why thank you, Herr Pagel. I think we must discover why the professor takes such pains to protect this particular piece." He made a snapping gesture with one hand. "Arrest this man," he ordered the ever-watchful guards.

Three of his soldiers converged on us. Eckart's first impulse was to run, but I knew if we ran, we'd be dead. Or rather he would. I just managed to keep my host from making that mistake. One man came to stand in front of us while the other two took up flanking positions on either side.

"Give it to me," the first soldier ordered and snatched at the tray.

We resisted, but it was futile, and I knew it. I prodded Eckart to let go of the tray. He did. The guard fell backward, tripped over another artifact, and hit the floor with a windy, "Oof!"

Eckart and I both heard the sound of something rattling inside the tray and saw the fine rain of coarse dust that sifted onto the soldier's uniform. Only one of us knew what it meant: The papyrus was disintegrating. We felt the grasp of strong hands on our arms. As much as I hated to do it, I abandoned Eckart and fled back to Manhattan to regroup.

I came out of the time dive, eyes open, mind leaping in fifty directions at once. After years of subjective time with no sign of the other diver, he shows up again. Why? More importantly, how? How would he know the artifact might be in Salzburg? The only answer I had to that wasn't one I liked: The saboteur was part of Project Backstory after all.

I also took some precious mental processing time to register the fact that I'd just exposed the fib about what I'd been looking for. I'd essentially painted a big fat target on Imhotep's canopic tray, and if my adversary hadn't figured out that the papyrus itself was now in play, he'd get it when he pried apart the tray and found the moldering remains.

Now, I took quick stock of who was in the Backstory lab and who wasn't. My surprise was momentary; then it made a sort of sense ... if I was right. The absence could be sheer coincidence.

There was only one way to be sure. The question at that point became where I'd be the most effective—searching the institute for a second transference rig or doing what I probably should have done instead of following the trail to Salzburg.

"There may be another GCT setup in the building somewhere," I told Vic, "and I need to dive again, right now."

She nodded and turned toward her computer. "Initiate August transference."

I didn't hear the sound of metal on metal that sent me back along my ancestral line. I was too busy praying I'd end up where I intended.

21

THERE AND BACK AGAIN

menaru and I strode into the necropolis at Saqqara as if we were on a mission from God, even though underneath our priestly robes we were sweating like crazy and surprised at our own *chutzpah*. The guards treated us to disinterested glances and gave sloppy salutes, barely even pausing their conversation. We were just a priest doing whatever it is that priests do around tomb complexes. Apparently no big deal.

Of course, poor Amenaru's idea of what we were doing was sketchy, to say the least. I'd caught that he didn't like Nebemakhet all that much and felt he'd make a far better companion for the Doctor-God. With some prompting from me, he had come to the conclusion that, whether he did anything about it or not, he very much wanted to know what great, mysterious knowledge the high priest had that he was being so miserly with.

So, late on an afternoon, we marched past the guardians of the necropolis and I got my first look at the City of the Dead in all its glory. The walls of the Djoser complex were intact and glowing with vivid color in the lowering sunlight. The pyramid of Djoser was still clad in a gleaming sheath of white limestone. I was in awe of the place, but I relied on Amenaru to act like he'd been here—and he had been here on occasional memorial days to lay offerings on an altar at the base of the Djoser pyramid.

At this point in the life of the monument, the slab that hid the entrance of Imhotep's tomb was indistinguishable from all the other slabs that covered the lowest course of the stepped structure. I did some quick calculations, using the itty bitty mastaba in the front corner of the larger pyramid as a reference point. I also took a calculated risk; I gave my host a swift flash of memory of the line drawing of the pyramid as etched into the hidden underside of Imhotep's amulet. He'd seen it, of course, the night we destroyed the medallion, but he'd relegated the knowledge to dream status. Now, I used it to give him an "aha" moment and the realization that the entrance to Imhotep's tomb was hidden beneath a piece of the pyramid's limestone cladding.

Amenaru supplied the surprising knowledge that he was familiar with the lever system used to seal such discreet entrances. I'd come across references to it in some of my online research, but all I had was speculation about how such doors had worked. My ancestor had studied engineering drawings done both by Imhotep and his daddy, and had actually seen some of these doors in operation. Question was: How was *this* door opened? I was pretty sure "open sesame" was not going to do the trick. I'd only seen this part of the complex as a pile of rubble and a hole in the ground, so I wasn't much help. But I did know that the hole in the ground lay along a nearly straight line from the western corner of the little mastaba.

I gave Amenaru a gentle poke and we slipped into the notch behind the mastaba and turned to face the pyramid. This was in deep shadow; late afternoon wasn't a bad time for a little breaking and entering. We walked forward until we stood where we could see the faint lines that marked the edges of a slab five feet tall and six feet wide. We scanned the lines, looking for some indication of the locking mechanism. We found it roughly a third of the way up the left edge of the slab—an almost invisible scoring in the limestone that made a perfect rectangle about the size of a brick.

Amenaru's pulse quickened and, without any help from me, he put his hand on the rectangle and pushed. It scraped downward about an inch, then stopped. He pressed again, but nothing happened. Leaning closer, we realized that there was a gap between the main slab and the smaller block big enough to insert three fingers. We did just that, and pulled. The block moved out, and the limestone slab rotated on a fulcrum, leaving a slot barely big enough for a man to slip into if he bent double.

We glanced around. To our right, we could see the bulk of the "front" side of Djoser's pyramid and the open courtyard before it. To our left, we could see to the end of the notch. There were no guards in sight on either side.

We dug in our satchel for one of the hand lamps we'd brought. Amenaru lit it expertly using flint and steel, then we ducked into the darkness of the tomb's entry. Now we were dependent on my memories of being here with Omari—on my sense of how far we'd had to venture down the corridor before taking that first right-hand turn. I found myself superimposing the rubble-filled tunnels I'd encountered over this almost pristine hallway with all of its sharp lines and squared corners. Our little hand lamp didn't afford much light. I would've killed for even something as low-tech as a Coleman lantern.

We counted cross-corridors and turned right at the fourth one. In another thirty feet, we were offered a choice of left or right and chose right again. And again. And again.

When we reached it, the door of the burial chamber was bracketed by stands containing lamps darkened long ago. There were a dozen of them on each stand, but only five of them had oil. We lit those and filled four more from a flask in our satchel.

By their light, we were able to find the locking mechanism for the inner chamber. We'd never seen it activated, but Amenaru understood the locking mechanisms from the designs that Imhotep himself had devised. It wasn't unlike the mechanism of the outer door. A particular block pushed in and over, and we were then able to shove the door to one side in a stone track. It took almost every ounce of strength in Amenaru's body, but we managed to push the door back enough to squeeze inside.

A narrow fan of light from the brace of lamps in the corridor fell across the floor of the chamber and onto the sarcophagus. We reached back through to grab a second hand lamp and went straight for the head of the stone coffin. We set both of the lamps on the altar, then knelt to peer into the shelf that contained the canopic jars in their fancy tray. The etchings and jewels in the tray glittered in the lamp light.

We reached in and pulled the tray out, and I have to say, I almost quaked with the expectation that someone was going to appear to rip it out of our hands again. I couldn't let myself think like that. I shook off the sense of dread. We took the canopic jars out of the tray and placed them gently atop the sarcophagus—one at each corner, because Amenaru wasn't content to just put them any old where. Things had to be done according to his sense of ritual.

With that done, we turned back to the altar to examine the tray. The bottom of the thing was a bit thicker than it needed to be to hold the jars. It had a false bottom. We pulled out a dagger we'd brought, but the tip was too thick to fit into the tiny line where two pieces of brass had been joined together. We needed something thinner. Something like ...

We looked around. Laid out on the altar were some of the Divine Doctor's surgical implements. We snatched up one that had a wide, paper-thin blade and used it to pry the false bottom from the tray. I thought we were going to have to force it, but when we got the surgical knife wiggled around to one corner of the shallow box, there was a *tick!* sound, and the bottom simply came off.

I could hardly believe it. After all I'd been through (and all I'd put various ancestors through), I was finally going to lay eyes on this elusive scrap of history. It wasn't all that impressive to look at: a thin folio made up of maybe a dozen sheets of papyrus held together by a simple wooden clamp. Amenaru was every bit as excited about this as I was. His hands shook as he laid the folio out on the altar and began to read it by the light of the lamps.

I didn't understand half of it, but that wasn't necessary to my being able to reproduce the images, and Amenaru understood enough of the contents to provide context. Yes, Imhotep believed he could transfer a human brain from one body to another.

Having done a few postmortems as Nebemakhet's sub-priest, Amenaru understood the principles well enough to grasp the overwhelming nature of the great man's research. The first pages of the papyrus laid out the basic principles of the surgery; the rest went into great detail about the task of reconnecting the "life lines," as Imhotep called the nerves and veins. He didn't describe an entire surgery, but rather described the reattachment of one nerve and one vein in excruciating detail.

It was stunning reading and, like I said, I didn't understand the half of it. I just took the best mental snapshots of the pages I could. Even with my lack of medical knowledge, I could see how this revolutionary stuff could become a moral nightmare in the hands of the unscrupulous and greedy. I debated destroying it— first with myself, then with Amenaru, who was not at all down with desecrating the sacred.

I compromised. We tucked the pages into our satchel, then swiftly reassembled the canopic tray and returned it and the jars to their proper place.

It should be dark above ground now. If we were lucky, we'd

get away clean with the papyrus and hide it someplace that would keep any future someones from being able to retrieve it without specific knowledge of where it was. We were reasonably crafty guys, me and Amenaru. I figured we could come up with something.

As we squeezed back out through the stone door of the burial chamber, we heard movement in the darkness of the corridor we'd have to pass through to do that whole getting away clean thing. It was a very faint sound and made all the hair on our body stand up in waves of awareness that we were in a dark, claustrophobic place with tons of rock overhead. On top of that reality, given all the twists and turns in the passages, that sound could be coming from anywhere in the maze.

We snuffed all the little lamps but one, then rushed back up the corridor, taking the turns in the opposite direction, our entire focus on breaking through to the clean desert air. When we could see moonlight peeking through the half-open entrance of the tomb, we jogged toward it.

With the suddenness of a gasp, the moonlight disappeared, which could only mean one thing—something or someone was blocking the entrance. We slid to a stop, bringing our knife to hand, but keeping it out of sight. "Hello?" we said.

A man dressed in priestly robes stepped into the flickering light of our hand lamp. For a moment I feared it was Nebemakhet. If the high priest caught Amenaru creeping about his lord's tomb at night there would be hell to pay.

But it wasn't Nebemakhet.

"Well, Abet, old friend," I greeted him, shoving past my host's surprise, "or should I address you as Drew?"

After a prolonged moment of total stillness, Abet asked, "How did you know?"

"It pretty much had to be someone on the team, Professor. The other time diver showed up in Salzburg not long ago. When I got back to the lab, you were the only one who wasn't in the room. I figure you must have your own sweet little setup somewhere in the MIN building. Right?"

Abet-Drew blinked. "Really? You think you can get me to monologue like a bad movie villain? I'm not your arch-nemesis, Detective. I'm just a man trying to save someone he loves."

"Your daughter," I guessed. "Her condition is more serious than you've admitted to anyone."

"My daughter," my adversary agreed. "The bionic tech I planted in my genetic timeline helped her a great deal. She has a mesh exoskeleton that has kept her muscles from atrophying and allowed her to continue to go to school, but eventually, the disease will destroy her joints completely, and when it does, she will waste away and die." Tears slid down the big man's face. They glistened in the light of my lamp. "So, Peter, I'm sure you understand why I have no more time to chat. You will give me the papyrus."

As Amenaru wondered who the hell Dru and Peeter were, I said, "Why would I do that?"

Abet brought a sword out from behind the folds of his robe.

"Good argument," I said, "but nope. I can't let you have it. Not sure what you'd do with it anyway. I mean it's not like you can take snapshots—"

"You're not the only member of Backstory with a photographic memory."

"Ah. Well. In that case—" We dashed our hand lamp to the stone floor where it shattered, spewing oil and flame. A knee-high wall of fire shot up between us and Abet. We pulled out the papyrus and flung it into the flames.

Abet and Amenaru both shrieked with horror and Abet dove after it, but it was already too late. As he scrabbled on the floor, trying to collect enough sand to smother the flames, I took the opportunity to get poor, confused Amenaru to safety. We leapt the flames and scrambled out of the tomb. Behind us, we could hear Abet weeping. I pointed Amenaru back toward Memphis proper, and willed him to go home to bed, suggesting this was all a weird dream. Then I sang my way back to the lab.

"Drew!" The name was out of my mouth before I'd completely resurfaced. "He must have a time diving setup somewhere in his offices."

Everyone gaped at me. That is, everyone but Harald. He and Drew were both gone this time.

Gaping aside, no one doubted. They followed me down to Drew's third-floor offices. The small lab he shared with Harald was empty, as was his personal office, but as we crossed his office to the door of his private study, Harald squeezed out through the doorway to block our entry.

"You can't go in," he said. "The professor is in the middle of an experiment."

"Yeah, I know," I said. "I was there. Come on, Harald. Unless you've got some hidden kung fu we don't know about, I doubt you're going to keep me out of there."

I could see the wheels turning behind his cornflower blue eyes. I recognized the moment he decided to take a swing at me, so I was already responding to the wild punch he threw before he threw it. I grabbed his arm, shoved my hip against his, and flipped him onto the floor between me and the others. Otis and Sophie sat on him.

I pushed through into Drew's private sanctum, gesturing for the others to stay back. I had no idea what to expect. Drew Hastings was an aloof individual. Instinct told me he wasn't the kind to go on the attack, but grief can make people act in bizarre and dangerous ways.

Drew Hastings was still connected to his transference rig, weeping uncontrollably.

Victoria came through the door behind me, and shot me a puzzled look.

"It's his daughter," I said quietly. "She's sicker than he's let on."

Drew spoke then, his voice tight and strangled sounding. "She's dying. By inches. Because of you. Because of you, there will be no lifesaving transplant. No chance for her to live beyond the time allotted to her disintegrating body."

Another look from Victoria. "I knew she was ill, but ... what's wrong with her, Drew? Why have you done all this?"

"*Ankylosing spondylitis,*" Drew said. "It's degenerative and incurable. Right now, we keep ahead of it with physical therapy and her exo-suit. But she's only eleven. By the time she's twenty, her life will effectively be over." He opened his eyes and sent me a glance that was completely without anger. I saw only despair. "You've made sure of that."

"You introduced the bionics research somewhere, though, didn't you?" Victoria pressed. "Peter says that robotics and bionics are significantly more advanced now than when he started time diving."

Drew nodded, seeming to wilt into his chair. "Yes. I got it into the works of Al-Razi. But his research was tangential to the European Renaissance, not foundational like the work of Ibn Sina."

"So, why didn't you go back and try Ibn Sina?" I asked.

"You left me no time ... or perhaps I made poor choices. I felt I needed to follow you or try to get ahead of you when I knew where you were headed. And now, the precious knowledge of Imhotep—which might have put medical knowledge ahead by centuries—is gone. Utterly erased."

Well, maybe not utterly erased.

I turned to look at Theron Cornell, who stood in the doorway of Drew's study. "What now, boss?"

"Call the police?" Otis suggested from the outer office.

Harald responded with a strangled, "No!"

"I *am* the police," I observed, "and I can tell you right now, I wouldn't even know what charges to press. On either of you," I added, raising my voice so Harald could hear me.

"Let's go back up to the lab," Theron suggested. "All of us. We need to consider our options carefully."

Back upstairs in the main lab, Theron shut Drew and Harald in his office while the rest of us gathered around the conference table in Vic's. I described my last two encounters with Drew through his ancestral hosts, then Theron explained to Otis and Sophie about the steps we'd taken to not tip our hand to the unknown time diver. They both seemed to understand why we'd had to keep them in the dark.

"The question before us now," Theron said, "is: What do we do about Drew and Harald?"

I wasn't so sure that was the question. "Look, I know what Drew did was … reckless, dangerous, possibly unethical, and undoubtedly some things I haven't even contemplated yet. But I think the question is, what do we do about Drew's daughter?"

"What *can* we do about Drew's daughter?" Victoria asked.

I said what I was thinking. "Drew said he'd been able to get the bionic tech in front of Al-Razi, but that kept it from going mainstream. Let me go back and put it in a more prominent place. Let me give it to DaVinci or, better yet, Ibn Sina."

She stared at me for a long moment, during which none of the others even made a peep. She turned to look at Theron. "Ibn Sina's work would put the principles of biomimetics solidly in the mainstream."

"You want to do this?" Theron asked me. "After everything that's happened? He might have killed Amenaru before his time."

"It's his *kid*, Theron. His little girl. I can't imagine something I wouldn't try if someone I loved that much was dying right before my eyes and there was something I could do about it. And it's not just her. Think of all the other lives tech like this could save."

Theron looked around the table at the group of solemn faces. "What do we think?" he asked them.

Otis and Sophie shared a glance, then Otis said, "How soon do you want to dive?"

I smiled. "As soon as you can have Drew get me some drawings to memorize."

Otis grinned and hopped up from the table. "I'm on it. C'mon, Soph. You explain to Drew what we're doing; I'll grab an iPad and a stylus."

Theron, too, rose. "I don't know about the rest of you, but I'm starving. I'm going to brief Drew and Harald, then order us up something to eat."

Vic and I watched them scatter to their various missions.

"It's too bad about the Imhotep papyrus," she said wistfully. "To lose all of that knowledge..."

"It's not lost," I told her, tapping my temple. "It's all in here. Eidetic memory, remember? I made a point of going over the papyrus—or papyri, rather—page by page. I don't understand it, but I can reproduce the glyphs and drawings and translate them for someone else to use."

"Brain surgery? Brain *transplantation?* We can't—"

"Not all of it. That's knowledge I agree would be dangerous even now. But there's something else, Vic. Imhotep also had some very concise notes about making repairs to the spinal column and even nerve bundles. I think maybe some good could come of that. Maybe I could, you know, leak a little of that to Ibn Sina while I was at it..."

She slid forward in her chair until we were nose to nose. "You're amazing, Peter August. Brave and kind and funny ... and sexy."

I felt heat sweep up my neck ... and a few other places. "Wow. All that?"

"But wait," she said, "there's more."

She kissed me. Thoroughly enough that I wished with every molecule of my body that it was quitting time.

"I have a surprising confession to make," she said when we'd stopped kissing. "I'm in love with you, Detective."

"God, I should hope so." I stood and held out my hand. "Let's go time diving."

She stood and took it. "I wish I *could* time dive with you. I wonder if that would be possible—to link two minds during a dive."

"You mean kind of like those tandem skydivers? It's an interesting thought. But it would only work if we had ancestors in the same area of the world."

"You realize, of course," Victoria told me as we set off to change history a bit more, "that you'll be the only one who sees the change. The rest of us will think whatever tech evolves has been here all along."

I laughed. "Well, that will be novel: Peter August, lowly detective, will know something all the brains in the Manhattan Institute of Neurology don't."

EPILOGUE

Now, you're wondering what happened with Drew's daughter. Well, I can tell you that the biotech, when I got back from my visit to Thabit in Ibn Sina's school, was significantly more advanced. Eva Hastings didn't just have an exoskeleton that kept her limbs working, she had permanent biomimetic joints and a completely repaired spinal column that would grow with her body as she matured. They were sustained by a network of bionic implants that kept her body from giving into entropy. I didn't understand a lick of it, though Drew and Theron both tried to explain it to me. I just smiled and nodded.

You're probably also wondering what happened with Drew. The changes Thabit and I made to the timeline had apparently rewritten enough of our shared adventures that when we got back he had just returned from a voluntary sabbatical to attend his daughter's recovery from her final surgery. His last threat to do me violence—which I seriously doubt he and Abet would have carried out—was remembered only by the two of us. We came to an understanding that there was no reason to enlighten the others.

"You read Imhotep's papyrus, didn't you?" he asked me.

I nodded. "Yeah. I did."

"Don't share it with anyone. You all were right. That information should never see the light of day. At least not at this point in human evolution."

We shook on it.

There were other evidences of the tech explosion, as well. The institute's security force was supplemented with robotic units, everything was voice activated and/or read your biometric profile, which meant that doors opened when you approached them if they "knew" you, cars read your profile and knew when you needed to go to the hospital or what you meant when you said "home," the coffee AI at Morning Grind knew what my "usual" was, and my cognitive transference rig was an AI with a VR module that could actually record what I saw so that the team in the lab could *see* history, not just hear about it after the fact.

And I had an onboard damping unit with a recall circuit. No matter where I was, or who I was with, Otis's clever device would distort any sound that fit the trash can profile so that the most I experienced was a little jolt of walking-over-your-graveness. That discovery gave me goosebumps because it meant that I might be in a position to ask for my old job and my old partner back.

I had something else, too. I had a new residence. When I left for Hamadan on my dive into Thabit again, I was living in a one-bedroom apartment with my cat. When I came back, I was living in a two-story brownstone with my cat and my fiancée.

Yeah. That.

I will admit here and now, that every time I came back from a dive, I was afraid that something between me and Vic would have changed radically. Well, it finally had, but in none of the ways I'd feared. That gave me a boost of confidence that allowed me to take dealing with the other weird and wonderful changes in daily life in stride ... although I often felt like I was living in an episode of *Star Trek*.

A morning came, not long after my visit to Hamadan with Drew's drawings and notes, that I had myself delivered to the NYPD's Major Crimes Division HQ and did two things: I put in my application for reinstatement, along with a note from my doctors (Greg Orlov and Victoria Shehata). After that I wandered by Detective Melchior Duarte's office on the second floor. He was there, wearing what looked like a minimalist VR visor and murmuring under his breath.

I stopped in the doorway. "Well, hell, Mel," I said, "playing games on the tax payers' dime? That's not the Melchior Duarte I know."

He froze for a moment, then took off the visor and looked over at me. I could tell by the expression in his eyes that he wasn't sure how to react to my presence. In the end, our long friendship (and maybe our months of separation) trumped whatever else he felt, and he smiled.

"Augie, it's been a while. What've you been up to?"

I shrugged and came into the office. "Oh, you know, wrecking the space-time continuum, righting wrongs, making the world safe for democracy. The usual."

"Just dropping by for a visit?" He waved me toward the chair next to his desk.

I sat down and sobered up. "I just submitted my app for reinstatement. I'm ready to come back to work."

His eyes got big. "Seriously? You, uh ... you solved that problem you were having? The blackouts?"

"They weren't exactly blackouts."

"Then what?"

"The specialist I saw called it genetic cognitive transference. It's complicated, and partly classified, but the short form is that whenever I heard a particular type of sound ... I sort of checked out. So, they found a way to keep me from hearing that sound.

In the rare event that I *do* hear it, they gave me a device that, um, brings me instantly back online."

Mel gazed at me for a long moment. His wounded shoulder twitched ever-so-slightly, and I knew what he was thinking. "So, what happened that night at Free Spirits—"

"Will never happen again. I just wanted you to know."

I stood, then, hoping he'd just blurt out, "Great! Then we can be partners again!" He didn't, so I started for the door. In the doorway, I turned back.

"Oh, and in other news, I'm getting married. Can I interest you in a gig as best man?"

He looked as if he thought I was spoofing him. "What? Married? Augie, you haven't had a date since we— I mean, you weren't even seeing anyone. What happened?"

"Dr. Victoria Shehata happened. She's gorgeous in a slightly geeky way, smarter than I will ever be in my wildest dreams, and for some reason I can't fathom, she loves me … and my cat."

He dropped his gaze and nodded. "Wow. Best man. Yeah. I'd be honored, Aug." He met my gaze again and smiled. "Congrats."

"Thanks." I sketched a salute and started to leave again.

"Hey, Augie."

"Yeah?"

"It's getting along toward lunchtime. Wanna grab something at the diner?"

"Sure thing," I said, grinning like a kid.

It wasn't "we can be partners again," but it was a step in the right direction. Who knew? Maybe it was all just a matter of time.

ARE THOSE REAL PEOPLE?

Some of the characters appearing or mentioned in *The Time Machine Gene* are actual historical figures. Such as…

Francis X. Aubry, Pony Express rider. As Peter tells us, "He went by FX, thought of himself as Fox, and hated that other people called him 'Little Aubry' because of his small stature. He was a young daredevil out to make a fortune carrying mail across the plains. Despite the fact that the Colt .45 was the most famous handgun in the old West, Aubry carried a Pietta .44." Peter is historically correct.

Imhotep, 27*th* century BC (3*rd* Dynasty Egypt), was a High Priest of Ra, architect, polymath, general genius and chancellor to the Pharaoh Netjerikhet (aka Djoser), Imhotep was so influential that he was elevated to godhood upon his death. His name means "one who comes in peace". Ironically, he's better known in the West as an Egyptian Rasputin type who breaks sacred mores and ends up becoming a cursed mummy with really bad karma. He's been most famously played on the silver screen by both Boris Karloff and Arnold Vasloo.

Flavius Anthemius was a statesman of the later Roman Empire. He moved swiftly upward in rank and responsibility during the reigns of Emperor Arcadius and the child emperor Theodosius II, and was raised to the station of Consul of the Eastern Roman Empire in 405 AD. He also supervised the construction of the first of the Theodosian Walls. Rising yet higher in Roman government, he was elevated into the ranks of the Patricians, and was appointed as a Praetorian Prefect, second in rank only to the Emperor. The Visigoth king, Alaric, who also plays a part in the book, was a thorn in Anthemius's side even as the Prefect passed laws to contain pagans, Jews, and alleged Christian heretics. Alas, he could pass none to contain the Visigoths.

King Alaric I of the Visigoths really was an intrusive nuisance to the Roman Empire. Rome hadn't been successfully invaded for roughly 800 years, but, after three tries, Alaric finally took the great city in 410 AD. It was a relatively peaceful sacking. The populace opened the gates to him for three days of material plunder, after which he simply left, leaving the people of Rome pretty much unscathed and their city largely intact. Alaric died of a sudden illness on the road to Sicily.

Ataulf was also a real person and brother-in-law of Alaric. He succeeded Alaric as King of the Visigoths and raised his people from a group of "barbarian" tribes to be a great political power in Europe.

Ibn Sina was an eleventh-century Persian polymath and philosopher. Incredibly prolific. He is often referred to by his westernized name: Avicenna. We still have about 40 of his medical texts and more than twice as many of his philosophical works. His volumes on human physiology were taught in all of the great European Universities of the Middle Ages, and became the foundation of modern medicine.

Ibn Rushd was a Muslim polymath and natural philosopher (what we now call a scientist) who authored more than 100 books and treatises on a variety of subjects, including philosophy, theology, medicine, astronomy, physics, psychology, mathematics, neurology, Islamic jurisprudence and law, and linguistics. In the realm of philosophy, he wrote numerous commentaries on Aristotle. In the West, he became known as The Commentator and Father of Rationalism. Ibn Rushd's name was Latinized to Averroes for the European market.

Baba Tahir was a great 11th-century dervish poet from Hamadan, Persia, which was then part of the Seljuk dynasty under Tugril. We know his full name—Baba Tahir Oryan Hamadani—but very little else, except that he lived a reclusive (read: mysterious) life. Although the prefix "Baba" may be a title of endearment (as in the case of Polish grandmothers), "Oryan" had become his most popular nickname by the 17th-century.

Ludovico Maria Sforza was Duke of Milan from 1494 to 1499. He built a reputation as the "arbiter of Italy". He really was the patron of Leonardo Da Vinci and Bernardo Bellincioni and a sponsor of many works of civil engineering. He was a real go-getter who managed to rule Milan, even though, as the fourth son of the prior duke, he had no legitimate claim to that rarified position. It seems the chosen heir, his nephew, Gian Galeazzo, met with an untimely end, thus allowing Uncle Ludo to assume the duchy. Some people claim that there's a Sforza to blame—a charge Ludo denies.

Bernardo Bellincioni really was the court poet of Ludovico Sforza. When he wasn't writing poetry—mostly sonnets—praising his patron, he was indulging in literary fisticuffs with other poets whose work he felt was too low brow and commercial.

Leonardo Da Vinci ... Need I say more?

READ A SAMPLE
FROM A SEA OF STARS AND TROUBLE

1 / BIRTHDAY

He was born as he walked the road into Porphyry.

At least, that's where he was when he remembered that his name was Ridley. Three steps later, he remembered that Ridley was his first name and that Matthews was the surname that went with it. Other than that, he knew of his newborn self only that he was wearing a once-blue shirt, gray breeks, and tall boots covered by a disreputable knee-length coat of indeterminate color that was vented at the sides and back.

He patted the vents over his thighs and had the vague sense that something was missing. A money pouch? A holster? A scabbard for a laz-blade? He glanced down at his hands. No rings. No tattoos. Nothing but a faint scar that ran along the inside of one wrist. He couldn't remember how he'd gotten it.

The air roared with the distant lift-off of a starship. He stopped and watched it soar toward the clouds—through them —its keel gleaming blue. The port was straight ahead, behind the walls of a city that sat on and among a range of low, rolling hills. He estimated the distance to the wall at about 400 meters and change.

Ridley knew something else about himself then—he wanted to get to the spaceport and off this world.

Which was ... what?

He did a 360 on the shoulder of the unnaturally smooth road. It had no potholes, cracks or blemishes and somehow he knew the surface was smooth to the millimeter, though he had no idea how he knew it. Beyond the road lay chaos; brackish fields and wetlands stretched out behind him; a forest of towering, crooked trees lay on one side of the road; a fen with waving reeds twice his height spread out on the other. Ahead of him, the dingy gray walls of the huge citadel rose in front of him and disappeared into the equally gray distance in both directions.

Ah. There was a sign over the gate this roadway led to: *Welcome to Porphyry.*

Right.

Porphyry. A port town on ... he racked his brain.

Nothing.

His lack of coherent memory didn't bother him too much. It would come to him eventually, he figured. He faced the city gate and began walking again, assiduously trying not to be mowed down by a variety of vehicles that were scurrying out of the twilight into the safety of the city.

He glanced back over his shoulder at the tall, waving grasses of the fen. Why was everybody in such a hurry? Did the gates—

He heard a siren go off ahead. Yellow lights flashed along the top of the gate that bracketed the roadway.

—close at dusk?

He ran, the tails of his coat flapping in the dank air. As he slipped through the pedestrian gate, barely saving the tails of his coat, he remembered something else about himself—he was running from something. Not whatever lived in the marshes beyond the city, but something else. Suddenly, his lack of coherent memory bothered him a great deal. He stepped into the shadow of the wall and searched his pockets. He found nothing. Not a credit tab, no ID, no weaponry.

The gate he'd entered through had been roughly three meters wide and constructed of aging stone with a newer metal insert. Clearly not a main access to the city. The section of Porphyry within it was a maze. This might be good, given his impression that he was on the run from … something. The streets were narrow, the buildings old, huddled together, and decrepit. Their layout was jumbled and confusing—like a random scatter of toy blocks.

He knew about toy blocks, he realized. Knew small children played with them. Knew the sound of a child's laughter. He scrambled after the happy/sad thought, then let it go in favor of dealing with his immediate situation. He seemed to recall that he trusted his sense of direction, but as darkness fell, he found he'd gone around in a convoluted circle without having realized it. It was like being lost in another dimension where the normal rules of geography did not apply. Or maybe the problem was in his addled brain.

He had apparently wandered into a dead zone. There was a distinct lack of lighting. Only the full moon, hanging huge and bloated in the sky overhead, cast its pale green light here. It was enough light to inform him that there was no one around to ask for the quickest route to the spaceport. There was no traffic. The shops were shuttered. The streets were deserted, as if the denizens of Porphyry had as much to fear within its walls as beyond them. Yet, in the distance he could hear the hum of a main thoroughfare, far-off sirens, the thunder of starship launch engines.

He looked up, scanning the facades of the buildings nearest him. Standing on a balcony some yards down the street was a cluster of robed figures, several of whom were looking right at him. Well, at least their hooded heads were turned in his direction. He couldn't see their faces. Unsettling. The ones that weren't looking at him were speaking into communicators of some sort.

P-comms, said his piecemeal memory. Short for ... something that started with a P.

The hair on the back of Ridley's neck rose, tingling, and he knew with sudden certainty that someone was behind him. He turned just in time to catch the merest glance of a gray-robed figure gripping a static-spitting staff before a jolt of freezing energy took him down. He hit the roadway like a rock and curled into a ball, bracing himself against the chill, tingling shock. Oddly, after a moment, the shock morphed into something eerily pleasant. In fact, he felt better than he had in a long time ... or at least for the past hour or so.

He'd had some expectation of the effects of the weapon based, he assumed, on prior experience—but the charge from this staff was causing his brain to explode, not with pain, but with a sense of contentment and well-being. He was suffused with a bliss so potent it was terrifying—or would have been if it didn't feel so damn good. Even the fact that he was probably about to die failed to penetrate the (insane) conviction that Ridley Matthews was profoundly right with the Universe and was fulfilling a purpose that surely had been preordained since the beginning of his existence—perhaps even the beginning of time. Everything he had ever done or experienced, whether or not he could remember it, had led inexorably to this moment, had put him just where he belonged.

He no longer felt any need to escape.

Like hell I don't, snarled a dissenting inner voice.

He ignored it. The thought of his imminent death cheered him; he wouldn't have to run anymore. He simply had to *be*, to allow events to unfold as God or the Universe had planned. So what if he didn't know who the hell he was? He was complete on every conceivable plane of existence.

Bull shit. Bull Shit. BULL. SHIT.

He *wasn't* complete. He was in a dangerous position for anyone to be in, even if they weren't a complete blank. His anger was as unexpected as the false joy, but at least it was an honest emotion, not forced on him by a neural weapon.

He was surrounded by robed figures now, all carrying similar meter-long staffs. They were swaying from side to side and chanting: "Burn, burn, burn away. Confusion, sorrow, doubt and pain. Burn away. Burn away."

Ridley gasped. Suppressing the alien bliss with a will, he stood, shaking hair out of his eyes. "Who are you? What did you do to me?"

The tallest of the monkish men—the one who'd zapped him —stopped chanting and stepped forward, seemingly surprised that their victim was speaking to them. His robe was decorated with symbols: crosses, pentagrams, cups, swords, several different kinds of stars and moons—a mishmash of religious icons from a dozen worlds and ages. Ridley could see the glitter of the man's eyes within the hood.

Good. He had a face … which Ridley was much inclined to punch.

"We are the Druud," the monk told him gravely. "The Brothers of the Rapture. We have shared the Rapture with you. You are blessed."

His companions—there were five, all dressed in similar attire —repeated the words, "Rapture. Blessed."

"Feel the burn, brother," the Druud told him. "Feel the layers of your soul sear away until your true self is revealed."

His true self. Did he want to know who or what that was? Something told him he'd been running for a while now, and until he knew what he was running *from* he'd just as soon leave his true self out of it.

"Why?" he gasped, feeling the burn. "Why attack me?"

The monk made a gesture with his staff. "We do not attack. We mean only to help you, brother." He sounded sincere.

Ridley understood. They just wanted him to join them—to be part of their cult. To belong. To them, this wasn't an assault, it was a conversion, not by faith, but by technology. Belonging wasn't bad. Belonging was good. It was necessary. He had belonged ... somewhere. Hadn't he?

Ridley locked his eyes on the glowing tip of the Druud's staff. Carrot and stick—both at once. Had they all been converted this way?

He had to wonder what made the conversions "stick"— frequent and repeated applications to weaken the mind and make it susceptible to the irresistible lure of inclusion? Was it a manipulation of the obvious loner's supposedly deep-seated desire to belong? Or was it addiction they were counting on— the mad urge to feel this overwhelming sense of wellbeing again and again?

Ridley eyed the staff, afraid the monk would use it on him— equally afraid he wouldn't. "Your rapture is false," he said through gritted teeth. He took a step, meaning to slip between two of the back-up monks, but the tall Druud cut him off, raising his staff menacingly.

"You must obey the law! Neither heathen nor holy may walk these streets at night without dispensation."

"What dispensation? I don't even live here, and I'm on my way off-world. For the love of God, just let me go!"

The tall monk looked him in the eye and lowered his staff slightly.

"I am not a cruel man. The Brothers of the Rapture is not a cruel order. We strive for justice and mercy—for harmony. Our streets are not to be walked by outsiders after the sun has set. This is the holy time, and our spiritual discipline is not to be disrupted by the presence of those who do not believe. This is the law. Therefore, you must believe."

Ah, the logic of insanity. Still, Ridley was cheered by the fact that Rapture Monk had not ended the sentence with "you must die". That was something.

"Let me see if I've got this right. You're zapping me into a religious experience because of a *zoning* ordinance?"

"Zoning ordinance? No," said the Druud. "These are the Proprieties of Herron's Hope. Here, in this sector of Porphyry, they are law."

Herron's Hope. *That* was the name of the planet. Right. He'd known that, hadn't he?

The Druud lifted his staff again and thrust it toward his would-be convert. This time Ridley grabbed it right behind the muzzle. Lightning crackled the length of his arm. He set his teeth against the overwhelming joy that came with it, wrenched the staff from the monk's grasp, and aimed a roundhouse kick at his head. Ridley's booted foot connected with a solid thud and the big man went down hard. A second monk leapt to his brother's defense, but Ridley completed his spinning move with a fist to the defender's face. He barely felt the blow on his knuckles.

When he finally stopped moving, he was outside the circle of monks, who stood and gaped as if they'd never seen anyone fight happiness with such determination. The man he had punched was warily pulling himself to his feet.

Ridley twirled the purloined staff as if it were a baton. "Go away," he said quietly, his voice a low rumble in his throat. He waited a beat, then added, "Please."

They went, scattering across the empty street, into the alleys and around the corners, three of them dragging their groaning leader to safety. The men on the balcony, who had been watching these events, withdrew to the shadowy recesses of the building.

Ridley didn't stick around to see if they were rounding up reinforcements. He started walking swiftly in the direction he surmised the spaceport lay, following the roar of engines. He'd gone several yards when the staff in his hand tugged at his thoughts. He glanced down at it. The deep feeling of contentment kickstarted by the staff remained, controlled only by the sheer force of his will. The desire to activate it again and siphon its primal energy coiled in his breast. His mind stood aloof, but emotionally he hungered to return to the pinnacle of faith and ecstasy he had attained in the moments after the monk had zapped him. Only innate stubbornness saved him from succumbing to the sudden addiction ... and perhaps the knowledge that this faith, no matter how intense, was artificial.

Leery of its insidious charms, he considered tossing the staff away into the darkness. Yet, he suspected that if he did, he'd regret it. This posed a quandary. He had no idea what he would have done under normal circumstances, but he was inclined to trust his instincts. Right now, they told him that his mind was in an altered state—the wrong state in which to make important decisions. He'd wait until his neural synapses had cleared of the staff's effects, however long it took, then he'd decide what to do with it.

As he strode briskly through the deserted streets, he analyzed his escape from the Druud. That told him something more about himself; he was a man with quick reflexes, not a little strength, and some knowledge of martial arts. What had he done back there, some sort of *kung fu?*

He flexed his hands, realizing that the one he'd used to punch the Rapture Monger didn't hurt at all. He was about to attribute that to the effects of the staff when he glanced down at his knuckles and realized they weren't swollen or abraded, as he'd expected. And the scar he'd noticed on that wrist earlier was nearly gone.

He looked at the staff with respect. Wow. That was something. It made you feel good and healed whatever ailed you. Powerful stuff. He glanced back over his shoulder, wondering if the staff's owners would be putting in an appearance soon to reclaim it, or if their beliefs would keep them from leaving their sector.

It was with a sense of relief that Ridley approached a district of bright, beckoning holosigns, crowded and noisy streets, and music pulsing from small cramped buildings. He felt oddly comfortable in the midst of all these strangers. Indeed, he felt almost as if he belonged among them ... until he became aware that they were staring at him, occasionally whispering to each other as he passed them. More than a few gave him a wide berth. At first, he thought they were looking at the staff, but they weren't; they were glancing up at his face. He made a point of nodding and smiling. While being sociable seemed to come naturally (how could he know?) he suspected his internal struggle was doing something funny to his face; his smiles seemed to spook the passers-by rather than reassure them.

He slowed to peer at himself in the dark front window of a closed-up shop and smiled into the reflective surface. The man who leered back at him was disheveled, dirtied, and torn. His hair—too long, too thick and wild—framed an angular face in which pale, almost silver eyes gleamed like tiny moons and on which the twisted smile looked downright sinister. Given that he was over two meters tall, he looked like a threat going somewhere to happen. But what bothered him most about this face was that it seemed only *almost* familiar.

He put a hand to his chin, seeking proof that this really was his face. It was smooth, even after however long he'd been wandering the byways of Herron's Hope before he regained a sense of self-awareness. In any event, it indicated bio-enhancements, or at least depilatory treatments.

How do I know that? How do I know that I know that?

He tried the smile again, tilting his head up, trying to exile the crazy from his eyes, and smiling broadly. His teeth were even and white. Eh, better, but still...

Something tugged at his consciousness. Something similar

to the sensation he'd felt when the Rapture Bros were casing him. He peered into the window, no longer looking at himself, but at the people passing behind him on the walkway. His eyes darted from face to face, but he saw no one overtly watching him.

What he did see was a drunken man, with a wild thicket of white hair and a matching gold-trimmed one piece suit of some silky-looking material, walk straight into a lamppost. The drunk, who was holding a credit tab in one hand and a drink in the other, gaped at the lamppost as if it had jumped out in front of him. Then he leaned against it and tried three or four times to slip the credit tab into his breast pocket before finally succeeding. He looked this way and that, then lurched forward, taking a couple of steps before promptly bumping into a pedestrian.

Ridley swung around, his senses suddenly and tightly focused on the interaction. He was certain the pedestrian had intentionally angled into the collision. (Why did he think that? Was he, himself, a common thief? Or a policeman?) He was equally certain the pedestrian had stolen that credit tab. He hadn't seen the actual pilfering of it, and of course the drunken mark suspected nothing as he tottered off into a nearby tavern called the *Nebula*.

Ridley kept his heightened attention on the pickpocket. He was easy enough to track—he was bald, with decorative patterns tattooed on his scalp in gleaming ink. He wore a dark gray long-coat, fitted breeches, and the high boots of a spacer. Ridley followed him up the street at a discreet distance, wondering if his peculiar interest in the theft was instinctual or an effect of the Druud rapture staff. By now he had found the buttons that controlled its power charge, but he still didn't know the sequence that set off the endorphin flood. It looked like he would have to do things the old-fashioned way. When the pickpocket turned right, into an alley, Ridley stepped in after him. In two strides he'd come up behind the other man and given him a short, sharp jolt to the kidney with the butt end of the staff. The pickpocket stumbled forward, fetching up against a stone wall. He hesitated, then held up his hands as if he thought this was going to be a simple robbery.

Ridley drew up close behind him and prodded him with the staff. "You've taken something that doesn't belong to you," he observed.

"Oh, you mean this?" said the pickpocket with a nervous laugh, holding up the tab. "You misunderstand, my friend. That fellow's a friend, and this is a bad neighborhood to be drunk in. I took his tab for safekeeping until he has a chance to sober up."

"Your altruism is commendable," said Ridley. He snatched the tab, then knocked the pickpocket unconscious with one deft chop to the back of his neck. Handy skill, that. He wondered, again, where he'd learned it.

He felt that "watched" tingle again and pivoted toward the street, catching the swift movement of withdrawal—a blur of black, gray, and white. Shaking off spookiness, he returned to the *Nebula*'s entrance, where a big, burly gentleman with bio-engineered tusks and knife-sharp teeth kept a watchful eye on the patrons coming and going. Judging by the wary way he eyed Ridley, he was more bouncer than doorman.

"A street hood," Tusks said, "wearing a swell's breeches and carrying a Druud staff—not something you see every day, and not someone I think will enhance the dignity of our establishment."

Someone pushed between Ridley and the bouncer—an aging spacer dressed in an old-school dress uniform in shades of black and gray. He was short, not much more than a meter and a half in height, and his skin had the slightly waxen pallor of someone who'd rarely been out in daylight. His hair was gray with streaks of white, receding in front, but flowing down to his shoulders in the back. Ridley was struck by the absurd conviction that this was the person who'd been watching him rough up the pickpocket.

"Excuse me," the spacer mumbled.

Tusks nodded. "Yeah, sure, Cap'n."

Ridley leaned on the staff. "Why does he get in without the inspection?"

"He's a regular. You're not."

"Y'know, from what I've seen of this town so far, if you banned everyone irregular from your classy drinking establishment, it'd be empty all the time. Besides, I have business with someone inside. He lost this." Ridley guilelessly held up the credit tab.

The bouncer reached for it. "Give it to me. I'll see that the proper gentleman gets it."

"Off-worlders are wrong about the people of Porphyry," Ridley replied. "It seems they really do have a sense of humor."

Damn, but I'm a glib sonofabitch.

The bouncer eyed him, then laughed and jerked his thumb toward the interior, signaling to Ridley to go in. He did, experiencing a disquieting sense of camaraderie that was offset by suspicion and an instinctive heightening of his senses.

The place was crowded, dimly lit, and noisy. People were talking, laughing, arguing. They were also eating, drinking, and smoking a wide range of substances, most of which at least marginally bad for one's health. Or so his vague memory informed him. He'd rather have more useful information at the moment, like who he was, beyond a name, and why he was here, and how he had gotten here.

The majority of the men in the room, and some of the women, were dressed in casual attire; some displayed logograms, badges, roundels and other insignia, indicating allegiance to various factions or ... no, alliances. Alliances and Guilds. Ridley noticed sigils for a handful he realized he recognized: Consonance, the Filial Pact, the Heartworlds Alliance, the Freeman's Guild, others.

Those who weren't obviously spacers tended to dress in a manner that showed off various physical assets. There were, inevitably, prostitutes of all types, some so alien in appearance, it was difficult to think of them as human. Yet they were human. In all of mankind's spacefaring history, no sentient alien species had yet been found—which could be seen as either a blessing or a curse. These were bio-engineered humans, modified to possess any number of inhuman qualities. But they *looked* alien, and that was enough to excite their adventure-seeking clients.

Their presence reminded Ridley to consider his own possible modifications—eyes that seemed to take in every movement, even in the dimmest corners of the room, ears caught and sorted through the babble of voices, extracting intelligible dialogues, skin that prickled with awareness of movement and attention. A trio of hookers had turned to watch him as he moved deeper into the room, their heads swiveling.

One of them—a woman with black hair and eyes so large and dark they seemed like rounds of polished jet—detached herself from the group and moved as if stalking him. Under the smoky light of the bar, her skin glowed golden—a counterpoint to the pale, body-hugging tunic she wore. Likely she'd seen the interaction with Tusks over the credit tab. Possibly she wanted to relieve him of it. She smiled, teeth flashing white in the golden face.

Hope springs eternal... He'd heard that somewhere.

The smell of food assaulted him then, and he forgot about the black-eyed hooker. He was suddenly ravenous. He had no idea how long it had been since his last meal. He would have to do something about that soon, but his errand came first. He scanned the tavern, finally spotting a familiar shock of white hair on a gentleman standing at the bar. The man was gesturing wildly, and Ridley had the distinct feeling he had ordered something and only now discovered he had no means of paying for it.

Ridley smiled and pushed his way to the bar, where he tapped the white-haired man on the shoulder. The old guy whirled as if someone had set him on fire, then his eyes widened as he saw the credit tab Ridley held in front of his face.

"Lose something?"

"By the Maw of Hell! You found it!" White Hair exclaimed. He presented it to the bartender as if it were a trophy. "See? I told you I'd lost it. Now I can pay for that drink!" He turned to Ridley. "And you! I definitely owe you a drink! Or three! And can I buy you something to eat?"

Ridley hesitated. This was literally *terra incognita*, but he was so damned hungry. Besides, he had performed a service; this was merely a grace.

"Come to think of it, the dishes do smell pretty decent," he said.

"That they do! What would you like? Biftek? Some fried eggs?"

Ridley shrugged. "How can I refuse?"

A few minutes later they were sitting at a table waiting for their food. The Druud staff leaned against Ridley's chair. Two beers—reportedly the best local brew—sat on the table. Ridley's new "friend" picked up his beer and gestured for him to do the same. He had just lifted his glass when someone jostled him, knocking the Druud staff to the floor. He reflexively reached down to retrieve it, glancing up briefly as he did.

The old spacer, again.

"Excuse me," the old guy mumbled, barely meeting Ridley's eyes. "It's a bit crowded in here, isn't it?"

Ridley felt the urge to explain to the fellow that he didn't rough up complete strangers without good reason. Instead, he just smiled and said: "Hope that means the food is good."

The duffer bobbed his head and shuffled off into the crowd.

"A toast!" White Hair said, words slurring.

"A toast." Ridley repeated. They clicked glasses.

"Life is good," said White Hair.

Much to his astonishment, Ridley Matthews found himself agreeing with the sentiment. He was on the run, with no memory of who or what he was, and it felt as if all was right with the universe. How wrong was that?

He felt anger trying to crawl up from his stomach. Would the effects of that damned staff never fade?

"Life is good," he agreed. He took a big swallow of beer. It was excellent.

"What may I call you, my new friend?" White Hair asked.

"Name's Ridley." He hesitated as another memory emerged. "But I go by 'Trouble.'"

"Trouble," repeated the old guy. "Now that is a most portentous sobriquet."

"I hope so," Trouble Matthews said, and was surprised to realize he knew what a portentous sobriquet was.

His meal came then, and he tucked in with a vengeance.

Get A Sea of Stars and Trouble at the BVC bookstore!

COMING NEXT YEAR
FROM BOHNHOFF & FRANGIONE

LIGHTS OF LEMURIA

Rio Temesa's high school field trip to Peru morphs into a waking nightmare in which a gang of armed insurgents is the least of the dangers Rio and his companions must face.

ABOUT MAYA KAATHRYN BOHNHOFF

Maya Kaathryn Bohnhoff is the New York Times Bestselling author of *The Antiquities Hunter* (a Gina Miyoko Mystery) and *Star Wars Legends: The Last Jedi* (with Michael Reaves).

She became addicted to science fiction when her dad let her stay up late to watch *The Day the Earth Stood Still*. Since then her short fiction has been published in *Analog*, *Amazing Stories*, *Century*, *Realms of Fantasy*, *Interzone*, *Paradox* and *Jim Baen's Universe*. Her debut novel, *The Meri* (Baen), was a Locus Magazine Best First Novel and Crawford Fantasy Award nominee. Since, she has published over a dozen speculative fiction novels.

Maya lives in San Jose where she writes, performs, and records original and parody (filk) music with her husband (and awesome musician and producer), Chef Jeff Vader, All-Powerful God of Biscuits. The couple has produced three children (all of whom have performed with them) and eight music albums:

RetroRocket Science, Aliens Ate My Homework, Grated Hits and *Shrödinger's Hairball* (parody), and the original music CDs *Manhattan Sleeps, Möbius Street, I Remember the Rain* and *Labyrinth*.

Following the lead of one of her heroes, Ray Bradbury, Maya's goal is to make reality behave by pretending to look the other way.

Visit Maya's writing website Making Reality Behave: htpp://www.mayabohnhoff.com

Visit Jeff and Maya's music site: https://jeffandmayabohn hoff.bandcamp.com

You can find their parody videos at: https://www.youtube.com/@mysticfig

ABOUT ANTHONY FRANGIONE

Anthony Frangione (on your left) was born in the Bronx, NY in the 1950's.

He watched every game of the 1964 World Series on the family's black and white Zenith because his 3rd grade teacher said that if the Yankees won there would be no homework for a week.

Given no option for guitar or piano early in life, he learned to play the accordion. And, although his great uncle was a revered priest who hoped his nephew might follow in his footsteps, Anthony's crushes on several girls hinted that the seminary might not be a good fit. He attended a secular college instead, completing undergraduate and graduate degrees.

He began writing as a therapeutic pursuit later in life, scribbling his ideas, longhand, in a series of notebooks. One notebook became twenty, and their contents became a book.

Anthony's dive into authorship accelerated with a writer's conference in Sanibel Island, Florida. It was not the influence of authors, professors or literary agents that finally convinced him to take his writing seriously, but the perseverance of a box turtle. Watching the little creature trek from street, to sidewalk, to grass, to sand, and finally into the water, Anthony understood the role of sheer stubbornness in the art of writing.

This author has a simple maxim: Let your imagination play with history, then just write.

ABOUT BOOKVIEW CAFÉ

Book View Café is a professional authors' publishing cooperative offering DRM-free ebooks in multiple formats to readers around the world. With authors in a variety of genres including mystery, romance, fantasy, and science fiction, Book View Café has something for everyone.

Book View Café is good for readers because you can enjoy high-quality DRM-free ebooks from your favorite authors at a reasonable price.

Book View Café is good for writers because 90% of the proceeds goes directly to the book's author.

Book View Café authors include New York Times and USA Today bestsellers, Nebula, Hugo, Lambda, Chanticleer, Crawford, National Reader's Choice, and Philip K. Dick Award winners, World Fantasy, Kirkus, and Rita Award nominees, and winners and nominees of many other publishing awards.

BOOK VIEW CAFE

ALSO BY
MAYA KAATHRYN BOHNHOFF

SHAMAN

(A Collection of Short Science Fiction)

Book View Café

ALL THE COLORS OF TIME

(A Collection of Short Science Fiction)

Book View Café

Gina Miyoko Stories

"Tinkerbell On Walkabout"

a Book View Café novelette

"Tinkerbell and the Storybook Murder"

a Book View Café novelette

COPYRIGHTS & CREDITS

The Time Machine Gene: A Peter August Mystery

Maya Kaathryn Bohnhoff and Anthony Frangione

Copyright © 2024 by Maya Kaathryn Bohnhoff and Anthony Frangione

ISBN 978-1-63632-347-3

Book View Café 2025

Chariot Books 2025

Production Team

Cover designer: Maya Kaathryn Bohnhoff

Cover elements: Deviant Art, Freepik

Proofreader: Irene Radford

Formatters: Jennifer Stevenson / Maya Kaathryn Bohnhoff

Print edition: 20250829mkb

Book View Café

304 S. Jones Blvd, Suite #2906

Las Vegas NV 89107